FREEDOM'S SONG

FREEDOM'S SONG

A Novel

KIM VOGEL SAWYER

THORNDIKE PRESS
A part of Gale, a Cengage Company

LIBRARY OF CONGRESS CIP DATA ON FILE.
CATALOGUING IN PUBLICATION FOR THIS BOOK
IS AVAILABLE FROM THE LIBRARY OF CONGRESS.

ISBN-13: 978-1-4328-9570-9 (hardcover alk. paper)

Published in 2022 by arrangement with WaterBrook, an imprint of Random House, a division of Penguin Random House LLC

Printed in Mexico
Print Number: 01   Print Year: 2022

For *Kristian,* my songbird;
for *Kaitlyn,* my joy bringer;
and for *Kamryn,* my champion
of the underdog

If the Son therefore shall make you free, ye shall be free indeed.

— JOHN 8:36

1

Thunderous applause. Cries of "Encore, encore!"

Fanny Beck bowed her head in humble acknowledgment and gratitude. Da had told her she'd been given a special gift by the Almighty to use for His glory. Ever since she was a wee girl, she'd relished enthusiastic responses to her singing, seeing the praise as an offering to the One her parents had taught her to love and honor.

With memories of Da and Ma warming her heart, she lifted her face, held her arms in a graceful position as if bestowing an offering, and burst into the song she always saved for when the audience clamored for an encore, " 'Come, let us join our cheerful songs with angels round the throne.' "

This hymn by Isaac Watts, offering adoration to the Lamb of God, wasn't a favorite of Sloan's. He often reminded her that her voice belonged to him because he'd indentured her, but he had given her permission to choose her own encore. She sang all five stanzas with heartfelt thanks for her Lord and Savior.

She sang the final note an octave higher than written and then dropped into a deep curtsy. While the audience proved their appreciation with resounding applause for several minutes, she remained in the pose she'd learned from the woman Sloan had hired to tutor her. The accolades continued, but Fanny's limbs began to tremble. She straightened and caught sight of Burke, her assigned watcher for the evening, gesturing to her from the edge of the riverboat's stage.

Standing behind a fall of shimmering red velvet, he was concealed from the audience. But Fanny was aware of his presence. Of the unwavering glare beneath his thick gray eyebrows, the scowl framed by untamed whiskers, and — mostly — the unspoken warning. If the applauding attendees could see his dour face or the stern jerk of his arm that signaled, *Come here now!* would any of them ponder why the young singer billed as the Darling of the *River Peacock* was kept under constant observation and summoned so harshly?

She faced the still clamoring crowd, touched her fingertips to her lips, then swung her arms wide, as if showering them with kisses, the way Sloan had instructed her to bid farewell. Then she pulled the folds of her black velvet cloak over her dress. As heavy and cumbersome as the cloak was to wear, she welcomed its coverage. Her performance dresses, all commissioned by Sloan in bawdy colors with plunging necklines, left her feeling exposed and indecent. Neither Da nor Ma would have approved indenturing her to Sloan if they had known she'd be dressed up like a strumpet.

With another bow of her head to her admiring audience, she left the stage, mindful of the rolling motion of the riverboat beneath her feet. The wind must be stout tonight. The moment she reached Burke, he grabbed the hood of her cloak and jerked it over her head.

She frowned. Sloan didn't want her wearing the hood. He'd said the cloak's red satin lining was too pretty against the rich black velvet to stay fully hidden. "Besides," he'd added, his gaze roving over her the way men examined a horse before purchasing it, "part of your appeal is your bonny face and dark-brown hair shot through with strands of red-gold. Why not let the men admire one of God's most lovely creations?"

If he saw her with her head covered, he'd

11

rage at her. She reached to remove it.

"Leave it," Burke said.

Fanny paused with her fingers pinching the edge of the hood. "Why?"

"It's rainin'. We can't have you drippin' like a drowned rat. You're gonna need to look fresh for the eleven o'clock show."

She had a full hour to dry and refashion her hair. She could tell him so, but why bother? She never won arguments with Sloan or Burke. Sometimes she argued anyway, if only for the sake of entertaining herself and utilizing her wits. But the hour was late, the weather was foul, and she preferred to reach her room for a much-needed rest.

She stifled a yawn. If only she could eat a little supper, crawl into her warm berth, and not have to get out again. But nothing would entice Sloan to cancel the late-night Friday show. During the program reserved for the male passengers, wine and other spirits poured freely, and in their drunkenness the men tossed coin after coin onto the stage at her feet. Of course, she wasn't allowed to collect those coins. Stage workers gathered them up and turned them over to Sloan.

A shudder rattled her frame, brought on by guilt and worry. Sloan would be furious if he knew her secret. But she was furious, too. Her term of service should end in August this year. Yet on her customary daily supervised stroll around the deck a few weeks ago, she'd overheard him instructing a couple to be certain to cruise again at Christmastime, when Miss Fainche Beck would deliver a special concert. She'd asked her escort, an elderly man nearly crippled by arthritis and nicknamed Cricket for the way his hip joints creaked when he walked, to take her to Sloan. Cricket had complied and stood silently while she reminded Sloan she'd be off this boat well before Christmas.

She would never forget the fury in Sloan's green eyes or the way he leaned within inches of her face and growled, "I'll let you know when you're free to leave this boat, and until then you'll do as I say if you have any intelligence at all."

She'd proved her intelligence — or her cowardice — by holding back further words of complaint, but she'd continued to rebel in her mind. And apparently she'd won Cricket's compassion. Because after that, each time he was given charge of accompanying her on her stroll, he sneaked her a coin or two. At first she hesitated to accept the five-, ten-, and twenty-dollar gold pieces. If they were caught, they would

13

surely suffer dire consequences. But he told her, "These're some tossed on the stage as thanks for your pretty singin'. You earned 'em, Miss Fanny. Ain't ya gonna need travel money to get to yer folks?"

How many times had she prayed for God's provision for transport to the Manhattan borough of New York City, where Da, Ma, and her little sisters had settled? Who was she to say that God hadn't prompted the old man to lend aid? God often used unlikely means and people to further His will. Besides, Cricket was right. She had earned them. So she gratefully accepted the coins. Closed in her private room, she'd wrapped each coin with a bit of cloth and hid them in her muslin dimity pocket. Sloan had many rules for her and only one for the crew concerning her: "Hands off." The pouch, tied by a string around her waist beneath her layers of skirts, was safe from discovery. She wore it day and night, its pressure against her hip bone a silent promise that she would join her family someday.

Burke escorted her through the unlit corridor behind the stage and out to the covered deck. Lanterns hanging from overhead beams poked holes in the darkness, but they did little to cheer the night. Not a soul, not even the usual cigar smokers,

14

lounged on the chair-lined, gleaming teakwood-paneled deck. And small wonder, for lightning slashed the sky and thunder rumbled in the distance. Fat raindrops, blown sideways by gusts of wind, pummeled the water and the paddleboat's tin roof with nearly as much clamor as the applause she'd left behind. Not even her hood protected her face from the onslaught. She hunched forward and shivered, the leather soles of her embroidered silk slippers sliding on the wet deck.

Burke, amazingly agile for a man who must be as old as Da, cupped her elbow and kept her upright. At the entry to the lower level, Burke released her arm. She stood shivering while he lifted the angled door built of thick planks joined with metal bands, his arm muscles bulging against the faded gray fabric of his shirt. He left the door open and led her down the warped wooden stairs to the lowest level — the level reserved for the lowliest of the crew — where Fanny had spent the majority of her life for close to seven years. The moist, cool breeze followed them.

He snagged a flickering lantern from a hook at the base of the stairs and gestured her to go ahead of him down the narrow hallway, light from the lantern bouncing off the damp walls like flashes of lightning. At her door, he hung the lantern on a nail pounded into the doorjamb and removed a ring of keys from his trousers pocket. He grunted as he twisted the key in the iron lock. *Click!* The rusty lock released.

Burke swung the door open and gave her a little nudge into the tiny space. "One of the cook's helpers left a cold supper beside your bed."

The lamp burning on the little table next to her cot cast a dim glow over three shriveled slices of pinkish meat veined with fat, a biscuit, and some type of wilted greens, probably fried in the fat from the meat. The diners she'd entertained during the seven o'clock show had sat at linen-draped tables and feasted on roasted pork, glazed carrots, buttery mashed potatoes, and crusty rolls. The sight and aroma of those foods had stirred her appetite, but the cold offering on her chipped crockery plate quelled her desire to eat.

Burke nodded toward the table. "Fill your belly, then rest. Sloan'll expect you bright eyed an' ready to sing loud an' strong for tonight's show."

Fanny had no intention of filling her belly. Not only were the options on the plate unappetizing, but a full stomach would

16

prevent her from getting a full breath and, therefore, hinder her ability to sing well. She'd eat later, when hunger overrode her aversion. But now she would rest.

She sat on the edge of her cot. The moment her frame met the lumpy cotton-stuffed mattress, the boat lurched and shuddered. Burke stumbled sideways and slammed against the doorframe. She bolted to her feet. The boat gave another violent shake, and she nearly lost her balance.

"Stay here." Burke staggered into the hallway, retrieved the lantern from its nail, and left.

Fanny gaped. Had he truly left the door open? Not once in all her years on this boat had her cabin door remained unlocked, let alone open, when she was inside. Had God chosen this day to answer her prayer for escape? The plan she'd concocted weeks ago unfolded in her mind. Make it to the passenger deck and hide, perhaps behind the stage, until the ship docked, then mingle with the passengers as they disembarked. Once on land, locate a railway station, purchase a ticket, and travel to New York City.

The desire to be reunited with Da and Ma, Flossie, and little Moira propelled her to the opening. She peered out. Burke was gone, and the hall lay thick in shadows. The roar of the boiler and rhythmic groaning squeals of the massive paddle wheel were now silenced, but scrambling noises and shouts filtered from the levels above, sounds unlike any she'd heard during her long years aboard the *River Peacock*. A perfect opportunity for someone to become lost in the crowd.

Heart pattering in both apprehension and hope, she took a hesitant step into the dark hall. Her body trembled so badly she marveled she could stay upright. She paused, fully expecting someone — Sloan, Burke, or one of the many crew members who'd been given charge of her over the years — to storm up and force her back into her cell. But no one came.

She felt her way up the hallway toward the staircase. The boat pitched sideways, throwing her against the opposite wall. Her feet slid out from under her, and she went down. The shock of the fall stunned her for a moment, rendering her incapable of movement. But then the acrid stench of coal oil and smoke attacked her nose. Her eyes burned. She turned her face into the satin hood of her cloak and forced her confusion-riddled mind to calm and think, think.

Screeches, wails, shouts, and the thunder

18

of many footsteps filled her ears and painted a picture of panic. The boat must be on fire. She had to get out of the bottom deck before the vessel sank.

Mouth dry, lungs heaving, she struggled to untangle her layers of clothing and rise, but the slickness of the floorboards and the violent jerking motions of the boat forced her down again. Whimpering in terror, she shifted to her hands and knees and half crawled, half dragged herself the remaining distance to the stairs. *Let the hatch be open, me dear Lord,* her heart begged as she inched her way to safety and freedom. If Burke or someone else had closed the hatch, she'd be trapped. The door weighed more than a hundred pounds. She'd never be able to open it by herself.

The desire for escape pounded in her chest, giving her the strength to push to her feet and stagger the final few feet to the base of the stairs. Rain-scented air poured over her. The hatch was open! She scrambled upward on all fours and burst onto the deck into a dance of chaos. She was swept into the milling throng and carried with it.

"This way! This way to the lifeboats!"

The authoritative voice had come from behind Fanny, cutting through the storm's fury, women's wails, and men's fearful shouts. Yet no one seemed to heed it. Fanny hollered, "Turn around! Turn around! The lifeboats are behind you!"

The tide of passengers turned in the opposite direction, and Fanny got bumped aside. Her soles slid on the rain-wet deck, but she caught her balance and rejoined the throng. Someone slammed into her, sending her stumbling sideways. Her hip collided with the railing. Pain exploded through her lower spine. She gasped and instinctively arched her back. Her feet went out from under her and her body flipped, the cloak wrapping itself around her as she tumbled headfirst over the railing.

A piercing scream left her throat, and then the frigid river swallowed her whole.

2

Sloan folded his arms and glared at the charred, smoke-damaged deck of his beloved *River Peacock*. How had a bucket of oily rags caught fire in the middle of a rainstorm? Bad luck, the man who inspected the vessel had proclaimed. Carelessness, Sloan countered. One of the boiler crewmen must have been smoking, although none would admit it. Well, they'd been discharged from service. When the boat was repaired and ready to sail again, he'd put a new boiler crew in place — men who would guard against such reckless behavior.

He tilted his head back and examined the stars winking against a black sky. The heavy rain had washed away every cloud. If he didn't know a storm had recently raged, he'd never guess it from the peacefulness of this predawn hour. The passengers were all settled in rooms at local inns, and his crewmen were in their berths. Tiredness tugged

21

at Sloan, but he couldn't sleep. Too much irritation burned within his chest to allow him to rest.

Burke tromped up beside Sloan. Purple flesh sagged beneath his eyes. "It coulda been a whole lot worse, Cap'n."

Sloan aimed a disbelieving glower at the man. "How, pray tell?"

Burke scratched at the muttonchop whiskers growing wild on his jaw. "We got the fire out. The *Peacock* didn't sink. Didn't even need to lower the lifeboats. Then we got 'er safe to a port town where there's skilled boatwrights who can fix 'er up again."

Sloan snorted. "There are skilled boatwrights all up and down the Mississippi."

Burke lifted his cap, smoothed his graying hair away from his forehead, and settled the cap again. "Coulda lost some passengers. 'Specially the way they was all swarmin' the decks willy-nilly, purely panicked and senseless. But every last one of 'em is safe an' sound. The crew, too. Except for —" He looked aside.

Fanny. Sloan finished the sentence in his head. Remorse churned in his belly. How could she be gone? Several passengers had reported the same story about a woman in a long black cape falling over the railing.

22

Even though they described the cloak he had custom made for her and one of her beaded, embroidered silk slippers was found on the deck next to where she went over, he refused to believe the story. But then they'd accounted for every other person on the paddleboat, and he had to accept that Fanny was gone.

He balled his hands into fists. If only idiotic Burke had locked her in her cabin. Of course, if the boat had sunk, she'd have been trapped. He cringed, considering such a demise. Yet she'd drowned anyway. A strong man would have struggled to swim in that wind-tossed water. A woman wearing a heavy dress and cloak? Not possible. As soon as they'd docked, more than two hours ago now, he'd hired a pair of men he'd spotted lounging near the pier to take out a rowboat and search for her body. He should, at the very least, give her a decent burial.

A groan built in his throat. From the moment he'd heard her sing from the dais of the country church on the edge of the Scottish village of Inverness, he'd known she was the talent he'd been seeking to entertain passengers on his steamboat. That she was a child of only fourteen took him aback, but her tender age proved in his favor when he presented the opportunity for a seven-year term of service in exchange for her family's transport to America. Her father's exclamation — "Why, she'll be young enough tae raise a brood o' her own when she's dane" — accompanied their handshake. Then he'd placed his bold *X* on the document of agreement to service.

Of course, her father hadn't been able to read the print that stipulated seven years *per family member.* Thirty-five years in all. Not that Sloan had intended to hold her *that* long. Another thirteen or fourteen years, perhaps. Long enough to earn him enough money to purchase a home in one of Boston's finest neighborhoods, where he could look down his nose at the less fortunate the way the high-society ilk had always done to him. Or maybe enough to buy an estate in England, the country his parents left when they were young and foolish. He'd visited the city of London twice and found it pleasing. Would it happen now, without Fanny? She'd held a significant role in him attaining his dreams.

He had watched her mature from a sweet-faced girl into a comely young woman, and her presence made the *River Peacock* the most popular entertainment steamboat on the Mississippi. Oh, other boats had singers or bands. One even advertised a small circus. But no performer could outshine Miss Fainche Beck's crystal-clear voice and lovely appearance.

He clicked his tongue on his teeth, shaking his head. "Such a loss. An immeasurable loss."

Burke patted Sloan's shoulder, the action awkward and uncomfortable despite their many years of acquaintanceship. "It's a sorrowful thing, for sure. She was a fine girl."

Sloan shrugged off the man's hand. "She was a rare talent."

Burke gawked at him. "You'll find another singer."

Sloan didn't want another singer. The boatwright estimated he'd need three months to repair the vessel to its former glory. He could use those months to scour opera houses, saloons, and churches for Fanny's replacement. But he'd never find a talented performer who would sing, in essence, for room and board. He envisioned his profits decreasing, and he battled the urge to throttle someone. He'd had the perfect setup, and now —

"Cap'n, why don'tcha take a room at an inn? Or go to your cabin on the *Peacock*? Your cabin didn't suffer no damage. Sleep'll

25

do you good. Ain't nothin' more you can do for Fanny." Burke coughed a weak laugh. "I'd like to get some slumber, too."

Sloan flung his hand in the direction of the docked boat. "Go on, then. Rest your weary head." Sarcasm dripped from the command, and he inwardly berated himself. He shouldn't take his frustrations out on Burke. The seasoned deckhand had served him faithfully since the day Sloan purchased the riverboat. *"The labourer is worthy of his hire."* Was he now hearing his father's voice in his head? He must be overly tired if Father's penchant for reciting Scripture was invading his mind.

Releasing a heavy sigh, Sloan gestured again to the *Peacock.* "It's fine, Burke. Get some sleep."

Burke slid his hands into the pockets of his baggy pants and slunk away.

Sloan folded his arms, squared his aching shoulders, and fixed his gaze upriver. He'd wait at the dock until the rowboat returned. A worthy laborer deserved to be laid to rest. Once he'd given Fanny a decent burial, he would dredge up the wherewithal to seek a new singer.

Fanny lay belly down, her cheek plastered against a cold, damp surface. Something wet and stringy covered her face. Something wet and heavy held her flat. Where was she? With effort, she forced one eyelid open. Dove-gray shadows diminished her view. She squinted past the veil of her tangled hair but couldn't discern her location. She was too tired to care. She closed her eye again.

"She dead?" The whispered query in a child's high-pitched voice came from behind Fanny.

"Reckon so," said another voice, deeper in tone but equally hushed. "Fill the bucket, like Grandpap said."

Fanny wanted to turn her head and see who spoke, but her muscles refused to cooperate.

"Seems awful sad to leave her layin' here all by herself." True sympathy tinged the child's words.

"No need worryin' over her, Dathan. Her folks'll be searchin'. She git found by an' by."

"Reckon they'll find us, too?"

The child's panicky question sent Fanny's pulse into a skitter. Sloan! Would he find her? She had to get up, to hide, to save herself. But her muscles refused to move.

"We'll be gone by then. Just fetch that water 'fore the sun comes full up."

The swish of skirts let Fanny know the woman was moving away, even though her footsteps made no sound against the moist clay bank. Her ears recognized the gentle slosh of a bucket dipping up water, then the rustle of movement through brush. Silence fell, save the familiar soft flow of the river. The people were gone.

But Sloan might come. If he found her, he'd close her in her room again. He'd keep her beyond their agreed-upon length of service — maybe forever. She would never see Da and Ma or her sisters again. She needed to leave, too.

Fanny willed her elbows upward and planted her palms against the cool ground. Groaning with effort, she pushed herself to her knees. Dizziness assailed her. She remained on all fours, head hanging low and chest heaving, for several minutes. When the sensation of spinning cleared, she gritted her teeth in determination and struggled to stand. She swayed, the unmoving surface beneath her feet unfamiliar, but remained upright.

She glanced down her length. The cloak

was gone, but her many layers of water-logged clothing still weighted her. Her legs were wobbly, and she'd lost both shoes. Cold from the damp riverbank seeped through her thin, torn stockings. She shivered, yet the moist earth between her toes raised happy memories of her childhood, walking the garden rows with Ma. Even so, her soles were tender after so many years of wearing shoes. She'd need help to make it to a train station.

Still unsteady, she sent a cautious look up and down the riverbank. Sloan would certainly search by boat. No boats in either direction. She blew out a small breath of relief and forced her muddled brain to think. Finding a kind farmer who might be willing to transport her to the closest town was her best hope for escape, but no glimpses of rooftops or wisps of smoke trailing upward against the pale gray sky that might indicate a chimney directed her. She needed help, but how to find it?

She shifted her gaze to the thick brush lining the riverbank. Barely discernible indentions in the clay led to a gap in the bushes. Was this the pathway the two water fetchers had taken? They'd mentioned a grandfather. Would he be willing to assist her? She had no other choice. Sending up a prayer for God's protection and guidance, she turned herself in a clumsy half circle and staggered for the narrow break in the heavy row of bushes.

Her water-soaked clothing and trembling limbs slowed her progress, and it seemed to take years to push through the tangle of brush. But finally she stepped into a small clearing surrounded by trees with peeling bark. Their thin branches, sparsely decorated with leaves, formed a lacelike canopy over the open area.

Several people, their heads low, sat in a circle in the center of the clearing. Under the glow of moonlight, she made out a broad-shouldered white-haired man, three women of varying ages, a little boy, and a baby girl — six people in all, each wearing bulky layers of threadbare clothing. The man murmured something in a deep, husky voice, but Fanny couldn't hear the words. Suddenly she realized he was praying.

Instinctively, she bowed her head, too. She remained at the edge of the cleared space until she heard a chorus of soft amens. She lifted her gaze as those in the circle did so, and her eyes connected with the little boy's. He jerked as if bee stung, then scuttled backward like a crab.

As if synchronized, the others all looked

in her direction. The youngest of the women bolted to her feet, the skirts of her calico dress swirling. She rasped, "She — she alive!"

Fanny blinked several times, a smile pulling at the corners of her lips. She struggled against the weight of her drenched clothing and took a single step toward the group. "I am. I am alive. Oh, thank You, Jesus." Her voice emerged loud in the otherwise quiet early morning. Croaky but strong.

The white-haired man rose, shaking his head. "Shhh."

The utterance startled Fanny into silence. She set her lips tight and stared at the man. He was big boned and stern looking like Burke. Only the fact that she'd heard him praying kept her from gathering the strength to run away.

The little boy leaped up and scrambled to the old man. "What we gonna do, Grandpap? She done seen us. She can turn us in."

The frantic whisper and genuine fear in the child's eyes pierced Fanny. She hadn't meant to frighten anyone. She started to assure them, but the man spoke first.

"Hush that." He put his hand on the boy's shoulder and leaned sideways a bit, seeming to peer beyond Fanny. "You all by yo'self, miss?" Wariness colored his expression and soft query.

She nodded. "I . . . I need help." She lifted her hand in a gesture of entreaty. "Please, can you direct me to a railway station?"

The man stared at her hand for several silent minutes. The distrust in his eyes brought a swell of defeat. He was going to send her away without offering direction. Fanny turned toward the brush.

A heavy sigh sounded. "Miss?"

Fanny looked over her shoulder.

He stretched his leathery palm to the spot of ground he'd vacated. "Set down an' have some bread. 'Pears you could use some bolsterin'." He whispered, his low voice soothing in its delivery. "Talk'll come later."

3

NEAR PALMYRA, MISSOURI
FANNY

Fanny held the well-worn blanket, given by the youngest woman of the group, snugly around her shoulders. Its warmth was restoring her strength. Her chest felt as tight as a drumhead, probably from swallowing river water, and every muscle in her body ached. But she was alive. Alive and *free.*

Overhead, pink dawn inched across the sky, snuffing out the stars and signaling a new day. A delightful shiver slid down her spine. Her first day free of the *River Peacock.* Her first day free of Sloan's control. Oh, such a wonderful day.

The group sat in a tight cluster across the cold firepit and stared at her. No one said a word. Even the baby, a bright-eyed girl perhaps a year old — a little younger than Fanny's sister Moira had been the last time she'd seen her — made not a sound. Her head low, Fanny peeked around the circle at each person. They were weary looking.

And old. Even the boy, who couldn't have been more than eight years of age, seemed ancient.

She suspected she'd stumbled into a camp of escaped slaves, but where had they come from? How long had they been here? Where were they going? She longed to ask questions, but weariness tugged at her. Speaking would take energy she didn't possess. Her eyelids felt weighted. She couldn't keep them open. Holding the blanket in place, she curled on her side, closed her eyes, and drifted off to sleep.

When Fanny awakened, shadows surrounded her. She blinked in disbelief. The sun was slinking toward the western horizon. Had she really slept away the entire day? Cocooned in the wool blanket, she struggled to sit up, and when she finally settled cross-legged, she found herself under the perusal of several pairs of dark eyes.

The old man cleared his throat. "You hungry?" He spoke in a whisper, just as he'd done early that morning.

"I am, sir." She kept her voice soft, too.

He signaled the youngest woman with a bob of his head, and she dug in a leather pouch. She brought Fanny a few pieces of dried meat, some sticky raisins, and a chunk of bread. Fanny took the food and smiled her thanks. The girl gave a quick half smile and hurried to the old man. She sat close to him and pulled up her knees, staring at Fanny.

Fanny ate every bit of the food while the others alternately watched her, glanced at each other, and sent hopeful looks to the north. Her belly full, she sent a smile around the circle. "Thank you so much. You've been very kind to me."

The old man offered a grave nod. "You's welcome. But now I reckon it's time fo' you to tell us who you is an' how you come to be in the river."

Fanny licked her dry, chapped lips. "My name is Fainche Beck, but everyone calls me Fanny. I'm a singer on a riverboat — the *River Peacock.* The boat caught fire during last night's storm, and I got knocked overboard." She paused, anticipating a response, but no one said anything. She swallowed. "I don't recall much after that. Until I woke to voices." She risked a smile. "Thank you for feeding and sheltering me."

"Now that you's all rested up an' got some food in you, reckon you ought to go back to the boat."

Chills exploded over her flesh. "I . . . I can't." She forgot to temper her voice. The woman holding the baby hissed and the

35

man frowned, shooting worried glances right and left. Fanny swallowed against her dry throat and spoke in a fervent whisper. "Please. I can't go back to the boat. I need to find a railway station."

For several seconds, the man stared at her, his heavy white brows low. Then he tilted his head. "You runnin' from somethin', miss?"

Fanny's stomach fluttered. If she told them the truth, they might send her back to Sloan. Resolve filled her, and she straightened her shoulders. If they tried, she'd run away. The pressure against her hip assured her she hadn't lost her money pouch. She only needed to find a railway station and she could go to Ma and Da.

She looked straight into the grandfather's worried face. "The man who owned the riverboat indentured me when I was only a lass. We made an agreement, but he doesn't intend to honor it. If he finds me, he'll take me into servitude again." She sent a slow look around the circle, searching for sympathy or understanding. Only the old man met her gaze. Perhaps they could make a pact. "I mean you no harm. I promise I won't tell anyone about you. I only ask that you let me go on my way as if you'd never seen me."

No one spoke a word. Fanny waited

several minutes, then gathered up her courage and asked, "Who are you? And why are you here?"

The baby's mother cleared her throat. "We's —"

"Hush, Pazzy." The grandfather turned a fierce scowl on the woman. "Don't be tellin' her nothin'. How we know she ain't gonna turn us in? Master's gotta be lookin', an' he fo' sure put a bounty on our heads."

Fanny blinked across the circle at the girl and oldest woman, who huddled together and held the children close. Every pair of brown eyes was fixed on Fanny, and the fear glimmering in their irises broke her heart. She longed to assure them she'd never alert authorities to their whereabouts, but she didn't have a chance to speak.

"Who got us safe this far?" The old man's voice, although whisper soft, grated harshly. He poked his thick chest with his thumb. "I did. So I decides whether we trust this gal or not."

Fanny leaned forward so quickly the blanket slipped from her shoulders. "You can trust me. Truly, you can." A lump filled her throat. She couldn't honestly say she knew how they felt. She hadn't been born into forced labor. Her service, although restrictive, was by choice. But she knew the heartache of being kept prisoner and forced to work for someone else's benefit. Having experienced a kind of oppression, she would never contribute to someone else's enslavement.

A scripture formed in her memory and spilled from her throat without effort. " 'All things whatsoever ye would that men should do to you, do ye even so to them.' That's what my parents taught me, and I learned it well." Loneliness for Da and Ma brought the sting of tears. She swept her hand across her eyes and cleared them. "I won't turn you in. I promise."

The man chewed the inside of his cheek and glared at Fanny long and hard. Then, ever so slowly, his furrowed brow relaxed. He nodded, as if agreeing with himself about something, and sighed. "I vow we won't turn you in, neither."

Relief sagged Fanny's frame. "Thank you, sir."

The grandfather rested his elbows on the worn knees of his trousers. "My name's Enoch. Me an' my family's from Looziana. Itiah there" — he gestured to the oldest woman — "is my daughter."

Fanny gave a little start. Given the woman's aged appearance, she'd presumed Itiah was Enoch's wife.

38

"Kircie an' Pazzy — them's her girls. Now, Pazzy — she the mama of these young uns." Fondness warmed his features. "They be Dathan an' Baby Leona."

Fanny smiled at each family member by turn. Only Dathan smiled in reply, but Fanny didn't resent the women's reticence. They had reason to be distrustful. She'd simply have to prove herself trustworthy.

Enoch nudged Dathan. "Gonna need a fire fo' cookin' whatever's in our snare. Get it started. Kircie'll tend it while you check the snare. An' keep a watch fo' . . ."

Dathan nodded. He pulled a flint from his pocket and struck it several times against a rock. Sparks ignited the pile of dried pine needles and sent up a spiral of smoke.

The scent of pine — sweet and heady — filled Fanny's nostrils. She inhaled the aroma, so much more pleasant than the fishy smell of river water on her clothes.

Dathan slipped away into the brush.

Enoch looked after him for a few seconds, then settled his dark eyes on Fanny. "Me an' my family plant an' harvest sugarcane." He heaved a huge sigh and shook his head. "Hard work, Miss Fanny. Real hard work. But we was all together. We grateful to the good Lawd fo' that. But then the fellow who oversees the field, he tells me our master arranged to sell Kircie."

His gaze shifted to the girl, and Fanny looked at her, too. Shorter in stature than the other women and as round shouldered as if she carried something heavy on her back, she always kept her head bowed. In sadness, shyness, or something else? How old was Kircie? Fourteen? Fifteen, perhaps? Fanny swallowed a knot of agony. Young enough to still need her mother, the way Fanny had needed hers when Sloan took her away. She pulled the blanket around herself again, seeking its comforting warmth. If Da and Ma had known Sloan would keep her beyond seven years, they wouldn't have agreed to indenture her.

"Overseer say she gonna be sent to a cotton plantation in Mississippi." Tears glistened in the old man's eyes. "Lost my boy to fever near thirty years ago, befo' he was full growed. My missus, Loolie, grieve him all the way to her grave. I couldn't sit by an' watch Itiah suffer that way. She already bury her brother, her mama, her husband, an' two born-too-soon babies. All she have left is Kircie, Pazzy, an' Pazzy's chil'ren. Nuh-uh. Couldn't do it."

No wonder Itiah looked so life worn and weary. Hard work coupled with great heart-ache had aged her beyond her years. Gratitude that the family had made it away from the master who'd planned to separate Kircie from Itiah welled up. "Of course you couldn't."

Dathan returned. Enoch sent him a questioning look, and Dathan shook his head, then sat and wrapped his arms around his upraised knees.

"There be folks willin' to help slaves go to free states." Enoch went on as if there'd been no interruption. "So we snuck word to a fella, an' he squirrel us away from our master. Took us to a black man who buyed his freedom years back. He a riverboat captain now — got his own boat. He hid us an' brung us upriver. He leave us off here three days ago. Said a wagon was comin', would take us to Iowa. But it ain't showed."

Fanny sent an uneasy frown at Enoch. "What if the person doesn't come? What will you do then?"

Enoch shrugged, the motion slow and labored. "I don't rightly know. We got enough victuals to hold us another day if we careful, longer if we snare a rabbit or grouse." His stubble-dotted chin quivered, but hopefulness flared in his dark eyes. "But the good Lawd'll guide us. Freedom's waitin', an' we gonna claim it."

Freedom was hers to claim, too, as long

as Sloan didn't find her. She needed to get far away from the river as quickly as possible. She rubbed her chapped lips together. "I want to go to New York — to my family. But I'd feel safer if I didn't have to travel alone. I won't be a bother to you. I'll pay my own way." She fixed a pleading look on Enoch, sensing a compassionate soul despite his rough exterior. "May I ride with you to wherever you're going?"

Canton, Missouri
Sloan

A wavering ball of light seemed to float on the river's surface. Sloan rubbed his eyes and looked again. Was he seeing a ghost? Then the slosh of oars rhythmically breaking the water met his ears. Ah, a rowboat was approaching. Finally.

He stifled a groan and pushed to his feet. After he'd spent nearly the whole day sitting on a splintery, backless bench, his muscles screamed in protest. He wasn't elderly — only forty-four years old, the same age Father had been when Sloan had left home — but he felt as if he'd aged ten years in the past several hours. He forced his stiff legs to carry him to the end of the dock, and then he squinted through the evening shadows, tapping his foot as the vessel approached. It pulled close to the dock, and the wiry gray-haired man at the bow unhooked the lantern from the boat's short mast and set it on the warped decking near Sloan's feet.

"Where did you find her?" The question grated from Sloan's throat.

"We didn't."

Exhaustion and aggravation warred for prominence in Sloan's mind. "What do you mean you didn't? I told you not to return until you'd recovered her body."

The second man set the oars aside and nudged his partner. "Tie 'er up, Clyde, so we don't float off. I'm plumb wore out from rowin'."

Clyde secured the rowboat to a piling with a ragged length of rope, then heaved himself onto the deck. "Me an' Sam stayed out pret' near half o' last night an' all o' today, searchin'. Haven't had no food or water since we set out."

Sloan grunted. Their lack of preparation wasn't his concern.

"We didn't find a woman's body, but we found this." Clyde leaned toward the boat. "Gimme that thing, Sam."

Sam handed up a soggy, mud- and sand-smeared bundle of fabric.

Clyde straightened and held out the wad

43

of cloth. "Did this come from your river-boat?"

Sloan examined the bundle. Lamplight caught a flash of shimmering red. Recognition struck with such force that he staggered backward two steps and his breath caught in his lungs. Fanny's velvet, silk-lined cloak, the same one he'd ordered from a seamstress in Paris. "Yes. Yes, it did."

"It was hers?"

Sloan nodded.

Sam, as slender as the first man but probably half his age, leaped onto the dock and sent the rowboat into wild rocking. He stood next to Clyde and stared at the cloak. "Clyde seen it first. It was layin' on the bank, all a-rumpled. When he pointed to it, I thought for sure it was her layin' there." He shook his head and released a regretful sigh. "If she was wearin' that heavy thing when she went in, it prob'ly took her straight to the bottom."

Sloan stifled a shudder.

Sam stuck his hand out, palm up.

Sloan lowered his gaze to the extended hand, then settled it on the hand's owner. "What?"

"You said you'd pay us five dollars when we got back." He bobbed his hand. "We're back. Where's our pay?"

44

Sloan snatched the cloak from Clyde. "I said I'd pay you to find the woman's body. Does this" — he thrust the fabric toward the unkempt pair — "look like a woman's body?"

Both men's eyebrows descended into sharp V's.

Clyde spluttered, "Now, wait just a minute, mister. You can't blame us if her body ain't washed up. That there thing you're holdin' proves we went lookin'. Went lookin' hard for more'n twelve hours. Like Sam said, she prob'ly got took to the bottom. Might've got hung up on somethin' down there. Might not surface for days. You expect us to keep rowin' up an' down, up an' down, until then?"

Sloan shook out the cloak. The evening breeze caught it and it billowed like a flag. He reined it in and set to folding it neatly. "If you expect to receive five dollars for your trouble, yes."

Sam balled his hands into fists and arched forward like a fighting rooster. "Mister, I —"

Quick as a striking snake, Sloan dropped the half-folded cloak and pulled his Colt pistol from his boot. He aimed the barrel at Sam. "Accost me and I'll blow a hole in your belly."

45

Sam darted behind Clyde.

With one hand, Sloan kept the gun pointed at the men. He slid the fingers of his free hand into his vest pocket, pinched out a coin, and squinted at it in the minimal light. A Liberty dollar. He'd rather give them a fifty-cent piece, but he was too tired to dig for a different coin. He flipped the silver disk at the men.

Clyde caught it and jammed his closed hand into his trouser pocket.

"That will pay for a good dinner. Proper recompense for your trouble." Sloan pulled back the hammer with his thumb and held his pistol steady. He'd proven he had money on him, and the rest of the town was settling in for sleep. No one would bear witness or come to his aid if he got jumped. "If you choose to go out again after a time of rest, and if you bring back the body of the woman who wore this cape, I'll pay the remaining four dollars."

Sam snatched up the lantern, and then the two sidestepped around Sloan and took off for town.

Alone again, Sloan carefully uncocked the Colt and returned it to his boot. He gathered up Fanny's discarded cloak and folded it as best he could with only a faint glow of moonlight to guide him. With the bulky fabric square in his arms, he stared across the river. Tiredness tugged at him, a tiredness he hadn't known since the early days of his business, overseeing the complete renovation of the *River Peacock.* He hadn't slept much then, either, certain his absence would allow for shoddy workmanship.

A snort blasted from his throat. He'd erred by not participating in the search for Fanny's body. If he'd not been so overtaxed from dealing with the fire and then seeing to the many guests, he wouldn't have given such an important task to a pair of men who idled away their days at the loading docks. Incompetent fools. They'd probably found the cloak and stopped looking, thinking they'd swindle him out of the full payment.

The rowboat bumped against the piling and bounced off, then returned for another bump. Sloan frowned at the pale shape on the dark water, a plan forming in his mind. He'd need a lantern, a basket of food, a jug of water — he knew how to prepare for a day on the river — and someone to man the oars. He had no intention of rowing the thing himself. But if he wanted Fanny's body found, he'd have to do the seeking himself.

4

Fanny delayed blinking for as long as she could bear it. She didn't want to miss celebrating even one second of her new-found freedom.

Everyone else — except Enoch, who kept watch at the edge of the clearing — lay wrapped in blankets around the glowing coals left from their fire, soundly asleep. But after sleeping all day, Fanny was wide awake. The quiet let her mind relax. With the roar of boilers a thing of the past, her ears were open to the delightful sounds of this night. She wanted to absorb the delicate whisper of a breeze through the thick stand of bushes surrounding her place of sanctuary. How long had it been since she'd heard the mournful coo of doves, the hoot of an owl, or the chatter of squirrels? And, oh, the sights. She could gaze at the star-studded velvet sky forever. She'd forgotten how brightly stars twinkled and how the moon took on a halolike glow when filmy clouds drifted across its face.

The variety of scents also thrilled her senses. Such joy in breathing the crisp, cool air that carried the freshness of newly unfurled leaves. Even the scent of moist dirt became a perfume after filling her nostrils with the ever-present stench of mildew, river water, and cigar smoke that had permeated the riverboat. She might burst from drawing in so much pleasure at once.

She hugged herself, stifling a laugh. She longed to express her joy and appreciation in a song of praise and adoration to the One who'd answered her prayers for deliverance. Especially since, she was certain, morning would dawn on Sunday — a day set aside to worship the Creator. But she held the notes inside. She wouldn't give away her benefactors' locations. Their freedom wasn't yet complete.

They hadn't agreed to let her travel with them, but Enoch had told her she was welcome to stay and rest up as long as she needed to. For now, it was enough. She marveled that the old man had granted even that much favor. Especially since neither Pazzy nor Itiah seemed to approve. How had Enoch found the courage to trust her after spending his life bound by a man whose skin color matched hers? She had no qualms about trusting any of them. They understood forced servitude. They understood the desire for freedom. When she'd prayed to be set free from Sloan's control, she never would have imagined God using a fire, a near drowning, and a band of escaped slaves to rescue her. But here she was, under a canopy of stars with a group of people seeking exactly what she'd longed for.

A twig snapped, shattering the peaceful night.

Enoch abruptly ducked, and Fanny sucked in a gasp. He waved his hand at her, frowning fiercely, and she clamped her hand over her mouth.

Enoch tapped Dathan on the shoulder. The boy snuffled awake. His eyes went wide, and he tossed his blanket aside. The two inched on hands and knees to the edge of the clearing and remained there, faces aimed in the direction from which the sound had come.

Fanny shivered. If bounty hunters found their camp, they wouldn't bother with her. But they'd round up her newfound benefactors. She sent up earnest prayers for their safety. Her heart pounded so hard its steady beat filled her ears as thoroughly as the beat of the paddle wheel on the water had, and she strained against it for any other sounds of an encroaching predator. Whether it was two-legged or four-legged, how would they defend themselves against it without weapons?

Another rustle from the brush, louder than a wind rustle, raised gooseflesh on Fanny's frame. The owl that had kept them company ceased its persistent hoot, a sure sign it, too, sensed danger. She wanted to ask if they should hide in the brush. Wouldn't it be less likely they'd all be rounded up? Then she considered what would happen if some were found and some weren't. This family had suffered enough separation. Even if they were all found, at least they'd still be together. But what would she do?

Enoch tapped Dathan, then gestured wildly. Dathan nodded, rose to a crouch, and moved into the brush, still bent low.

The rustle in the brush intensified, and then the mutter of voices drew near. Pazzy, Kircie, and Itiah stirred, each sitting up and tossing worried looks at one another. Fanny couldn't stay seated. She clumsily rose. The heel of her foot caught on her underskirt's ruffle, and the fabric tore. Pazzy shot her a sharp look, and Fanny cringed. She grabbed up the blanket and wrapped it around herself, her body instinctively swaying slightly while she stared hard at the spot where Dathan had disappeared.

Moments later, Dathan broke through the brush. The lurking shadow of a tall man followed him. Dressed in black from his hat to his boots and with heavy black whiskers covering the lower half of his face, the man nearly disappeared against the backdrop of night. A band of white skin showing above his beard told her he wasn't another slave. But was he a slave catcher?

Dathan raised up on tiptoe close to Enoch and whispered, "Ransom."

Enoch gave a jolt, and then his spine seemed to wilt. He put his hand on Dathan's shoulder, as if too weary to hold himself upright, but a huge smile lit his face. "Ransom," he rasped, "we been waitin' for you."

Fanny's fear dissolved in a heartbeat, and gratitude filled her. Not a predator, but their rescuer. And what an appropriate name. She repeated it in a whisper as soft as thistledown. "Ransom."

The man jerked his gaze to her and pointed. "Who is she?"

Enoch's smile didn't dim. "Long story, mister. But she with us."

Fanny's pulse stuttered. She was?

Dathan tucked himself under Enoch's arm, his smile bright. Pazzy and Kircie rose and moved close to Enoch, their hopeful gazes locked on Ransom's face.

"Sorry it took me so long." Ransom yanked off his hat and twisted its brim in his hands. "There's other hidin' spots up an' down the river. I went to the wrong one first. Then the storm held me in place. The fella down the line's probably given up waitin', so you've got some walkin' ahead of you."

Pazzy shrugged. "Walkin' don't bother me none. Spent purty much my whole life on my feet." She waved her hand in Fanny's direction. "But she gonna have trouble keepin' up. She ain't got shoes."

Ransom aimed a quick look at Fanny's bare toes poking out from holes in her torn stockings. "Not havin' shoes could be a problem later on, but for now it's only a short walk to my wagon. After that, we'll be ridin' for some distance. Plenty of time to find her a pair of shoes. Have you got some rags or such to wrap around her feet to get by for now?"

Given the circumstances, Fanny doubted Pazzy had anything extra to spare. Besides, she'd promised not to be a bother to Enoch's family. "I'll use a ruffle from my"

— heat filled her face — "underskirt and see to my feet myself."

"Then get to it," the man said. "Folks, gather up your things quick as you can. We'd best be on our way."

Fanny turned her back on the group and sat on the ground. She busied herself with tearing loose the gathered lengths of rumpled linen from the hem of her undergarment and wrapping the strips like bandages around her feet, while the others packed their belongings.

"Kinda nervous about leavin' in the daylight, Mr. Ransom." Enoch's rumbling tone held more than a hint of concern. "If we get seen, we could get took back."

"That's a reasonable worry," Ransom said. "Our forger made certificates of freedom for each of you, but I'll be outright honest. There's some who, if they see you on your own, might not take the time to read 'em. There's others who don't care what the papers say." He sighed. "You'll be safe enough with me, but if my friend Standard isn't at our meeting spot, I can't go farther'n there. You'll hafta rely on prayer to get yourselves over the border into Iowa."

Fanny gave the fabric knots a quick tug and stood. The bulky wrap wasn't comfortable, but her feet were protected. She turned and faced the group. "I'm ready."

Ransom abruptly shifted his attention to her, almost as if he'd forgotten she was there. "You . . . you're traveling with 'em?"

Concern that he might refuse to take her swooped in. She lifted her chin the way she'd done whenever her sisters dared to ignore her instructions. "I am."

A slow grin climbed the man's cheeks. "Then I have an idea. I'll mull on it while I drive." He turned back to Enoch. "My wagon's waitin' in some trees over yonder. Ain't safe to stay in one spot so long. The Almighty's been watchin' over you folks, for sure. But it's best we get on our way."

Canton, Missouri
Sloan

Before the sun came up Monday morning, Sloan waited at the back door of a small café. After putting off his search for an entire day, he was in a surly mood. The folks in this town took resting on Sunday to the extreme. Not one person would row a boat for him on what they called "the Lord's day." The waiting around had reminded him of sitting on the parlor sofa with a book in his hand through the long Sunday afternoons of his childhood. He'd never understood why he couldn't run and play on a

55

day when school was closed. But Father had kept the rule all through Sloan's growing up.

Sloan snorted. He hadn't rested yesterday. He'd paced, inwardly stewing over the delay. Many times he'd heard people say there was closure to seeing a deceased loved one laid out in a parlor, hands folded, eyes closed. Looking peaceful. He'd never understood it, though. Maybe because he hadn't gone to his grandparents' funerals. How could he have? He couldn't leave the *River Peacock* for the time it would take to travel to Massachusetts and back. But if those people were right, maybe he'd be able to rest after he'd put Fanny to rest.

Whistling interrupted his thoughts, and he squinted through the morning mist at a pair of men sauntering in his direction. The whistler carried a bucket, and the second man held a pair of bobbing fishing poles on his shoulder. They reached the edge of the rock-slab stoop at the café's back door and came to a halt. The whistling ceased. The man carrying the fishing poles stuck both hands in the air, sending the poles clattering to the ground. The bucket carrier only raised his free hand.

"Don't shoot, mister." The one with both hands in the air squealed the plea. "We ain't got much to spare, but we'll give ya whatever we got. Just don't shoot us."

Sloan scowled. "Why would I shoot you?"

The man holding the bucket slowly lowered his hand. "Last fellow we found skulkin' around before full light stuck a gun in my face an' took every penny I owned. All kinds of ilk come off the riverboats." He angled his head and peered at Sloan. "You sure you ain't a robber set on pickin' us clean?"

"Of course I'm sure." Sloan pushed aside his jacket flaps and hooked his thumbs in his trouser pockets. Odd how standing on solid ground left him feeling less footsure than when he walked the decks of his vessel. "I'm the captain of the *River Peacock.* I have no need to rob the likes of you."

The second man's hands dropped, and he let out a huge sigh. "Sure am glad to hear it. Then what're you doin' back here?"

"Waiting for the owner to come and open up so I might purchase a basket of food."

A grin broke on the bucket carrier's face. He swiped his hand down his pant leg, then stuck it out. "Well, you're in luck, Cap'n. I'm the owner of this here establishment, an' I'd be plumb pleased to fix you up with a basket."

Sloan gave the man's slimy hand a quick

57

shake, then used his handkerchief to clean his palm. "I'd like enough sandwiches to last a full day — breakfast, lunch, and dinner — for two men. I also need a jug of water."

The man winked. "I can getcha somethin' better'n water."

Sloan sold liquor. It fetched a tidy profit for his till. But he never imbibed. His father had preached fiery sermons about drink stealing a man's brain. Although he didn't hold with much of what he'd heard from his father's pulpit, he'd seen proof of the maxim in other men. He needed his full senses to operate his business. "Water only."

"All right, Cap'n, if that's what you want." The man shrugged and stepped up on the stoop. He moved past Sloan, aiming a skeleton key for the lock. "Come on in an' I'll put Bobby here to work on them sandwiches. I gotta get these fish cleaned an' ready for fryin'."

Sloan peeked into the bucket. The floppy carcasses of channel cat and walleye lay in a heap. He wrinkled his nose. "You won't put those on my sandwiches, will you?"

A hearty laugh burst out. " 'Course not." He creaked the door open and stepped inside. "Got some smoked ham. Makes real good sandwiches on rye bread."

"That'll do." Sloan followed him in. "And be quick about it. I need to be on my way."

5

ON THE MISSISSIPPI RIVER,
NEAR LA GRANGE, MISSOURI
SLOAN

Sloan held his stomach and twisted his head back and forth, searching the banks, while the man he'd hired slowly rowed the rickety little boat up the middle of the river. The constant turning of his head and refocusing of his eyes was making him dizzy. Or was it the sandwich he'd eaten an hour ago? The ham had tasted . . . off. He didn't intend to eat another, and he hoped the one he'd already consumed would stay put. He'd never vomited over the edge of a boat, and he had no desire to do so with this common stablehand, who'd introduced himself as Rock, as witness.

A clear blue sky stretched from horizon to horizon. Sunlight dappled the water, and an occasional splash signaled a leaping small-mouth bass breaking its surface. Each time, Sloan jerked his attention toward the sound. The silver scales on the fish's underside sparkled like diamonds when caught by the sun's rays — a fetching sight.

A cool morning breeze touched his face, and on both sides of the mighty river, new leaves decorated trees and bushes, a lovely backdrop for the brownish water lapping at the bank. A beautiful day. Too beautiful, considering the grisly task to which he'd set himself.

As he scanned the banks, he alternately hoped for a glimpse of Fanny's body and dreaded finding it. He'd never touched a dead body before, and he didn't think he'd have the ability to do so today. Not with his stomach rolling like dice in a chuck-a-luck cage. But he could have the oar operator do it. A man who shoveled manure wouldn't be averse to placing a corpse in the bottom of a rowboat.

They drifted near the center of the river for nearly two hours without seeing anything more than birds, jumping fish, and a pair of deer drinking at the water's edge. Sloan's impatience grew. Maybe they were too far away from the bank for him to notice anything that could lead them to Fanny's body.

He pointed to the western shore. "Row closer to the bank."

"You see somethin'?" Eagerness colored Rock's tone.

Sloan understood. He, too, was weary of sitting in this rowboat. "Not yet. But I want to go up along this shore, then back along the other."

"Yes, boss."

Not a hint of eagerness this time. Only resignation. But the man was being paid well for his efforts. He wouldn't receive five dollars in wages plus food — such as it was — for a day's labor in the stable. He had no reason to complain.

The next hours of their slow progress a few feet from the shore proved no more successful than the earlier hours. Nausea added to impatience took Sloan from surly to outright uncivil, but he held his tongue. Rock was four inches taller and twice Sloan's girth. No good could come from goading the man. The noonday sun blazed down, warming the top of Sloan's head through his hat, and he shrugged out of his jacket. As he did so, he caught sight of something unusual out of the corner of his eye.

He froze, the jacket hanging from his elbows. "Look there."

Rock gave a backward jerk on the oars, slowing their motion, and turned his gaze toward the bank. "What?"

"That patch of ground. It looks stirred."

Something other than nausea rolled in Sloan's belly. "Do you see several foot-prints?"

Rock craned his neck and squinted at the bank. A smile spread across his square face. "I do." Then he scowled. "But ain't we lookin' for a body?"

Yes, they were. But Sloan wanted to investigate anyway. Besides, if this queasi-ness persisted and he emptied his gut, he would rather do so in the bushes. He lay his jacket over the plank seat. "Pull up to the shore."

Rock followed Sloan's order. The row-boat's nose slid onto the bank, and Sloan hopped over the side onto the moist, sandy clay. He walked slowly around the periphery of the area, holding his belly and examining the footprints — two sets from boots, one child-sized and the other larger. An unusual indention also marred the ground. The boot prints seemed to circle the indention, then trailed off into the bushes.

Sloan looked toward the brush where the prints disappeared, curiosity rolling in his mind. He turned to Rock, who remained in the rowboat. "I'm going to explore a bit."

"Mind if I eat some more o' them sand-wiches?"

Sloan didn't mind if he ate them all. "Go ahead."

Rock reached for the basket, and Sloan plowed into the brush, head low, scanning the ground for more prints. Dried leaves in various stages of decomposition littered the ground, hiding distinct footprints, but tiny broken branches and trampled spots led him onward. He broke through the brush into a clearing, roughly twelve feet in diameter, obviously not carved by nature. Bushes had been hacked down, their stumps barely sticking above the ground. Many of them seemed to have been pounded to splinters by a hammer. In the center of the cleared area, a circle of rocks surrounded the charred remains of a fire. Or, given the number of blackened chunks scattered in pale gray ash, many fires. A small stack of dried branches and pine needles lay next to the rock circle.

Sloan tapped his chin, scowling. Was this a fisherman's camp? Or a hunter's? Possibly. The ground around the firepit was mostly smooth and hard, as if it had been worn down the way pathways were by frequent passage. But the recent rain must have softened it somewhat, because when he crouched low and looked carefully, he made out several boot prints in various sizes and a few prints made by someone with bare feet. He couldn't imagine a hunter bringing his entire family along, but a fisherman might. He slowly scanned the area, still pondering the purpose for this carefully carved sanctuary, and something out of place caught his attention.

He rose and crossed to the far edge of the clearing. A torn scrap of cloth, dingy gray and wrinkled, was caught on one of the little stumps. He pinched it up and stared at it. After purchasing all items for Fanny's wardrobe over the past years, he recognized the fabric — a simple linen used for women's undergarments. But was it from one of Fanny's petticoats?

He raised it to his nose and inhaled, seeking the essence of Fanny's lilac toilet water. The foul smell of dead fish and decayed plants filled his nostrils. His stomach whirled, and he tossed the bit of cloth aside. He bent over and lost his belly's contents. Emptied, he spat several times, but the rancid taste remained in his mouth. He'd rinse it well with water from the jug when he returned to the rowboat. Which he needed to do. Miles of shore remained to search.

For two days, the man they knew only as Ransom — he had explained that those who aided slaves to freedom kept their names secret for their safety — transported Enoch's family and Fanny along the south fork of the Fabius River.

Initially she was surprised he made no effort to avoid established roadways. Even Enoch had asked why they weren't hidden under bags of cotton, as they'd been on the riverboat. But Ransom had assured them that to anyone they came upon, their group would look like an owner and his wife transporting field hands to another location.

"Nobody'll pester you while you're with me," he'd said with such conviction that Fanny believed him.

They'd slept in a barn the night before and enjoyed a hot meal cooked by a farm-wife. The woman had gaped at Fanny's tangled hair, sunburned face, and mud-stained, hopelessly wrinkled dress and then escorted her into the house. She said, "Honey, you stick out like a Scotch thistle in a rose garden. Nobody'll take you for a lady dressed thataway. Lemme get you fixed up." She brushed Fanny's hair and pinned it into a bun, tied a wide-brimmed bonnet

66

on her head, and even gave her a dress from her daughter's wardrobe.

The gesture touched Fanny deeply, especially because she saw how few frocks hung on the pegs. Fanny offered to pay for the dress, but the woman waved her hand.

"No, no. My Mary's close to growin' out o' that dress anyway. If we hadn't already passed her outgrowed shoes to a neighbor gal, I'd hand those to you, too. That cloth you're wearin' on your feet won't last for long." Then she had hugged Fanny and said, "You keep your money, an' if you get the chance to give to some needy person along the way, you do it an' think o'me."

The blue-checked frock with its simple button-up front and lack of embellishment was foreign yet oh so welcome after she'd worn stage dresses for so many years. She felt as if she was peeling away her identity as a riverboat singer and finding herself again. She vowed to do as the farmwife had asked — to help others the way she was being helped.

Now Fanny rode on the seat with Ransom. As the wagon bumped over the rough road, its rocking motion reminding her of being on the riverboat, Fanny prayed that the man called Standard would still be waiting for them even though they were two days past the planned rendezvous. But if he wasn't there, Ransom asked Fanny to maintain the role of a plantation owner's wife and accompany Enoch and his family to Iowa. He'd told her, "I can send 'em on alone. It's been done before. But only with one or two folks makin' the escape. A group as big as this one? It'll be a heap sight harder for them to stay hid. But I know you've got your own plans, so you aren't obliged to do it."

Fanny prayed for discernment. She had confidence in these men who'd previously worked together to help free slaves. Such an intricate system they'd developed! But she had little confidence in her ability to keep the family safe.

While they rode, Ransom concocted a story for Fanny to share in case she decided to travel on with them. He made her recite the details over and over so she'd be ready if anyone tried to accost her and remove Enoch and his family from her. She knew the words by heart, but would she be able to deliver them with heart? Da and Ma had taught her that bearing false witness was an affront to God. Lying had never come easily from her tongue, and Ma had laughingly told her she shouldn't bother trying to fib because her guilty face gave her away. Surely anyone could look at her and know she was spinning a tale. She prayed she wouldn't be forced to recite falsehoods.

But as soon as they were all safe, she intended to sing a song Pazzy had taught her. Fanny asked Pazzy where she had learned it, and she explained she'd been briefly loaned to a Mormon family as a wet nurse when the mother died in childbirth. The family's housekeeper often sang it while working, and Pazzy memorized it.

"We'll find the place which God for us prepared" seemed to speak a promise. Many other lines from the beautiful hymn also spoke to Fanny, such as "Though hard to you this journey may appear, grace shall be as your day." No part of her unexpected journey had been easy, and it didn't seem as if it would be easier ahead, but she'd seen evidence of grace every step of the way. Living under Sloan's control for those long, lonely years, she'd never guessed so many good-hearted people existed. But from old Cricket to each person she'd encountered since her fall from the *River Peacock,* God had aligned her pathway with folks who honored Him.

She held to the wagon seat and closed her eyes. With the sun warming her hair through the pink-flowered bonnet and the scent of spring pleasing her nose, she thanked God for His guidance, asked His blessing on each of the people who contributed to bringing Enoch's family and others to a place of freedom, and asked His protection for the remainder of their journey.

As she ended the prayer, someone tapped her shoulder. She turned partway on the bench seat and found Dathan standing behind her, his fingers curled over the seat's planked back. She smiled at him. "Were you needing something?"

"Yes'm. When we stop, wouldja show me some more letters?"

At their previous stops, she'd entertained Dathan by writing the alphabet in the dirt with a stick and telling him the sounds the letters made. She hadn't been able to discern whether the activity truly interested him, so her heart rolled over in joy at his request. "I surely will. And if yer mama approves, I'll show y' how to write yer name. Would y' be likin' that?"

He nodded hard.

She grinned. "All right then."

Ransom cleared his throat. "There might not be time for letter learnin'. Edina's just ahead — we'll be there in another hour or so. Our meetin' spot is in a thick patch of trees behind a boardinghouse on the north

70

edge of town. If Standard's not waitin', they'll need to push on. Closer we are to the border between Missouri an' Iowa, the more dangerous it gets. The longer they stay in one place, the more likely somebody'll notice them an' ask questions. Won't be time for much more'n walkin', eatin', an' sleepin'."

Dathan sank down, his lower lip poked out.

"An' one other thing . . ."

The hesitation in the man's tone sent prickles of apprehension across Fanny's scalp. "What is it?"

"Your speech. You . . ." He pulled in a breath, then blurted, "Right then you sounded Irish."

She couldn't resist a laugh. "Not so surprising. I am Scottish by birth." Sloan had discouraged her brogue, saying it made her sound ignorant. He'd hired a tutor not only to educate her but to train her to speak without the lilting rhythm of her homeland.

"Much as I hate to admit it, Miss Fanny, there's folks who don't hold much favor toward the Scots or the Irish." He glanced at her, then set his gaze forward, as if too embarrassed to meet her eyes. "That story I gave you to tell . . . well, it'll fall flat unless you sound like a planter's wife."

"And a rich planter wouldn't be marryin' up with a Scottish lass — is that what yer tellin' me?" She deliberately injected her brogue for the pleasure of hearing it.

He nodded. "That's what I'm sayin'." He shot a brief frown toward the back of the wagon, and then his hands tightened on the traces. "If you end up goin' all the way into Iowa with this family, you gotta be careful."

Her pulse skittered, and she shivered despite the sun's warmth flowing down. She sent up another prayer. *Let Standard be waiting.*

6

EDINA, MISSOURI
FANNY

Fanny's heart fell. No peddler's wagon — the conveyance Ransom had indicated Standard used to transport "cargo," their word for the people they helped — waited at the stand of maple trees growing well behind a large wooden structure Fanny perceived was the boardinghouse Ransom had mentioned.

Ransom sat for several minutes on the seat, staring ahead with his jaw clenched so tight his muscles twitched. Then he abruptly leaped to the ground.

"Stay here, folks. I'll be back." He stalked off.

Itiah slumped against Enoch, and he whispered to her while patting her shoulder. Kircie crouched on Itiah's other side, worry crinkling her brow. Pazzy sat stone faced with Baby Leona in her arms, and Dathan stared, wide eyed and silently, at his mother, as if waiting for comfort. She didn't offer it.

Ransom paced back and forth along the uneven row of straggly maples. His tense frame and angled head reminded Fanny of a sheepdog sniffing out a lost lamb. Suddenly he charged into the trees. She stared at the spot where he'd disappeared, praying the wagon was somewhere in those trees. If not, Ransom would again ask her to accompany Enoch and his family all the way to Iowa. But how long would that take? She wanted to reach New York City and reunite with her family as quickly as possible. Her heart ached with loneliness for Da, Ma, and her sisters. She'd already been away from them for almost seven lonely years. It seemed unfair to ask her to wait longer.

"Miss Fanny?" Kircie knelt behind the wagon seat, so close her warm breath touched Fanny's ear. "What you speculate he doin'?"

"I don't know." Fanny gave the girl a smile she hoped hid her own concern. "But Mr. Ransom, with God's help, has brought us safely thus far. Let's trust God to continue guiding him. And us."

Uncertainty glimmered in Kircie's eyes, an uncertainty with which Fanny empathized. The girl sat down without another word.

Moments later Ransom strode from the

trees to the side of the wagon and lifted his hands to Fanny. "Come on down from there." He assisted Fanny, then reached into the bed and swooped Dathan to the ground. "All of you, climb out an' follow me."

The wagon box creaked noisily as Kircie and Enoch scooted out the back on their own. Enoch helped Itiah and Pazzy, and they trailed after Ransom into the trees.

"Like I figured, Standard had to go on," he said. "A peddler wagon parked in one place for so long could draw attention. But he left me some notes nailed to a tree. An' a whole lot else, too. There's fresh clothes for all of you. Well, except for Miss Fanny because we didn't know she was comin'. He drew a map to follow, an' he hung a pack o' food from a branch." He chuckled. "The rope an' some edges of the pack are chewed. Looks like a squirrel or two tried their best to get to it, but the food's still in there."

He stepped aside and gestured to a wooden crate nestled at the roots of one of the larger trees. "Help yourself."

Enoch, Itiah, and Kircie looked at each other as if confused by the direction. But Pazzy handed Baby Leona to Fanny and hurried to the box. She pulled out the first item, a pair of wool britches. She sent a grin over her shoulder. "These oughta fit you fine, Grandpap. An' here's a jacket to match. You gonna look handsome as a preacher in this suit."

Fanny bounced Baby Leona on her arm and watched Enoch inch forward so slowly it seemed he slogged through ankle-deep mud. He took the clothes and stared at them. The true wonder in his expression brought the sting of tears.

Pazzy removed a dress and undergarments, held them up for a brief examination, and then gave them to Itiah. The older woman accepted the items with the same awe Enoch showed. Pazzy laid aside another dress for herself, then scowled into the box. "Mr. Ransom, whoever pack this box do real fine fo' Mam, Grandpap, an' me, but these clothes that're left ain't gonna work for Kircie or my boy. They all wrong."

Ransom moved close, shaking his head. "These were picked careful for you all." He turned to Kircie with an apologetic face. "The plantation owner from Louisiana" — Fanny appreciated his refusal to call the man their master — "could've sent an alert over the telegraph to sheriffs an' such to be on the lookout for an adult man, two women, a girl, and a small boy. By dressin' the youngsters different, it'll help disguise you."

Dathan's eyes bulged. "You sayin' I hafta wear a dress?"

Ransom's lips twisted into a sympathetic grimace. "I'm afraid so, son. But only until you get to Iowa. Then you can throw the dress away an' never look at it again."

"Nuh-uh, he won't." Pazzy spoke with conviction. "We gonna keep the dress. Someday Baby Leona'll be able to wear it. Besides" — tears winked in her dark eyes — "it'll remind us o' the kindness folks showed us."

Enoch scratched his stubbled cheek. "Mr. Ransom, what if somebody stop us an' don't believe Kircie here's a boy an' Dathan's a gal? How we gonna make 'em believe?"

Ransom turned to Enoch. "You show them the certificates I gave you. Kircie's says she's a boy named Peter, an' the one for Dathan says he's a girl named Esther. You an' Pazzy an' Itiah have new names on the papers, too. Memorize those names an' make sure you use 'em when you're around other folks. That should be proof enough."

Enoch hung his head. "They ain't a one o' us who can read them papers, Mr. Ransom. We won't know which one to show somebody who ask."

Ransom put his hand on the old man's shoulder. "Don't feel shame for not knowin' somethin' you ain't been taught. The shame belongs to them who kept you from learnin' it."

Enoch lifted his face and gave a solemn nod. "Thank you, Mr. Ransom."

"You're welcome." Ransom took a step away from the group, gesturing to Fanny to follow. "Miss Fanny an' me will let you all get changed into your new clothes. I'm gonna drive her into Edina so she can buy shoes. To be safe, you all stay here in the trees until we get back."

Pazzy took Baby Leona, and then Fanny followed Ransom to the wagon. Her limbs trembled, making her stumble. His leave taking was upon them. She needed to tell him her destination was New York City.

She touched his sleeve. "Mr. Ransom, I . . ." A worry attacked, stealing her intended statement. "Iowa is still so far away. Will they be able to safely reach it without the help of a knowledgeable guide?"

Ransom turned a somber look on her. "I didn't wanna scare Enoch an' the others, but those folks won't be safe even in Iowa."

His comment made no sense to her. "But isn't Iowa a free state? Enoch believes so."

"It is, but the Fugitive Slave Act says escaped slaves have to go back if they're found, even if they're found in a free state.

So the government lets slave catchers prowl in the free states, too. It's the law."

Fury filled Fanny, temporarily overpowering her fear. "It's a *bad* law, Mr. Ransom."

"Just 'cause somethin' is legal don't make it right. That's why me an' some others help folks like Enoch an' his family. An' we're all prayin' for the day when a law says slavery ain't right in any part of our country."

Fanny straightened her spine. "I'll pray with you."

A smile formed on the man's face. "I admit, Miss Fanny, when I saw you back at the river campsite, I came close to leavin' you behind. But I think God put you there, and I think He's gonna use you to help Enoch, Itiah, an' the others find freedom."

Tingles climbed Fanny's spine and tickled her scalp. Had God swept her to that very spot on the riverbank not only for her own rescue but for the family's rescue, too? *"We'll find the place which God for us prepared . . ."* The song Pazzy called her freedom song rang through Fanny's mind, the first word in the line — *we'll* — seeming to reverberate. And all at once she knew. God meant for her to be part of that "we."

"I'll go with them if it will help keep them safe." Staying with Enoch's family would delay Fanny's arrival in New York City, but

Da always said God's will was more important than any man's will. She offered a slow nod, building determination. "But if Iowa isn't safe, then where will they be free?"

"The farther they can get from the Missouri border, the safer they'll be. If they can get to Milwaukee, Wisconsin, there's a Baptist church not too far from the train station. The preacher there'll give 'em shelter an' protect 'em."

Fanny committed his words to memory.

"Then he'll send word to some other folks, an' hopefully they'll make it all the way into Canada. No slave catchers'll bother 'em there."

Fanny's mouth fell open. "Canada?" Did God expect her to go all the way to another country?

"But you don't have to go with 'em that far. Even Enoch told me you need to get home, too."

Enoch's concern for her touched her deeply. Fanny silently vowed to seek God's instruction concerning how long she should stay with Enoch and his family.

Ransom pulled a folded piece of paper from his shirt pocket and held it out to her. "This is the note Standard left. Read on through it. If somethin' don't make sense, ask now. Soon as you've got some shoes on your feet, I need to move on. Been away from my family more'n a week now. Folks are probably startin' to ponder why they haven't seen me workin' my fields, an' my wife's probably worried somethin' happened to me. This work we're doin' — it don't come without risks."

How thoughtless she'd been, only worrying about herself. She reached for the letter but placed her hand lightly on his wrist instead. "Thank you for all you've done for us, Mr. Ransom. I will never forget your kindness."

He blushed crimson. "Now, miss, no need for that. Just doin' what the Lord called me to do. I'm free because Jesus forgave my sins. I reckon I owe Him, an' helpin' a few folks find their way to freedom is a small price to pay." He put the letter in her hand. "Read that now."

Fanny unfolded the wrinkled sheet of paper. The writing, done in pencil, was smudged and ran in crooked lines across the page. Several misspelled words leaped out at her. She was a good reader, thanks to her tutor's diligence, but this might challenge her. She drew in a breath, squinted at the markings, and began at the top.

To whom it may cunsern:

To get to Iowa follow the South Fabius River. Make a wandering path stead of a strate one and stay outa site as best you can. Safer that way. Keep the river in site on yer right hand side and youll do fine. When you reech its end head due north. In about 20 miles youll come to the North Fabius River. Follow it to its end. Bout 25 miles. When you get there youll be in Iowa. Theres stage stops and some farms on the way but they aint friendly. Best to keep moving. Good luck and God bless you.

Below the letter was a rough map with long squiggly lines — rivers? — and a few *X*'s marking what she presumed were towns or stage stops. Each of those *X*'s meant people — even slave catchers? — would be found.

"They aint friendly."

She broke out in a cold sweat. She lifted her gaze to Ransom. "I . . . I want to help, but I don't know if I can do this."

His lips formed a grim line. "I thought the same thing when I picked up my first cargo an' carried it up the road. But, Miss Fanny, you got a whole lot o' people who're prayin' safety over the escaped slaves an' every person who helps 'em. That means they're prayin' for you, too."

When she lived on the riverboat, she would never have believed that people she didn't know would pray for her. But the experiences of the past days had shown her people's generosity and care. Her lips quavered into a smile. "Thank you." Worry crept in again. "But will the story you made up be enough to fool someone who wants to do Enoch and his family harm? I confess, I'm not a good storyteller."

"That's why I made you practice it. When you need it, you'll be able to tell it." He bent and looked her in the eye. "Do you believe it's wrong to keep people in bondage?"

She gulped. "I do."

"Do you believe God helps folks who are doin' good works in His name?"

Da and Ma believed it. They'd taught her she could rely on God's might when she felt weak and powerless. She'd relied on God's strength many times during her lonely years on the *River Peacock.* "I do, sir."

"Then you keep remindin' yourself you're doin' God's work. Trust Him to see you through."

Wasn't that what she'd told Kircie only a

few minutes before? She straightened her spine. "I will."

"Good." He straightened. "Now, you've got money to buy shoes?"

"I do." Her hand automatically went to the pouch and its comforting bulge. She crinkled her brow. How much would it cost to travel to New York? The coins Cricket had collected added up to seventy-five dollars, what Da would have considered a small fortune. She shouldn't squander it, but there were things besides shoes she would likely need for a lengthy journey.

Ransom folded his arms and tipped his head back slightly, peering at her with squinted eyes. "What kind of plot are you hatchin'?"

As Ma said, Fanny couldn't hide what she was thinking. She must work on maintaining a straight face should she need to make use of the tale Mr. Ransom had scripted for her. "I was only thinking of things we'll need if we're to take care of ourselves the whole way to Iowa."

He guided her to the wagon and helped her onto the seat. "We can talk about it on the way to town. Let's take that trip into Edina an' then get you folks on your way."

On the fifth day following the riverboat fire, Sloan sent the last of his passengers back to their homes. He'd had to strike bargains with the captains of a dozen different paddleboats to accommodate all who'd been aboard the *River Peacock.* Not all the vessels, including this last one, were intended to carry passengers. One man's particularly brusque objections still rang in Sloan's ears. Not that he'd been the only one to complain. Their impatience and ire served to increase Sloan's aggravation. Did they think he set fire to his own boat to inconvenience them? Couldn't they offer condolences in place of criticism, considering he'd temporarily lost his source of livelihood? And permanently lost Fanny, the Darling of the *River Peacock.*

He left the dock and trudged across the grassy shore to where his paddleboat was tied to cleats. There it would remain until all repairs were done. At least he didn't have to waste money on a hotel room. His cabin was unscathed, as were the crew's quarters. He'd sent most of the crew away, though, too. Why pay them to loiter about? He'd retained Burke and the old arthritic man, Cricket, who had no place else to go, and given them instructions to guard the boat from unwanted pests, whether man or creature.

As he neared the vessel, he caught sight of the gangplank for the middle level of the boat laid out on the ground as if the boat were sticking out its tongue. He gritted his teeth. Hadn't he told the workers not to leave it lying open? It invited invasion, and the boat's slight motions pushed the gangplank's end against the ground, which might damage the hinges. He stomped over the creaky plank, then pulled the ropes attached to pulleys and sealed it shut. He turned and found Burke in the hallway.

Surprise registered on the man's whiskered face. "Why, Cap'n, I thought you was sendin' off passengers."

"They're all gone." Just as Fanny was gone. Sloan waved his hand at the closed gangplank. "What have I told you about leaving this open?"

Burke held up both hands as if surrendering to the enemy. "Wasn't me who done it. Must've been the fellas hired to fix things up again. They're always comin' an' goin'."

Sloan would address the issue — again — with the shipwright in charge of repairs. For now, he needed to clean out Fanny's cabin. "Keep an eye on it."

Burke nodded. "Aye, sir."

Sloan pushed past the man, clomped down the stairs to the lowest level, and followed the hallway to Fanny's cabin. He'd finally given up on locating her body. After days of fruitless searching and finding nothing more than her other embroidered slipper, which he'd placed in a small trunk with her cloak and the slipper left on the deck, he conceded that she'd either been carried out to sea or was on the bottom of the murky river. He had to set his attention to securing a singer.

Fanny — so beautiful in voice, face, and form — had set a high standard. With her gone, his reputation as a provider of excellent entertainment was at risk of being destroyed. What was an entertainment riverboat without an entertainer? He must locate a singer of equal poise and ability. If one existed. As he'd told Burke, Fanny was a rare talent.

He reached her cabin and then came to a stop outside the doorway. His gaze fell on the little cot where she'd slept, sat to take her meals, and wrote in one of the tablets the tutor had given her to practice her writing. If he closed his eyes, he could picture her. Demure. Rarely complaining. Always giving her best effort to her performances.

And he'd intended to take advantage of her by keeping her beyond her perceived seven-year term of service.

But serving longer than a single term was only fair. After all, he'd brought her entire family from that lowly plot of land in Scotland to the United States. He paid for five people's passage in exchange for one person's employment. Then hadn't he educated her, housed her, clothed her, fed her? Seven years per family member was a more equitable exchange. But why worry over their agreement now? The girl was dead.

He pulled in a big breath of the mildewy, damp air, blew it out with a whoosh, and crossed the threshold. He began gathering Fanny's belongings and laying them on the cot. So few things to call her own and none of real monetary value, but he would send them to her parents anyway, along with a message about her passing. He doubted her parents would be able to read it, but Fanny's sister — the older one, Flossie — had learned to read and write during her first year in New York. She could tell them what it said.

A stack of envelopes bound with a length of pale-blue ribbon sat on the little table beside the cot. Each time the *River Peacock* docked in Kansas City, Sloan checked his mail. Three or four times a year, he found a letter from Flossie waiting. And Fanny always had one or two ready to send. He'd applied the postage and sent the missives on their way to the tenement building in the Lower East Side of Manhattan. Thanks to the sister's correspondence, he knew where to ship Fanny's belongings.

He started to pack her dresses, then changed his mind and returned them to their hooks. He'd invested quite a bit in her stage gowns. His next singer could make use of them. He placed the leather-bound Bible she'd treasured, along with the letters, tablets, and few books the tutor had left for Fanny, on top of her nightgown and under-things. A pencil rolled from between the pages of one of the tablets. He'd often seen the girl with pencil in hand, adding lines to the page. What had she found to write about?

Violating her privacy was no longer an is-sue. Would a dead person object? He picked up the top tablet and flipped it open. The first page contained nothing more than her given name, Fainche Ann Beck, written over and over in a neat, slanted script. His lips tugged into a wry grin. Such a pretentious name her parents had given her. Named for a saint, as he recalled. Perhaps that's why she'd been such a good-hearted, longsuffering soul.

He smacked the tablet into the trunk, chasing away the thought. Then he reached for the trunk's lid. But his hand paused midway, his gaze on the packet of letters. He should keep them. He needed the return address to know where to send the trunk. His conscience pricked. He could record the address on another sheet of paper and leave the letters in the trunk. Why keep missives sent to Fanny from her sister? Such a whimsical thing to do — keeping someone else's letters — and he was not a whimsical man. But he laid them aside and latched the trunk lid, sealing away everything else.

Then he went in search of Burke. He'd hand off the task of shipping the chest to Fanny's family. Sloan had a more difficult, pressing task awaiting him. He had to find a new singer.

7

NORTHEAST MISSOURI, NEAR THE SOUTH FABIUS RIVER
FANNY

Fanny felt as if she'd been walking for years. Her twice-daily strolls around the *River Peacock*'s deck had not prepared her to trek over miles of uneven landscape. She prayed for strength and hummed Pazzy's freedom song as a distraction and for encouragement, and somehow her weary legs carried her forward.

The first two days of travel without Ransom as their guide, Fanny saw wagons in the distance only twice. Both times, the group hunkered behind some bushes near the river until Enoch felt it was safe for them to continue. At Enoch's insistence, Fanny carried Standard's map, but Enoch was the true leader of the group, and she was grateful for him. His calm, rational responses to the others' concerns soothed Fanny's frayed nerves. At the start of each day, he asked the Lord to guide them, and at the close, he thanked Him for His protection.

She glanced at Enoch, who held the opposite handle on the crate of items Standard had left outside Edina. His skin glistened with perspiration, and his heels sometimes dragged in the grass, but even though he was at least three times Fanny's age, his pace remained steady hour after hour. Behind them, Dathan toted the bulkier of the two carpetbags Fanny had purchased in Edina's mercantile. Their mouse-eaten blankets plumped the bag the way grain filled a feed sack, making it impossible to carry by its handles. Such an unwieldy burden. But the boy balanced the load against his belly and never complained.

Kircie trailed Dathan and lugged the second carpetbag, which held their jackets and the cast-iron cooking pot Fanny had insisted on buying for cooking on the trail. When she added the pot to her pile of purchases on the general store's counter, Ransom had scowled in disapproval and said, "That's gonna be heavy." He'd been right, but they'd already made use of it.

The previous evening, Itiah and Dathan gathered a huge bouquet of purple flowers shaped like stars. While Fanny entertained Baby Leona by turning the blossoms into finger puppets, Itiah and Pazzy stripped the tiny leaves from the stalks, then broke the stalks into pieces. They boiled them with wild onions Kircie foraged near the river. If Fanny hadn't seen what went into the pot, she would have believed she was eating cooked turnips.

She'd been wise to buy the pot, and when she sent the family on their way without her, they would have one piece of kitchen equipment for their new life. She smiled, remembering the benevolent farmwife's encouragement to perform a kindness for someone as repayment for the dress Fanny now wore. She'd done so, and it felt good. What a parade they made — Dathan and Kircie with the carpetbags, Pazzy carrying Baby Leona in a makeshift fabric pouch on her front and the pack Standard had left for them on her back, and Itiah at the rear, constantly scanning the landscape. Was she scouting for possible edibles, for slave catchers, or both?

To Fanny's way of thinking, with their carpetbags and the trunk, they resembled a group traveling together, not a band of runaways. If they unexpectedly came upon a farmer or hunter, would he view them the same way and leave them be? In the event they were questioned, she would tell her story. The items they toted made it more believable. She continued to practice it, just as Ransom had instructed, but she still hoped she wouldn't be forced to use it. After all, in the eyes of the law, she was stealing the family members from the one who claimed to own them. She didn't want to add lying to her list of sins. But she'd do it if she had to.

"Grandpap?"

Dathan's plaintive query brought Enoch and Fanny to a stop. Enoch peered over his shoulder. "What you need?"

The boy dropped the carpetbag. "Somethin' in my shoe's pokin' me. Can we stop an' lemme get it out?"

"Best get to it."

Dathan plopped onto his bottom, tossed his frilly skirts aside, and wriggled his right shoe free.

Enoch glanced at the crate. "Set this thing down, Miss Fanny, an' take a little rest."

They lowered the trunk to the ground, and Fanny perched on its edge, stifling a groan. How good to sit, even for a few minutes. Were it not for Ransom's somber warning about slave catchers, she'd ask Enoch if they could make camp early. Her muscles screamed for rest.

Dathan bounced his shoe against the

ground, then stuck it back over his bare foot. He waggled his shoe in the air and grinned. "All better. No more pokin'."

Enoch pointed to the carpetbag. "Then pick that up an' let's go on."

The child heaved a man-sized sigh, but he obediently reached for the bag. Fanny stifled her own sigh and pushed herself to her feet. As she stood, a wonderful, savory scent reached her nose. She pulled in a full breath of the aroma.

Dathan must have smelled it, too, because he lifted his head and sniffed the air. He licked his lips. "Somebody cookin'."

Panic struck Fanny. If they were close enough to smell someone's supper cooking, they were in danger of being seen. Instinctively, she ducked low, and the others imitated her. They squatted in the thick grass, dark eyes pinned on her.

Enoch leaned in. "You see somethin' worrisome, Miss Fanny?" His husky whisper barely carried over the sound of the river's trickle and the wind's song in the grass.

"I don't see anything, but Dathan's right. Someone is cooking. They must be fairly close for us to smell it so strongly." The aroma was making her mouth water. If only Standard had marked a safe house on the map. She would knock at the door and ask

95

for a meal. Wouldn't they all benefit from a good, hot, hearty supper after their long day of walking?

Itiah pointed to the opposite direction of the river, what Standard had marked as east on the rough map. Fanny looked, too. A spiral of smoke lifted above the gentle rise. From a house or a stage-station chimney? Either way, Standard's letter said the people wouldn't be friendly. And they were probably too close to it for safety. They should push on.

Kircie tapped Fanny's knee. "Miss Fanny, how far you think we got to go yet?"

Standard had estimated a distance of forty-five miles from the spot near Edina to reach Iowa, but with their weaving away from the river and back, they'd probably added miles to it. For reasons she couldn't explain, being near the river made Fanny edgy, and she'd probably steered them farther from the ribbon of water than she should have. They still hadn't reached the end of the South Fabius River. "I don't know for sure." Whoever was cooking the food would probably know, though. The information could prove useful.

She removed the little embroidered purse purchased at the Edina store from the trunk and pulled out the tortoiseshell comb that came with it. "Kircie, would you pin my bun? Pazzy, please take the shawl I bought in Edina from the bag."

The two did as she asked even though puzzlement creased their faces.

Enoch scratched his heavily whiskered chin. "What you gonna do?"

Fanny sucked in her lips. The desire to treat everyone to a good meal as well as discover how much farther they had to travel pulled her toward the source of the aroma. But if Enoch forbade her, she wouldn't go. "I'd like to find the person who is cooking and ask how many miles remain to reach Iowa." She chose not to divulge her idea about buying food. Dathan was still licking his lips and pulling deep breaths in through his flared nostrils. She'd disappoint the boy if she failed.

Enoch's thick brows tipped inward. "That be wise, Miss Fanny?"

"We need to know, don't we? And I promise I'll be careful."

He didn't say anything else, which Fanny took as permission. She opened the purse again and withdrew a twenty-five-cent piece from the little pocket in the purse's lining. When she'd paid with a ten-dollar gold piece for the goods in Edina, the clerk's eyes had nearly popped out of his head. Ransom had told her afterward not to let anyone else know how much money she was carrying. Fortunately, she'd received a few smaller coins in change, and she chose one big enough to buy a good meal but not large enough to attract unwanted attention.

Kircie sat back. "All done."

Fanny smoothed her hand over her hair. The bun felt secure. "Thank you."

The girl gave a shy nod.

Fanny returned the comb to her purse, then removed the most expensive item she'd purchased in Edina. The simple gold band cost $1.70, but its presence would lend credence to the story Ransom had concocted. She slid it onto her finger, feeling like a fraud.

Pazzy held out the fringed shawl. "You want this?"

"I do. Thank you." Fanny wrapped it around her shoulders and tied the points in a knot. It would hide some of the dirt stains on her dress and make her appear more presentable. She held her hands wide to the others. "Well? How do I look?"

Enoch chuckled. "You look right smart." His humor faded into worry. "You be careful, Miss Fanny. Anybody give you trouble, you let out a shout. I'll come runnin'."

Dathan puffed out his chest. "An' me, too."

She'd have to be in dire need to call them out of hiding. She placed the purse into Enoch's hands. "If I don't come back, the money in there is yours."

He pressed the purse to his chest. "You make sure an' come back, Miss Fanny."

She smiled at his concern. "I will." Then she set off toward the gray trail of smoke drifting toward the heavens.

A dusty stagecoach, its rigging empty of horses, sat outside the long clapboard building, identifying the place as a stage stop. In a corral beside the building, six horses nibbled grass. They lifted their heads and snorted as she passed.

The closer she'd gotten, the stronger the enticing aroma of roasting meat had grown, and her stomach growled in hunger. She gripped the silver coin in her fist and covered the final yards to the building's front porch. A groan escaped as she stepped up on the wooden platform. Oh, how her muscles ached. But a hot, hearty meal would do her and the others much good.

Just as she reached the door, it swung open. A tall man wearing a sweat-stained tan cowboy-style hat and several days' growth of dark whiskers filled the doorway. He came to a halt and yanked off his hat, revealing a thatch of uncombed brown hair.

"Well, hello, ma'am." His gaze swept left then right and settled on her again. "Where'd you come from? You weren't on the stage."

Fanny twisted the ends of her shawl, willing her trembling limbs to still. "I was not."

"You needin' a ride?" He took one step toward her, his face set in a friendly grin. "I'm fetching fresh horses now. Gonna head out in about ten minutes. Gotta keep to the schedule, you know."

She didn't know but nodded anyway.

"There's an extra seat if you want it."

"I don't need a ride, thank you. I . . . I'm traveling with my husband" — her pulse pounded as she spilled the practiced story — "and our wagon lost a wheel." To her surprise, the man didn't even blink in doubt. Heartened, she extemporized a bit for the situation. "He smelled food cooking and sent me to buy a dinner since we'll likely not be home by suppertime."

The man stepped aside and swung his arm toward the doorway. "You come to the right place, then. Most o' the cooks at the home stations can't even fry an egg worth eatin', but Bill makes real good grub. Tonight he's got a pot o' beef stew simmerin'. You go on in an' have a plate. I gotta see to the horses." He slid the hat into place, stepped off the end of the porch, and disappeared around the corner.

Fanny pulled in a breath, silently thanking God for carrying her this far. She moved inside and found herself in a simple dining room dimly lit by oil lamps in cast-iron wall brackets. A lamp in the center of a trestle table sent a yellow glow over a pair of well-dressed older women sipping from dented tin cups and two rough-looking men scooping food from their plates with spoons. The men glanced over their shoulders at her, then turned their attention to their remaining dinner.

A big-boned man with a bald head and an apron tied around his middle stood facing a huge iron stove on the back wall of the room. He stirred the contents of a large kettle. Each swish through the kettle raised the savory aroma.

Fanny fingered the coin, gathering courage, then marched within a few feet of him. "Excuse me, sir?"

He turned around, the spoon gripped in his fist. His brows descended. "Who're you?"

"Mrs. Theodore Carlson." She gave the

101

name Ransom invented. "My husband and I were passing nearby and lost a wheel on our wagon. My husband smelled food cooking and sent me to ask about buying a meal." How skilled she was becoming at talebearing. She didn't know whether to be relieved or disgusted by how easily she spun the yarn.

He put the spoon on the edge of the kettle and wiped his hands on his apron. "I s'pose I could dish you up a plate. Fifteen cents for stew an' a biscuit. But you're gonna need to eat it here. I can't send it with you."

"Then what is my husband to do?"

Bill shrugged. "Go without, I reckon."

Why hadn't she thought to bring the pot with her? How else could she carry the food? Then she recalled the cook on the riverboat giving her an empty lard pail to hold her hair ribbons and combs. "Do you have a tin pail you're no longer using?"

Now his eyebrows shot up. "You want a whole pail of stew?"

She licked her dry lips and offered what she hoped was a convincing smile. "My husband has a big appetite. And your stew smells wonderful. How . . . how much would a pail of stew cost?"

He folded his arms and stared at her for a few seconds. "Six bits. Two for the pail, and four for the stew."

She cringed. She turned her hand over and opened it, showing him the quarter dollar. "I only have two bits."

"Then I guess you're either eatin' a plate here or carryin' away an empty pail."

The stagecoach driver came back in and ambled over. "Is Bill fixin' you up, ma'am?"

Bill pointed at her, his expression aghast. "She wants a pail o' my stew an' only has two bits with her."

One of the men at the table barked a guffaw. "You could have her sing for her supper." The women tittered.

Heat flooded Fanny's face, but hope ignited in her breast. She drew a full breath and sang, " 'Come again, bright days of hope and pleasure gone; come again, bright days, come again, come again.' "

Bill and the driver gawked at her. One of the women gasped, and the men spun around on the bench and faced her.

She'd sung "By the Sad Sea Waves" many times on the *River Peacock* and knew it well. She sang both verses and choruses, then dipped into a curtsy.

Those listening clapped, and one of the men whistled through his teeth.

She straightened and, by habit, tossed a kiss to her small but enthusiastic audience.

When she realized what she'd done, she gripped her hands and pressed them to her ribs. She was no longer a riverboat singer. She mustn't behave as if she still were.

The stage driver poked Bill on the shoulder. "I think that was worth *two* pails of stew. Whadda you think?"

"You're right." Bill wiped his eyes. "Miz Carlson, that was the purtiest singin' I've heard in my whole life. You earned your supper, for sure. If you buy the pail, I'll fill it for you."

8

DAVENPORT, IOWA
FANNY

The mournful whistle of a train engine carried across the landscape and penetrated the walls of the barn where an elderly farmer had given Fanny and her companions refuge. The sound, so different from the doves' coos that had lulled her to sleep, stirred Fanny to wakefulness. She sat up, the prayer she'd winged heavenward many times over the past days repeating itself in her heart — *Take us safely to freedom, please, dear Lord.*

On the tail of her silent prayer, the song she'd learned from Pazzy filled her mind and found its way to her lips. " 'We'll find the place which God for us prepared . . .' "

Although Fanny sang barely above a whisper, Pazzy stirred and sat up. She began to sing, too. " 'Far away in the West, where none shall come to hurt or make afraid.' "

The others awoke one by one and sat up, their faces pinned on the singers. Fanny's soprano blended beautifully with Pazzy's rich contralto, and the whisper-softness of their combined voices only added emotion to the heart-stirring lyrics. Together they sang all the way to the final words, " 'All is well! All is well!' "

"Amen," Enoch said.

Dathan shifted to his knees and blinked at Fanny, hope shining in his dark eyes. "You think it's gonna be all well, Miss Fanny?"

She fought tears. A boy his age shouldn't have to wonder such a thing. Not on a sunshiny spring morning. She grabbed him in a hug and pressed a kiss on the top of his head. "Doesn't your great-grandpa keep telling us God's brought us safely this far?"

Dathan nodded. "An' He gonna take us safe all the way to our new home."

"That's right."

"An' when we get there, I can wear britches again."

Fanny laughed and released him. "You certainly can."

Enoch cleared his throat and pushed to his feet. "But that ain't gonna happen 'less we get ourselves outta this barn an' off to the train depot." He brushed bits of hay from his clothes. "What day you 'spect this be by now?"

Fanny had been keeping count. "If my

memory serves me correctly, today is Friday, April twenty-seven." A full two weeks since the storm had knocked her overboard and sent her on this unexpected journey.

"April twenty-seven." Enoch stared ahead as if he saw something the rest of them couldn't see. "Fou'th day o' May, Baby Leona'll be one year old." He turned his face and met Fanny's gaze. "Figure we'll be all the way to our new home by then?"

Fanny didn't know, but she smiled. "That would be something special, wouldn't it?"

He huffed a breath and nodded. "Sure would be." Then he gestured to the others. "Pick up them blankets an' such. Farmer say we gotta be out with the sunrise."

While the others shook their blankets free of hay and packed the carpetbags and crates, Fanny moved to the window facing the town of Davenport. She folded back the shutters and looked to the dusky pink sky dotted with puffs of white. On the other side of those clouds, God resided in the heavens. Was He looking back at her, aware of the worry churning in her belly?

Over the days of travel, she had discussed with Enoch the wisdom of taking the family straight through Iowa as quickly as possible. Iowa, being so close to the Missouri border, was a likely place for slave catchers to prowl for escaped slaves. The family needed to get as far from slave states as possible. Which meant traveling by something other than their feet.

Someone touched her elbow, and she turned. Enoch stood close by. "After what happen in Muscatine, mebbe it's best you buy all the tickets. It'd make folks wonder, I reckon, how we all come to have that kinda money."

An involuntary shudder rattled Fanny's frame. Oh, how frightened she'd been when the scowling lawman stopped them on the road two days ago and asked what business they had in his town. She'd prayed silently for God's favor while he listened to her fabricated explanation and examined the freedom papers. To her great relief, he'd returned the documents to her and sent them on their way without further interference.

As much as she hated to admit it, Enoch was probably right. She wouldn't risk putting them in harm's way. "All right. If you want to give me your ticket money, I'll do all the purchasing."

His brow furrowed. "We ain't got ticket money."

She drew back. "Y-you don't? Ransom didn't give you money?"

Enoch shook his head. "He give you the map. I figure he give you the money."

Fanny faced the window and leaned against the sill. Ransom must have expected them to walk all the way to Milwaukee. It had taken them more than a week to travel from Edina to Davenport — roughly two hundred miles. How much farther was it to Milwaukee, where the Baptist preacher would lend aid?

She rested her forehead against the cool glass, closed her eyes, and envisioned the remaining coins Cricket had gathered for her on the *River Peacock*. She'd spent almost eight dollars in Edina, but since then, despite visiting three different stagecoach stations to gather information that would assist them on their journey, she'd spent only twenty-five cents at the first stop. The other two times, she earned a pan of corn bread or a basket of fried catfish by singing. She still had a little over sixty-six dollars. If she were traveling alone, it would most likely be more than enough. But would it cover train tickets, meals, and whatever else Enoch's family needed to get far, far away from Missouri?

"Miss Fanny?"

She turned from the window and met Enoch's worried gaze.

"Ransom didn't give you no money?"

She swallowed. "He did not."

Enoch sucked in his lips and seemed to examine the barn rafters for a few minutes. Then he looked at her again, and a resigned smile formed. "Then I reckon we got some more walkin' to do."

Fanny stared at the map tacked to a board on the depot wall. The map was large — double the size of the banquet tabletops on the *River Peacock* — and showed not only the Mississippi and Missouri Railroad routes but the train routes for the entire Unites States of America. She could scarcely believe her eyes. She'd never imagined there were so many places for people to go by railway.

Enoch stood near, but the others clustered at the edge of the raised boardwalk with their small pile of belongings, quietly talking amongst themselves and trying, as Fanny had encouraged them, to look as if they hadn't a care in the world.

Although several of the other passengers milling around the red brick building serving as a depot had stared or pointed at the group, no one had approached them. But the threat hung over Fanny like a cloud of foul-smelling smoke. The family needed to get out of Iowa. They were still too close to Missouri.

She held Standard's crude map against the wall and, with a sliver of coal, attempted to draw a map leading from Davenport to Milwaukee. "See here, Enoch? I think the best way to reach Milwaukee is travel east to Chicago, then straight north. It means going south a bit, but if we can stay fairly close to the railroad track, we'll be less likely to get off course." She scowled at the smudgy lines on the paper. They looked nothing like the map on the wall. Would it make sense when they'd left Davenport?

"Now, Miss Fanny, you stop sayin' *we.*" Enoch's expression turned stern. "You come far enough. Me an' mine, we just fine. You get to yo' folks. Is there train lines runnin' all the way to New Yo'k City?"

She slid her gaze along the lines signifying track. The route seemed complicated, but trains could carry her to Chicago, then around Lake Michigan, through Indiana and Ohio, and finally alongside Lake Erie. But at the end of the line, she would reach New York.

She stared at the name of the state, and without conscious thought, she leaned toward the words, as if being closer to the map would bring her closer to her family.

"There is a route."

"Then take yo'self to the ticket counter over there an' get yo' ticket."

She turned and looked into Enoch's kind eyes. An ache settled in the center of her chest. As much as she missed her family, she wasn't yet ready to bid farewell to Enoch, Pazzy, Kircie, Dathan, and Itiah. They'd come to mean so much to her.

Enoch gestured in the direction of his family. "C'mon, Miss Fanny. Like Mr. Ransom say, we can't be stayin' still fo' too long."

He was right. With a sigh, Fanny nodded. She and Enoch joined the group waiting in the shade. Fanny put her hand on Dathan's narrow shoulder. "Well, I —"

" 'Scuse me."

The voice came from behind Fanny. She turned slightly and found two filthy, gruff-looking men glaring at Enoch and the others. She angled her chin in a haughty pose, praying her fear didn't show on her face. "May I assist you gentlemen?"

They turned their scowls on her. The first one, wearing a worn leather vest over a plaid shirt with patches at the elbows, gestured to Enoch. "Not unless you're with these uns."

She folded her arms. "These *people*" — she hoped he caught the emphasis behind the word — "are traveling with me."

He flicked a disparaging look across the entire group. "Where you all from?"

"A little town in Wisconsin." She pressed her memory for the name of one of the towns she'd seen on the depot wall map. "Oak Creek. Have you been there?"

The man shook his head.

"It's a nice place. Perhaps you'd like to visit it sometime." She reached for one of the carpetbags.

The man stuck out his grubby hand. "Hold up, there. I ain't done with you."

The second man, his clothes even more worn and dirt stained than the first's, circled the group, his narrowed eyes slowly roving over them one by one. Fanny caught a glimpse of terror in Dathan's eyes, but the others maintained a stoic expression. She inwardly praised them for their fortitude. She felt certain she would dissolve into a puddle of fear any moment.

"Sir, I need to purchase tickets if we're to board the next train." She forced a firm yet pleasant tone. "What else do you need from me?"

"Don't need nothin' from you exactly, but I need plenty from them." He jerked his chin, indicating Enoch and the others. "Me an' Frank are huntin' a group of slaves who

113

escaped from Louisiana. These uns sure look to be about right." A menacing gleam entered the man's eyes. "An' even if they ain't, they might belong to somebody. We aim to find out."

She would not release Enoch, Kircie, Dathan, or any of the family to these men. Not as long as she drew a breath. She released a huff full of honest disdain. "I am Mrs. Theodore Carlson. These people are employed by my husband and me."

The man's lips curled in derision. He folded his arms over his chest. "You tellin' me these're your hired workers?"

She lifted her chin. "That's right."

"Then you must be wealthy folks."

She gripped her purse. "Indeed we are."

"Then how come you all look like you been sleepin' in a barn?"

Why hadn't she considered their appearance? Although they'd washed their hands and faces at a pump behind the barn before setting out for the train station, their clothes wore dust from the days of walking. She searched for a plausible explanation, and unexpectedly the truth came out. "Because we slept in a barn last night."

The man barked a laugh. "Well, then, lady, I wanna know how come somebody rich enough to travel with a passel of *em-*

114

ployees ended up sleepin' in a barn."

"We came from Oak Creek to Muscatine to visit Theodore's sick brother." Fanny embellished the story Ransom had invented. "Theodore brought some of our workers with us to take over the household duties during our visit so my brother-in-law's servants could be temporarily relieved of their duties. They've been overly taxed of late, seeing to my brother-in-law's needs. He's been ill for a long time."

The man's thick brows dipped together. He waved his dirt-encrusted hand at Dathan, then pointed at Baby Leona, snug in the wrap securing her to her mother's chest. "You tellin' me them're hired by your husband?"

Fanny tsk-tsked. "Any fool can see they're too young to work. But they're also too young to be left on their own, so they traveled with their mother."

The man's scowl had darkened at the word *fool.* He leaned in slightly. "I'm still waitin' to know why you all slept in a barn."

"Because the man hired to transport us to Davenport didn't bother to inspect his wagon thoroughly before setting out. One of the axles broke, and we were forced to continue our journey on foot. We arrived very late yesterday evening." Suddenly she

115

was speaking more truth than not. "A farmer on the edge of town graciously allowed us to spend the night in his barn."

For several seconds the man glared down at her, his eyes spitting venom. "Where's your husband now? I'd like a word with him."

Fanny's chin quivered. Fear brought the tremor, but she prayed he would read the reaction as grief. "He's seeing to his brother's estate, now that our dear Bertrand has gone to be with his Lord." Surely God would strike her dead any minute for the lies so effortlessly spilling from her mouth. If God would forgive her for these, she vowed she'd never tell another falsehood once Enoch's family was safe. "It will likely take several days, and he told me I should go on home. You're welcome to call on him at my brother-in-law's house in Muscatine. Would you like the address?" She held her breath, fully expecting him to see through her ruse.

The second man tromped back to the first one, his boot heels thundering against the wide boards. "C'mon, Stokes. These ain't our runaways. We've pestered this lady enough." He tipped his grimy hat. "My condolences on your loss, ma'am. Safe travels to you." The pair sauntered to two saddled horses at the edge of the street and rode off without a backward look.

Enoch whispered, "We all right."

Kircie and Pazzy exchanged relieved glances and released slow breaths. Itiah stroked Baby Leona's head, as if gaining comfort from the child. Dathan slumped against Fanny, and she slid her arm around his shoulders. She made a snap decision. None of them would walk to Chicago. They would ride on the train. And they would leave as quickly as possible.

9

NEAR SHELBYVILLE, MISSOURI
SLOAN

Sloan tossed his carpetbag onto the rear boot of the dusty stagecoach, stifling a groan. He pressed his hand to his lower spine. Of all the ways to travel, a stagecoach must be the least comfortable. Less, even, than riding astride a horse. But these rattling conveyances made more frequent stops than trains, giving him an opportunity to explore even the smallest of towns for his next entertainer. Although he'd secured enough Wells, Fargo & Company drafts to fund a monthlong search, he hadn't intended to venture so far from the *River Peacock*.

He'd taken a crisscross path over middle to eastern Missouri, visiting churches, saloons, and even a brothel, but his search had proved futile. Many young women claimed to be singers, but none he encountered could hold a candle to Miss Fanny Beck. Not in appearance, and certainly not

118

in vocal ability. Today marked his tenth day of searching. Shouldn't he have found someone by now?

He growled under his breath, "It's likely useless."

"What's that you say?"

Sloan jerked his gaze in the direction of the speaker, embarrassment striking when he found the affable stagecoach driver a few feet away. Only the witless talked to themselves, and he'd never considered himself witless. He wouldn't allow this young man to presume so, either.

He snapped, "I was only yawning."

"Hmm." The man, who'd introduced himself to the passengers as Chris, frowned. "Coulda swore you said words." He fiddled with the straps of the coach's rigging. "Somethin' about useless."

Of course the man would have excellent hearing. Sloan opened the coach door, braced his foot on the iron bar serving as a step, and caught hold of the doorframe.

"That mean you're givin' up on your search?"

Sloan paused. "What do you know about my search?"

Chris shrugged and gave the closest horse's rump a pat. He brushed his gloved palms together, raising a small cloud of dust. "Not much o' nothin', 'cept you gotta be lookin' for somethin'. Otherwise you wouldn't keep ridin' from town to town, never stayin' put. Ever'body else's got a destination in mind. You? You're just ridin'."

Sloan had underestimated the man's intelligence. But he had no desire to share his personal dealings with a stranger. He pulled himself into the coach and slid onto the cracked leather seat. A spring poked him in the rear, and he shifted slightly, grunting in displeasure.

Chris propped his elbow on the window ledge of the wide-open door and peered inside. "If I knew what you was lookin' for, I might be able to help. I been all over the state, from one side to the other. I've seen just about ever'thing Missouri has to offer."

Sloan considered Chris's statements. Perhaps he should divulge the nature of his business. It could cut this traipsing journey short if the stagecoach driver directed him to a talented singer. "I'm the captain of a riverboat, and I need someone to provide entertainment for my passengers. Have you encountered a comely young woman who sings well?"

Chris drew back, shock registering on his face. "Is that what you're wantin'? Well, then, I can say I sure have."

Eagerness quivered through Sloan's frame. "Where? When?"

The man shifted his battered hat aside and scratched his head. "As I recall, it was the stop near Lancaster. Yessir, the Lancaster home station. I remember now, 'cause Bill was doin' the cookin', an' she came in lookin' fer a meal. That's how she come to sing for us all. She didn't have enough money to buy food, so Bill let 'er sing for it." He chuckled, his eyes twinkling. "Had ol' Bill nearly blubberin' in his stewpot by the time she was done. That little gal sang pure an' sweet as . . . well, I don't rightly know what. Just know it sure did please my ears to hear it. An' she was comely, too. Had a face that'd stop a man dead in his tracks just to admire it."

Sloan twitched with impatience. "The Lancaster stop, you said? And she lives near it?"

Chris shrugged. "I reckon so. She come in on foot. Told me how her an' her husband was headin' home an' somethin' busted on their wagon. That's why she needed to buy some food. They wouldn't get back 'til late."

Dismay washed away Sloan's initial excitement. "She was married?"

"Yes, sir. She said so." Chris scratched his head again.

121

Sloan was beginning to wonder if the man had lice.

"Seems like she told us her husband's name, but I can't recall it." Chris brightened. "But Bill might remember. He was real taken with her singin'."

Sloan sat back and pinched his chin. He preferred to hire a young unmarried woman, but if this woman and her husband had a hardscrabble life, they might both agree to work on the *River Peacock*. It was worth pursuing. Especially if Chris was accurate in his assessment of her appearance and vocal ability. "How far is it to Lancaster?"

Chris shrugged. "I got a scheduled stop there next Tuesday, the first day o' May."

"And that's the soonest I can get there?"

" 'Fraid so."

Sloan flicked his hand at the driver. "Then let's get going."

Near Seneca, Illinois
Fanny
The rocking motion of the train reminded Fanny of being on the riverboat the night of the storm. She'd intended to travel the full distance to New York by train, but after being tossed back and forth since yesterday morning — and suffering through nightmares each time she fell asleep — she

122

wondered if she'd be able to bear traveling the full distance in a railcar. Unless the swaying wasn't as noticeable in the actual passenger cars.

Indignation roared to life again within her breast as she recalled the stationmaster in Davenport eagerly taking six dollars per person except the baby for the ride to Chicago but then saying her companions wouldn't be allowed to utilize the passenger cars. Confused, she'd asked where they were supposed to ride.

"In the cattle cars," he'd said, then added with a wink, "but you're more'n welcome to take a nice padded bench in a passenger car, little lady."

How could the man even suggest she ride in comfort while her friends were shuffled into an animal crate? She'd paid full price, so they should ride in the same car as any other passenger, but she couldn't protest without calling attention to her companions. So she stomped off, tickets in hand, and they'd all climbed into the cattle car.

Although they were forced to endure days in a rattling car with smoke-tainted air constantly streaming through the slatted sides and the stench of manure rising from the floorboards, she consoled herself that at least they were off their feet. The past weeks had been difficult. In fact, the past years had to have been difficult for Enoch and his family. But better things waited if they could make it all the way to Canada.

At the opposite end of the long car, Enoch encouraged Dathan to scratch letters with a stick in the grime caked on the floorboards. The boy obliged, his mouth set in a determined line. She looked to her left at Pazzy, who cradled a fussing Baby Leona. Pazzy hummed softly, a mournful melody Fanny had no desire to learn. Beyond Pazzy, Kircie sat on her knees next to Itiah and ran her fingers through her mama's hair. Itiah's eyes were closed, her face puckered as if a pain gripped her.

Enoch rose and crossed to Fanny, bouncing his hand along the slatted side of the car to steady himself. He sank down and heaved out a huge sigh. "You doin' all right?"

She shook her head, gaping at him. "Enoch, why does it matter to you how I'm faring?"

He offered a slow shrug, confusion pinching his wrinkled face. "Don't seem right takin' all the things you been givin' an' not at least spend some worry time on you." He toyed with the brim of his hat. "Don't rightly understand how come you stay with us. Seems to me it's a heap o' trouble. You coulda gone on soon as Ransom dropped us off. Didn' hafta travel with us. Didn' hafta use yo' money to buy us food an' tickets. There ain't much else I can give you 'cept my regard. An' mentionin' you in my prayers."

His concern and his prayers were more than she'd received from anyone since she'd been a young girl. Tears distorted her vision. "That you would care about me and speak to the Lord about me is . . ." She squeezed his callused hand, unable to find words to describe her gratitude. "Thank you for being my friend."

His chuckle rumbled. He slid his hand free and placed it in his lap. "You welcome, Miss Fanny. Reckon that goes the other way, too." He crinkled his brow. "Been worryin' on somethin' else." He glanced at the others, as if ascertaining whether they were occupied, then leaned a little closer to her. "Been watchin' you pull out coins an' buy our lunches an' such at the stops." He spoke so quietly she had to strain to hear him over the rush of wind through the slats and the *clank-clank-clank* of iron wheels against the track. "There gonna be enough left to take you all the way to yo' folks? 'Cause, 'cept for the little uns, we don't gotta eat more'n once a day. Can even skip a day if it'll help."

She'd watched the amount in her purse dwindle, too. The price of food at the stations was more than she'd anticipated, especially since they offered such simple fare. Fifteen cents for slivers of cheese between two slices of stale bread? Five cents for a wrinkled apple? The train was due to arrive in Seneca late this afternoon. Since the trains didn't run on Sundays, they'd spend this night and all of the next day in the town before boarding again Monday morning. How much would a safe place to hole up and several meals cost?

Her mind whirled, considering how many more meals they'd need by the time they disembarked in Chicago by noon on Tuesday. How many days of travel would it take for the family to reach Milwaukee? They had to eat during those days, too. Worry plagued her, but she wouldn't burden Enoch with her concern about not having even enough money left to buy their tickets to Milwaukee. If possible, she would send them on by train. As much as she wanted to reach Da and Ma, she wasn't in any danger. They were.

She gave him a firm look. "I have no intention of letting my friends go hungry."

A smile twitched at the corners of his lips, and it lifted her spirits.

"Thank you, Miss Fanny." He got up and made his way back to Dathan.

She peered between slats at the landscape. Strange how it seemed as if the ground moved while she sat still. The sensation made her stomach roll, and she closed her eyes. When she was a child, one of her favorite Bible stories was about the widowed mother whose oil jug never ran dry. Da aways said God would provide for His own. Might God increase the coins in her purse?

Let there be enough, me dear Father. Please let there be enough.

10

The Chicago station teemed with activity, reminding Fanny of the busy milling on the *River Peacock*'s deck when passengers disembarked after a cruise. Fanny, Enoch, and his family took a winding path from the railcar to the large depot, toting their belongings. Wind blew dust in their faces, and Dathan repeatedly sneezed.

Other passengers skirted around them, either crinkling their faces in disgust or holding their noses.

Fanny's chest burned with humiliation. They looked awful after weeks of travel, including days stuck in a cattle car. The time in the Seneca stable had done them little good. Based on the reactions of those they encountered, they smelled even worse than they looked. But how to rectify it? A bath, certainly. But where would they bathe? And why bother, when most likely they'd be placed in yet another cattle car for the ride

128

to Wisconsin? People would simply have to keep their distance. Which was safer, anyway.

She smiled, hoping to ease her companions' embarrassment. "Almost to the depot. Let's stay together."

At least thirty people already waited in the ticket line. Enoch gestured everyone to the far side of the building and set down his end of the crate. The others put down their loads and turned expectant looks on him.

"Miss Fanny, it be all right with you if we all stay here while you see to the tickets?" Enoch smoothed the front of his rumpled jacket. "Mebbe it'd be easier fo' you to stand in the line by yo'self."

Fanny didn't want to spend one minute of their remaining time together away from her friends, but she understood his reticence. They had so little to call their own. She could at least allow them a small element of dignity by being spared the disparaging looks they'd surely receive if they joined the line.

"Of course. But if someone bothers you, have Kircie or Dathan" — she flicked a nervous glance over her shoulder — "er, Peter or Esther fetch me. I'll return as quickly as I can with the tickets."

Clutching her purse snug against her hip,

she took her position at the end of the line. Those in front of her scooted forward, and those who joined behind maintained a gap of a few feet. But she had bigger worries than offending the noses of these travelers. Would the money in her purse be enough to take Enoch, Itiah, and the others all the way to Milwaukee?

Perspiration made her flesh prickle, and the stout wind drove dust beneath her sleeves and under her bonnet. Hours seemed to pass as she waited her turn, shifting from foot to foot on the ground that constantly vibrated from the many trains coming and going. Such a busy station! And noisy. When she finally reached the ticket window, her ears rang from the repeated whistle blasts.

"Destination?" The young man on the other side of the counter snapped the single word.

Fanny placed her purse on the edge of the wood surface. "Milwaukee, Wisconsin, please. There are six travelers in all, but one is an infant."

"Infants ride free. Three dollars each for the others."

Fanny nearly collapsed with relief. She had enough. She withdrew the last two ten-dollar gold pieces from her purse and slid them to the man.

He exchanged her coins with a single five-dollar piece. With his lips puckered, he chose a stamp from a box near his elbow and smacked the stamp on an ink pad and then on squares of stiff paper one by one in a rhythmic motion that spoke of great familiarity. He stacked the tickets into a neat pile and handed them to her. Leaning sideways, he hollered, "Next!"

Fanny held up her hand. "Wait, please. I also need one ticket to New York City."

He reached for a stamp. "Twenty-five dollars, please."

Fanny's mouth went slack. "Did you say t-twenty-five dollars?"

A scowl formed on his narrow face. "Yes, ma'am. There's at least thirty stops between here and there."

She gulped. "And how many days of travel?"

"All goes according to schedule, a little over two weeks."

She sagged against the counter. Food for two weeks of travel, even if she ate only one meal a day, would cost between three and four dollars. Enoch and his family needed food money for the next couple of days, too. She stared at the remaining coins in her purse, her mind racing. She would have enough for herself if she turned in the tickets for Milwaukee. Could Enoch and his family walk the rest of the way?

Guilt swooped in. How could she even think of leaving Enoch and his family stranded? There had to be another way to get to Da and Ma. God had met her needs thus far. She inwardly begged her heavenly Father to advise her now.

"Miss, other folks are waiting. Do you want the ticket or not?"

Fanny lifted her head and met the man's scowl. "What's the first stop on the way to New York City?"

He glanced at a chart of some sort attached to the wall of the ticket booth, then turned to her again. "Baileytown, Indiana."

"And how much is a ticket to Baileytown?"

"Dollar sixty-five."

Two five-dollar gold pieces, three Liberty dollars, two dimes, and a nickel remained in her purse. After a moment's contemplation, she pinched out a five-dollar coin and gave it to the agent. "One ticket to Baileytown, please."

She received her ticket and the change due her and placed everything in her purse. Then she scurried to the spot next to the building where Enoch and the others

132

waited. She held up their tickets. "Here you are — five tickets to Milwaukee." She pressed the tickets into Enoch's hand with a quavering grin. "According to the date on the tickets, you'll arrive in Milwaukee on the morning of Baby Leona's birthday."

"That so?" Enoch beamed at Pazzy, and Pazzy released a joy-filled laugh.

Fanny turned a serious look on Enoch. "Remember to look for the Baptist church when you reach Milwaukee. Ransom said it isn't far from the station, so you should be able to find it."

Enoch nodded, then tapped his white temple. "I remember, Miss Fanny. Find the church an' the preacher. He gonna help get us on into Canada."

"That's exactly right." Fanny removed all but the dimes and nickel from her purse. She curled her fist around the coins for a moment. In her soul, trust in God's provision warred with the fear of being stuck in a strange city without resources to care for herself. But Da and Ma had taught her to trust. She wouldn't disappoint them now.

She extended her hand and offered the coins to Enoch. "You won't eat like kings, but I hope this will be enough to buy some sandwiches and milk on the way to your new home."

Enoch raised his hands as if under arrest. "I don't want yo' money, Miss Fanny. You already bought the tickets. Don't seem right to take somethin' more."

Fanny turned to Itiah. "Dathan and Kircie have to eat. So does Pazzy if she's to nurse Baby Leona. You and your father can't go without, either. Please take it." She bobbed her open hand in silent encouragement.

Itiah sent Enoch an uncertain glance and then stared at the coins. Her hand slowly lifted, pausing every few seconds as if her joints were too stiff to allow unfettered movement. Finally she closed her fingers around the coins and met Fanny's gaze. The corners of her lips tipped upward. With her free hand, she grazed Fanny's upper arm — a touch so light, if Fanny hadn't seen Itiah's hand move, she might have thought she imagined it.

"Thank you, Miss Fanny." Itiah's voice rasped in a barely discernible whisper. "God bless you."

Fanny had never seen Itiah smile and had only heard her murmur to the children. Of all Enoch's family, she'd remained the most distant. For her to reach out, to speak directly to her, was a gift Fanny hadn't expected to receive. It made every penny she'd just sacrificed worth it.

She blinked back tears and beamed, cupping her hand over Itiah's. "You are welcome. God bless you, too."

Enoch cleared his throat. "What about you, Miss Fanny? You got a ticket an' food money fo' yo'self?"

Fanny patted her little purse. "It's all in here." At least her words were true, even if they were slightly misleading. She turned toward the street. The hands on the four-sided clock mounted on a pole outside the depot showed a little after eight, and the train to Milwaukee would leave at eight thirty. Their time of separation drew near.

She forced a cheerfulness she didn't feel. "We need to find Engine Forty-Two. It pulls the train that will take you all the way to Milwaukee." She sent a quick look left and right, assuring herself no one was close enough to overhear. "Do you have your freedom papers in case anyone questions you?"

Enoch touched the left breast of his jacket. "They all in my inside pocket. Got 'em ordered from oldest to youngest so I can keep 'em straight."

Fanny tapped the brim of Dathan's bonnet. "If they get mixed, ask Dathan. He's learned to spell your names, and he will help you."

The boy puffed up, as proud as a peacock showing off for its mate. "I can 'cause I know 'em. I know 'em all, Grandpap."

Enoch put his hand on the boy's shoulder. "Eases my mind considerable, bein' able to call on you fo' help." He flashed a grin at Fanny, then grabbed a handle on the crate. "Catch hold over there, Dathan, so we can be goin'."

Dathan took the other side of the crate. Itiah carried Baby Leona, and Kircie and Pazzy each lifted a carpetbag, while Fanny grabbed the pack.

Enoch nodded to Fanny. "We ready."

Fanny repeatedly blinked back tears while accompanying the family past several tracks to the train that would transport them to Milwaukee. As had happened in Davenport, the uniformed man who took their tickets pointed to a cattle car hooked near the end of the train. Fanny swallowed her resentment and kept walking.

At the car, Enoch slid the side door open and pushed the crate across the bed. He reached for Dathan, but the boy in a calico dress and ruffled bonnet jerked away from his great-grandfather and flung his arms around Fanny's middle. His shoulders shook with hiccuping sobs.

136

She dropped to her knees and held the weeping child, certain her heart would break, but she rocked him side to side and whispered as reassuringly as she could, "Shh, now. You'll be fine. You'll be just fine."

Dathan pulled back and swiped his eyes with his fists. His lower lip poked out. "Gonna miss you somethin' fierce, Miss Fanny. Wish you was comin', too."

Enoch squeezed the boy's shoulder. "Miss Fanny's gotta get to her folks, son. Be plumb selfish fo' us to keep her when she ain't seen her mam or pap in so long."

Dathan nodded, his expression forlorn. He blinked at her, his eyelashes forming moist spikes. "I . . . I love you, Miss Fanny."

Fanny kissed the boy's cheek. "I love you, too, Dathan." She did. She loved all of them. She rose and swept her gaze across each dear face. "I am so grateful God brought us together. I am blessed to call you my friends. My prayers go with you."

Abruptly Dathan closed his eyes and gripped his hands beneath his chin. "Dear Lawd, go with Miss Fanny an' take her safe to home an' freedom."

She'd never heard a sweeter prayer. She grabbed the boy in another hug, then reluctantly released her hold. "Goodbye, Dathan."

"Bye, Miss Fanny."

Enoch helped the others aboard. Fanny stood to the side, offering tremulous smiles and nods and whispered goodbyes. The whistle blared, and Enoch glanced in the direction of the sound. Then he looked Fanny full in the face. "You been God-sent, fo' sure, Miss Fanny. I ain't never gonna fo'get you."

Fanny bit her lip. The pain in her chest was so great that she marveled she could draw a breath. "Nor I you, Mr. Enoch."

He grabbed the sides of the train and heaved himself in. Pazzy moved to the opening and smiled down at Fanny, her eyes shimmering with unshed tears. "You an' us — we all gonna find the place which God fo' us prepared."

The lines of the song wound through Fanny's heart and spilled from her lips. She continued singing even as the train began its chugging motion. The whistle's blast, the whoosh of steam, and the creak of the wheels on the track drowned out her voice, but she sang as she waved. Dathan and Kircie hung their arms out between slats and waved, too, until the train rounded a bend and hid them from her sight. As the caboose made its turn, Fanny finished, " 'All is well! All is well!' "

She remained in place for a few more minutes, sniffling and wiping her eyes. When she felt composed, she returned to the depot.

Vendors lined the street, peddling various wares. She had twenty-five cents in her purse. An apple might stave off her hunger for a while. She ignored the upturned noses and huffs of disgust offered by those whose path she crossed and roved the stands, seeking the best deal. She came upon an old man selling items crafted from tin. She paused at the display. Apparently not put off by her cattle-car stench, he scuttled to her side.

"See somethin' you like, miss? I made ever' single thing m'self. All first quality. You want a little play horse? Makes a fine present for someone. Or mebbe a pretty barrette for your hair?"

Wouldn't Baby Leona love the toy horse? And the barrettes were lovely, with flowers or birds impressed in the buffed metal. But she couldn't squander her money on such things. "Thank you, but —" Her eyes fell on a cup, and a memory rose up with such clarity that she released a little gasp. When she, her family, and Sloan had arrived in New York, she'd seen a man on a street corner blowing a tune through a small flute while making a puppet dance at the end of several strings. A tin cup sat on the ground near the man's feet, and as people passed, they tossed coins into the cup. She'd asked about it, and Sloan explained that the man earned his living by entertaining the passersby.

Nearly breathless, she pointed to the shiny cup. "How much?"

"Five cents."

She pressed her nickel into his eager hand, and he gave her the cup along with a toothless smile. Gripping the cup against her ribs, she hurried toward the station. Surely God had stirred the recollection. Hadn't she sung for supper at several stops along the way? Now she would sing at depots in exchange for coins from passengers. She could earn train fare with her voice.

Prayers of gratitude rose from her heart. All was well. With God's help, she would sing herself all the way home.

11

"Mister, you got any idea how many people come through this station in a week? How can you expect me to remember all their names?"

Sloan fisted the coffee mug the way he wished he could squeeze the portly station cook's neck. "I'm not asking you to remember all of them. Only the woman who sang in exchange for a meal."

The man laid slices of pork in an iron skillet. Steam rose in a cloud, bringing a savory scent with it, and the grease sizzled as loudly as heavy rain on a roof. "I remember the singin', that's for sure. A voice like a nightingale, my ma would've said. She was Mrs. Somebody. Seems like it started with a *K*. Or maybe a *C*." He angled a sheepish grimace at Sloan. "I ain't never been too good with spellin'."

Or remembering, it seemed. Sloan took a sip of the stout coffee, hoping the liquid

141

would drown his irritation. Father always preached patience and goodwill, and while Sloan didn't follow the instruction as much as his father preferred, he had learned over the years a person could catch more flies with honey than with vinegar.

He drained the cup, then ambled to the trestle table where the other stage passengers awaited dinner. "Any of you folks from around these parts?"

A man Sloan had figured for a traveling salesman, based on his pin-striped suit and the large wood case he lugged by its leather handle everywhere he went, shifted on the bench and faced Sloan. "Don't hail from here, but I come through right regular. Have visited most folks in the area."

Yep, a traveling salesman, for sure. Probably sold snake oil out of that case. "I'm looking for a pretty young woman —"

The man barked a laugh. "Ain't we all?" He bounced his grin at the other passengers. The lone woman pursed her lips, but the other two men snickered.

Sloan cleared his throat. "I heard about a pretty young woman from this area who has a lovely singing voice. Bill over there" — he bobbed his head toward the cook — "says her surname likely starts with either a *C* or a *K*. Does that sound familiar to you?"

"Well . . ." The man scrunched his face as if deeply thinking. "There's a Kaufman family. Live on a farm east of Lancaster. Then seems like in the city, I met up with some Christiansens."

Sloan filed the names away in the back of his mind. "Anyone else?"

"Hmm, not that I can think of offhand." The man gave the tabletop a light smack with his palm. "You know what you ought to do, mister? Visit the Lancaster mercantile. Nearly every mercantile gives credit to local folks, and the owner should have the names of every family in town on his book — least the ones who shop his store. Folks in town'll probably know who sings pretty, too."

Bill scuffed to the table, balancing plates on both arms. "Here you go, folks." Sloan took one of the plates and sat. Bill handed around the remaining plates, then swished his palms together. "Anything else I can get you folks? More coffee? Jam for them biscuits?"

The salesman looked to the other end of the table. "Only thing I need is pepper. Say, Carl, wouldja hand the pepper shaker this way?"

The man named Carl lifted the shaker, and at the same time, Bill let out a loud gasp. He clapped his hand on Sloan's

143

shoulder. "Carlson. That was the name she said. Mrs. Carlson."

Excitement stirred in Sloan's chest. "Are you sure?"

"Sure as shootin'. It just come to me like somebody bellered it in my ear." His grin stretched from ear to ear. "That gonna help you out any, mister?"

Sloan nodded, his lips pulling into a smile. "It should. It most certainly should." He picked up his fork and dug into the fried potatoes, pork chop, and boiled carrots on his plate. He'd fill his stomach, retrieve his bag from the stagecoach's rear boot, then find a way into town.

Mishawaka, Indiana
Fanny

Fanny glanced at the round clock on the depot wall. The conductor warned they'd have only a thirty-minute rest before moving on to the next station, and half that time had already slipped by. At each previous stop, she'd received enough contributions to pay for a ticket and buy a bit to eat. But the people of this city, for the most part, seemed unwilling to give her even three or four cents. They barely gave her attention.

Anxiety speeding her pulse, she linked her hands over the pointed ends of her shawl and began to sing what had become her song of deliverance — Pazzy's song. Enoch and the others were never far from her thoughts or prayers. She carried a permanent ache in the center of her heart, the result of loneliness. She couldn't be with her friends anymore, but her family waited. How she pined for them.

As she sang, she scanned the faces of the passersby, looking for a hint of interest or compassion. Most acted as if they couldn't see or hear her. A few paused long enough to drop a single penny in her cup, but she needed more than pennies to purchase food and a ticket to the next stop. Frustration rose, tangling her vocal cords. Mishawaka was the largest of the four stops since she'd left Chicago. Shouldn't people in larger cities be more generous than those who lived in smaller towns?

She finished, " 'All is well! All is well!' " and dipped into a curtsy, her head bowed.

The toes from a pair of polished black boots entered her line of vision, mere inches from her cup. She straightened abruptly and found herself under the perusal of a middle-aged man. His formal black suit, white gloves, and silk top hat marked him as a gentleman. Heat flooded her face. Compared to his fine tailored clothes, how slovenly she must appear in her smelly, wrinkled dress. She grabbed the tails of her shawl and crisscrossed them over her bodice.

He tipped his hat. "That was a lovely song, miss."

"Thank you, sir." She sneaked a glance at the clock. Only ten more minutes before the train was scheduled to depart. Could she raise enough for a ticket in that amount of time?

"As lovely as your face, if I might be so bold to say."

Something flickered in his eyes. The heat in her cheeks increased. Warning bells clanged in the back of her mind. She'd seen the look before, usually from men who'd imbibed too heavily and lost control of their senses. But back then, Burke or Sloan or another crew member was close by to offer protection. Who would protect her today if the man tried to touch her?

She scooped up her cup and took a shuffling step away from him.

He advanced the same distance, his narrowed gaze pinned to her face. "You seem to be in need of financial assistance." He dropped a meaningful glance to the cup and then met her eyes again. "How much have you gathered there?"

Fanny dared a peek. At quick count, she surmised perhaps fifteen cents had been deposited during her quarter hour of singing. Not nearly enough to take her to the next station. She bit the corner of her lip.

His chuckle drew her gaze. "That little, hmm? Well, perhaps I could assist you."

A wealthy man like him, if he liked the song, might give her a dollar. Or even two. Fanny gripped the cup tightly to her pounding chest. "I have an extensive repertoire. I'd be happy to sing something of your choosing."

He pushed his jacket flap aside and slipped his hand into his trouser pocket, an action she'd seen Sloan do countless times. His hand slid free with a five-dollar gold piece pinched between his finger and thumb.

Fanny stared at the coin. Five dollars might take her all the way through Indiana and into Ohio. "What song would you like, sir?"

He slowly shook his head. "I confess, my dear, your voice is pleasant, but a song isn't what interests me."

She stared at his leering face. Her flesh exploded with prickles. He might dress like a gentleman, but now she knew better. She backed up several inches, her pulse scampering into double beats. "I am not — I would never —"

His lecherous gaze traveled from her face to her feet and up again. A smirk curled one side of his mouth. "I wouldn't be too hasty, my dear. Given your, uh, unladylike appearance, I doubt anyone else will make a better offer." He rotated his wrist, making the gold coin catch flashes of sunlight. "This should be the easiest five dollars you ever earn."

And the fastest way to lose her self-respect. Fanny gave an adamant shake of her head. "I am a singer." She straightened her spine. "And a lady, no matter how I may appear."

His lips twitched as if he held back laughter. "A lady, you say? Perhaps looks can be deceptive."

Fanny tipped up her chin and glared at him. "They certainly can."

He shrugged, pocketed the coin, and adjusted his lapels. "Very well, then. Good luck to you." He turned and sauntered off.

Fanny nearly collapsed with relief. She was safe. For now. She sent up a prayer of gratitude for God's hand of protection, then made a hasty decision. She wouldn't raise enough money for a ticket here. But hadn't she proven her ability to walk long distances? Traveling by foot without her companions was a dreary undertaking, but even so, she'd walk every one of the remaining miles to New York all by herself over what the so-called gentleman proposed.

She tipped the coins into her purse and set off in search of a food vendor. She would buy a sandwich or some crackers and cheese. Then she would follow the tracks to Elkhart, the next town with a train station.

Fanny pushed her bonnet back and let it dangle by its strings on her back. She swiped the sweat from her forehead. The air held a nip, but in her eagerness to escape the attention of the man with the top hat, she'd set a good pace for herself. The train had chugged past at least an hour ago, if she judged the position of the sun correctly. When she traveled with Enoch and his family, they'd covered fifteen to twenty miles a day, depending on the terrain. Why hadn't she taken the time to ask the number of miles between Mishawaka and Elkhart? If she knew the distance, she might be able to discern how much farther she had to go, as well as what time of day she might arrive at the town. It seemed likely she'd need to find a place to spend the night since tickets could be purchased only during daylight hours.

Her stomach rumbled, reminding her that the few crackers and cluster of raisins she'd purchased before leaving Mishawaka hadn't satisfied her hunger. If Itiah was there, she would probably scavenge some edible roots, berries, or plant stalks. How she wished Itiah and all the others were still with her.

After so many years of loneliness, having the company of Enoch's family had been such a joy. And after experiencing the joy of companionship, being alone again was even more painful. Tears stung, and she gave her eyes a quick swish with her fingertips. Would crying help anything? Of course not. Even Baby Leona had seemed to understand that truth, because the little girl had rarely fussed. Only once, when a bee stung her on the foot, had she truly cried long and hard. She must be missing the family more than she realized. She even heard Baby Leona's cries in memory.

Or was it in memory?

She halted and scanned the landscape, straining against the rustle of the wind in the grass and birdsong from the thick brush nearby. She nearly convinced herself she'd merely imagined hearing a baby's wails, but then the sound came again. Her heart rolled over. Someplace not too far away, a small child was in distress. She remained rooted in place, waiting for the cries to stop. Surely the child would receive comfort, wouldn't it?

Apparently not, because the wails continued, growing louder and more frantic by the minute. Fanny looked east, at the lines of silver track leading to Elkhart, then south, from which the plaintive cries seemed to come. She couldn't ignore the child's anguish. Even if it meant delaying her arrival in Elkhart, she had to offer comfort or, at the very least, assure herself that someone else was trying to soothe the child.

She changed direction and set off toward the heartrending sound.

12

NEAR GIDEON, INDIANA
FANNY

Fanny topped a grassy rise, worked her way through a tangle of overgrown trees and brush, and found herself in a broad clearing. Ahead, a small cabin stood near a log barn with an attached corral. She tipped her head, listening. The wailing came from inside the cabin. She remained in place for several seconds, seeking evidence that someone other than the distraught child was nearby. No people anywhere. Only a spotted cow nosing at tufts of grass at the base of a corral post and a pair of chickens pecking in the dirt outside the cabin.

She trotted to the cabin. The side facing north had no windows, only a rock chimney centered on the long log wall. She rounded the east side and found windows — a square one near the roof's peak, and a larger one two panes wide and three panes high. The larger one's ledge was perhaps four feet above the ground. She cupped her hands and peered through one of the lower panes, then grunted in annoyance. Was there no window on the west side to allow in light? The interior was so dark that she made out only shadowy shapes.

She didn't need to see inside, however, to know the child hadn't finished crying. The wails had changed to shuddering sobs, reminding Fanny of Dathan's tears when they'd said goodbye in Chicago. A lump filled her throat. She'd been helpless against the boy's sorrow. She would somehow ease this child's unhappiness.

Swallowing the knot of sadness, she hurried to the front of the cabin. A flat slab of rock served as a stoop in front of the single planked door. A bucket with a dipper handle sticking out of it waited at the edge of the stoop. She stepped past the bucket and thumped her fist on the door. Silence fell from within for a few seconds, and then a new wail rose — this one shrill and filled with desperation.

Overcome with sympathy, Fanny searched for a door handle. A rawhide string dangled from a drilled hole. She grabbed the string and pulled. To her relief, the door swung inward, and she stepped inside. Afternoon sunshine painted a weak, slanted beam to the northeast corner and cast light on a tiny barefooted girl standing inside a pen of some sort. The child reached one hand to Fanny, her lower lip quivering. Her eyes, a vivid blue, swam with tears, and moist tracks rained down her cheeks.

Fanny dashed over and lifted the child into her arms. The little girl clung, burying her damp face in the curve of Fanny's neck. Fanny patted her back while turning a slow circle and searching every nook of the single room. This child was much too young to be left alone. Surely her mother or father was here somewhere — asleep, perhaps, or sick in bed. But a cursory search proved the little girl was, indeed, all alone.

Alone, and penned like a goat or a duck. How well Fanny knew the awful feeling of being trapped in a space not of one's own choosing. At least she'd been old enough to find ways to entertain herself when the walls seemed to close in. This little girl wouldn't be able to distract herself from her imprisonment, making the act even more cruel.

Indignation burning in her chest, Fanny carried her outside, sat on the warm flat rock, and placed the child on her lap, where she could get a better look at her. The sight turned her stomach. The little girl's curly hair was plastered to her head with sweat and mucus. She'd chewed her fist, leaving behind a welt on her knuckle. Her reddened cheeks looked chapped, perhaps from the cascade of salty tears she'd shed, and the front of her simple frock was damp. Obviously she'd been crying for a long time. She smelled bad, too. She needed a napkin change.

Indignation blossomed into hot fury. Who could be so heartless as to lock a child — hardly more than a baby — in a dreary enclosure and leave her all alone for what must have been hours? She pulled the little girl snug to her breast and kissed the top of her head. "Don't worry, wee one. I'll see to you. I won't leave you by yourself."

Carrying the child, she reentered the cabin and snooped around. Shutters locked out the sunlight on the west-facing window. She folded them back, and the additional light proved helpful. A simple shelf attached to the wall with a pair of iron brackets held several tins. She popped the largest one open and discovered crackers. She gave one to the little girl, who gnawed on it with an eagerness that stung Fanny's heart. A simple bed filled a corner of the cabin, and a cradle waited at its foot. Fanny hurried over and peeked in the cradle. To her relief, she found a stack of cloth squares inside. She snatched up two of them and laid the little girl on the bed.

A scream left the child's throat, bringing with it a little flow of mushy cracker crumbs and saliva. She launched herself at Fanny.

Fanny whisked her into her arms again and bounced her, uncaring about the paste-like smear deposited on her shoulder. "Now, now, didn't I say I wouldn't leave you? I only need to lay you down so I can change your napkin. You've soiled it, and we need to clean you up." She singsonged the words and smiled into the little girl's fear-filled face. After a few minutes of gentle jostling and comforting the child, Fanny tried again to place her on the bed. This time, even though the girl whimpered, she lay still.

Chattering a steady stream of nonsense to keep the little girl occupied, Fanny whisked off the stained dress and filthy napkin and tossed both items out the door. She used one cloth, after dipping it in the water bucket, to wash the child, then picked up the second to use as a napkin. She paused, napkin in hand, and frowned. She'd removed the child's soiled napkin so quickly that she hadn't taken note of how it was fastened. Many years had passed since she'd diapered her littlest sister, and Pazzy had left Baby Leona unclothed beneath her little frock.

"Hmm," Fanny muttered under her breath, "Ma always said where there's a will, there's a way." Fanny certainly had the will. Now to find the way. After a few fumbled efforts, she folded the fabric into a triangle, pulled the center point up between the child's legs, then drew the other points over the girl's belly and knotted them.

When Fanny was finished, she sat the child up, and the little girl broke into a dimpled smile that exposed eight perfect little pearl-like teeth. She lifted her arms, and Fanny scooped her up for a hug. She rested her cheek against the child's head and sighed. "Oh, such a darling you are. How could anyone go away and leave you here to fend for yourself?"

The little girl toyed with the top button on Fanny's bodice, and Fanny chuckled. "I wish I knew your name."

"Nay-nay-nay," she babbled, then pointed a chubby finger at the cracker tin.

Fanny fetched another cracker, then carried her outside and roamed the area around the cabin. Not a soul was around. She entered the barn, half hoping to find someone and half dreading it. If someone was there but unable to answer the child's cries, what would she do? She searched every corner, but the barn was as absent of caretakers as the house.

She bounced the child on her arm and organized her thoughts. The little girl seemed well fed and the grounds appeared cared for. The only true sign of neglect was the pen in which the child had been left for heaven only knew how long. But such a horrible thing to do. And how often was she left there? Every day? Prickles attacked her flesh. She'd never forget the first weeks of being closed in her tiny cell on the boat, only allowed to come out to perform or take a meal in the kitchen under the cook's supervision. She'd been trapped like an animal in a cage.

The shrill call of a train whistle drifted over the plain. She instinctively turned toward the sound, her heart skipping a beat. She needed to reach Elkhart, hopefully before sundown, and locate a safe place to spend the night. The sun hung heavy in the western sky, seeming to grow larger as it descended. How many hours before dark fell? Three? Four?

A pudgy hand patted Fanny's cheek, drawing her attention. The little girl offered a crinkled-nose smile, then babbled nonsensically. Fanny hugged her close, protectiveness welling. Elkhart would have to wait. She would not return this child to that awful pen. She planted a kiss on the little girl's forehead and headed for the cabin. "Let us find a clean gown for you. Then I'll try to fix you a decent supper." Surely there were food items besides crackers in those tins. "And then we'll wait for your ma or da to come take care of you."

And when they came, she'd tell them exactly what she thought about them leaving their baby alone in a pen.

Walter Kuhn

If he'd broken his leg, it wouldn't bear weight. Walter was no doctor, but he knew that much. Even though planting his right foot against the ground sent a shaft of pain from his knee to his hip, he could walk. The realization should comfort him. But it didn't. He'd been gone too long. Far too long. He needed to hurry home to Annaliese, his precious *Liébling.* She must be crying with hunger by now.

He finger combed his thick beard, as he always did when he worried. What would he give her for supper? In his tumble over the ridge, he'd not only wrenched his knee but also lost the three plump rabbits meant to stretch their food supplies.

159

A failure, that's what he was. A failure as a father, who should be able to provide for his child. And a failure as a husband, too. Didn't the newest grave in the church's small cemetery prove it? He squeezed the wavy whiskers growing from his chin and forced the remembrances into hiding. He took another limping step. Starlight twinkled overhead, and a sweet breeze filled his nostrils. He should find pleasure in this evening. Hadn't he accomplished what he'd set out to do when he left New York City five years ago? Yes, he'd carved a life from the rugged, open land far away from the smelly, crowded streets of his boyhood city. Many times, he'd stood beneath the broad expanse of sky, whether the robin's-egg blue of noonday or dusky gray of night, and thanked God for the blessing of this place. But no pleasure filled him tonight.

"I cannot do this alone, God." His prayers were most often complaints these days, but he'd been taught to speak to God, and so he did. But he couldn't help wondering if anyone listened. Or observed. If God were watching, He would already know that Walter needed help. He'd written to *Vater* and *Mutter* four months ago. A week after Grete's death. When would his parents send back word about finding him a new wife?

He struggled up the final rise between him and his cabin, a sigh of relief easing from his throat. Almost home. At the top he paused and smiled at the glow of lamplight behind the windows. Ah, such a welcoming sight. Then he gave a jolt. Lamplight? But how? His nose twitched. Did the smell of smoke hang in the air? Yes, yes — smoke from a fire. Panic exploded within his chest. Had Annaliese somehow escaped her enclosure and set something ablaze?

"Dear Lord in heaven, have I not lost enough to flames?" The words groaned from his dry throat. He could not lose his baby girl, too. Gritting his teeth against the throbbing agony in his injured leg, he half stumbled, half ran the final distance to the cabin and charged in. With terror pulsing through his veins, he staggered to the corner where Annaliese should be safe inside her pen.

She wasn't there.

Walter turned in a clumsy circle, his frantic gaze jerking from the glowing lamp on the mantel, to the crackling fire in the fireplace, to the filthy stranger sitting in the rocking chair — in *Grete's* rocking chair — with Annaliese asleep in her arms.

Fear dissolved and anger ignited within him, as hot as the flames dancing in the rock fireplace. He took a limping step in the woman's direction. *"Wer bist du?"* He barked the query in his native German.

Her fine eyebrows came together in a scowl. "I do not know what you said, and neither do I care." The chair's rungs grated a steady rhythm against the hard-packed earth floor. "What kind of person are y' to leave a wee bairn all alone for more than half a day? Had I not come along, she would still be crying in that . . . that *cage.* 'Tis a shameful thing to have done, sir!"

He cringed. She spoke softly, hardly more than a whisper, but her words speared him through and through. Even this stranger knew he carried the weight of shame like a millstone. But why should she sit as judge and jury against him? She didn't know his circumstances.

He limped to the woman and took his sleeping Liébling from her. Annaliese released a little whimper, but she quickly quieted when he formed a cradle with his arms and gently rocked her to and fro. He aimed a frown at the stranger and commanded his tongue to speak the English his parents had insisted he learn. "The pen is to protect her. To keep her from wandering away or reaching things that could harm her."

The woman's eyebrows relaxed a bit, but

her lips remained clamped tight.

"And I did not intend to leave her for so long. I only meant to check my snares. An hour — two at the most — while she took her nap. But I fell and hurt myself. For a while I couldn't walk. I crawled to the creek and soaked my leg in the cold water until the swelling went down. Then I came home." He kept secret the lost rabbits. He'd made himself seem inept enough.

The stern pucker of her lips eased. She put the rocking chair into gentle movement.

"Who are you?" He repeated his earlier question, this time in English. He shuffled a few more inches closer to her. "Where are you from?" Her wild appearance made him nervous about her being around his Liébling. "Why are you here?" He wanted her out of Grete's chair.

"My name is Fanny Beck. And yours?"

"Kuhn. Walter Kuhn."

"Have you had any dinner, Mr. Kuhn?"

He gave a start. Had he heard her correctly?

"There is porridge in that pot by the fireplace. It will be thick as clay by now, but it should still be warm. I wouldn't call porridge a hearty meal, but I did the best I could with what I scavenged from the containers on the shelf and the milk from

163

your cow."

She'd milked his cow? And gone through his food stores? How long had she been in his cabin?

"I looked for eggs, but I didn't find any."

Of course she didn't. The chickens laid their eggs wherever they chose, and black snakes usually found them before Walter could.

"I put the chickens in the barn," she went on in a soft, somehow musical voice. "They'll likely escape again by morning. They're wily enough to find their way out between the gaps in the logs."

So he hadn't chinked the rebuilt barn yet. Didn't he have more important tasks, taking care of a house and a child and preparing a field for planting and everything else that needed doing on this homestead? He'd chink the barn before winter set in. If his new wife came by then.

"Perhaps you should build a coop."

Would she also advise him on how to plant and harvest his corn? And she still hadn't answered his questions or budged from Grete's chair. "Fräulein, I —"

"Eat some porridge, sir. It will likely be spoiled by morning." She slowly rose, her tender gaze on Annaliese's sleeping face. "Would you like me to tuck this wee one

164

into her cradle? Then, when you've finished eating, perhaps we can . . . talk."

13

THE KUHN HOMESTEAD
FANNY

Fanny sat in the rocking chair beside the fireplace. Such a comfortable seat. She could sleep in it, if its owner granted permission.

At the rough-hewn table in the center of the room, Mr. Kuhn sat on a stool crafted from a slice of tree trunk and four thick pieces cut from branches. He ate the porridge directly from the pot. His explanation had cooled her fury. She believed his intentions had been good. But she still found his choice to leave his very small daughter unattended for an hour or so — even while she slept — reckless, foolish, and inexcusable.

Despite her disapproval, she'd said all she intended to about the matter. If she made him angry with her, he would send her out into the night. If she couldn't sleep in this chair, she hoped to sleep in his barn, such as it was with its gaps between the logs. The structure resembled a giant birdcage. But it was a shelter. And in the morning, maybe he'd share a breakfast with her before she set off for Elkhart.

He tipped the pot sideways and scraped the remaining bits of hardening oats, sugar, and milk mixture from the sides. Then he released a sigh and set both spoon and pot aside. He looked at her, and a frown marred his brow. The frown concerned her. Now that he'd rested and filled his stomach, he'd likely gained enough strength to order her away.

He shifted slightly on the stool, wincing as he did so. Sympathy pinched Fanny's chest. His leg must be paining him. He said he'd soaked his knee in creek water. If comfrey grew near the creek, she could grind the leaves and make a compress. Itiah had made one for Enoch's back several evenings while on their journey, and the treatment seemed to give him comfort.

"I would like to know how you came to be in my home, cooking at my fire and caring for my Annaliese." The food had definitely revived him, because his tone now carried a command.

Fanny set aside thoughts of a comfrey poultice and offered him a mild frown. "I was passing by on my way to Elkhart, and I heard *your* Annaliese crying. I couldn't ignore a child in distress" — to her satisfaction, remorse pursed his face — "so I investigated. I was very surprised to find her all alone. I couldn't bring myself to put her back in the . . . the pen and leave her by herself, so I stayed and fed her. Then I waited for you." Suddenly something occurred to her. She shot a quick look left and right. "Where is Annaliese's mother?"

His face contorted. He thrust his fingers into his thick beard and bent forward as if someone had dropped a boulder on his back. "She is dead."

His words emerged so flatly and emotionlessly that if she hadn't witnessed his physical angst, she would think he didn't care. But he did care. His grief was palpable. As Itiah's had been. Fanny whispered, "I'm so sorry."

He sat up abruptly and dropped his hand from his whiskers. "Do you live in Elkhart?"

She swallowed a laugh. "I do not. I've never been there. I was going to the train station to buy a ticket. I'm trying to get to my family in New York City."

His eyebrows rose. "You are a long way from home."

Truthfully, New York City had never been her home. She'd stayed in the city only one night before traveling with Sloan to Missouri. But Da, Ma, Flossie, and Moira were there. They were all she needed to make the city feel like her home. "I am."

"How have you come to be so far away from your husband?"

Confused, she shook her head slightly. "I have no husband."

He glanced at her left hand.

She'd forgotten about the ring. All the lies she'd told during the past weeks stung her conscience. She would be truthful with this man. "It's only a piece of jewelry. I am not married."

He sat for several seconds with his lips sucked in. The gesture made the whiskers beneath his chin stick straight out, like Flossie poking out her tongue in sassiness. Did Flossie still do such a thing? Probably not. She was a young lady of sixteen already. Fanny had witnessed her sister's growing up through letters.

Letters! Fanny leaped from the chair, losing her shawl with the sudden motion, and clapped both hands over her mouth.

Mr. Kuhn drew back, his expression uncertain. "What's wrong?"

How had she forgotten about the letters she'd received and carefully hoarded over the years? Even in the stress of travel, she should have thought of them before now.

The messages penned by her sister had become so much a part of her that in her mind they were always with her. But they weren't any longer. She didn't care about the frocks she'd worn on the *River Peacock*'s stage, but her letters — and Ma's Bible — were lost to her now. The loss struck with as much force as her body smacking the surface of the water the night of the storm. She groaned behind her hands.

Mr. Kuhn pushed himself to his feet and stared at her. "Are you going to be sick?"

She was already sick. Sick at heart.

"You're trembling. Sit down."

She started to sit, but a whimper from the cradle caught her attention. She turned and spotted Annaliese sitting up, her little arms reaching. Mr. Kuhn turned toward the child, but Fanny hurried to the cradle and lifted the baby into her arms. She held the child close, giving comfort but also receiving it. She'd lost almost seven years of being with her family. Now she'd lost the things that had kept her linked to them during those long, lonely years. And she'd never get them back.

Walter

Walter limped forward and plucked Annaliese from the Fräulein's arms. The baby set up a howl, stretching one little hand to Fräulein Beck. He turned his back on the woman and bounced Annaliese, murmuring *shh, shh,* but she continued crying and reached over his shoulder.

His leg throbbed, but more than that, his heart hurt. He'd always been able to comfort his Liébling. This stranger in his house needed to go. But how would he force her out when it pained him to even take a step?

" 'There was a man lived in the moon, lived in the moon . . .' "

Walter's thoughts stilled when the Fräulein began to sing. Such a ridiculous song. No man lived in the moon, but Annaliese quieted and stopped fighting against Walter's hold. He slowly turned around and faced the woman. As the song went on, about the man wearing a hat of cheese, Annaliese's blinks slowed and her eyelids eventually closed. Still humming, the woman held out her arms.

If Walter crossed to the cradle, he might jolt his Liébling awake with his jarring limp. With reluctance, he allowed Fräulein Beck to place the baby in the cradle. For a few seconds, the woman remained bent over, the way Grete had when tucking Annaliese in, and then she straightened and turned. Her gaze met Walter's, and her dirt-smudged cheeks turned pink.

"You . . ." He swallowed. "You sing quite well, Fräulein."

She lowered her head. "I was a singer on a riverboat."

"But not now?"

"Not now."

He limped to the stool and sat. "You are very good with Annaliese."

She aimed a fond smile toward the cradle. "She's a sweet bairn. She reminds me of my little sisters." Sadness pinched her dirty face. "I haven't seen them in a long, long time."

"How far have you walked?"

The pink deepened to red. "From Missouri to Iowa. Then I rode a train, in a cattle car, as far as Chicago, Illinois."

The unpleasant smell clinging to her clothes now made sense.

"But my money ran out when I got to Mishawaka. That's why I was walking to Elkhart when I heard Annaliese cry." She moved toward Grete's rocking chair.

Walter stood. "Here." He gestured to the stool. "Sit here." She gave him a puzzled frown, but she sat on the stool. He limped to the other side of the table and sat on the second stool.

Outside the window, full dark had fallen.

She wouldn't be able to see her way to Elkhart until morning. Another thought entered his mind. "If you ran out of money, how were you going to buy a ticket in Elkhart?"

A sad smile formed. "I planned to work for it." She pointed to a little tin cup on the dry sink, sitting atop a beaded purse he'd never seen before. "People put coins in my cup when I sing. I sing until I have enough for a ticket. Then I go to the next town." She shrugged. "It worked well until I reached Mishawaka. I pray it will work well in Elkhart and in the cities after it. So I can get all the way to New York City."

Her singing voice was lovely. He understood why people had given her money in exchange for a song. But her present appearance would put people off. He doubted she'd have any more luck in Elkhart than she'd had in Mishawaka unless she cleaned herself up.

She stood. "Mr. Kuhn, would you allow me to sleep in your barn tonight? I'll leave for Elkhart first thing in the morning."

He couldn't let a lady — even one who smelled like cow manure — sleep in his barn. He shook his head.

She sighed. "Very well." She headed for the door.

He rose and held out his hand. "Wait, Fräulein." She stopped with her back to him. "You cannot sleep in the barn. But you can sleep in the house. I will sleep in the barn."

She slowly turned around. "That's kind of you, but I'll be fine in the barn. I've slept outside or in barns several times over the past weeks. It won't bother me to do it again."

"The least I can do after you saw to my Annaliese is let you sleep in a bed tonight." He'd need to air his sheets afterward. He didn't care to put his nose on sheets that carried the foul cattle scent. He limped to the door. "Sleep well. I will see you in the morning."

Walter made a bed by spreading a blanket over a pile of straw — as comfortable as his straw-stuffed mattress on the rope bed inside — but his throbbing knee kept him up most of the night. Being awake while stars twinkled, coyotes yip-yipped and howled, and night birds cooed gave a man plenty of time to think. By the time the sun peeked over the eastern horizon, he'd made a decision.

He would talk to the Fräulein about staying. Not for good. Only until his parents' letter came with word about his new wife. Fräulein Beck wanted to get to New York. She would get there faster if she didn't have to stop and earn a ticket at each station, so he would pay her to care for his house and his daughter. This would solve problems — for her and for him. Pride swelled his chest. He might be only a homesteader, but he'd come up with a good plan. Now to convince her it was a good plan.

With effort, he got to his feet, fetched the milking stool and bucket, and set to relieving Carlotta of her full udder. Such a sweet-natured beast, she didn't even try to shuffle aside when he stuck his injured leg straight out beneath her. But he probably shouldn't be surprised by the cow's gentleness. Grete had treated the animal like a pet, spoiling her with carrots from the garden and brushing her with the horse's curry brush every evening. Walter brought the cow a carrot now and then, but he never brushed her. Carlotta probably missed Grete. As did Walter.

He stopped the steady squeeze-pull, squeeze-pull for a moment. Would asking the Fräulein to stay dishonor Grete? He shook his head. No. No more than bringing a new wife here would. And finding a new wife or hiring Fräulein Beck wouldn't be necessary if only he'd been brave and strong enough to —

Walter pressed his forehead to the cow's warm, smooth flank and returned to milking. No sense in thinking about what was past. He couldn't change it. He had to go forward. For Annaliese, and for himself. If he were lucky and Fräulein Beck agreed to his scheme, she would be able to go forward, too.

Yes, this was a good plan. A very good plan.

14

LANCASTER, MISSOURI
SLOAN

Sloan folded his nightshirt into a neat square and shoved it into his travel case next to his shaving kit. Seeking out the woman named Mrs. Carlson had seemed like a good plan, but he'd lost patience with it. According to the schedule he'd seen on the wall of the telegraph office when he sent a message to Burke, alerting him to Sloan's current location, the stage picked up or delivered passengers at seven in the morning. He intended to be waiting to climb aboard.

For three days, he'd crisscrossed the town and ventured into the surrounding countryside. The only Carlsons he'd located ended up being a middle-aged couple. They were friendly. Even invited him to stay and have supper with him. Which he did, because the food from the restaurant in his hotel was hardly palatable. But after hearing the woman hum at the stove, he knew he hadn't found the singer.

In case Bill's memory wasn't as accurate as the man had presumed, Sloan visited the homes of people whose surnames sounded like Carlson — Karlsson and Karlsen — as well as those similar to Carlson. He'd knocked at the doors of the Carsons, Carltons, Karlins, Garsons, and Colsons. And he still hadn't located the pretty young woman who'd sung, as Bill said his ma would describe it, like a nightingale. He might have more success if he went hunting the goose that laid the golden egg.

He swung his bag from the end of the squeaking mattress, took a step toward the door, then stopped. Was he giving up too soon? Maybe he should give Lancaster one more chance to produce the singer. The city was a good size. There could be a talented woman in the community. This was Saturday, when many people did their weekly shopping. Sunday was worship day. What if he put up notices at the post office, the general mercantile, and each of the churches in town? The majority of people would see it, and those who didn't might hear about it. People liked to talk. If he scheduled an hour or two for singers to come to the hotel's lobby and audition for him, he might draw out the woman who'd sung at Bill's stage stop or another one with equal talent.

He tossed his bag into the corner, settled his hat over his hair, and went in search of a newspaper office. The town would come to life in another hour or so. There was no time to waste.

The Kuhn Homestead
Fanny

Fanny peeked out the west window. Beneath a rose-tinted sky, the cow grazed in the enclosure behind the barn. Her slack udder signaled that Mr. Kuhn had seen to the morning milking. What else was he doing out there? She couldn't leave until he returned to the house.

Impatience stirred within her. She'd risen before dawn and dipped rainwater from a barrel outside the house into the biggest pot she could find. After heating the water over the fire, she'd given herself a thorough wash. The water turned the color of mud from her travel-dusted body and oily hair, which mortified her. She'd never been so filthy. But now she was clean from head to toe — at least underneath her dress. If only she'd had time to wash and dry her underthings and single frock. Then she could leave for Elkhart all-the-way clean and not smelling like cattle. But she couldn't risk

Mr. Kuhn seeing her wrapped in only a blanket while her clothes dried next to the fireplace.

She turned back to the table. Annaliese sat in her chair and gnawed a hard biscuit. Such a mess she made, dribbling food across her round, bare tummy, but Fanny smiled and toyed with a curl behind the little girl's ear. Caring for the wee lass, even for such a short time, had brought back so many pleasant memories of helping Ma, first with Flossie, born when Fanny was five years old, and then with Moira seven years later.

A hint of sadness intruded upon her sunny reflections. Would Flossie and Moira even know her anymore? They'd been so young when she'd left with Sloan. Flossie might, because of the letters they'd exchanged over the years, but little Moira would probably see her as a stranger.

Fanny darted to the window and peered out again. Wouldn't the man hurry so she could be on her way? Then remorse struck. Of course he couldn't hurry. He'd hurt his leg. Had the swelling returned during the night? He might be sitting out in that birdcage-looking barn, overtaxed from seeing to morning chores, unable to walk.

Urgency fueled by worry propelled her to

the table. She used a moist cloth and washed the mess from Annaliese's face and tummy, then perched the child on her arm and crossed the hard ground on bare feet to the barn's double doors. They stood slightly ajar, and she gripped the edge of the right one. But a voice stopped her — Mr. Kuhn's low voice, laced with emotion. She tipped her ear to the gap between the doors and listened.

"I know I have no right to ask this after what I've done."

Fanny frowned. To whom was he speaking?

"But the Fräulein is right that my Annaliese must be cared for better than I am doing."

Fanny pressed a kiss on Annaliese's rosy cheek. Indeed, she deserved better than being left in a cage by herself. At least her father realized it.

"So I ask, Lord, that . . ."

Fanny's heart fired into her throat. He was praying! She shouldn't listen to a man's private prayers. She inched backward.

". . . whatever she says when I ask, let it be what is best for me and my Annaliese."

Suddenly Annaliese bounced on Fanny's arm. "Fa! Fa!"

Fanny whirled and took a few stumbling

steps toward the cabin.

"Fräulein?"

Stifling a groan, she turned and faced him.

He stood in the barn's doorway holding the end of his dark, wavy beard, his thick brows low.

Annaliese babbled and reached her pudgy arms for her father.

Fanny considered putting the child down and running off. If she'd put her shoes on before leaving the cabin, she would have. She must seem like an eavesdropper. She should apologize. Then put on her shoes and run off.

He limped to her and took Annaliese, who jabbered happily in his arms, and fixed an embarrassed frown on Fanny. "You were looking for me?"

"I was." She linked her hands against her rib cage. "I saw the cow in the fenced-in area, but you didn't come to the cabin. I was worried."

His brows dipped lower. "Worried? For me?"

"I thought your leg might keep you from coming inside."

He nodded. "It is slowing me down this morning. But I've finished all my chores and my morning pray —" Red streaks appeared above the thick growth of whiskers on his cheeks. "I am ready to go to the house now."

She moved toward the cabin, and he walked beside her, his gait slow. "I fixed breakfast, and Annaliese has eaten a biscuit."

He shot her a quick look. "Where did you find a biscuit?"

"I made some." She cringed. "They aren't very good. It's been a long time since I did any baking. And I couldn't find butter or jam to flavor them. But Annaliese didn't seem to mind."

The semblance of a smile, perhaps inspired by his fondness for his daughter, twinkled in his eyes. "She has learned not to be picky. I am not a good baker, either."

They reached the cabin, and he gestured for her to enter first. Once inside, he pointed to the table. "Fräulein, would you sit, please? There is something I would like to discuss with you."

She wanted to put on her shoes, gather her few belongings, and be on her way as quickly as possible. After his kindness in giving up his bed for her, though, the least she could do was listen. She sank onto one of the stools.

He took the other stool, stretched his hurt leg straight, and set Annaliese on his good knee. "Fräulein, thank you for seeing to my

Annaliese yesterday." He pulled the little girl closer and briefly touched his cheek to her head. "Leaving her alone isn't the best thing to do. But she is over a year old now. Too big now for me to carry all the time, as I could right after . . . after her Mutter died. And yet she isn't big enough to keep up with me as I go about my work."

The pain in his blue eyes — it suddenly struck her where Annaliese got her stunning blue eyes — stung Fanny. She nodded. "I understand. I'm sorry for speaking to you the way I did when you came in. I had no right to condemn you when I didn't know the reasons for her being left by herself."

"*Dánke* — thank you — Fräulein, for your understanding."

Annaliese wriggled, and he set her on the floor, then turned his attention to Fanny again. "You said you have little sisters. You helped care for them?"

A smile tugged at the corners of Fanny's lips as memories flooded her mind. She'd been Ma's best helper — Ma always said so — and she'd relished the position. "I did. Flossie is five years younger than me, and Moira twelve. Your Annaliese isn't much younger than Moira was when I last saw her." She gazed at the girl, envisioning Moira playing on the dirt floor of the cot-

184

tage in Scotland.

"I don't want to keep leaving Annaliese alone."

Fanny shifted her attention to Mr. Kuhn.

"But without someone here to take care of her, I have no choice. So, I wondered . . . if you might stay and care for my Annaliese."

She sucked in a startled breath. "S-stay?"

He crunched his beard with his fingers. "I know you want to reach New York. But this plan of yours to sing at each stop and earn money . . . it might not work out."

He could be right. It hadn't gone so well in Mishawaka.

"If you stay, I will pay you." He paused, pulling in his lips and making his whiskers poke out. "I can offer a dollar a week." He lowered his head. "I know it isn't much. I know I'm asking a lot of you." He met her gaze. "But it won't be forever. A new wife is coming, and when she gets here, you can go. Because then Annaliese and I will be fine."

His final statement about him and Annaliese being fine seemed forced. Did he mean to convince Fanny or himself? And what difference did it make? She folded her hands on the edge of the table. "That's good. I'm happy for you. When will she arrive?"

"I don't know."

She found his answer less than satisfactory. Sloan had intended to keep her beyond their agreed-upon length of service. If she stayed, would Mr. Kuhn expect her to remain as Annaliese's caretaker for mere weeks, several months, or even years? She tilted her head and fixed him with a steady look. "You don't know?"

He shook his head. "But soon, I hope."

Fanny hoped so, too. She couldn't bear the thought of Annaliese alone day after day in that despicable pen. But neither did she want to delay her departure for New York. Her thoughts bounced back and forth, considering the options to stay or go. The singing had worked well most of the time. But when it didn't, it delayed her progress. If she earned enough for a full ticket — no more having to stop at each depot and sing — she might reach her family sooner in the end.

Then the gentleman who propositioned her in Mishawaka flitted through her mind. Although she sensed Mr. Kuhn was not a lecher — he'd been very respectful to her and seemed tender toward his little daughter — she should fully understand his expectations. She forced her dry throat to release words. "What would you ask of me to earn the dollar a week?"

"Take care of Annaliese and see to house-hold chores." He spoke in such a rush that she suspected he'd been holding back the comment until she asked.

"I would stay here in the cabin with her?" He nodded.

"And you would stay . . ."

"In the barn, as I did last night." Then he released a heavy sigh. "I know you have no reason to trust me. Not after coming here and finding my little girl crying and alone. But I'm not a bad man, Fräulein." He winced, as if a pain suddenly gripped him, and then his expression cleared. "If you can wait another day to decide, I will take you to church tomorrow. The town of Gideon is three miles south of my homestead, and the chapel is halfway between. Annaliese and I walk to service each Sunday."

She suddenly realized she hadn't seen a horse or wagon on the property. How did he plow his fields, go to town for shopping, and do all the other things a farmer needed to do, without a horse or wagon? But she could ponder that later. Her heart fluttered. A chance to go to church sounded wonder-ful. She hadn't attended a service since she left Inverness for America. Even when the boat was docked, Sloan kept her under his watchful eye. And he never went to church.

"You could talk to my minister or to others in the congregation who know me well. If they say something that makes you uneasy about staying, you can leave. I won't argue with you. And I'll give you a little bit of money for the time you've already spent taking care of Annaliese."

At her name, the child sent a nose-wrinkling smile over her shoulder. She rose and went to her father, arms reaching.

He picked her up and settled her on his knee again. "What do you think, Fräulein?"

Fanny gazed at little Annaliese. Two desires warred within her — to keep Annaliese safe until Mr. Kuhn's new wife arrived, and to reach her family as quickly as possible and reacquaint herself with her parents and sisters. She considered his suggestion about speaking to his minister. A man of God would be able to counsel her.

She looked into Mr. Kuhn's eyes. The hopefulness in his expression became her undoing. "I can wait one more day to make a decision."

Walter

Such relief smote Walter that he sagged on the chair. "Thank you, Fräulein."

"You're welcome, Mr. Kuhn." She gestured to the dry sink. "There are biscuits

188

under the napkin if you would like some breakfast."

"I would."

Before he could set Annaliese on the floor, she quickly rose. "I'll serve you."

Already she was seeing to their needs. He watched her choose a plate from the shelf and stack three biscuits on it. Her graceful movements brought back memories of Grete moving around the cabin. Those first months after her death, every memory of her brought such pain that he'd tried not to think about her. But over time, the memories had become bittersweet. Eventually would even the bitter part disappear?

Considering how she'd died, probably not.

Fräulein Beck carried the plate to the table and set it in front of him. "Biscuits by themselves are a sad breakfast. If there are eggs somewhere, I could fry them for you."

His mouth watered. Fried eggs tasted so good. But he shouldn't trouble her. Being demanding might chase her away. He smiled. "The chickens lay their eggs wherever they please. I think they hide them on purpose to tease me. I didn't win their find-the-eggs game yet this morning, but I'll look again soon. Maybe we can have eggs for lunch."

She glanced at his wounded leg. "Would

189

you like me to search for the eggs? We had chickens when I was a little girl, and I gathered the eggs for my ma."

"No, no. Collecting the eggs is my job." Although it had been Grete's. He ignored the pang of sadness. "The biscuits are fine for my breakfast. Thank you, Fräulein."

She nodded and returned to the dry sink, humming as she went.

Walter ate his dry biscuits, sharing a bit now and then with Annaliese. Such a relief to know he wouldn't need to worry about his little daughter's care anymore. After Fräulein Beck spoke to Reverend Lee, she would decide to stay, because the kindly man would say good things about him. The reverend's affirmation and her affection for Annaliese would keep her here. He started to send up a silent prayer of gratitude, but the words wouldn't form. Not even in his head.

Yes, Reverend Lee would say good things because he didn't know everything about Walter. What might the reverend tell the Fräulein if he knew that Walter had killed his wife?

15

GIDEON BIBLE CHAPEL
FANNY

Fanny sat on a backless bench in the middle of a simple, homey sanctuary and blinked repeatedly against tears. Happy tears had threatened the moment she spotted the cross on the clapboard building's steeple. She'd wanted to break into a run and enter the building standing alone but proud in the middle of the prairie as quickly as possible, but Mr. Kuhn's limping gait had slowed their passage.

A breeze whisked through the open windows and ruffled the pages of the Bibles on parishioners' laps. She had no Bible to hold since the one Ma had given her had been left behind on the riverboat, but — oh! — the joy of being in God's house was bliss beyond description. Not until she was able to join a congregation in singing hymns of praise and listen to a preacher share from God's Holy Book did she realize how much she'd missed being with fellow believers.

Going to church did her heart much good. She didn't regret postponing her departure for New York.

She smoothed the wrinkled skirt of the rose-colored muslin dress she'd donned that morning. To her shock, before he'd gone to the barn last night, Mr. Kuhn brought down a trunk from the cabin's loft space, opened it, and invited her to choose a dress.

"You'll want something clean to wear to church, won't you?" he asked, and she couldn't deny he was right. The dresses likely belonged to his dead wife. His generosity in sharing them touched her deeply. Fanny had taken the top dress, rather than digging through the trunk, and thanked Mr. Kuhn for his kindness. His shy smile in reply lingered in her mind's eye. She would be very surprised if the soft-spoken, white-haired preacher didn't confirm Mr. Kuhn's claim that he was a good man.

The service ended with a hymn and a prayer. Fanny presumed everyone would leave for their homes and Mr. Kuhn would take her to the preacher, but people swarmed her bench. After so many years of being mostly alone or separated from people by the stage, being surrounded by even such a small and friendly crowd made anxiety prickle her frame. She instructed herself to smile, as she had when she performed in front of the large audiences on the ship.

The folks introduced themselves, offered warm welcomes, and complimented her voice. Fanny shared her name and returned their hellos, but the compliments embarrassed her. She hadn't intended to sing so loudly that everyone heard her. Ma and Da would say she'd behaved boastfully. She thanked the people for their kindness and made a secret vow — if she returned next Sunday, she would temper her joy and sing more quietly.

The minister came last, and when he smiled at her and enclosed her hand between his warm palms, she felt, oddly, as if she'd been accepted into his fold.

"It is a real treat to have a visitor this morning," he said. His eyes, pale brown as the honey Ma harvested in the fall, shone with sincerity. "I am Reverend Lee. And you are . . . ?"

"Fainche Beck." Why had her given name rather than her common one slipped out?

"*Fine*-cuh." He released her hand and seemed to sample her name. "How lovely. I've never heard it before."

"It's Scottish." Her explanation emerged in full Scottish brogue, turning *Scottish* almost into *Scootish*. She cringed, recalling

Ransom's comment about some people's perception of those from Scotland or Ireland. Quickly she said, "Everyone calls me Fanny."

"Very well. It's nice to meet you, Miss Fanny."

Enoch and his family had called her "Miss Fanny." Loneliness for her friends created an ache in the center of her heart. She prayed they were safely on their way to Canada and doing well.

Mr. Kuhn had stayed near but silent during all the greetings. Now he cleared his throat. "Reverend Lee, I've asked Fräulein Beck to be Annaliese's caretaker until my new wife comes. Because she is new in Gideon, I told her she should talk to you about whether or not it was a good decision for her." He limped to the end of the center aisle of the small chapel. "I'll take Annaliese outside and let you two talk privately."

Fanny watched them leave the building, then turned to the preacher. "I hope I'm not keeping you from your dinner."

"My dinner can wait. How can I help you?"

His openness put Fanny so at ease that she spoke without hesitation. "I hadn't intended to stay in Indiana. I'm traveling from Missouri to New York, where my family lives. I've been away from them for almost seven years, performing on a riverboat."

His snow-white eyebrows rose. "Ah. That explains the lovely singing I heard from the congregation this morning. You are a riverboat singer?"

"Was." She shuddered. "I'm not anymore, and I don't want to be again. I . . ." She swallowed a knot of agony. "I want to be with my family. But I also want to take care of little Annaliese." If she told the man how she'd found the child trapped in a cage all alone, he might change his opinion of Mr. Kuhn. She decided to remain silent about it. "She's such a bonny lass. I've become fond of her already. Mr. Kuhn promised to live in the barn and allow me to live in his cabin with Annaliese. He said he would pay me to take care of her and do the household chores." Sloan had made promises, too, but he hadn't kept them. She clasped her hands together to control their sudden tremble. "Can I trust him to honor his word?"

"Oh, yes." Reverend Lee nodded as he spoke, adding extra emphasis to his affirmation. "I have known Walter Kuhn since he claimed the plot of land north of Gideon five — or is it six? — years ago. Since his arrival, he's faithfully attended service here.

Even though coming now means walking the distance, he's never missed a Sunday. He always trades fairly with his neighbors, pays his bills in a timely manner, and lends a helping hand wherever it is needed. He has a fine reputation in Gideon."

Fanny didn't realize she was holding her breath until it eased from her lungs in a sigh of relief. Maybe if her parents had asked others about Sloan's reputation before agreeing to indenture Fanny to him, she would still be with her family. "This is good to hear."

"Yes, Walter is a trustworthy man." He tipped his head. "He is also a trusting man. How long has he known you?"

The question emerged in a friendly tone, but the sharpness of his gaze spoke of his concern. "I came upon his cabin this past Friday afternoon."

" 'Came upon'?" He folded his arms, but his pose seemed more curious than stern. "How did that happen?"

Fanny briefly explained her intention to sing her way to New York and her failure to earn enough money for a ticket to Elkhart. She didn't tell him Annaliese's wails drew her to the cabin, though. "Since it was late, he allowed me to stay the night in his cabin while he slept in the barn. Then yesterday morning, he asked if I would stay and care for Annaliese. But only until his new wife arrives."

The minister's face pinched into a frown of sadness. "When he suffered the loss of his wife in the barn fire" — Fanny stared at the man, shock jarring her — "people from the community came together and helped build his new barn without him even asking. Their response to his tragedy says as much as my words to his standing in the community."

She pressed her laced fingers to her heart. "He said his wife had died, but he didn't say it was in a fire. How awful." Sympathy for the man filled her, and at the same time, questions flooded her. Wasn't the barn a man's domain? Why hadn't he, instead of his wife, been trapped in the fire?

"It is. To lose a young wife and mother at all is sad, but in such a way." Reverend Lee shook his head. "It was I who first encouraged Walter to send a request to his parents about finding him a new wife. Women from the big cities are eager to carve better lives on the open prairie, and Walter has much to offer, given his land holding and his gentle nature. I've been praying for the woman who comes. That she and Walter will learn to love each other and live together in harmony. But, of course, it's taking a while. Maybe longer than either of us expected." The minister pinned Fanny with another intense look. "In the meantime, here you are."

She wasn't sure how to respond, so she waited. As did he, for several seconds, his gaze never wavering from her face. Then a smile softened his expression.

"Miss Fanny, a stranger in our congregation is a rare treat, so I observed you this morning. You appeared to drink in every word I spoke. Your face, while singing the hymns, glowed. Are you a believer in the Lord and Savior, Jesus Christ?"

The same joy she'd experienced during the time of worship returned, and she nodded with emphasis. "I am, sir. Me da and ma taught me to serve Him, and He has been my source of strength and comfort during my years away from them." Loneliness smote her. "I am keen to be with them again, but Mr. Kuhn's promise to buy me a ticket to New York when his new wife comes seems more secure than me begging for coins at train stations."

"I see." He tapped his lower lip with his finger, thoughtfulness creasing his brow. "It could be God has sent you in answer to a prayer."

Fanny tilted her head. "What prayer?"

"For Annaliese to be safe and well cared for." He linked his fingers together and rested them on his knee. "Walter did the best he could, putting her in the enclosure and checking on her frequently."

The minister knew about the cage? Fanny received a second shock.

"But we both knew it wasn't ideal. Not for Annaliese, and not for Walter. A man can't complete his chores if he has to leave every half hour or so and go to his house, especially when he must work by hand, since the plow and horse were also lost in the fire." Reverend Lee sighed. "If Annaliese was a year or two older, there'd be no problem. She could accompany her father. But she's little more than a baby, and —" A rueful grin lifted the corners of his lips. "Listen to me, sharing my concerns for my friend with you instead of letting you speak. Is there anything else you need to know, Miss Fanny?"

Truthfully, he'd told her all she needed to know. Walter Kuhn was an honorable man who loved his little daughter and did his best for her. But, through no fault of his own, his best wasn't good enough. He needed help. And she needed ticket money. It seemed Reverend Lee was correct that

God had brought them together. Should she argue with the Lord Almighty? Neither Ma nor Da would approve such behavior. Besides, the dear lady who gave her the dress had asked her to do kindnesses for others along the way.

"Nothing else. Thank you." She stood and extended her hand. "I enjoyed being with your congregation this morning, Reverend Lee. You're a fine preacher, and hearing the Word of God read aloud was like drinking a cup of cool water after a long time in the desert."

He shook her hand again, beaming at her. "That's the nicest thing anyone has said to me in a long time. Welcome to our community, Miss Fainche Beck. I believe you are going to be a blessing to Walter and Annaliese, and to all of us here at Gideon Bible Chapel."

His kind words were another cool drink to Fanny's parched soul. "Thank you. I suppose I should —"

"Before you go, let me pray for you."

Enoch had prayed for her, as had Dathan. Now the preacher wanted to pray for her. In all her years on the *River Peacock,* no one had ever offered to pray for her. Although traveling with Enoch's family and remaining in Gideon wasn't part of her plans, God must have orchestrated her crossing paths with these people, to encourage her and remind her of His presence.

She closed her eyes and bowed her head.

Walter

Walter wanted to pace in nervousness. What was taking so long in there? But his hurt knee still needed to carry him home. He shouldn't wear out his leg by pacing. He sat on the edge of the chapel's porch, watching Annaliese toddle after beetles in the grass and waiting for the Fräulein and Reverend Lee to come out.

What would he do if she decided not to stay? He wouldn't blame her if she chose to leave. Why take care of someone else's child? Why see to the home of such a lowly man? Maybe the reason no new wife had come yet was because Vater and Mutter couldn't find someone willing to marry him. He had very little to offer other than a piece of land, a cabin, and the guarantee of hard work for a lifetime. He shouldn't have let himself get his hopes up. He'd only be disappointed in the end.

The door hinges squeaked. He shifted sideways and looked toward the sound. Fräulein Beck stepped onto the porch first, followed closely by Reverend Lee. The minister wore his usual soft smile of contentment, but the Fräulein's cheeks were as pink as Grete's dress. He half rose, but his knee gave way and he sank down again, grimacing. He couldn't even stand on two good legs. He must seem to need caring more than Annaliese did.

She came down the steps and paused next to him. "Mr. Kuhn, if your offer to pay me to take care of your house and your daughter is sincere, I would like to accept it."

His mouth dropped open. "You . . . you would?"

"I would." She fingered the lace at the neck of the dress. "Until your new wife arrives, or until I have enough money for a ticket to New York City. Reverend Lee thinks it will be close to twenty dollars to travel from Elkhart to New York."

Twenty dollars meant twenty weeks. Roughly five months. Walter finger combed his beard. Surely his wife would come before then. If she came. He pulled himself upright and balanced his weight on his left leg.

"Thank you, Fräulein. I'm glad you will stay." Glad, yes. Relieved. And even a little confused. God had answered his prayer with a yes? Maybe He was listening more than Walter thought.

"But there is something I would like to ask you."

He braced himself. If she asked about Grete's death, what would he say?

"Fräulein is a very hard word for Annaliese to say. So instead would you call me Fanny? Then she'll know what name to use."

He gazed into her gold-flecked brown eyes and saw nothing but warm acceptance. He turned to Reverend Lee. "Would it be all right, Reverend?" He didn't want to be accused of being improper.

The corners of the older man's eyes crinkled with his smile. "I believe you and Miss Beck will become friends as you work together. Calling friends by their first names is acceptable. So, yes, it would be all right."

Walter looked at Fanny and gave a quick nod. "Very well. I will call you Fanny. And you can call me Walter."

She put out her hand. For a moment, he stared at it, uncertain. Then he realized she was offering to confirm their agreement with a handshake. Heat flooded his face. He hoped his beard hid the blush.

He gave her hand a quick shake and then stuck his hand in his pocket. He shrugged, flicking a look at Reverend Lee. "I . . . I guess now we go home."

She shrugged, too. "I guess we do."

Reverend Lee gestured to his buggy and horse, which waited in the slash of shade beside the church. "May I give you a ride to your cabin?"

Walter should say no. The minister had already overstayed his time at the chapel. But his leg would appreciate a rest. And suddenly he was shy about being alone with Fanny. But why? They'd been alone at the cabin for a full day and part of this one already. Nothing had changed. He was being foolish, but he couldn't shake the odd feeling. "Thank you, Reverend Lee. We would appreciate a ride."

The minister smiled. "Let's go, then."

16

THE KUHN HOMESTEAD
FANNY

Fanny suspected that Walter's acceptance of a ride in the preacher's buggy had to do with his leg hurting him. In order for him to work, his knee needed to heal. So after a simple lunch — sliced potatoes fried in lard with the last of the onions from a bushel basket in the cellar — she set off for the creek he had mentioned.

At first, he'd balked at letting her go, claiming concerns about wild animals. But when Fanny asked whether beasts would prowl in the middle of the day, he crushed his beard in his hand and agreed she'd most likely be safe. Then he gave her directions to the creek.

With the woven handle of a reed basket hooked over her arm, she skirted the plowed patch of dark soil where she presumed Walter would soon plant a crop and headed over a gentle rise, keeping a steady northeasterly direction. As she went, she scanned the area for any of the flowers or plants Itiah had harvested during their walk from Missouri to Iowa. Walter — odd how quickly she'd come to think of Mr. Kuhn as Walter — had few food items on the shelves in his cabin. He'd shown her the smoked ham, for which he'd bartered with a neighboring farmer, and the root vegetables left over from last year's garden and stored in his cellar. She'd make use of those foods, but the fresh greens Itiah had prepared tasted so good.

As she went, she gathered a few leafy plants, but she didn't want to spend too long foraging. She needed comfrey for Walter's poultice.

The melodious gurgle and fresh scent of water captured her attention before she saw the creek. She pushed her way through a tangle of brush and found herself on the bank of a narrow winding ribbon of crystal-clear water. The sun's rays bounced on the water's surface, shimmering like thousands of diamonds. She paused for a few moments and admired the sight, a smile lifting the corners of her lips without effort. The creek was so small compared to the Mississippi River but lovely all the same. Maybe even more so, since she was free to stand on solid ground and gaze for hours if she wanted.

Delight fluttered through her chest. She

was no longer held captive in the belly of a boat. She was free. Truly free. But standing there admiring the view wouldn't put comfrey in the basket.

Pulling her bonnet brim forward to better shield her eyes, she scanned the sunniest areas of the creek bank, the most likely place for comfrey to grow. She spotted several of the leafy plants on the other side. The creek wasn't deep, but she didn't care to soak her shoes and stockings. She sat, tugged them off, and left them on the bank. After gathering her skirt in one hand above her knees, she walked gingerly over the pebbles at the creek's edge and stepped into the gently flowing water.

She came to a startled halt and hissed through her teeth. Mercy, the water was cold! As it had been the night she went overboard. Shivers broke out, rattling her from her scalp to her toes. She clung to the basket and forced her fear-riddled mind to calm. The gently moving water sparkled with sunshine, not stirred by fierce rain and dappled with moonlight like the night she went overboard. The creek was only as deep as her ankles. She wouldn't be submerged even if she fell. She was safe. *Safe.* And if she didn't get out of the water, she would catch a chill.

Holding her breath, she crossed to the other bank as quickly as her tender soles allowed, then waited for the warm breeze to dry her feet. When her body no longer shuddered with chills, she moved to the comfrey plants, squatted, and removed leaves from the stalks. Uneasy tingles climbed her flesh as she worked. Every surface of the comfrey was covered in tiny hairs. She wouldn't call the hairs spiny, as they didn't pierce her fingers, but neither was it pleasant to handle the leaves. Only knowing how much the poultice would help Walter kept her from stepping away from the task.

She emptied eight plants of their leaves, then swished her hands free of the tiny hairs in the creek. As she turned toward her shoes, she spotted the slender grasslike leaves of wild onions. Remembering how good onions had tasted with the stalks Itiah had cooked in their single pot, Fanny added a handful of them to her basket. They'd make a fine addition to the stew she hoped to cook for their supper.

She lifted the hem of her skirt, drew in a breath of fortification, and splashed across the creek. She walked slowly to her shoes, partly to choose the smoothest patches of ground and partly to give her feet a chance to dry. As she pulled on her stockings and shoes, she noticed a thick bunch of egg-shaped leaves with jagged edges growing beneath a fairly large tree near the creek. Her heart gave a hopeful flutter. Could it be? She bounded to the plants and knelt. She flipped over a leaf and laughed aloud. The whitish underside gave the plant away. It was lamb's quarter.

Her mouth watered. How often had Ma wilted the tender leaves in the grease left behind after frying pieces of mutton? The wild plants had been a mainstay in her diet all through her childhood. She plucked the leaves and piled them on top of the comfrey and onions in the basket. As she pinched the leaves free, memories of Ma's slender hands, always chapped and dotted with calluses, flashed in Fanny's memory. Loneliness for her mother, as well as for Da and her sisters, swelled in her chest.

At that moment, the wind whistled through the tree limbs, the sound similar to the telltale *woo-woo* of a train's stack echoing from afar. She sat back on her heels and instinctively turned in the direction of the tracks, her pulse scampering. Temptation to leap up and run to the nearest depot pulled with such ferocity that she rose up on her knees. The wind died and the sound floated away. She sank onto the mossy ground, tucked her feet to the side, and stared across the rolling landscape, imagining her family far, far away.

"Oh, Ma and Da, I miss you," she whispered to the trees, brush, and burbling creek, knowing her secret was safe. "I want to come to you. But I'll stay and care for wee Annaliese, as I said I would." Indeed, she wanted to go. Desperately. But she'd committed to staying, and Da had taught her to always keep her word. Even if others didn't keep theirs, she should be true to herself and keep hers.

An idle thought flitted through her mind. Had she dishonored herself by leaving Sloan before her full term was served? She pushed the reflection aside. It would be foolish to retrace her steps back to Missouri now. She needed to press forward.

She hugged the basket to her chest, heart aching, and looked skyward. "Father in heaven, bring Walter's new wife quickly so I can go home."

Walter
Walter limped to the east window of his cabin and peered out again. Fanny had left after washing their lunch dishes and putting Annaliese down for her afternoon nap. His Liébling had awakened an hour ago already

and now played happily in her pen with a rag doll and a few blocks he'd made from the leftover pieces of lumber used for the cabin's window frame. More than three hours Fanny had been gone. More than enough time to walk the half mile to the creek, fill her basket, and return. Had she gotten lost?

He groaned and turned from the window. There were many dangers in the untamed areas of this state — black bears, wild cats, even wolves. Any were large enough to attack a person. Fanny had been correct that the animals normally didn't prowl during daytime hours, but what if she'd come upon a den? A protective mother would defend her cubs or pups.

His mouth went dry from fear, an unwelcome but far-too-familiar emotion. Ever since he was a boy living in the tenements of New York City, fear had been woven into his very flesh. He wasn't a large man now, and he'd always been small for his age. His size, as well as his German tongue, made him a target of bullies. Fear was part of the reason he'd left his parents' home and come to Indiana. No bullies chased him, threw rocks at him, or stole his pocket money here. He'd thought he would leave his fear in New York, but it had come with him.

Mostly it stayed hidden, the way his body stayed covered by his clothes, but it rose to taunt him at unexpected moments.

As it had the night the barn caught fire.

He broke out in a cold sweat. He still carried fear, and now he carried guilt on top of it. If Fanny didn't return, his burden of guilt would grow heavier because she'd gone in search of a treatment for his leg. He slapped his thigh, angry at his clumsiness. If he hadn't tumbled over the ridge, he wouldn't have hurt his leg. If he hadn't hurt his leg, Fanny wouldn't be lost. He pressed his hand over his eyes, groaning. If something had happened to her, he —

"Walter, are you all right?"

He lowered his hand and jerkily turned toward the voice. Fanny stood in the cabin's doorway. She wasn't lost. She was back. He limped toward her, joy and relief bringing a smile to his face. "I'm fine. And you are . . . fine, too?"

"Fine as corn silk." She came all the way in and put the basket on the table. After whisking the bonnet from her head, she dropped it on the edge of the table and smoothed sweat-damp strands of hair from her forehead. She retrieved two bowls from the shelf and began transferring leaves to them from the basket.

Walter examined her closely. She said she was all right, but her red-rimmed eyes and splotchy cheeks made him think she might be telling an untruth. He moved closer to the table. "You are sure?"

She barely glanced at him. "Of course I am. A little weary from all the walking today. Walking to church, then walking to the creek and back."

But she'd walked from somewhere in Missouri all the way into Iowa. Would such short distances, compared to the miles and miles she'd covered before coming here, be enough to wear her out? He wanted to ask, but something — fear again? — held his tongue.

He gestured to the leaves. "Did you find what you went looking for?"

"And more." She glanced up again, her lips tipping into a quick smile, and then she focused on the basket's contents.

"Do you want my help?" He had no idea what she was doing, which leaf was for what, but courtesy dictated he should ask.

She paused, pushed some stray bangs aside with her sleeve, then nodded. "I'll need a pestle."

He frowned. He hadn't heard the English word before.

She must have interpreted his confusion,

because she ground her fist into her opposite palm. "A pestle. For crushing things."

"Ah. A *Stößel*."

Her red-brown eyebrows rose. "A what?"

He mimicked her actions and repeated the German word. *"Stößel."* Then he held out his hands in a gesture of defeat. "I do not have a . . . a pestle."

"Oh." She sucked in her lips for a moment. "Well, I need to crush the comfrey leaves. Itiah used a rock. Do you have a rock? One perhaps the size of your fist."

How many rocks had he unearthed when turning the ground for planting? More than he could count. He had at least three piles of them on his land. He turned toward the door, then paused. Should he take Annaliese with him? She was content in her enclosure for now, but he knew how quickly she could lose interest in her toys and want attention. Fanny must need to concentrate on the leaves. She couldn't seem to look up from what she was doing.

He changed direction and scooped his daughter into his arms. She laughed and patted his whiskered cheek. "Fa." He pressed a kiss into her little palm. She giggled and patted him again. Smiling, he turned toward the door. From the corner of his eye, he caught Fanny staring at him. He stopped again and faced her. "Did you need something else?"

She shook her head very slowly, her gaze seemingly locked on Annaliese's little hand. "My baby sister would pat my cheek that way, and I would kiss her hand. Then she would giggle the way Annaliese just did." Tears winked in her brown eyes, and she offered a wobbly smile. "I'm missing her is all."

"I'm sorry, Fanny." He meant it. His heart hurt witnessing her unhappiness. Was he being unfair, keeping her here when she'd been away from her family for so long? He should ask if she'd changed her mind about working for him. If she said yes, he'd have to either not work or leave Annaliese alone again. The question refused to form.

He said again, "I'm sorry," and limped out the door. Not until he reached the closest rock pile did another question enter his mind. Who was Itiah?

Fanny

By the time Walter and Annaliese returned with a speckled rock slightly larger than a man's fist, Fanny had brought her emotions under control and regretted allowing herself to become so weepy. She must have looked as silly as a turkey, sniffling over a simple

215

kiss on a little girl's chubby hand. Da always said turkeys were too stupid to come in from the rain and would stand outside and drown. She'd tried to drown herself with tears on her walk from the creek to the cabin. But the time for tears was done. She was needed here. She would do the job for which she'd been hired, and she would do it heartily as unto the Lord, the way Ma and Da would expect of her.

Walter sat with Annaliese on his lap. The two of them seemed content to watch her mash the comfrey leaves until they looked like pulp and had excreted a small amount of pale-green liquid. She scooped the leaves into a square of muslin from his wife's trunk, folded the flaps over the soggy mess, then handed it to Walter.

"Keep this on your leg while you sleep." She pointed at the poultice. "See where the cloth is getting moist? Put that side against the sorest place on your knee. By morning, some of the pain should be gone."

A puzzled frown marred his brow. "Why should I wait until I sleep? Does it only work at night?"

Itiah had placed the poultices she made for Enoch against his skin under his shirt. A grown daughter could look at her father's bare back and no one would blink in consternation. But how could Fanny tell a man she hardly knew, even if he was her employer, that he'd need to bare his leg before applying the poultice? Polite people didn't talk about baring limbs — their own or anyone else's.

"Well . . ." She waved her hand at the blotching fabric. "You see, the medicine . . ." She gulped and turned her back. Talking to the window was easier than talking to him, even if the action did make her appear as silly as a turkey. "It needs to touch your skin, and right now, you . . . you're wearing . . ."

He cleared his throat. "I understand."

She nearly collapsed with relief. But she couldn't face him yet. Not until the blush had faded. She scurried to the dry sink and picked up the bowl of lamb's quarter leaves. "I'm going to the well for water. These need to be washed before I can add them to the pot." She escaped out the door, her gaze on the leaves.

At the well, she set the bowl on the ground, brought up the bucket, then splashed a little water on her warm cheeks. She had lived a third of her life on a riverboat with mostly men. Then she spent more than two weeks traveling with Enoch, an old man. But she hadn't dealt with as much discomfort and embarrassment as she'd just suffered instructing Walter on how to use the poultice. This arrangement wouldn't work unless she relaxed around him.

She unhooked a dipper hanging from a wire hook on the side of the well, then poured water over the leaves before returning the dipper to its hook. Tomorrow would be easier. Walter would spend his day away from the cabin. She'd see him only at breakfast, lunch, and suppertime — the same amount of time she'd generally spent with the crew on the *River Peacock*. Certainly tomorrow would be easier.

Balancing the bowl in her hands, she walked slowly toward the cabin doorway, singing under her breath, " 'All is well! All is well!' "

17

LANCASTER, MISSOURI
SLOAN

Sloan poised his pencil over the page. "Name, please?"

"Myrtle Miller."

Sloan wrote her name. "And what are you singing today?"

The girl glanced toward the crowd of people bunched together on the opposite side of the hotel lobby. "Mama said I should sing 'All People That on Earth Do Dwell.' "

Sloan stifled a snort. The hymn must be popular in this town, because at least four girls before her had already performed it. He recorded the title, then lifted his gaze to her. "Very well. You may begin."

After peeking at the crowd again, she cleared her throat. Then, eyes aimed upward, she drew a full breath and began. A woman at the front of the group of spectators beamed with pride, mouthing the words along with the girl.

Sloan hid a yawn behind his hand. He'd

219

expected ten, maybe fifteen young women to come to the hotel lobby for an audition. But Prospect Twenty-Six now stood in front of him, wearing her best dress, no doubt, and sporting garish streaks of rouge on her cheeks. He'd wager she was unaccustomed to applying makeup, and he was surprised Mama had allowed it. He rested his chin in his hand and tapped the pencil on the pad of paper in beat with the hymn. The girl had a passable voice. Maybe the best he'd heard so far. Not bad looking, either, if a person ignored the rouge and imagined her in one of the elaborate gowns he'd purchased for Fanny. He scanned her from head to toe. She might even fit Fanny's gowns with a few alterations. But she was young — probably no more than sixteen — and he suspected that if he hired her, he'd get Mama in the bargain. No, thank you.

Myrtle finished and dropped into a deep curtsy. The spectators clapped, Mama the most enthusiastically. After Sloan thanked Myrtle, she scurried to Mama, who hustled her to the back of the group.

Yet another prospect crossed the floor and stepped into the slash of sunlight pouring through the hotel's plate-glass window.

Sloan picked up his pencil and then turned to the crowd. "How many more intend to audition?"

Four women raised their hands.

He flicked his timepiece open with his thumb and frowned at the hands. No wonder his lower back ached. He'd been sitting in this chair for three hours already. And the lunch hour was nearly over. He'd be stuck at least another half hour listening to the remaining five singers. Well, they could wait while he took a deserved break.

He stood. "Auditions will resume at two o'clock."

A few people in the crowd murmured, but they all milled in the direction of the front door. When the room cleared, the hotel's manager strode to Sloan, his arms swinging and his lips set in a scowl.

"Mr. Kirkpatrick, when you asked if you could use the lobby for auditioning singers, I didn't know you'd occupy it the whole livelong day." He folded his arms and tapped his foot on the floral carpet. "The maid needs to clean this area."

Sloan shrugged and headed for the hotel dining room. "Then tell her to clean it."

The manager trotted behind him. "Only to have another crowd come in and dirty it up again? This entire situation has become inconvenient. I'm afraid you'll have to listen to the final singers somewhere else."

Sloan stopped and swung around to face the man. "Sir, I have spent a significant amount of money in this establishment for the privilege of sleeping on an uncomfortable bed in cramped quarters and eating barely digestible food in your dining room. Yet I have offered not a single word of complaint." He pointed at the manager's bulbous nose. "You told me I could hold auditions in the hotel lobby. I paid for announcements with your hotel's name printed on them. That's advertisement for you, and I didn't ask a penny in exchange for it." Sliding his hand into his pocket, he cocked one eyebrow and stared the man down. "If you are a gentleman and an honest businessman, you will honor your word to me. Are you sure you want to send me elsewhere?"

The manager's face turned brighter than Myrtle Miller's rouge-reddened cheeks. He shook his head.

Sloan patted the man on the shoulder. "Wise decision. Now, please excuse me. I have very little time remaining before the last of the performers return. I'd like to have some lunch, unpleasant as it may be." He turned on his heel and strode off.

He ordered a bowl of ham-and-potato soup with a side of buttered bread. Surely the cook couldn't sabotage something as simple as soup. While he waited for his lunch to arrive, he scanned the list of names and considered each of the prospects by turn.

Myrtle Miller had the best singing voice of the lot, but he'd rather not book someone named Myrtle. Not that he personally held anything against the name. His mother's youngest sister was named Myrtle, and he had fond memories of visits with her when he was a boy. But Myrtle wasn't a name that rolled off the tongue. Besides, the girl belonged behind a school desk, not on a stage.

As had Fanny. He scowled. Why on earth would he consider such a thing? He shook off thoughts of Fanny.

Such a shame Splendora Whittingham couldn't hold a pitch. He'd been taken by her name and her appearance. She was quite lovely — tall, slender, with shiny dark hair and eyes as green as clover, the way Mother had described Sloan's eyes. He could market a girl named Splendora, especially one who looked as regal as a princess. Yes, posters sporting her face would draw people in. But as soon as she opened her mouth to sing, they would leave the performance room in droves. He'd barely sat through her three-minute audition without grimacing.

The server arrived with a crockery bowl of soup and a small plate holding a stack of bread slices and a walnut-sized mound of butter. "Anything else, sir?"

"Tea. With cream and sugar."

"Yes, sir." The man scurried off.

Sloan set the pad aside with a sigh. Maybe in the last five auditions, he'd find a passably attractive woman with a passably pleasant voice. Not another Fanny Beck, but someone . . . passable.

He broke a slice of bread apart and carried a piece to his mouth. Had the trunk of Fanny's belongings reached her parents by now? He'd instructed Burke to enclose a note explaining what had happened to her. He inwardly berated himself for giving Burke the task. He should have written the note instead. Burke wasn't known for tact. He probably included a single line, something such as *Fanny drowned in a storm, so here's her things.* She deserved better after so many years of faithful service.

The bread turned to sawdust in his mouth, and his hunger dissolved. He wiped his mouth with the napkin. The server returned with the tea, but Sloan waved him away. He dropped a few coins on the table and ambled toward the lobby. If he were still a praying man, he'd send up an appeal for one of these remaining women to be both skilled in voice and enticing in appearance. But he'd given up praying a long time ago.

Snippets of the hymn sung by Myrtle and some other girls rang in his memory — *"Know that the Lord is God indeed . . . We are the flock he surely feeds . . ."*

Maybe at one time he'd been part of God's flock, but not now. Not since the day he'd shouted at his parents that he wanted more out of life than barely scraping by.

Father had pointed to the door and said, sorrow in his voice, "Then go. Seek your fortune. See if it satisfies you." And Sloan had gone. He'd sought, and he'd found success. With it had come a sizable fortune.

His feet slowed to a stop, an odd thought trickling through his brain. Had it truly satisfied him? With a snort, he set himself in motion again. Of course he was satisfied. Losing Fanny had rattled him, but he'd find his footing again. As soon as his boat was repaired to its former glory and he had an entertainer who would entice travelers aboard, all would be well.

The Kuhn Homestead
Walter

Walter stopped the wheelbarrow and cocked his head toward the cabin, listening. Was Annaliese crying? No. She was squealing. With laughter. A welcome sound. His little daughter was fine because Fanny was there.

A smile tugged at the corners of his lips. After months of always worrying, always listening for her cries, how good to be able to remind himself that Annaliese was cared for.

He gripped the handles and pushed the wheelbarrow in motion again. Digging sandy clay from the creek bank and hauling it home — so tedious. Maybe he should have built his cabin closer to the creek. Many of his neighbors had chosen to build close to a creek on their property. But it hadn't seemed necessary. Why dip water from a creek when the well right behind the cabin was so convenient? Between his well and the rain barrels — Indiana skies produced plenty of rain in the spring and summer — he had good access to water. But water was only one ingredient needed for chinking. It would take a lot of clay mixed with his collected ashes from the fireplace and a fair amount of good, rich Indiana dirt to make enough chinking to close all the gaps between the logs of his barn.

He rolled the wooden cart near the growing hill behind the barn and tipped it up. Moist clay, as thick as the oat porridge Fanny had served for breakfast, oozed out and added another layer to the pile. Some stuck to the bottom of the barrow. Using a garden trowel, he scraped out all the bits. The wheelbarrow's box empty, he stuck the trowel into the mound and then aimed the cart for the creek. He'd brought back three loads already, and he wanted one more before he went in for lunch.

The morning breeze was cool, thanks to the sun hiding behind a covering of clouds, but sweat dampened his flesh anyway. Proof of hard work, Vater would say. At least his leg wasn't paining him as badly this morning. Keeping Fanny's poultice on his knee overnight had helped. He'd told her so at breakfast, and she'd blushed crimson. Then she told him from whom she'd learned the remedy. He shook his head in wonder. She'd traveled with a family of former slaves? The woman was full of surprises.

Some people might think ill of her for staying in their company, but he didn't much care who'd taught her. He was grateful it had done some good. He'd been able to bend his knee when milking Carlotta that morning, and he could walk without wincing with every step. A big improvement.

She promised to make another poultice if he brought back more of the leaves from the creek. He promised to do so.

He reached the creek, grabbed the shovel he'd left there, and filled the wheelbarrow's wooden box again. Then he gathered leaves and jammed his pockets full. He returned to the wheelbarrow and reached for the handles. He paused for a moment, thinking ahead. He planned to stay at the cabin awhile and have some lunch after dumping this load. Depending on whether Fanny needed his help with the washing this afternoon, he might not come back to the creek again today. He wedged the shovel into the box. A man never left his tools out in the elements overnight. Blades could become rusty, and small animals might gnaw on the wood handles, making the tool weak and useless.

Not only tools could be defined as weak and useless. He gritted his teeth and gave the wheelbarrow a mighty push. Even if Fanny didn't need his help with the wash, he'd need his shovel to turn the soil in the garden plot. It was the second week of May already. The potatoes should be in the ground by now. He huffed a breath. How had he forgotten something so important? Until this year, Grete had done the gardening. The familiar ache of loss filled his chest again, followed by the weight of guilt and shame. He increased his speed, ignoring his knee's complaint, and forced his thoughts away from Grete. He couldn't go back and change the past. He could go only forward. So he would prepare the garden plot and plant potatoes to feed him and Annaliese and his new wife over the winter.

As he topped the final rise, a train whistle echoed from the tracks. Strange how the sound carried such a distance. Inside the cabin, he never heard the whistle. The sturdy, solid north wall with its rock fireplace facing the tracks blocked the sound. When he was outside the cabin, no matter where on his property, he heard it. He'd always liked the sound, the reminder of the country's progress. Someday — hopefully soon — his new wife could come by train.

And Fanny would go.

As if his thinking of her could make her appear, she rounded the corner of the cabin. She carried the basket Grete used for their laundry, moving slowly, and little Annaliese trailed after her. His heart caught. How trustingly his Liébling accepted the one she'd begun to call "Nee." How beautiful

229

they both were with sunshine on their faces and bare feet scuffing through the grass.

Fanny looked in his direction. A smile broke. She put the basket down and crouched, her hand stretching to Annaliese. She drew his daughter close, settled her between her knees, and pointed at him. Annaliese, with a finger in her mouth, lifted her sweet face to him. When Fanny waved, Annaliese stared. Fanny laughed, then pulled Annaliese's hand from her mouth and manipulated it into a wave. Annaliese giggled.

A lump filled Walter's throat. What a sight they made — as if they belonged together. He waved in reply. Instantly, an image of Grete waving to him as he returned from a day's toil flashed in his mind. His hand trembled. He grabbed the wheelbarrow handle, squeezing until his fingers ached. After what he'd done, he didn't deserve sweet memories of Grete. He didn't deserve Fanny's kindness. He didn't deserve a new wife, either.

Please, Lord. Please, Lord.

Please, what? He didn't know.

18

THE KUHN HOMESTEAD
FANNY

The morning of Fanny's first full day as Annaliese's caretaker passed in a flurry of activity. Many chores relating to housekeeping had gone neglected. She understood the reason why, and she didn't fault Walter for ignoring the dusting and sweeping. But Ma had told her uncleanliness invited vermin to make themselves at home. Fanny couldn't bear the thought of Annaliese living with fleas, beetles, or mice. She gave every square inch of the little cabin, including the loft, and each piece of furniture a thorough scrubbing that morning.

While in the loft, she discovered folded paper packets marked with vegetable names, such as cabbage, onions, peas, squash, and beans. She showed them to Walter at lunchtime, and he told her they were seeds his wife had collected for future planting. For a moment, they'd both sat in silence — she uncertain how to proceed, and he, she presumed, caught up in memories. Then he'd cleared his throat and advised her which seeds could be planted now and which should wait until midsummer.

Armed with knowledge and a determination to keep food on the table, even if she wouldn't be there to eat it herself, she set aside her afternoon plans to wash bedsheets and towels. Instead, she and Annaliese spent the afternoon in the garden. Years had passed since she'd worked the soil with Ma at their cottage in Inverness, clear across the ocean from where she now resided, but she remembered how to chop the larger chunks with a hoe and crush smaller clods with her hands.

Before Walter left with the wheelbarrow again, he cut several potatoes into chunks, each containing at least one eye. Fanny buried the potatoes in the rich dark soil sparkling with minerals, then carved neat rows and planted the seeds for cabbage, onions, carrots, and radishes. The beans, peas, and squash seeds could wait. Annaliese helped by patting the dirt over each seed the way Fanny showed her.

Fanny found such pleasure in the planting. As she worked, she imagined tiny shoots peeking through the dirt, and her mouth watered when she thought about eating tiny green peas. If she was still here when the peas were ready for picking, she would remove some new potatoes from the roots and cook them with the peas in a cream sauce, the way Ma had done. Was there anything better than creamed peas and potatoes? Not when the vegetables were fresh from one's own garden.

After splashing each row with water from the well to entice the seeds to plump and grow, she gave Annaliese a good wash, then fed her a simple early supper of crackers, boiled eggs, and sliced apples from the nearly empty bushel in the cellar.

Annaliese fussed and twice fell asleep at the table between bites. Fanny vowed she would make sure Annaliese took an afternoon nap from then on. As soon as Annaliese finished eating, Fanny tucked the drowsy little girl into bed.

Walter limped into the cabin shortly after dusk fell and glanced around. "Where is Annaliese?"

Fanny hid a smile. He looked as droopy and sounded as cranky as his daughter had been. She spoke softly. "The poor little bairn had a long day. She was so tired I put her in her cradle."

He crossed to the cradle and peered into it. Fanny waited a few minutes, then gave a

233

gentle *ahem.* He looked over his shoulder at her.

"Are you ready for your supper? I put a pot of beans with some ham by the fire after lunch and let it cook all afternoon." She gestured to the pot hanging to the side of the flames.

He nodded and limped to the table. He moved to sit, but then straightened and dug in his pockets. "Oh, I forgot to give these to you at noon. I picked some comfrey leaves, like you asked." He put the crumpled scraps of green on the table and sank down on the stool, releasing a heavy sigh.

She bit back a chortle. After spending hours in his pockets, the leaves were mashed almost as well as if they'd been pressed by her rock. She scooped them into a wooden bowl, then grabbed a plate from the shelf. "While you eat, I'll make the poultice."

Walter took a bite, chewed, swallowed, and sent an unreadable look in her direction. "Have you already eaten?"

Fanny twisted the rock on the leaves. "Not yet. I'll have my supper later."

He nodded and continued eating without speaking, seemingly too tired to talk. She stayed quiet, too, while she turned the leaves into pulp and then folded the mushy mess into a square of muslin. She finished the poultice at the same time he swallowed the last bite.

She held the poultice to him. "Here you are."

He put down the spoon and took it. "Thank you. And thank you for the supper."

"Did you get enough?"

"Yes."

She picked up his plate and spoon and carried them to the dry sink. She glanced in the pot. "I think there will be enough left over for tomorrow's lunch."

"I won't be in for lunch tomorrow."

She turned, frowning. "No lunch? Why?"

He rested his elbow on the table and fiddled with the folded edge of the poultice. "I must get my corn crop planted. I have the field prepared. I readied the ground during April in snatches of time between checking on Annaliese."

She could imagine how difficult it had been, given the distance between the cabin and the plowed patch she'd passed on her way to the creek yesterday.

"But now that you're here" —

Heat filled her cheeks. Such a simple statement, but so laden with gratitude, it both embarrassed and pleased her.

— "I can plant the corn. It's a tedious

chore. I'd been saving up to buy one of those automatic corn planters, but . . ." He shifted his gaze toward the east window. Even in the dim light from the lantern on the table, it seemed the color drained from his face. "It takes a horse to pull one. I don't have a horse anymore, so there's no sense in buying the machine." He looked at her again. "Planting by hand takes a full two days to get all forty acres planted, so don't worry if you don't see me much. Once the corn is planted, I will start chinking the barn." He stood and picked up the poultice. "Thanks for this. The first one helped quite a bit."

She'd suspected it would. "I'm so glad. What else can I do to help you?"

He ran his fingers through the short length of his beard. "If you'd be kind enough to put some food stuff — maybe an apple and some carrots — in a sack tomorrow morning for me to carry to the field, I'd appreciate it."

She'd planned to bake biscuits for tomorrow's breakfast. She would make extra and use them to make ham sandwiches for his lunch. "I'd be happy to fill a basket for you." She started to tell him how few apples remained in the cellar, but he started talking again.

"And pray the rain holds off."

She drew back in surprise, honored by his request. He not only trusted her to care for his little girl, but he trusted her to lift his concerns to the Lord Almighty.

His lips pinched into a scowl. "God has been good to bring clouds but no rain. The clouds help hold back the heat, but if it rains, I won't be able to keep planting."

She couldn't resist a smile. "But we need rain to make the plants grow." Unbidden, memories of the last rainfall she'd experienced tiptoed through the recesses of her mind. A slight shiver rattled her frame.

"That is true."

Fanny returned her focus to the present.

"But I hope He'll wait until all the corn is in and my barn is chinked. If He brings rain on Saturday, that would be fine."

Saturday she would clean and bake. She'd be safe inside the cabin, where the rain wouldn't touch her, so she wouldn't mind rain then. But she didn't want to walk to church in the rain on Sunday. "I'll say a prayer for God to bring rain on Saturday." She didn't realize she'd spoken aloud until a grin brightened his face.

"I won't argue against such a prayer." He went to the cradle, bent down, and kissed Annaliese's forehead, then straightened and aimed a weary smile at Fanny. "Thank you, Fanny. Good night, now." Poultice tucked in the bend of his elbow, he headed outside.

Fanny latched the door behind him, then scooped a serving of beans into a bowl. She sat and bowed her head in prayer. She prayed for her family, for Walter and wee Annaliese, and for Enoch's family, then asked God to protect the people helping slaves find their way to freedom — things she prayed for every day. She asked Him to wait until Saturday to bring rain, as Walter desired.

She finished with, "And please prepare his new wife's heart to love and care for him and his baby. Amen."

Her prayers done, she ate a spoonful of beans. They crumpled between her teeth, feeling as if wood splinters filled her mouth. She spat them back into the bowl, then stared at the pot. Were they overcooked or undercooked? How had Walter managed to choke them down? Had he requested a basket lunch because he didn't want to leave the field, or because he didn't want to eat her beans again?

True to his word, Walter spent all of Tuesday away from the cabin. Fanny spent much of the day bent over a washtub. She might not be able to cook a pot of edible beans, but she knew how to get clothes clean. She'd done her own laundry on the *River Peacock*.

She started with the sheets and blankets from the beds and draped them over bushes behind the cabin to dry. Then she washed all the clothes — Walter's, Annaliese's, and the dresses from the trunk because he'd told her on Sunday, before going to the barn for the night, that she could make use of them. The row of bushes took on the appearance of a long patchwork quilt with all the items laid out to dry.

Determined to serve Walter a hot supper, she put chopped potatoes, carrots, and a chunk of pork side meat with a few splashes of water into the pot and left it to cook at the edge of the fire while Annaliese napped and she searched for eggs.

Silly hens. Walter was right about them — they did seem to intentionally turn gathering eggs into a hunt each day. She scoured the side yard, where she'd found them the day before, but there were no eggs. Had a black snake made off with them again? She wouldn't blame it if it did. After all, snakes had to eat, too, and if the hens were careless enough to lay their eggs in the grass, they were giving snakes an invitation to dine.

She checked on Annaliese and found her

peacefully snoozing. She could look some more. She headed to the barn. As she moved along the stone foundation, she noted a few small pieces of charred wood. Probably remnants of the barn that had burned. She shuddered, imagining the terror Walter's wife must have experienced with flaming logs falling. Once again, she wondered what Walter's wife had been doing in the barn. Maybe looking for eggs. The thought saddened her.

To her relief, she located both eggs in Carlotta's stall. She put them in her apron pocket and scurried for the cabin, grateful to be out of the barn. She put one of the eggs in a bowl under the dry sink but used the other in batter for corn muffins. They'd go well with the stew.

Annaliese awoke from her nap happy and ready to play. Fanny took her outside and walked with her to the bushes to check the clothes. The distance of perhaps four hundred feet — twice the length of the *River Peacock* — took quite a while to cover. Annaliese wanted to stop and examine flowers, bugs, and leaves along the way. Fanny didn't mind. The little girl's interest in nature pleased her.

With Annaliese toddling on her heels, Fanny went down the row of bushes, pinching and patting the items. A few of Walter's shirts and all of Annaliese's little gowns were dry. She gathered them up and carried them to the house. While Annaliese bounced her rag doll against the floor and jabbered at it, Fanny checked each clothing item for rips or missing buttons before folding them into neat stacks on the bed.

Walter came in from the field near dusk just as Fanny, with the large woven basket and Annaliese in tow, headed to the bushes to fetch the remaining laundry. He changed direction and hurriedly limped to her.

"Fanny, let me help you."

She looked him up and down. His clothes were sweat stained and dusty. If he took the laundry, the items wouldn't be clean anymore. "There's no need. I can get everything myself."

He shook his head, a stubborn jut to his chin. "You and Annaliese shouldn't be out here this time of day. Predators could be hiding in the brush. Give me the basket and go to the cabin. I'll collect the clothes."

She chewed the corner of her lip. The droop of his shoulders spoke of weariness. He'd put in a full day's work. He shouldn't do her work, too. Not when he was paying her to do it. "If you're worried, stay close." She bobbed her chin toward Annaliese.

"Play with your daughter. She's hardly seen you the past two days. It will do both of you good to have time together."

The pinch of his brow let her know he was ready to argue. Before he could voice a word, she trotted to the far end of the row. She plucked a sheet free and wadded it into a ball, then looked back at him.

Walter sighed and sat in the grass next to Annaliese. He picked a stem of long grass with a shaggy tip and tickled her with it.

Fanny smiled. She collected the clean-smelling laundry while Annaliese's laughter and Walter's low-toned chuckle provided harmony to the birds' chirps and cheeps. Her basket was heaped to overflowing by the time she added the last item. She struggled to balance it against her stomach.

Walter clumsily pushed to his feet. "Here. I'll take one handle and you take the other."

She had carried the crate with Enoch the same way. The remembrance created a bittersweet ache in the center of her chest. She walked with Walter, the basket between them, and Annaliese clung to her father's free hand. They moved slowly, tempering their strides for Annaliese's sake and, she secretly, for Walter's.

Fanny enjoyed the leisurely progress. The evening was so pleasant with its spring-scented breeze and a white moon sliding upward against a graying sky. She pulled in full lungs of the air, savoring its freshness, and scanned the landscape from horizon to horizon. She turned her head and discovered Walter watching her.

A shy smile lifted the corners of his lips. "You like being outside?"

Fanny nodded. "I do. When I was a child, my ma often scolded me because I ignored my chores to go traipsing. So many times while I lived on the riverboat, I longed to feel the grass beneath my feet or push my toes into moist earth."

His eyebrows dipped. "You said you sang on a riverboat. You lived on it, too?"

She didn't want to remember those lonely, isolated years. But courtesy dictated she should answer his question. "I did. But now I don't. And . . ." She kicked one bare foot from beneath the hem of her dress. "See? I am going without shoes, the way I did when I was a little girl."

His smile remained, but worry glimmered in his blue eyes. "This time of year, as nice as the grass feels under your feet, you should put on your shoes when you wander. I don't see them often, but there are rattlesnakes in Indiana. If you startle one and it strikes, you're safer with shoes on."

She cringed. "I'll remember from now on."

"Good."

They reached the cabin. He let go of Annaliese's hand and took the basket. Fanny picked up the little girl and opened the door. The savory smell rising from the pot of meat and potatoes filled her nostrils. He must have smelled it, too, because he sniffed the air, then licked his lips. He set the basket on the floor near the door.

"I'll wash up at the well and be back."

By the time he returned, his face shiny from its scrubbing, she had set the table and secured Annaliese in her chair with a length of toweling tied around her waist. She put the pot of stew and the plate of muffins in the center of the table. As he'd done at every meal they'd shared together, Walter thanked God for their food.

At his "Amen," Fanny reached for the serving spoon.

He held out Annaliese's little bowl. "While we eat, there's something I need to tell you."

Could it be he'd received word about his new wife? If so, her heart should leap with joy. But it didn't. Rather, an odd weight of dread seemed to fall on her. She swallowed and gave a quick nod, dispelling the strange internal reaction. "All right, Walter. I'll listen."

19

THE KUHN HOMESTEAD
WALTER

Walter broke one of the muffins into pieces over the steaming stew on his plate. His first bite had been a big improvement over last night's beans. If Fanny had lived on a boat for many years, she probably hadn't cooked in a fireplace. He should have told her to put more water in next time. But maybe she had figured it out and put the extra water in tonight's stewpot. The vegetables were nearly mush. He wouldn't complain, though. It was nice having someone else do the cooking.

He stirred the chunks of cornmeal muffin into the vegetables. "Tomorrow, like today, I will plant corn. But on Thursday, a friend of mine — his name is Hugh Moore — will come and help me chink the barn."

Her brown eyes widened. "It will only take a day to chink the barn?"

He chuckled. "It will take several days, and lots more clay from the creek, but we hope to at least get the gaps between the lowest logs filled. It will block the wind from bothering Carlotta, and little wild creatures will have a harder time getting in." It would benefit him, too, since he was living out there temporarily.

She lifted a spoon of stew and blew on it. "Is there a way I can help with the barn? Or do you only want me to keep Annaliese out of the way?"

Since she'd told him how she liked being outdoors, he would feel guilty telling her she had to stay inside all day. Thank goodness he didn't have to tell her so. "No, because you won't be here."

She drew back slightly, and a frown marred her forehead. "Where will I be?"

"In Gideon."

She put down her spoon without taking the bite. "Walter, you aren't making a great deal of sense."

Of course he wasn't. He'd never been good at talking with strangers, especially strange women. Not that Fanny was a stranger. Not anymore. Although she'd only been in his home a few days, he already trusted her. Maybe he even saw her as a friend. Or, at the least, Annaliese's friend. His tiredness scattered his thoughts, making it hard to explain himself.

He set his spoon on the table and took a big breath. "Ever since I lost my wagon and horse" — he inwardly prayed she wouldn't question how — "Hugh and his wife, Josephine, have taken me into town twice a month with them for shopping. While Hugh helps me on the barn Thursday, Josephine will take you shopping. So tomorrow I need you to look through the cellar, the food shelves, and the loft. Make a list of things you need for cooking and seeing to Annaliese's or your own needs for the next two weeks."

Her mouth fell open. "How am I to know what you need? I've never stocked shelves or . . . or bought things for a little girl. Or even for myself. I'm afraid I'll request the wrong things and you'll have to do without what's needed for half a month before you go to town again."

He hadn't intended to frighten her. He knew how fear felt. He reached across the table and put his fingertips lightly over her fingertips, then quickly removed them. "Please don't worry. Look in the tins and kegs and baskets. You'll know what was stored there. If something is close to empty, write it down."

"Like apples?"

Her level voice let him know she'd set

248

aside her fear. "Yes. If we need apples, write it down. Write down flour and sugar and whatever else. Make a list. The mercantile owner and his wife know how much to send."

She blew out a dainty breath, and a smile quavered on her lips. "All right. I can do that."

"I know you can. And if there is something you need that wasn't in . . . in Grete's trunk . . . put it on the list." He swallowed. She'd arrived wearing a dress and carrying only a small purse and a tin cup. There was much she must need. He wasn't worried about the cost, but why hadn't she packed her belongings before she set out for New York? "If the mercantile has it, add it to my account."

Fanny

Was there no end to this man's generosity? She'd only concluded her second day of working for Walter, and he was already treating her as if she mattered to him. What a kind man.

He toyed with the handle of his spoon. "Do you have any questions?"

She searched her mind for things she'd need to know. "What time will your friend come on Thursday?"

"Early. By eight in the morning, for sure."

Walter ate breakfast closer to seven. The friend probably wouldn't need to eat breakfast here at the cabin, but what about the men's lunch? "Should I have a lunch prepared for you and him?"

He shrugged. "If it isn't too much trouble."

She'd have to scurry in the morning, but she wouldn't complain. Not when he was being so unselfish with her. "It will probably be a cold lunch since I won't be here to keep the fire stoked. I doubt you'll want to leave your work to check on it."

He chuckled, a sheepish sound. "You are right. A cold lunch will be fine. Thank you."

He never failed to thank her for her efforts, even for those awful beans the other night. He would probably thank her for this stew, too, although she'd cooked nearly all the flavor out of the vegetables. His consideration reminded her of Enoch. Enoch and Walter were so different from Sloan, who'd rarely praised her. With each expression of gratitude, she felt as if more and more of her past life was sloughing away. She celebrated its departure.

They finished eating in silence — not the cloying silence she'd suffered in her little room, closed away from everyone else on the *River Peacock,* but a companionable silence.

Walter pushed his plate aside, leaned over and kissed Annaliese's head, then stood. "Thank you for the supper." An odd expression flitted across his face. He smoothed his beard with his fingers. "There is one thing more I would like you to do when you are in Gideon. Please go to the post office and ask if there are any letters for me."

Sympathy rose in her breast. How impatient he must be for word concerning his new wife. Especially if she was a good cook. Would he be happy to send Fanny on her way? Probably. And she should be happy to go. So why did the thought hurt?

She forced a nod. "I will be sure to ask."

His shoulders slumped, she presumed in relief. "Thank you."

Fanny followed him to the door, then watched him stride to the barn. He still favored his right leg, but the limp wasn't as noticeable as it had been. Still, she should make at least one more poultice. As long as she was here, she would do her best to make his life easier. If she went to the creek and gathered comfrey leaves, she could also pick more lamb's quarter and maybe more wild onions. Foraging cost nothing except time. Wouldn't Walter appreciate spending less

251

on food stores? Tomorrow, after she finished mending the rips she'd found in the clothes, she would walk to the creek.

She turned toward the table, intending to clear the dishes, and her gaze landed on little Annaliese pushing a lump of carrot around in her bowl with her finger. She released a little huff of self-recrimination. How could she go to the creek with Annaliese? She dogged Fanny's steps all over the cabin and yard, but she'd never make it all the way to the creek. And if Fanny carried her, she wouldn't be able to tote the basket.

She crossed to the little girl and coiled a soft curl around her finger. "Well, my bonny hen, I suppose I'll put my traipsing plans aside until your papa is home and can stay with you." If he returned as late as he had this day, he wouldn't approve of her going. Not during an hour when animals prowled.

She frowned. She needed those leaves. An idea seemed to drop from the ceiling and bop her on the head. Laughing, she scooped Annaliese from her chair. "Tomorrow after my chores, you and I will go to the creek, my bonny hen."

Annaliese pulled Fanny's hair, bucked, and squalled in protest. Fanny didn't blame her. She was ready to shout in aggravation, too.

How had Pazzy made carrying Baby Leona in a piece of cloth look so easy?

Fanny sat on the edge of the bed and untied the fabric she'd used to strap Annaliese on her back. Annaliese plopped onto her bottom, then crawled to the head of the bed and stared at Fanny, distrust in her big blue eyes.

Fanny sighed and tweaked one of Annaliese's bare toes. "I'm sorry, wee one. I'm not trying to anger you. But unless I find a way to carry you and still have my hands free, we cannot go leaf gathering."

She shook out the rough length of toweling and stared at it, envisioning the way Pazzy had crisscrossed it around Baby Leona and her own torso and shoulders. Fabric under the baby's bottom, tails crossed in the front and looped over her shoulders and then crossed over the baby and tied in the front. But when Pazzy carried the pack on her back, she put Baby Leona in front. What if Fanny carried Annaliese in front of her? Would she be happier if she could see and touch Fanny's face?

Fanny laid the fabric across her lap and then beckoned, "Come, my bonny hen. Sit on Nee's lap."

Annaliese took two wobbly steps on the lumpy mattress and flopped into Fanny's arms. Fanny snuggled the little girl, laughing softly, then settled her straddle-legged on the cloth and performed the actions she'd viewed in her mind's eye, talking all the while. "My, you're a bonny hen, and Nee loves you very much. I don't want to hurt you. I want you to be secure while we go traipsing to the creek." She gave the tails of the cloth a firm yank, cupped her hand beneath Annaliese's bottom, and stood, holding her breath.

The wrap held. Fanny's breath released in a whoosh. She kissed Annaliese's forehead. "Isn't this nice? And look — I can use my hands!" She moved both arms up and down and smiled when Annaliese chortled and imitated her. "All right, now that you're secure, let's fetch the basket and we'll go."

With the basket handle hooked on her arm and Annaliese jabbering in her ear, Fanny set off beneath a sky heavily layered with big puffy clouds.

Walter had been right about the clouds holding back some of the heat. Although it was early afternoon, the mild temperature made for a pleasant walk. Everywhere she looked across the horizon, she saw green. Green grass, green leaves on bushes and trees. Varying shades of green that reminded her of the hillsides of her childhood home.

Odd how two places so far apart resembled each other, but the sight made her less lonely for the place where she'd been born.

She topped a rise. Below, the large square of turned ground Walter had prepared for planting a crop created a dark-brown island in the sea of green. He was in the middle of the island, a plump bag slung over his shoulder and a thick stick in his hand. She paused and watched him thrust the end of the stick into the ground, drop a seed into the hole, smooth the spot with the toe of his boot, then take a step and repeat the motion.

Her heart rolled over in her chest. What a hardworking man he was to plant seeds over the entire expanse in such a way. She'd surmised he would scatter the seed the way Ma had done with flower seeds she harvested from dying plants, giving their cottage riotous color all spring and summer. But his planting was meticulous, intentional. And no doubt wearying. No wonder he'd seemed so tuckered when he returned to the cabin the other evening.

Seeing his efforts made her all the more determined to make the pain-relieving poultice and gather more lamb's quarter and wild onions. He'd praised the addition of the greens in Sunday's stewpot. He would enjoy them again at supper. A man who worked so hard needed a hot, hearty, tasty meal at the end of the day.

Annaliese bounced her heels against Fanny's hip and babbled, "Fa, Fa, Fa!"

Walter stopped and lifted his gaze in their direction. A smile broke on his face. He waved to them, giving the action the full swing of his arm.

Fanny took Annaliese's hand and helped her wave a reply.

His smile grew even brighter. He pushed back his hat and leaned on the stick. "Where are you off to?" He hollered the question.

Fanny cupped her hands over Annaliese's ears before shouting, "To the creek. For comfrey leaves."

He patted his knee and nodded. "Thank you."

She nodded, too, then waved a goodbye and slowly descended the grass-covered rise, one arm wrapped around Annaliese. She couldn't see her feet, and if she stumbled, she didn't want to spill the baby or, worse, fall on her. On more level ground, she heaved a sigh of relief and grinned. "Here we are. Safe and sound."

Annaliese babbled in response and laid her head on Fanny's shoulder. Fanny put a quick kiss on the top of her curly head and strode off again, singing, " 'There was a man who lived in the moon . . .' "

20

THE KUHN HOMESTEAD
WALTER

Walter poked the ground and dropped a seed into the indention. While he pushed dirt over the spot, he glanced over his shoulder at Fanny and Annaliese. How had Fanny secured Annaliese to her frame? Clearly his Liébling didn't mind. Her little head lay on Fanny's shoulder, the same way she'd snuggled in Grete's arms. As she did with him when he rocked her.

The two of them disappeared behind the huge blackberry bramble, but he heard Fanny's voice from the other side of the bushes, its tone as sweet as the aroma drifting from the bushes' abundant tiny white blooms.

He smiled, chuckling softly, and turned his full attention on where to place the rod. He wished he could pay her more than a dollar a week. He'd expected her to cook, clean, and care for Annaliese. He hadn't expected her to worry over him and his needs. Or to love his Liébling. Because she did. He witnessed it in the ways she smiled down at Annaliese in the cradle, the gentle tone she used, and the light touches she gave the baby's hair or cheek as she passed Annaliese's chair. Fanny could have only fed her and kept her clean. But she did more. She truly *cared* for Annaliese. How did a man fairly pay the person who gave so selflessly and tenderly to someone he loved more than life itself?

Was it fair of him to keep Fanny here? She'd been away from her family for so long, more time even than he'd lived on this homestead. A lifetime, it sometimes seemed. She'd go to town tomorrow and do his shopping and check his box at the post office, too.

His pulse stuttered. Would there be a letter from Vater and Mutter? It hadn't taken nearly this long for his parents to reach an agreement with Grete's father. Why such a delay this time? He'd never gone so many months without word from his folks. A letter would assure him they were well. A letter would assure him a new wife was coming. He needed both assurances.

A soft sigh of reflection left his throat. How young they'd been — he nineteen and she seventeen. But both sets of parents had given their blessing for not only the union but also his taking Grete far away from New York. Although they'd had to labor hard, they'd been happy. Especially after their precious Liébling was born.

A new worry suddenly presented itself. He stood very still and stared at the blackberry bushes, picturing Annaliese's little head snug on Fanny's shoulder. Fanny loved Annaliese, but it surely seemed as if Annaliese loved her Nee, too. If Annaliese got too attached to Fanny, she might not accept his new wife. That could cause problems.

He shook his head, clearing the thought. If Annaliese accepted Fanny so readily, she would accept the new wife. Wouldn't she?

Fanny

Fanny gave the tails of the toweling a good yank, assuring herself Annaliese would stay secure for the ride to town. She'd never forgive herself if the baby fell out of the Moores' wagon and hurt herself.

While Annaliese played with the collar of the blue-checked dress Fanny had donned for the trip to town, Fanny stacked slices of cheese and cold boiled pork on a plate and added watercress she'd found during her forage along the creek. She covered the plate with a cloth napkin and set it on the table next to the bowl holding the last three apples from the bushel basket in the cellar. Such a paltry lunch. She hoped the food would be sufficient for the men.

She moved to the stoop outside the door and looked for a sign of Walter's friends. No wagon yet. Thumps and thuds from the barn told her Walter was busy in there. How did a person get ready to chink a barn? She didn't know, but she trusted that he did.

She turned to go back in, and the sound of a train's whistle captured her attention. Her heart leaping, she hurried to the corner of the cabin. The *hoot-hoot,* haunting as it echoed across the plains, raised a long-buried memory of the day a train carried her away from the New York City station to Kansas City, Missouri. In her mind, she could still see Da, with Moira in his strong arms, standing close to Ma and Flossie on the boardwalk, all of them teary eyed and waving. She'd pressed her face to the window, held back her own tears, and waved, too.

As if it had a will of its own, her hand lifted in a fleeting farewell.

Suddenly a small arm waved back and forth beside her face. Fanny caught hold of Annaliese's dimpled hand and pressed it to her lips. Oh, how this little girl had stolen a piece of her heart. A train would carry her to her family, but it would carry her away from Annaliese. Would she be able to bear bidding this child — and the child's kind, patient father — goodbye? Her heart flipped in her chest.

The soft clip-clop of horses' hooves accompanied by the rattle of a wagon chased away the painful reflections. Mr. and Mrs. Moore were here. She scurried inside and grabbed the basket she'd used yesterday for leaf gathering and quickly checked its contents. Two muslin squares and a fresh baby gown rested on the bottom in case they were needed. The shopping list she'd made was tucked under the layers of cloth, where it wouldn't blow away if the breeze turned stout. She was ready.

Annaliese patted Fanny's cheek and grinned her crinkled-nose grin. "Nee."

Fanny tapped the end of the little girl's button nose, her chest constricting with mixed emotions. "The time will come when I must go far away, but for as long as I'm here, I'm going to love you, my bonny hen." She squared her shoulders. "All right. Let's go shopping." She headed out the door.

The wagon was beside the barn. A woman perhaps three or four years older than Fanny sat on the seat, the reins in her hands. Wavy light-brown hair peeped from beneath the brim of her pale-pink bonnet, and freckles dotted her nose, giving her a girlish look. Walter and a tall, stocky man with a shock of thick blond hair and an easy smile leaned against the wagon box, chatting. The woman leaned sideways, her head tipped, apparently listening in on the men's talk.

As soon as Fanny reached the wagon, Walter's friend stepped forward and plucked the basket from her arm. "Lemme put that in the back for you, miss. Looks to me like you're already totin' enough." He set the basket in the wagon's bed, then turned around and tapped Annaliese on the tip of her nose, waggling his eyebrows. "Hey, little lady. You look snug as a bug in a rug." He shifted his cheerful gaze to Fanny. "You probably don't remember 'cause so many people came at you, but we met at church last Sunday. I'm Hugh Moore, and that's my wife, Josephine."

Fanny offered each of them a shy smile. "I do recall seeing you, but I'd forgotten your names. It's good to meet you again, Mr. Moore."

"Just Hugh is fine." He took a step backward and tilted his head, surveying the cloth rigging. "That's pretty clever the way you've got Annaliese tucked in tight. The only other time I saw somebody carry a baby that way was when I was a little fellow. Me an' my pa saw a Shawnee woman with her baby strapped into some kind of cloth pouch. But she carried him on her back." He stood up straight and aimed a curious grin at her. "You learn how to do that from the Shawnee?"

Fanny rocked back and forth slightly, patting Annaliese's bottom. "I did not. I learned from a friend who carried her baby this way. She —" She cringed. She'd said too much. She wasn't ashamed of her friendship with Pazzy. She'd told Walter about Enoch's family after he asked how she'd learned to make the comfrey poultice. But later she'd regretted it. Speaking of her friends could endanger them. She needed to end this conversation quickly.

She looked past Hugh to Walter. "How long will it take to reach Gideon?"

"A little over an hour."

She drew back in surprise. More than an hour?

Hugh laughed. "There's no established road between here an' town. You could walk it faster'n the horses'll pull the wagon 'cause you'll cover so many little hills. They slow the horses. But you gotta have a wagon to tote your purchases home."

Fanny vowed to exercise caution in what she said to Josephine. She thanked Hugh, then gave Walter what she hoped was a lighthearted smile. "Would you help me onto the seat? I'm a little clumsy with Annaliese blocking the view of my feet."

Walter's cheeks above his beard flushed, but he took hold of Fanny's elbow and escorted her to the front of the wagon. He pointed to an iron bar on the back of the seat. "Can you take hold of that?"

Fanny tried, but her reach was too short. "I cannot."

"All right. Put your foot on the step, then."

She peered around Annaliese. "What step?"

Josephine tsk-tsked and shook her head. "Walter, we ain't gonna get to town at all if you don't help this girl."

His pink flush became flaming red, but he bent over and guided the placement of her foot. Then he caught her waist and gave a boost. Josephine grabbed Fanny's hand and pulled, and with their help, she made it aboard.

She slumped into the seat. "Thank you very much."

Walter backed away from the wagon. "You're welcome. Have a pleasant day." His words and tone were casual, but his blush and his fingers raking his beard spoke loudly of discomfort.

Josephine released the brake and wriggled her fingers at Hugh. "See you later." She flicked the reins, and the pair of horses jerked the wagon into motion.

Fanny resisted turning around on the seat to see if Walter was watching after them. She cupped her hands around Annaliese and aimed a shy smile at Josephine. "Thank you for taking me into town. Wal—" She was Walter's employee. Just as she shouldn't talk about Enoch's family, she shouldn't use his given name around others. "Mr. Kuhn asked me to fetch his mail from the post office while we're in town. I hope that won't inconvenience you."

Josephine laughed, the sound merry. "I always check the mail slots when I'm in town. I have two sisters. One lives in South Bend an' the other in New Carlisle. The only way we talk is through letters, so I'm always eager for word from them." She glanced at Fanny. "Where does your family live?"

Annaliese squirmed, and Fanny automatically smoothed the little girl's hair. "In New York City. I'll be going to them as soon as Mr. Kuhn's new wife arrives." Too late, she

266

wondered if Walter preferred she didn't talk about his new wife. She set her lips in a firm line.

Josephine tugged the reins, and the horses pulled the wagon into a slight curve. "There's some folks who thought you might be Walter's new wife when they seen you in church last Sunday."

One of the wheels hit a bump, jarring her sideways. In that moment, she relived the fearful plunge over the side of the riverboat. Her mouth went dry and her pulse scampered. She planted the soles of her shoes firmly against the floorboards, steadying herself, and prayed she wouldn't fall over the edge. The wagon moved in a straight course again, following lines of flattened grass that lay like railroad track over the prairie. The conveyance continued to rattle and shake, but she no longer worried about being tossed to the hard ground.

She sighed a relieved breath. "I am only Annaliese's caretaker."

"Well, I can see she's lucky to have you." Josephine angled a lingering look in Annaliese's direction. Longing glimmered in her hazel eyes. "When Grete died, me an' Hugh offered to take Annaliese in. We . . ." She paused, shifting her gaze forward. "We want children, but so far the good Lord hasn't blessed us."

Now Fanny understood Josephine's woeful expression and Hugh's attention to Annaliese back at the cabin. She touched Josephine's sleeve. "You're young yet. There's time."

A wry chuckle left Josephine's throat. "Lots of folks have told me so. But we've been married nine years already, an' I'm getting mighty impatient. Since me an' Grete were such good friends, I thought maybe Walter would let me see to the baby, but he said no. I don't hold it against him. Annaliese is all he has left of Grete. But my heart pines for . . ." She sucked in a big breath and then let it out in a whoosh. "Mercy, here I am blatherin' away. Not very polite of me, especially considerin' you're a newcomer. So how about you tell me somethin' about yourself. How'd you get so far away from your family? They're in New York, you said?"

Fanny didn't mind setting aside talk of Grete. "They are. We came from Scotland" — should she mention Scotland? — "when I was fourteen. I was indentured to a man in Missouri."

"So young." Josephine shook her head. "But I was only a year older'n that when I married Hugh an' we left New Carlisle an' settled our land near Gideon." She flashed a sympathetic grin at Fanny. "I s'pose we've both been away from our families for a long time."

Their shared experience, although for different reasons, bonded Fanny to Josephine. "I suppose we have."

"Was your job difficult?"

Fanny blinked twice, confused. "Job?"

"You said you were indentured. What work did you do to earn your transport from Scotland?"

Relieved her place of birth had brought no offense, Fanny answered promptly. "I sang for passengers on an entertainment paddleboat called the *River Peacock*. It sailed up and down the Mississippi River."

Josephine's eyes widened. "Sailin' on the river? Singin' to entertain folks? My goodness, Fanny, what a life you've had!"

It must seem so to someone who didn't know the truth. And Fanny wouldn't share the truth. She preferred to forget. She forced a smile. "I have."

"And now here you are, livin' outside little Gideon, Indiana, takin' care of a baby." A frown lowered her brows. "How did that come to be? If you don't mind me askin'."

The wagon jounced again, this time bouncing them up off the seat and down again with a hard bump.

Annaliese grasped Fanny's neck and wailed. Fanny soothed the little girl. She regretted Annaliese's fear, but she couldn't help being grateful for the distraction. She couldn't talk about her journey from the riverbank to the train tracks leading to Elkhart without mentioning Enoch's family.

She gently rocked Annaliese to and fro, humming in her ear and hoping Josephine would set aside the topic of Fanny's employment with Walter. She'd have to be careful. Josephine was very amiable. Fanny would find it easy to form a friendship with her. But forming relationships in Gideon wasn't wise. Not when she needed to keep Enoch's family's whereabouts secret. And not when she was only passing through.

21

Sloan gritted his teeth and bit back a groan as he ducked and exited through the small door of the coach. His feet met the ground, and he stepped out of the way of the other disembarking passengers while grinding his fists into the small of his back. When he finished his search, he would never ride in another stagecoach for as long as he lived.

The familiar scent of river water met his nostrils, and he turned his face to the breeze to better capture the aroma. Most people found smells rising from a river unpleasant, but to him, the scent meant home. And profit. The fishy smell and the sight of wispy black tails from the smokestacks of steamboats on the Missouri River created a different reason to groan. He'd spent three weeks jouncing across the miles in stagecoaches and mostly sleeping in louse-infested stagehouses. He was ready to return to his beloved *River Peacock* and once more

271

travel the Mississippi in comfort. Once more invite people aboard to enjoy the pleasures his cruising vessel provided. Once more add to his coffers.

He turned his focus to the town of Jefferson City. From its lengthy street of businesses and blocks of residential houses, many of which spoke of considerable wealth, it seemed he'd entered a bustling, well-populated city. He scanned the opposite side of the wide dirt street and discovered a hotel constructed of limestone blocks. The two-story building loomed larger than any of the other hotels in which he'd spent a night during the past weeks.

At the other end of the block, a small square building displayed a Telegraph Office sign. Good. He would send Burke a telegram informing him of Sloan's current location and reminding him his boss hadn't dropped from the face of the earth. By now Burke must be wondering when he'd return. Sloan had hoped his search would be short and productive. Since it hadn't been, he was grateful he'd had the foresight to bring so many bank drafts. He'd visit a bank and cash another before he left town.

He fingered the folded drafts tucked safely in his jacket's interior pocket. Would he spend every last one of them before he found Fanny's replacement? Maybe he'd expected too much from the singers he'd auditioned thus far. After all, Fanny had a unique voice. Perhaps if he lowered his standards a bit and listened with an unbiased ear instead of comparing the singers to Fanny, he could end this search.

"Twenty-minute stop, folks." The driver tromped toward the small group of passengers gathered near the coach, dust rising from his tan trousers. He gestured to a small building bearing a fresh coat of whitewash. "There's an outhouse out back for y'all's use. If you're hungry, go on in the café. Lorna — she's the owner — always has sandwiches an' pie ready for folks passin' through."

Sloan's mouth watered. Pie sounded good. The other passengers apparently thought so, too. They all headed for the café. He'd get some when the others cleared out. He followed the driver to a water barrel next to the building.

"Driver, if I decide to stay in Jefferson City for a day or two, when will the next stage stop here?"

The lanky man dipped a bucket into the barrel and headed for the horses in a wide-legged, swaying gait. "Stages stop in Jefferson City every day but Sunday. Got regular stops in the mornin' around ten, like we done today. Then on Tuesdays, Fridays, an' Saturdays, they roll through here twice. A second one comes in late afternoon around four. Always a twenty-minute rest time." He held the bucket to the closest horse and angled his face to Sloan while the horse sucked up water. "You got kin to visit in these parts?"

His business didn't concern the driver. "Is the woman who owns this café trustworthy?"

The man's eyebrows rose. "Why, sure. Lorna's like a ma to every person who comes through here."

Sloan didn't need another ma, but at least he believed his belongings would be safe with her. "When you're done watering the horses, remove my bag from the storage boot and set it inside the café door. I'll retrieve it from there when I return from my errand. I doubt I'll finish before you leave again."

The driver offered the bucket to a second horse. "Sure enough, mister. Be glad to do that for you. Hope you enjoy your stay in Jefferson City."

Sloan tipped his hat in reply and strode in the direction of the hotel, formulating a plan as he went. First, reserve a room. Second,

274

gain permission to hold auditions in the lobby on Saturday morning. Finally, ask directions to a reputable printer. If he had posters in hand by midafternoon, he could have them hung up and down this main street by evening, Friday morning at the latest. Word should get around fairly well, and he could anticipate a decent turnout for Saturday. In a city of this size, surely he'd find a talented singer.

He grimaced. Hadn't he thought the same thing in Lancaster? Maybe he should have hired Myrtle Miller after all. At least he'd be done with this search and he could return to the *River Peacock.* But it was too late for that now.

He set his jaw in a determined angle. He'd spent enough time wandering the state. He would hire a singer from this town, one old enough to be away from her parents. One who was pleasant to look upon and pleasant to hear, even if she didn't possess a voice as pure and memorable as Fanny's. He would contract her to work for him for room, board, and a pittance. The promise of performing on a stage was proper enticement for many attention-hungry young women.

He stepped up on the boardwalk fronting the hotel, paused to adjust his lapels and brush dust from his jacket front, then gave the brass doorknob a twist. He gave the sizable lobby a quick perusal, then smiled. Yes, this room would do nicely for auditions. He crossed to the counter.

The slender young man behind the desk smiled. "Mornin', sir. What can I do for you?"

"My name is Sloan Kirkpatrick. I need a room, and when that's settled, you may fetch the manager for me. I'd like to discuss a business proposition with him."

"Yes, sir."

Sloan propped his elbow on the counter and released a sigh of satisfaction. Yes, by the end of Saturday, he would hire a singer. And then go home.

Sloan rolled the two dozen posters into a tube and strode up the boardwalk toward the little café next to the stage stop. He'd left his belongings with the woman named Lorna far too long. He hoped his bag was still there, undisturbed.

He entered the café, sweeping his hat from his head as he crossed the threshold. Only three round tables, each draped with a blue cloth that matched the curtains in the windows, sat in the center of a dining room not much bigger than his berth on the *River*

Peacock. He placed his hat on the table nearest the front door. A doorway with another blue curtain centered the back wall. The sounds of pans clanking together and a woman humming filtered through the curtain. Probably the proprietress washing up the last of the lunch dishes.

His stomach rumbled. He'd missed out on pie midmorning and hadn't taken a break to eat lunch, and now the hour was approaching suppertime. Even as hungry as he was, filling his stomach would have to wait. He must retrieve his bag, put it in his room at the hotel, then start hanging the posters.

He glanced around the small room. The two front windows facing the street let in enough sunlight for him to see into every corner. Where was his bag?

He stifled a groan. What if the stagecoach driver forgot to unload it? He should ask Lorna. He started for the curtained doorway, making a weaving path around the tables. When he was halfway across the floor, the curtain flew to the side, and the largest woman he'd ever seen filled the doorway. Or maybe she only looked large because her apron had ruffles at the shoulders, on the bodice, and on three sides of the skirt.

Her gaze landed on him, and a smile as big as the rest of her filled her face. She balled her hands into fists and plunked them on her well-padded hips. "I didn't hear nary a soul come in. I'm sure sorry for it, too. Welcome to Lorna's. Wouldja like a piece o' pie? Got half a buttermilk pie an' one big slice o' mince in the kitchen. Or mebbe you'd ruther eat some fried catfish an' grits?"

It all sounded good to Sloan. Temptation to sit and ask her to fix him a plate wheedled him, but he had posters to distribute. He'd come back later. "Thank you, ma'am, but I'm here to collect my bag. The stagecoach driver said he'd put it in your café. Do you still have it?"

Her fists left her hips, her hands splayed wide, and she held them up as if someone had given her a huge surprise. "Why, are you Mr. Kirkpatrick?"

"Yes, ma'am."

"Then I sure do." She pointed a thick finger at him. " 'Fore I fetch it, though, you're gonna need to tell me what it looks like. I don't put up with no shenanigans in my place. I don't aim to give somebody's personal belongings to nobody but the rightful owner. So . . ." She folded her arms over her chest. "What's that bag look like?"

He should be grateful she was taking precautions, but her cautiousness was wasting precious time. Stores would start putting up their Closed signs soon. "Light-brown leather with a wooden handle and a wide strap with a brass buckle."

Her stern pose relaxed, and another smile lit her face. "That sure enough sounds like the bag I got." She turned sideways, cupped her hand beside her mouth, and bellowed, "Podrick? Fetch that bag Delton left an' bring it out." She smiled at Sloan. "Podrick's my grandson. He helps out around here. He'll have that bag for ya right quick." Suddenly a scowl marred her brow. "You sure you don't need somethin' to eat, mister? You got a hungry look about you."

She could see his hunger? Little wonder the stagecoach driver had said this woman was like a ma to everyone. He shook his head. "No, really, I'm fine. I just need my bag and I'll be on my way."

The curtain was tugged to the side, and a boy — or was he a full-grown man? — entered the room with Sloan's bag hanging from his large hand. He clomped to Sloan and shoved the bag at him. "Here ya go, mister. Same as you left it."

Sloan took the bag and nodded at the youth. Podrick was certainly the size of a

279

man. He nearly matched his grandmother in height and girth. But pimples dotted his whisker-free face, giving mute testimony to his young age. Sloan wagered no other boys in town challenged this one to fisticuffs. "Thank you." He shifted his attention to the woman. "And thank you, ma'am, for keeping hold of it for me." He tucked the roll of posters under his arm and slid his hand into his pocket.

Lorna raised her hands again. "If you're fixin' to pay me for storin' that bag, you can keep your money. 'Round here, we don't charge for courtesy." Impishness glistened in her eyes. "But we do charge for a catfish dinner. You sure you don't wanna sit an' eat a good meal?"

Her request reminded him of his own mother, who, despite their limited resources, shared a plate of food with anyone in need. The fond reflection almost made him say yes. He caught himself and chose a different reply. "I appreciate it, ma'am, but I have some work to do before the stores close."

"What kinda work would that be?"

The courtesy she'd mentioned required a reply. He bobbed the roll of posters. "Asking store owners to hang these in their windows."

She shuffled forward and took the posters

from him. She unrolled the pages the way biblical priests must have opened scrolls, then scanned the words from top to bottom. "Mm-hmm, considerin' you're gonna hold auditions mornin' after next, these need to go up."

Sloan held out his hand, but she turned to her grandson. "Podrick, take these things around to the businesses. Go in the front door, long as it's open. If it ain't, knock at the back. If you can get 'em all delivered by six, I'll save that mince pie for you." She winked. "I know you been eyeballin' it."

Podrick's pimply face glowed. "Sure thing, Granny." He reached for the posters.

"Wait." She pulled one sheet free and handed the rest to him. "Now scoot. Don't dawdle."

"I won't." He bounded out the door.

Sloan gawked after the man-sized boy, then at the woman. How had he so quickly lost control of the situation? "I — You — He —"

Lorna bumped his shoulder on her way to a front window. She wedged the poster into the window's sashing, then turned and peered down her nose at him. "Reckon the words you're seekin' are 'thank you.' "

"Thank you," he said without thinking. Yes, indeed, this woman was everyone's ma.

She grinned. "You're welcome. Now, I can't offer you that mince pie 'cause sure as my name's Lorna White, Podrick'll be back here an' wantin' it for himself before the bell on the Episcopal church tolls six times. But I can bring you a nice wedge of buttermilk pie, and you can eat that while I fry some catfish. Got my own tank out back. I scoop them catfish out, clean 'em, then fry 'em in a cornmeal batter."

The same way his mother had prepared catfish. Except he and Father had fished them from a creek behind the church.

"Your dinner'll be ready by the time you finish the pie. Sound good?"

His own mother had never offered dessert first. He slid into a seat. "Sounds wonderful. Thank you, Lorna."

She brought him a mug of steaming coffee and a slice of pie so large it must've been a good quarter of the whole. He ignored the coffee but savored every bit of the buttermilk pie. Laden with cinnamon and nutmeg, the flavors ignited his hunger.

He was swallowing the last bite when Lorna came through the curtained doorway carrying a chipped crockery plate. She set it in front of him, and he laid his eyes on six crisp-fried catfish filets, two corn muffins, and a scoop of grits with butter melting on top. Simple fare compared to the meals the cook on the *Peacock* served, but the aromas rising from the plate made his stomach roll over and beg.

He licked his lips and pushed the empty pie saucer aside. "Thank you, ma'am." He picked up his fork and aimed its tines for the grits.

She pulled out the chair across from him and sat.

He paused, his fork hovering two inches above the plate, and peeked at her. Was she going to sit there and watch him eat?

She waved her hand at him. "Go ahead. Eat up. Just wanted to talk to you some about that poster. What for are you needin' a singer?"

Between bites, Sloan told Lorna about his damaged riverboat, his lost singer, and his need to find a replacement to entertain his passengers. "I've been in no fewer than twelve cities over the past three weeks, but I still haven't found a young woman with the qualities I'm seeking." Should he have said such a thing to this big-boned woman? He didn't want to offend her, especially not after she'd been so kind to him.

She pointed to his untouched cup. "You gonna drink that?"

He shook his head.

She picked it up and took a noisy slurp. "You ever heard of the singer they call the Swedish Nightingale?"

Certainly he'd heard about Jenny Lind. She was renowned in Europe and America. "I have, but I couldn't afford to hire her to sing on my boat."

Lorna laughed. "I reckon not. But I heard talk from some folks who come off the train last week." She shrugged. "I hear lots of things. Folks seem to like talkin' to me."

He believed it. She'd put him at ease, and that was no mean feat.

"Seems this couple was goin' through Chicago an' they heard a lady singin'." Lorna leaned in, her eyebrows high in either wonder or disbelief. "Said she was standin' betwixt the tracks, right close to a cattle car, an' singin' to some folks ridin' in the car." She clicked her tongue on her teeth and sat back again. "They found it a mite odd, her singin' an' wavin' as the train pulled away, but they said she had the purtiest voice they ever did hear. The man said she sang as good as the Swedish Nightingale herself."

Sloan frowned. Previously he'd looked for the woman the stage-stop cook said sang like a nightingale. Now someone else used a similar description. Was it possible the couple had heard the same woman? The people who'd heard her sing at the stage stop thought she lived nearby, but maybe they were mistaken. Maybe she'd been only passing through. Excitement stirred in his chest. Should he cancel his room at the hotel and check train schedules instead?

Podrick burst into the café, his face red and dotted with perspiration. "All done. I gave out every last one o' them posters, mister, an' there was some folks in the Feed an' Seed who got all excited when they read the words. They're gonna bring their daughter in to sing for you."

Sloan thanked the boy, and Lorna told him his pie was waiting. He galloped off, his footsteps vibrating the floorboards. Lorna looked after him, an indulgent smile tipping up her lips, and then she faced Sloan again.

"I reckon if you don't find a singer you're wantin' here in Jefferson City, you could take the train to Chicago. There's a heap o' stops between here an' there, but the rails'll carry you the whole way." She pushed her bulk from the chair and picked up the dirty dishes, then fixed him with a stern look. "Reckon you better wait until after Saturday, though. Wouldn't be fittin' to invite girls to audition an' then not be there to listen to 'em. A man oughta stay true to his word."

Sloan squirmed. Had she read his thoughts about skedaddling out of town? But did he really want to go on what could very well be another wild-goose chase? Hadn't he decided he would choose the best singer from Jefferson City and be done with his search?

He met Lorna's unwavering gaze and gave a nod. "Yes, ma'am. I'll be here for those auditions."

22

THE KUHN HOMESTEAD
FANNY

Fanny awakened early Saturday morning to a soft thunk outside the door. She tossed the quilt aside, padded across the floor, and cracked open the shutters. A shadowy figure — one with a barely discernible limp — was striding toward the barn. Suddenly she knew the source of the sound. Walter had brought the morning's milk to the house.

She waited until he disappeared into the barn, and then she brought the two-thirds-full tin bucket of frothy milk into the cabin. She smiled as she carried it to the dry sink. On their drive back from Gideon Thursday afternoon, with a load of food items but no letters for either Josephine or Walter, Fanny confessed she could make biscuits but not bread. Josephine kindly offered to teach her on Saturday and told her to have six cups of scalded milk ready. Fanny informed Walter of the conversation, and he promised to have the milk to her in time to scald and cool before Josephine's arrival. He'd kept his promise. His keeping his word in even such a small thing did much to help rebuild the trust Sloan's dishonorable intention had stolen from her.

As she measured milk into a kettle, she recalled Walter's crestfallen expression at the news that no letters waited in his box. Although a full day had passed since she told him, she still felt guilty about it. A silly emotion since she had no control over someone else penning a letter and mailing it from New York to Indiana. Or maybe she felt guilty about adding such a large amount to his account at the mercantile.

Josephine hadn't even hesitated in putting on Walter's account forty-eight pounds of flour, two ten-pound bags of cornmeal, a gallon of molasses, twenty pounds of white beans, ten pounds of rice, five pounds of white sugar, three pounds of brown sugar, a whole smoked ham, ten pounds of side meat, a wheel of hard yellow cheese, two dozen eggs, three pounds of butter, and thirty pounds of apples. She assured Fanny every last bit of it would be used and Walter wouldn't protest, but Fanny worried all the way home.

But her worry was for nothing because Walter unloaded the purchases from the wagon without a word of complaint. Which made it even harder to tell him there'd been no mail waiting.

She hung the kettle's handle on the iron hook and pushed it directly over the glowing coals in the fireplace. The wood box was full, thanks to Walter's diligence. She chose two large pieces of wood and carefully layered them over the coals. On her hands and knees, she blew gently into the space between the logs. The coals flared like sheet lightning behind clouds in a night sky, and on her third puff of breath, a tiny flame rose up and licked the underside of one of the logs. She watched it for a few seconds and, assured it wouldn't die out, rose and dressed.

Her stomach quivered with anticipation. Even though the uppermost logs of the barn still lacked chinking, today Walter planned to build an enclosure for the chickens. When it was complete, he'd buy two more laying hens and a rooster. "It'd be nice to raise some chickens for the stewpot or frying pan," he'd said, hanging his head. "These hens are the only two left after the . . . the barn burned down. It's time to build the flock again."

She'd then volunteered to be the chickens' caretaker. Before coming to the United

States, she'd been responsible for Ma's small flock of Dumpies. Although American hens looked nothing like the short-legged black-and-white chickens from Scotland, she anticipated taking good care of Walter's chickens, of building his flock so he needn't ever purchase eggs at the mercantile again.

Nor would he have to purchase butter as long as she was here, because Fanny had located a churn in the cellar. She would put it to good use. Carlotta produced close to five gallons of milk per day. Much more than they could drink, and even more than she needed for cooking. Walter traded some of it with neighbors, but Fanny had witnessed him pouring much of it out behind the barn. Such a shameful waste! She vowed to find the means to make use of every drop of milk.

She woke Annaliese, changed her napkin, and then put her in her chair with the last of the previous day's biscuits to keep her occupied. Then she mixed a pot of cornmeal mush, using milk instead of water, and dropping in several spoonfuls of brown sugar. She checked the kettle of milk and released a squawk of alarm. A film had formed on top — the sign Josephine told her to watch for. She used her apron to protect her hand and removed the kettle from the flames. She hoped she hadn't scorched the milk. Would bread taste foul if the dough contained scorched milk?

The worry was still rolling in the back of her mind when Walter tapped on the door. She scurried over and opened it for him. How awkward for him to seek permission to enter his own cabin. She pushed the rock they used as a doorstop into place, silently berating herself. She needed to remember to prop the door open after she was fully dressed so he'd know he could come on in.

He sniffed the air, his nostrils flaring. "What have you been cooking?"

"Milk." She laughed at his puzzled expression. "Remember? Josephine told me to scald the milk."

Walter sat in his chair next to Annaliese and stroked her silky blond hair. "Ah, yes. It's been so long since someone baked bread here in the cabin, I'd forgotten how milk smells after it's been heated to scalding."

"Thank you for bringing it to the cabin early. I'm sorry it smells unpleasant, but I'm sure you'll be happy to have bread instead of always eating biscuits." She spoke as she ladled thick mush into bowls, grabbed spoons from the crock on the dry sink, and placed the items on the table. "I'm sorry, too, for such a simple breakfast. I wanted to make something I could quickly clean up so I'd be ready when Josephine arrives."

"Mush is fine. It fills the belly, and that is what matters, my Vater would say."

She smiled. "Your . . . fodder" — she hoped she pronounced the title correctly — "sounds a lot like my da."

He smiled, then folded his hands around Annaliese's hands and bowed his head. After delivering a short prayer of thanks, he picked up his spoon, his expression turning serious. "Never apologize for what you cook, Fanny. I appreciate not having to see to it myself. Having you here has been very helpful."

Heat filled her face, and it wasn't because she sat close to the fire. Such a kind thing to say, especially considering how many of the things she'd cooked had been less than enjoyable. Hadn't she always been Ma's best helper? Da laughingly said Fanny had come into the world armed with determination. Ma sometimes huffed that Fanny was too stubborn for her own good. The trait — whether determination or stubbornness — had always helped her persevere, even through the loneliest, most trying days on the *River Peacock*. But so many years had passed since she'd stirred a stewpot over an open fire, she was woefully inept. She'd keep trying, though. And she would learn to bake bread. Walter had pleased her with his kindness. She wanted to please him in return.

He spooned up a bite of the mush, then swallowed. "I am very sorry, though, that no letter came."

An uneasy feeling attacked her middle. She looked at him. The true sorrow in his eyes pierced her. "I am sorry, too. I know you're eager to hear from your parents."

His brows pinched. "Maybe when you go to town the next time, one will have arrived. That would be good. Then you —" The rattling sound of an approaching wagon interrupted. "Here is Josephine now. We'll talk more later." He gulped down huge bites of the mush, rose from his chair, and headed for the doorway. One foot inside and one on the stoop, he looked back at her. "Enjoy the bread making, Fanny. I'll see you at lunchtime." He hurried off.

Fanny stared after him, certain he'd planned to say, *Then you can go to New York.* He appreciated her help, sure. But he wanted her replacement to arrive. The realization was as painful as if she'd been stabbed through the heart.

Sloan heard the slender young woman sing a ballad in a sweet, timorous voice, but he wasn't really listening. He couldn't shake Fanny from his thoughts. Trapped in his hotel room for an entire day, waiting for Saturday morning's auditions, he'd wiled away the hours reading her sister's letters.

He had watched Fanny grow up on the *River Peacock,* witnessed her blooming from a lovely girl to a beautiful young woman, yet he hadn't known her. Not beneath the surface. Reading the words penned by Flossie, words clearly responding to questions sent by Fanny, had revealed the totality of who Fanny was. So much more than a singer of songs.

Many of the entries referred to her family — how they missed her and wished they were all together. Flossie also recorded memories of their years in Inverness. Treasured years, even though they scrabbled for a living there. Those posts didn't haunt him nearly so much as the ones hinting at the longings of Fanny's heart.

Snippets tiptoed through his memory.

Must you always stay on the boat? Can't you get off and run through the grass on your bare feet and laugh at the sun shining down on your head?

I'm sorry you're so lonely in your room. Ma says she'll pray someone will come onboard who you can call a friend.

Happy birthday, Fanny! Twenty already. That seems so old. I'm almost fifteen now. Da says I should be praying about the man God has picked out who will take me as his bride. Do you ever think about getting married?

What had Fanny written in reply to the question about marriage? Not that it mattered. Because of the fire on the vessel, she'd never realize her hopes and dreams.

"Sir?"

Sloan gave a start. The singer remained a few feet from him, her hands still clutched in front of her but her song silent. He cleared his throat. "Are you finished?" Titters rolled from someone in the small crowd of people either waiting their turns or listening to the auditions.

The girl nodded, her expression uncertain. "Yes, sir. Unless you'd like me to sing something else. I prepared two songs."

He couldn't honestly say he'd heard the

first one. He should give her another chance. He flipped his hand in a silent invitation.

She raised her chin and began one of the songs Fanny had sung for her repertoire. A poor choice. Although this young woman was appealing in appearance, her voice couldn't possibly compare to the way Fanny's had run the scales as effortlessly as a hawk floated on the evening breeze.

He let her sing all the way through, thanked her for her time, then glanced over his shoulder at those waiting. "Who is next?"

A red-haired girl with an abundance of freckles stepped forward. "I am, sir."

"Name?"

"Clotilde Strong."

He shifted in his chair, pencil poised to record her name in his record book. The previous singer was still standing in the middle of the rug he'd told those audition-ing to pretend was the stage. Why was she still there?

She linked her hands and rested them at her waist, the pose similar to the one he'd taught Fanny to hold when she performed. "Mr. Kirkpatrick, may I ask a question?"

He wanted to bring the next singer to the rug. The auditions were tedious, and he was ready to leave this chair. To leave this city.

But the watching audience compelled him to mind his manners. "Yes, you may."

"When will you post the name of the one who'll be the new singer on your boat?"

He rubbed his chin with his knuckles, pondering the best reply. There were several papas in the crowd, and some of them were as large as Lorna's grandson. He didn't care to tangle with any of them. He forced a genial tone. "I'm auditioning singers from a variety of cities. Jefferson City is only one on my list. When all auditions are complete, I'll make a selection, and I'll post a notice in the local newspapers."

"How many more cities are you going to visit?"

He chuckled. "Well, Miss" — he consulted his paper — "Mitchell, that depends on whether or not a singer from Jefferson City stands out as the clear winner of this contest."

The girl smiled, bobbed a quick curtsy, and scurried from the rug.

Clotilde Strong took the previous girl's place and, without preamble, launched into "I've Left the Snow-Clad Hills."

Sloan was very familiar with the number, and he was also familiar with the name of the singer who'd made it popular. Jenny Lind, the Swedish Nightingale, was rumored to have sung the song for the queen of England. He couldn't validate the rumor, of course, because he had no close relationship with the queen. He could verify for himself that this girl, although singing on pitch and with enough volume to reach the rooms on the second floor, was no Swedish Nightingale.

But somewhere in Chicago, Illinois, apparently there was a singer comparable to the well-known, well-celebrated vocalist. He glanced over his shoulder. By quick count, another six or seven girls waited their turn. He could sit through six or seven more auditions. Maybe he'd be lucky and one of them would sing with such skill and heart that he'd hire her on the spot. But if one didn't, he'd purchase a train ticket for Chicago.

The telegram he'd received from Burke yesterday indicated all was proceeding well with the *River Peacock* and Sloan wasn't needed in Canton, Missouri. He'd lost the Darling of the *River Peacock*. If there was a chance of hiring a singer he could book as the Mississippi River Nightingale, he had to take it.

23

THE KUHN HOMESTEAD
WALTER

The aroma of fresh-baked bread carried from the cabin to the back side of the barn. Walter sucked in full breaths through his nose, savoring the scent while working on the chicken coop. Only the longest wall yet to complete, and then he could go inside and have some bread. He should hurry, but for more reasons than enjoying a slice of bread.

He sent another skyward glance. The morning had dawned clear and bright, but in midafternoon, clouds had gathered and their bellies were turning gray. Rain would come before the day ended, just as he and Fanny had prayed it would.

Rain was good. Good for the garden, good for his corn seeds, good for the prairie. A dry prairie was a dangerous place. He would welcome the rain, but he wanted to have the coop done before the clouds opened and spilled the moisture.

This enclosure for the chickens was a much simpler structure than the first one he'd built. He made use of the same rock foundation, four feet deep and six feet long, tucked snug against the back wall of the barn. Not having to lay a new foundation saved time. He couldn't afford to purchase one-by-twelve boards and windows a second time, but walls built of lath strips would do.

He took a step back and examined the partially constructed coop. Lath dictated a shorter ceiling. The wood frame stood only four feet high. He grimaced. Small? Certainly. But it would provide adequate shelter for the flock he intended to raise. He'd already topped the framework with a solid roof angled to shed water or snow, but he placed the lath for its sides a scant quarter inch apart. A coop needed ventilation.

When the walls were done, he'd build a little door on one side for the chickens to go in and out and a larger door on the other side for Fanny to enter. She'd cared for her mother's chickens when she was a child, she'd told him. Did that mean she knew how to pluck and cook one? He released a soft grunt. He needed to think about his work instead of chicken dinners. Or Fanny.

A niggle of guilt rolled in the back of his heart. The look of betrayal on her face as he'd darted out the door that morning haunted him. He should have stayed in the cabin long enough to finish telling her he understood her desire to go to her family. He wanted her to know that he wouldn't make her stay if she'd changed her mind. But he hadn't wanted Josephine to come in and hear some of the conversation. His and Fanny's arrangement was between only them.

His nose received a stronger whiff of bread. His mouth watered. Wouldn't the fresh bread taste good with the rabbit stew Josephine had brought along for their supper? When he'd gone to the cabin for his lunch, at least eight pans with rising lumps of dough sat on the dry sink. Fanny had served him a cup of buttermilk and biscuits heavily slathered with creamy, freshly churned butter, along with stewed apples and fried side meat. The most satisfying lunch he'd enjoyed since Grete died.

When he praised her, she sheepishly confessed that Josephine had prepared lunch while Fanny kneaded the dough. The white streaks of flour decorating Fanny's left cheek and the front of her apron from bib to skirt hem proved her industriousness.

And here he was, letting Fanny crowd into his thoughts again. The clouds wouldn't hold off forever. He shifted his attention to adding another slat.

Laughter trickled from the cabin. Even though Josephine was there, he knew who'd released the laugh. Fanny sang beautifully, and somehow her speech and even her laughter sounded like music. In only a week, he'd become familiar with her voice. Her kindness. Her servant's heart. Before he turned in for the night, he would fetch a dollar coin from the can tucked in a hole in the corner of the barn and give it to her as her first week's wage. He'd tell her then what he should have said that morning. He hoped the assurance would return the smile to her face.

He liked Fanny's smile.

With a stern jerk of his arm, he snatched up another piece of lath. No more thinking. He needed to work.

Fanny

Fanny protected her hands with a clean towel and lifted another pan bearing a nicely browned loaf of bread from the kettle. Seeing the beautiful loaf where a ball of dough had been before seemed like magic. And she'd performed the trick — well, she and Josephine — by combining flour, milk, eggs, salt, and baking powder into a sticky dough, then kneading in more flour until the dough became a smooth lump that plumped all by itself.

Josephine had closely supervised while Fanny mixed the dough. She had said — and Fanny agreed — that Fanny would remember better if she performed the steps herself. But after Josephine readied their lunch, she had taken over the kneading because Fanny wasn't forceful enough with the dough.

"You gotta fold an' push hard, Fanny, if you want the loaves to rise. They might've ate unleavened bread in the Bible times, but to my way of thinkin', bread that's flat as a pancake ain't worth eatin'," Josephine had said.

Letting Josephine do what was supposed to be Fanny's work stung her pride. But she'd discovered in the past week that cooking on her own was hard. And kneading dough, something she'd never done even for Ma, was very hard. Sharing the chore with Josephine, who knew what the dough should feel like when it had been kneaded enough, seemed prudent. After witnessing how the dough had risen above the pan's rim into a smooth, crusty dome after baking inside the largest cast-iron cooking pot, and smelling the enticing aroma now permeating the entire cabin, she was glad she'd shared the task.

Fanny carried the latest loaf to the window and set it next to two others cooling on the sill. The opposite windowsill held three loaves, as well. Two more to bake, and both she and Josephine would have enough bread to last them a full week. She gazed at the perfect-looking loaves and licked her lips. Wouldn't the bread taste good at suppertime, smeared with the butter she'd churned while Josephine entertained Annaliese? Although it had been years since she'd rhythmically plunged a beater up and down in a churn until clumps of butter floated on the surface of the milk, she remembered how to do it. How many times had she stood on the little stoop outside her family's cottage and worked the beater in Ma's crockery churn? Doing so that morning, even though she'd been inside a cabin on the Indiana prairie, had brought back pleasant memories.

Fanny put the last two pans of bread into the pot, settled the lid in place, and pushed the pot closer to the fire. As she straightened, a roll of thunder echoed from the distance. She scurried to the doorway and looked out. Suddenly she understood why the cabin's interior seemed dim for midafternoon. She'd been so busy she hadn't realized clouds were building. Rain would fall today, just as she and Walter had prayed. Her pulse quickened.

Holding Annaliese, Josephine stepped next to Fanny. "Oh, good. Rain is coming. We need it. But maybe I should go home. I don't care to get soaked."

As she finished speaking, the first fat raindrops met the grassless patch in front of the stoop.

Fanny offered Josephine a penitent look. "It's too late. You'll surely get wet now."

Josephine huffed. "And so will the bread if we don't get it off those sills an' close the windows."

Annaliese twisted in Josephine's arms. "Nee. Nee."

Fanny reached for her, and the little girl tumbled against her.

Josephine hurried to the east-facing window. "I'll get these, Fanny. You get the others."

Thunder rumbled again, louder this time. An unexpected chill — one carrying a spark of remembrance, distant yet intense — tiptoed down Fanny's spine and sealed her in place. She shivered and held Annaliese close, seeking comfort.

"Fanny! The bread's gettin' wet." Josephine darted to the opposite side of the cabin.

A breeze flowed through the doorway, bringing the strong scent of rain and rain-wet earth into the cabin. The smell filled Fanny's nostrils. More chills attacked, and a memory flared to life, transporting her to the deck of the *River Peacock.* Her limbs went weak. She staggered to the table and sank onto a stool, still cradling Annaliese.

Scarcely aware of Josephine thunking pans of bread onto the table, closing windows, and lighting a lantern, Fanny stared at the mesmerizing curtain of water trickling over the edge of the roof. Beyond it, rain fell softly, not heavily as it had the night of the boat fire. It came straight down, not blown sideways by a raging wind. She clung to Annaliese and told herself she had no reason to be afraid. But the scent, so much stronger than the aroma of bread she'd relished only minutes ago, convinced her otherwise.

Annaliese pushed against Fanny, and she set the little girl on the floor. She stared at the falling rain, memories of her last minutes on the *River Peacock* flashing in her mind's eye and raising waves of terror. Her stomach whirled.

Josephine crouched in front of Fanny and

took her hand. "Fanny, what's the matter? You've gone pale as bread dough. Are you ailin'?"

She would be sick if she couldn't rid herself of the scent and sight of rain. She whispered hoarsely, "Close the door."

Josephine tilted her head. "What?"

"Close —"

Walter burst into the cabin, scattering water droplets from his clothes and hair. "The clouds really opened up. What a good rain. The Lord answered our prayers." He kicked the rock doorstop aside and sealed the door into its casing. He turned to the table, and his bright countenance instantly faded. "What is wrong?"

With the solid door closing her away from the torrent of moisture, she should be fine. But she wasn't. Shame pressed down on her, and she hung her head.

Josephine squeezed Fanny's hand. "Fanny's not feelin' good." Keeping hold of Fanny's hand, she shifted to her knees. "Fanny, what is it? You were fine earlier. You were fine until we heard the thunder. Are you scared of thunder?"

Fanny looked up, ready to answer Josephine's question. Walter stood behind Josephine, dripping. Raindrops had dripped from the hood of Fanny's cloak the same way the night of the boat fire. She stared at him, unable to form words.

He glanced down at himself and grimaced. "I'm making a puddle."

Her gaze followed him to the row of pegs holding towels. He retrieved the largest one and rubbed it over his head and clothes as he moved to the rocking chair and started to sit. But then he caught Fanny's eye. He stepped away from the rocker. "You are shivering. Come, sit here by the fire's warmth."

Fanny's legs trembled, but they carried her to the chair. She slid onto its smooth seat, pressed her spine against the high back, and gripped the handrests. The sturdy chair offered security and stability. The fire offered warmth and comfort. But she continued to shiver.

Walter sat on the stool she had vacated, and Josephine moved to the second one. Fanny sensed their fervent study, but she couldn't meet their gazes. How weak and foolish she must appear. One of Da's favorite scriptures from the book of Isaiah offered assurance that God gave power to the faint and increased the strength of those without might. She'd often assured herself with the words during the first difficult weeks away from her family, but now she couldn't recall the chapter and verse. She wished she still had Ma's Bible. She would look for the words in God's Holy Book and read the promise again and again.

She turned her focus to Annaliese, who sat in her play corner, stacking blocks.

"Fanny?" Confusion and concern colored Walter's soft tone. "What is troubling you?"

Glancing at him, she lifted her hand and gestured to the door. "The rain. The . . . the smell of it. And the sound. It reminds me of the river."

Josephine's brow pinched. "But you lived right on the river. You were scared of it?"

Fanny shook her head hard. "Not the river. I am afraid of . . . what it makes me remember." She covered her face and moaned behind her hands. Why wouldn't the images abate? Would they stop when the rain stopped?

"What do you remember?" Walter's gentle voice, as tender as Ma's hand stroking her hair when she was young and frightened by a dream, penetrated the emotional wall Fanny had erected.

She slowly lowered her hands to her lap and laced her fingers the way she did when she prayed. Instinctively she begged, *God, me dear God . . . help me.* Then she drew in a shuddering breath and forced herself to speak. "A storm. The *River Peacock* was on the Mississippi, and there was a storm. Rain, wind, thunder . . ."

As if cued, a rumble of thunder vibrated against the log walls.

She gulped. "And there was a fire."

Walter abruptly sat up. He clamped his hands over his knees so tightly his knuckles glowed white.

Touched by what she perceived as his sympathy, she wanted to smile at him, but her quivering lips refused to cooperate. "It was dark. And the deck was slick. The passengers were all frightened and moving about in a panic." A warm tear rolled down her cheek. "They . . . one of them bumped me." A shudder shook her frame. "I fell over the railing into the river."

Josephine gasped. "Oh, you poor thing!" She hurried to the rocker and patted Fanny's shoulder. "Thank the Lord they got you out before you drowned."

Fanny winced. "They didn't get me out. They might not have even known I fell, it was so dark and noisy. I don't know why I didn't drown. God must have sent angels to save me. I awakened the next morning on the bank." An intense, cold chill rattled through her.

Josephine grabbed the quilt from the bed

and draped it around Fanny's shoulders with an awkward sideways hug. "I'm gonna check the bread. I don't want it to burn."

Fanny closed her eyes and pulled the quilt snugly around herself. With the snapping fire and the heavy quilt, why did she continue to tremble like a rabbit cornered by a fox? God had spared her life. She was far from the Mississippi River, far from the *River Peacock*. How childish to sit in this secure cabin and quake in fear.

A hand curled over her knee, and she opened her eyes.

Josephine was crouched beside her. She took one of Fanny's hands between her palms and rubbed it. "You must've been scared outta your wits when you went tumblin' over the rail. Is that why you're not singin' on the boat anymore? Because you were afraid you might fall in the river again?"

"I didn't go back because —" But she couldn't tell Josephine the full truth. She needed to protect Enoch and his family, who had illegally escaped their bonds, and she also needed to protect herself. She'd inwardly condemned Sloan for planning to break his agreement with her, but she was no better. By running away before her term was done, she'd broken the agreement.

311

She turned her face toward the dancing flames in the fireplace, too ashamed to face Josephine and Walter, who were being so sympathetic.

Walter cleared his throat. "Josephine, if you would like to borrow my oilcloth cape, it should keep you dry for your ride home. By now Hugh is probably watching for you and worrying."

She sighed. "You're likely right. Besides, he'll go hungry if I don't come home. He's helpless when it comes to cookin'." She released a wry chuckle.

"I backed your horse and wagon into the barn so it will be easy for you to drive out."

"That was good thinking, Walter. Thank you." Suddenly her arms were wrapped around Fanny's shoulders, her cheek against Fanny's temple. "If it's all right with you, I'll leave the loaves here tonight an' come for my four tomorrow after church. If it ain't rainin' then. Those two in the pot should be done about the time you're ready to dish up the stew."

Fanny nodded, but the knot in her throat didn't allow a reply. From the corner of her eye, she observed Walter fetch a bulky wad of heavy cloth from the box under the bed. He gave it to Josephine, and she shook it out and slipped it over her head. After

312

adjusting the hood, she straightened her spine as if preparing for a confrontation. "All right. Ready." Walter opened the door, Josephine scurried out, and he quickly closed the door behind her.

Fanny frowned. Why didn't he watch to see if she made it safely to the barn? It was the gentlemanly thing to do, and Walter was always a gentleman. But maybe he was being gentlemanly by closing out the sound and scent of rain.

Annaliese toddled from the corner, gripping a block in each pudgy hand. She held them to Walter with a crinkling grin. "Bock?"

Walter went down on his knee and cupped his hands around his daughter's. He manipulated her hands into gently tapping the blocks together. Annaliese giggled, and he smiled at her with both affection and pride. A lump filled Fanny's throat. What a kind man he was. To Annaliese and also to her. He'd been so supportive and had entrusted her with the care of his precious baby girl. Would he change his opinion of her if he knew she was still legally bound to Sloan?

Annaliese pulled free of her father's hold and plopped onto her bottom. He stood and turned toward the table. His gaze collided with Fanny's and held for several silent seconds. Warmth flooded her frame. Not from the fire, but from within. Could she trust him with her secret? Her heart told her she could. She gathered her courage, took a breath, and said, "Walter?"

He tilted his head. "Yes?"

"Nee!" Annaliese pushed to her feet, ran to Fanny, and lay her head in Fanny's lap. Fanny ran her fingers through the little girl's silky curls, her gaze still locked on Walter's unsmiling face. She swallowed and tried again.

"Walter, what —"

"Fanny, would —"

They both stopped. He waved his hand and sat on the closest stool. "Go ahead."

But now she didn't want to ask if he thought she was wrong for not returning to the River Peacock. What if he said she should go back? How could she return to the boat when the remembrance of her last minutes on it brought such fear? Would it swoop in on her again, the way it had tonight, leaving her weak and trembling?

She sighed. "It isn't important. What did you want to say?"

"We can talk later. When you feel better."

Such a kind man. She hoped his new wife would appreciate his gentle nature. "Very well." She shifted Annaliese from her lap and urged the child toward Walter. "Go to Fa, Annaliese. Nee must check the bread."

24

THE KUHN HOMESTEAD
WALTER

The thick slice of warm, fresh-baked bread oozing with butter didn't please Walter's tongue as much as he'd thought it would. He ate it, though, along with a big serving of stew swimming with chunks of tender rabbit, peas, potatoes, and carrots. He wouldn't disappoint Fanny by refusing to eat, even though his hunger had fled.

Before they sat down to supper, he'd dredged up the courage to tell her he wouldn't hold her to their agreement if she wanted to leave.

She had listened quietly to his assurances, and he thought she would give him an answer — either "I will stay" or "I will go." Fanny never said yes or no. She'd surprised him by saying, "I want to think and pray about what is best for you and Annaliese." Pray first. Pray for what was best — not for herself, but for him and his little daughter. Yes, she was a woman of faith.

When they finished eating, he bathed Annaliese and dressed her in a clean gown. Then he sat in Grete's chair and rocked his daughter to sleep. Her little head snug on his chest felt so good. He held her even after she fell asleep, unwilling to put her in the cradle. He sensed Fanny looking over at them from time to time while she cleaned up their supper dishes. He sneaked glances at her, too. She no longer quaked, but she hadn't released all her fear yet. He knew, because for the first time all week, she didn't hum while she washed, dried, and put away the dishes.

Finally, when the little carved German clock on the mantel chimed eight times, he pushed from the rocker and carried his sleeping child to her cradle and covered her with the little patchwork quilt Grete had sewn. Then he moved toward the door. Slowly. Quietly.

"Walter?"

At Fanny's soft, musical voice, he stopped. He turned his head and met her gaze. "Yes?"

She twisted a damp towel into a rope in her hands. "Do you think the rain will be gone by tomorrow morning?"

He hadn't heard thunder in quite a while. The rain clouds must be moving on. "Most likely, yes."

"Will we walk to church?"

"If the threat of more rain is gone, then yes, we will walk to church." His heart fluttered. If she wanted to go to church, she must be considering staying longer. He shouldn't hope so. It wasn't fair to her. But he was selfish enough to hope anyway. He paused, arguing with himself, but decided to risk the question. "Do you want to walk to church tomorrow?"

"I do." She replied so quickly, so adamantly, he couldn't hold back a smile. She untwisted the towel, gave it a shake, and hung it on a peg. "I haven't brought in water yet for my b-bath" — her face glowed as bright red as if she'd stuck her head in the fireplace — "and hoped you might stay with Annaliese while I . . . fetch it?"

He needed a bath, too, but his would be a cold one, the same as last Saturday. He couldn't very well bathe in the house with Fanny there. If he carried a couple of pans of hot water to the barn, he could warm up his tub, but it took time to heat the water. Did he want to keep her up so long when she looked so tired?

He grabbed the crossbar and lifted it. "I'll bring in several buckets for you. You're probably worn out from . . ." He shouldn't mention her emotional response to the rainstorm. "You worked hard today."

"So did you."

Why did the simple comment warm him so? "*Ja,* well, you fetched the water for washing the dishes, so I'll bring water now." He left before she could disagree. When he returned with the first bucket of water, she had pots waiting. He filled one, then made two more trips.

As he poured water into the last pot, she stepped close. "Thank you, Walter. Will you need the tub for . . . for . . ."

He couldn't climb into a washtub she'd just sat in. "There's another in the barn. Good night, Fanny." He darted out, leaving the door open behind him.

The rain had moved on, but its freshness remained. The scent of damp earth warmed by the sun filled Walter's nostrils. Birds sang happy songs from trees and bushes. If not for his worry about Fanny, he would have called the day perfect in every way. But she was not her usual self this morning.

As they crossed the soft, moist ground on their way to the chapel, he carried Annaliese, but she had reached for her Nee several times already. Fanny didn't seem to notice. Very unlike her. And she didn't hum. Not at breakfast, and not now. Had last night's storm stolen the song from her heart? Was she still afraid of rain? Or was she so fervently considering the answer to the question he posed last night that her present surroundings seemed far away?

He glanced at her again. Her rosy lips were set in a firm line, and her brow was furrowed, yet he didn't believe she was worrying. His gaze dropped briefly to her hands pressed at her bodice with her fingers laced. Praying. She was praying. She'd said she wanted to do what was best for him and Annaliese. Not thinking of herself. She humbled him.

All of his prayers were for himself. For the rain to fall on a certain day. For Annaliese to be safe. For his new wife to come. For him to be brave. God honored some, such as the prayer for rain. He was still waiting for his new wife. As for being brave, Walter had decided God said no and would leave it at that. Probably as punishment for the night his cowardice had taken the life of someone so precious.

Out there on the grassy landscape, beneath a morning sun while birds formed a joyful choir, the ugly memories roared through his mind again. Memories of the night lightning struck the barn and started the roof on fire . . .

Grete stood on the stoop of the cabin, eyes wide with horror and hands folded on her breast. "Oh, Walter, what of Hans? And Carlotta?"

How dearly she held the animals. He squeezed her arm and said, "I'll save them. I promise." And he pounded across the ground on bare feet and dashed into the burning barn.

The chickens squawked and ran in circles. He inwardly cursed himself. Earlier that day, he'd found a fox-dug hole next to their coop, so he had put them in the barn for the night. One chicken, the fool bird, darted back and forth under Carlotta's feet. The cow mooed and stamped the floor. On the other side of the barn, Hans — the big, beautiful gelding Grete's father had given her as a gift — reared up, his fear-filled scream carrying over the awful crackle and whoosh of wood being consumed by flames. So much noise. So much confusion. The scene dizzied him, making it hard to think.

He flapped his arms at the chickens. Some darted under the wagon, but two escaped out the door. Carlotta's stall was closer than Hans's. He jogged to it and urged the cow toward the opening with a hard smack on her rump. Head bobbing, loudly bawling, she trotted to freedom. Then, coughing and half-blinded from smoke, he staggered to Hans's stall. He yanked the horse's mane, slapped his flanks, pushed against the mighty beast with all his might. But Hans, his eyes rolling in terror, backed himself into the corner and refused to budge.

A sharp sound like a rifle shot came from above his head. Then another. He squinted upward, trying to make sense of what he'd heard, and realization exploded through him. The beams were cracking. The roof would fall. And when it did, he'd be trapped. Heart racing, hands trembling, he tried once more to grab hold of Hans's mane. The horse swung his head and knocked Walter to the hay-strewn floor.

Another ominous crack.

Fear propelled Walter to his feet. Sobbing out, "I'm sorry, Hans — I'm sorry," he staggered through the smoke to the yard.

Grete met him, looked into his eyes, and screeched, "No!" Then she lurched toward the barn.

Walter grabbed her. "It's too late! The roof beams, they're —"

"I can't let him burn to death!" She broke free of his restraining arms and ran in. Moments later, the roof collapsed in a deafening crash. A brilliant shower of sparks rose and briefly lit the dark sky.

He watched the barn burn to the ground, his mind numb and his legs unmoving. His lungs heaved while tears streamed down his face. He should have gone in after her. Even if it meant dying, too. He didn't deserve to live after being too cowardly to try to save her.

A whimper escaped his throat. A tiny hand touched his beard, and he looked down into his daughter's sweet face. The present whooshed in, and he found himself standing on rain-moist grass beneath a bright morning sun while birdsong and a fresh breeze filled his senses. The memories scuttled to the far recesses of his mind, and an awareness he'd never considered before dawned. If he'd died that night, along with Grete, Annaliese would be orphaned. It wouldn't be right for her to lose her mother and her father.

He kissed her little hand and then her temple. Maybe he'd been saved for Annaliese. With the ugly remembrances tucked away, he sent a hesitant look at Fanny. She gazed at him, her head tilted slightly, her hands now at her sides.

"Is your leg paining you? Do you want me

to carry Annaliese?"

He hugged his daughter and shook his head. "No. No, I am fine." *Now.* "Let's . . ." He nodded in the direction of the chapel.

They moved onward, she matching him step for step with her gold-dotted brown eyes pinned on his face. He read both curiosity and concern in her expression. He could satisfy her curiosity by telling her the truth about Grete's death. If he did, how quickly would her concern change to condemnation?

He shifted his attention ahead to the spot where the wooden cross on top of the chapel's steeple seemed to poke up out of the thick green grass. He kept his eyes locked on it for the remainder of the distance.

Gideon Bible Chapel
Fanny

When the church service ended, Fanny worked her way through the small gathering of people and reached Josephine. Josephine was in conversation with another woman, so Fanny stood quietly and waited for them to finish.

Midway through a sentence, Josephine seemed to notice Fanny and held out her hand. Fanny took hold, and Josephine drew her forward.

"Eliza, have you met Fanny Beck?" Josephine beamed at Fanny. "Fanny, this is one of my dearest friends, Eliza French." She turned to Eliza. "Fanny is takin' care of Annaliese until Walter's new wife comes to Gideon."

Eliza tsk-tsked. "We thought sure she'd be here by now." She looked from Josephine to Fanny and back while she spoke. "Why, Tom Tucker sent for a wife two Januaries ago, remember? An' his Mary came by the first of March. Not even two months later. Grete's been dead, what? Almost five months now? Walter wrote to New York for a new wife not long after she was buried. Heaven knows he needs somebody to help him take care of that little girl of his. I can't imagine what's takin' so long." She settled her attention on Fanny. "I reckon he's sure happy to have you lookin' after Annaliese."

Fanny's stomach churned in nervousness. How should she respond? She'd seen women in pairs or in small groups on the *River Peacock* with their heads together, talking and sometimes laughing softly. But she'd never participated in such a get-together. Sloan would've had a fit if she'd tried befriending any of the passengers. Uncertain what to say, she offered a smile.

325

Eliza sighed. "I'd sure like to stay an' gab, but my husband's probably out there in the wagon wranglin' the children an' wonderin' where I am. I best skedaddle." She backed toward the open doorway. "Nice to meet you, Fanny. I hope we can talk again some other time." She turned and hurried out.

Josephine squeezed Fanny's shoulder and leaned close. "I'm real glad to see you here today after . . ." She sent a quick glance around the nearly empty room. "Well, after you had such a hard evening."

Fanny shuddered. She preferred to forget the hard evening, as well as the memories that had prompted it. "I wanted to ask, since you're coming to the cabin for your bread, would you want to stay and eat with us?"

Josephine reared back. "That's real nice of you, but ain't it too much?"

"It isn't." Fanny pressed her clasped hands to her stomach. "You've been so kind and helpful to me. I'd like to repay you." Especially since she might not see Josephine again after tomorrow. With the coins she'd collected in Mishawaka plus Walter's dollar, she had enough for a ticket to at least the next town. If she went, she'd trust God to provide for her the rest of the way. If only she knew for certain if He wanted her to go.

Josephine looped her arm through Fanny's and propelled her toward the front door. "There's not one single thing you owe me for. But if you're willin' to share a meal with Hugh and me, we'll gladly sit an' enjoy it with you." She paused inside the church door. "I'll be real honest with you, Fanny. When Hugh told me how you showed up at Walter's cabin like you fell from the sky, I was plenty worried."

Walter must've talked to Hugh when they chinked the barn together. Fanny wished she knew exactly what he'd said. It might help her decide what was best — leave for New York now, or stay until Walter's new wife came.

"Invitin' a stranger into his home? Givin' her charge over Annaliese?" Josephine shook her head, her eyes wide. "I declare, it didn't seem like something Walter would do. He's always been a little — how should I put it — timid about things."

He hadn't seemed timid when he'd burst into the cabin and barked at her in German. She almost smiled in remembrance.

"But then I reflected on that time we had together, when we drove into Gideon to do the shoppin'. I watched you with Annaliese. You were real kind an' patient with her, an' she seemed right at home with you. Then

327

yesterday I seen how nice you're keepin' the cabin. How you're takin' care o' Annaliese, sure, but Walter, too. So I got to thinkin' maybe it didn't matter so much where you came from. You're exactly what Walter an' Annaliese need."

A flutter of joy whisked through Fanny's chest. "I am?"

"Yes, ma'am, you are."

"Why?" The simple question emerged on a breath of wonder.

Josephine released a laugh. "I reckon it'd be hard for you to know the Walter we've been seein' ever since Grete died. He was a sad man, always worryin'. Worryin' about Annaliese, worryin' about gettin' the crop in, worryin' about somethin' else bad happening. But Hugh an' me have both seen a change in him since you came. Knowin' his little girl's cared for has rolled the worries right off him." She gave Fanny a quick hug, then stepped back. "You're his godsend."

"You been God-sent, fo' sure, Miss Fanny." Enoch's voice whispered in Fanny's memory. Enoch believed — and Fanny did, too — that God had brought his family and her together. They'd helped each other find freedom. Had God also brought her to Walter's family for all of their good? She'd prayed and prayed last night before falling

asleep, begging God to reveal what she was to do.

"You're his godsend."

The words Josephine chose seemed like God speaking through her. Caring for Annaliese and all the household chores was a big responsibility. She couldn't know how long she would be needed. But in that moment, she made a decision.

For as long as she was needed, she would stay.

25

THE KUHN HOMESTEAD
FANNY

Fanny presumed that when they finished eating the fried ham, rice — which wasn't crunchy, to her relief — and tomato preserves from a jar in the cellar spooned onto slices of bread, Hugh and Josephine would go home. But as soon as Fanny cleared the dishes from the table, Walter got out a tin box and spilled little ebony rectangles onto the middle of the tabletop, challenging Hugh to a game with a smirk.

On the *River Peacock,* men entered dominoes tournaments and bet against each other. Sometimes the racket of fights and arguments filtered through the floorboards of the main deck and disturbed Fanny's sleep in her little room below. But only laughter and good-natured teasing accompanied the game in the Kuhn cabin. She hadn't realized people played merely for fun. She smiled and sometimes chuckled to herself while she washed the dishes.

Josephine rocked Annaliese, frequently instructing the men to *shhh*. They didn't. Somehow Annaliese fell asleep anyway. Josephine tucked her into her cradle, then crossed to Fanny. "Can I help?"

Fanny lifted the last pot from the dishpan. "As soon as this is dry and put away, I'll be done."

Josephine took the pan of murky water. "Let me empty this an' rinse it for you. Then you an' me can maybe get in the wagon an' go visit Eliza." She tossed a grin at the men. "These two'll likely be at it the rest of the afternoon. It's near impossible to peel Hugh away from a table when dominoes are bein' played."

Hugh snickered. "She's right, Fanny. You gals might as well find somethin' to entertain yourselves up until suppertime."

Josephine carried the basin of water out the door and disappeared beyond the doorjamb.

Hugh slid a domino into place, then aimed a grin at Fanny. "I hear Walter keeps you as busy as an ice cutter in December." Walter blushed crimson and fiddled with his dominoes. Hugh winked at Fanny and went on. "But this is Sunday, when a body's supposed to rest. Would you like it better if we cleared out?"

Josephine returned with the empty wash pan as Hugh asked his question. She stopped and turned a regretful grimace on Fanny. "I didn't even think about us keepin' you from restin' up. We can sure go on home if you want us to."

Fanny knew what she wanted. She turned to Walter. "Would it be all right with you if we walked to the creek?"

Walter looked up, his fingers poised to pick up another domino. "Are you sure you want to go so far?"

"I am. I'd like to pick more lamb's quarter and dig some wild onions." She also wanted comfrey for a poultice. Her shoulders were sore this morning, probably from the kneading she'd done yesterday. But he didn't need to know that. "If you're worried about Annaliese waking up and disturbing your game before we get back, we won't venture so far."

He glanced in the direction of the cradle, a fond smile lighting his blue eyes. "If my Liébling wakes up, I'll see to her. She's more important than a game of dominoes."

His tenderness toward his little daughter always touched her. She took the basket from its hook and slipped its handle over her arm. "Then I'll not hurry, and I'll fill the basket to the brim. We'll have lamb's quarter for several days' meals."

He gave a little jolt, and his finger left the domino. "We . . ." He seemed to search her eyes. "We will?"

She offered a hesitant nod. "If that is all right with you?"

Relief flooded his features, and she knew he'd understood what she meant but hadn't said. She would stay. "Yes. Yes, it's all right." He stroked his fingers through his beard, and his cheek whiskers twitched into a lopsided grin. "If you ladies want a real excursion, fetch the fishing pole from the barn before you go. Josephine can catch some bullhead."

"Oh, what a grand idea!" Josephine touched Fanny's arm. "You ever fixed bullhead before?"

Fanny had eaten the fish while on the *River Peacock.* The cook prepared simpler meals for the crew. Freshly caught fish were a staple, as they'd been when she was a child. But she'd never cooked fish herself. "I have not."

Josephine licked her lips. "It's easy as fallin' off a log. I dredge the meat in flour and cornmeal, then fry it in lard. They're real tasty, every bit as good as river catfish. Hugh likes bullhead filets for breakfast." She nudged her husband with her elbow, grinning at him. "I ain't had a chance to drop a line in the water yet this spring. Hope I ain't lost my touch."

Hugh looped his arm around her waist and pulled her snug to his side. "Don't fall in the creek, Jo. It's still too cold for swimmin'."

She laughed, wriggled loose, then bent and gave him a peck on the lips. "I don't intend to go swimmin' until you can go, too." She grabbed her bonnet from the little table near the door and tied it over her wavy brown hair. "C'mon, Fanny, don't dally. I've got a real hankerin' for some fried fish."

Fanny followed Josephine across the sunny yard to the barn. Inside was dark now that most of the logs were chinked. Only a tiny bit of sunlight sneaked between the logs closest to the roof. After so many years of living in a windowless room, Fanny preferred staying out in the sunshine. She waited near the doorway while Josephine disappeared into the shadows. Minutes later she emerged with a slender pole over her shoulder. "I got Walter's fishin' pole an' some string to keep hold o' the fish I catch. Let's go."

Fanny pointed. "The creek's out this way."

Josephine set off, a smile on her face. "Oh, I know where the creek is. That windin' creek's the border between our land an' Walter's. I go there regular, but it's been a while since I been there from this side. Me an' Grete did plenty of sittin' on the bank, dippin' our toes an' chatterin' away, tryin' to get bullheads to catch our hooks." A wistful expression flitted over her face. "Least we did before Annaliese was born. After that, Grete stayed close to home. Can't say as I blame her. Havin' youngsters changes things for folks."

Fanny didn't know what to say in response, so she stayed quiet.

They passed the new chicken coop. The pair of hens pecked in the dirt outside the slatted enclosure.

Josephine nodded at the coop, as if giving her approval. "Now that the coop's rebuilt, Walter should put up a fence made from some of that newfangled chicken wire. Probably ought to do it before he adds to his flock. These two know where home is, but it'll keep the new chickens from trying to wander off. Is he plannin' on puttin' up a fence?"

Fanny shrugged. "I don't know. He hasn't said." She didn't expect him to discuss his plans with her. But she wished he would.

"Well, I'll have Hugh get a roll of wire fence the next time he goes into Gideon."

Josephine kept a brisk pace, the fishing pole bobbing on her shoulder. "Not that I think Walter ain't smart enough to think of it himself. He's a real smart man. Went all the way through the twelfth grade in New York City. But since Grete died, he's been a little lost an' uncertain. Grief'll do that to a person."

Fanny thought she understood. Although she hadn't lost her family to death, she remembered the lonely days after Sloan took her away. She missed Da, Ma, Flossie, and Moira so deeply it hurt to breathe. If it hadn't been for Sloan pushing her to learn the songs for the shows and do her studies with the tutor, making her think of something other than her broken heart, she might have withered up and died. Maybe that was why Walter had kept Annaliese with him instead of letting the Moores care for her. He'd needed to keep himself busy.

It struck her how well Josephine knew Walter. Maybe as well as family members knew each other. Maybe more than she knew her parents and sisters now. "You and your husband spent a lot of time with Walter and Grete?" The question popped out before she had a chance to think about it.

"Oh, we sure did." Josephine caught the skirt of her dress and hiked it above her ankles as they climbed the first rise. "See, our cabin is a half mile or so on the other side of the creek. When they came to Indiana, their wagon went right through our land, so we met 'em even before their cabin was built."

They topped the rise. Josephine stopped and loosened the ties on her bonnet. "Hugh an' me had been here a good half-dozen years already, so we knew pretty much everybody. Hugh rounded up men to help Walter build his cabin an' barn, an' I helped Grete learn to cook over a fireplace." She laughed, a sound laced with affection. "Grete'd been born into a more well-to-do family, so she'd never had to do any real housekeepin'. But she was downright clever with a needle an' thread. Made all her own clothes."

Fanny looked down at the green-sprigged muslin dress she'd donned that morning. Had Grete made this dress? Walter was very unselfish in sharing his wife's things, but what would Grete think about Fanny wearing her clothes?

"I teased her that if she could stitch up supper instead of cookin' it, she an' Walter would eat better'n kings an' queens." Josephine's expression turned contrite. "Not that Walter ever complained about anything she put on the table, mind you. He's always been a patient man for as long as I've known him. And smiley. Whistled all the time, even when he was workin'. I guess when he lost Grete, he lost his whistler, too." She sighed, shaking her head. "Oh, them were good days. Us an' the Kuhns, we got along as good as . . . well, as beans an' molasses, I guess." She set off again.

Fanny hurried after her. Beans and molasses? That was something she hadn't tried.

Josephine released an airy sigh. "Me an' Hugh helped Reverend Lee talk Walter into sendin' for a new wife right away. He wanted to wait a spell. Didn't like the idea of replacin' Grete."

A knot of sorrow filled Fanny's throat. She swallowed.

"But we told him it didn't make sense to be alone. Not when he has a farm to run an' a baby who needs a mama." Furrows formed briefly on Josephine's brow. "Me an' Hugh are prayin' that Walter an' his new wife'll grow to love each other as much as him an' Grete did an' be real happy together." A sheepish shrug briefly lifted her shoulders. "I confess, I'm also prayin' her an' me will be good friends. I miss havin' Grete to talk to."

Was that why Josephine hardly ever

stopped talking? Grete had been gone for several months. Josephine had a lot of pent-up words to share. Fanny lightly squeezed Josephine's arm, hoping she communicated sympathy.

"Sure wish the woman would hurry up an' get here." Her grin in Fanny's direction seemed sad. "Reckon you do, too, so you can be on your way."

Fanny nodded. She didn't trust herself to talk.

Josephine came to a sudden stop, then whirled and faced Fanny. "There's somethin' I've been ponderin'. Can I ask you a question?"

What might the gregarious woman ask? Fanny wondered at the wisdom of granting permission, but she said, "You may."

"You said you were indentured to a riverboat captain. You said you fell overboard in a storm. An' you said you didn't go back to the boat."

Fanny nodded slowly, her pulse scampering.

"If you're indentured to him, you signed a contract, didn't you?" Josephine's eyebrows dipped in the center, giving her a worried look. "Ain't it illegal for you not to go back?"

Defensiveness roared through Fanny, carried on a wave of anger. "Me da put his *X* on the contract next to Sloan's signature. We agreed to seven years of service. I counted every one of those days, always looking to the last one, when I'd be free to go to Da and Ma and me little sisters. But Sloan didn't intend to let me go. He planned to keep me on his boat. To keep me locked in me room when I wasn't singing, as he'd done since me very first days on the *River Peacock.*" She trembled from head to toe, recalling the helplessness of being trapped all those days and weeks and years. "Indeed, I fell overboard before my time was served. But if I go back to him, I will never be free. I will *not* go back."

Josephine's eyes had widened as Fanny spoke, and her jaw hung slack. She gaped for several silent seconds, then dropped the fishing pole and grabbed Fanny in a hug. "Oh, Fanny." A sob broke from her throat. "I didn't know such things could happen to a person."

Fanny leaned into the comfort Josephine offered. Such things did happen. And not only unfair servitude like Fanny's. Hundreds of people like Enoch, Dathan, and Pazzy were still trapped in slavery. Fanny was free, and she had to trust, given the way the Lord had blessed and protected them, that Enoch and his family were, too. But what of the others? While Josephine held her, Fanny closed her eyes and prayed success for Ransom, Standard, and all the people working to guide slaves to a place of freedom. And she prayed for freedom for all those caught in bondage.

"I'm so glad you got away from him." Josephine released Fanny and wiped her eyes. "Ain't it somethin' how it happened, though? Bein' in a storm an' gettin' knocked into the river." She shook her head, wonder blooming on her face. "My ma liked to say God works in mysterious ways, but I never would've thought of Him usin' a near drownin' to set one of His children free."

Fanny pulled in a big breath and released it slowly, willing the rise of fury to leave with it. "Nor would I. But I prayed and prayed for deliverance, and He gave it to me."

Josephine bent over and grabbed the fishing pole again. She flung her free arm across Fanny's shoulders and escorted her forward. "An' soon you'll get to see your folks again. I'm happy for you, Fanny."

Worry nibbled in the back of Fanny's heart. As much as she longed to be with her family, how would she leave her wee bonny hen, sweet Annaliese, behind?

26

THE KUHN HOMESTEAD
FANNY

Fanny awakened Monday morning with an awareness. She'd formed a friendship with Josephine. Their hours at the creek — talking nonstop while Fanny gathered leaves and scavenged for wild onions and Josephine pulled six plump, mud-colored, whiskered fish from the creek — had sealed it. There was no retreating from it. And Fanny didn't want to retreat.

She hummed as she followed the directions Josephine had given her to prepare the bullhead filets. She dipped them in flour, then milk, then in cornmeal and laid them in the lard sizzling in the frying pan. When the edges seemed brown, she flipped them. Some of the cornmeal coating fell off with the action, exposing the white flesh of the fish. The cheerful melody died in her throat. Was that supposed to happen?

Walter stepped onto the flat stone outside the cabin door a few minutes before seven, just as Fanny pulled the pan of fried fish filets from the fire.

He sniffed the air. "What do I smell?"

She put the pan on the dry sink and reached for a plate. "I fried the bullhead filets Josephine left for us."

He crossed to the dry sink and seemed to watch with interest as she transferred the crisp, browned, shriveled strips to the plate. She handed him the plate, and he stared at the contents. He didn't speak, but his expression worried her.

She tangled her hands in her apron skirt. "What's the matter?"

"Nothing." He put the plate on the table and sat in front of it. "May I have a fork?"

Why hadn't she set the table? Because she was watching the fish turn brown. "I'm so sorry." She handed him a fork and a napkin.

"Thank you." He tucked the napkin in his shirt collar and looked up at her. "Aren't you having any?"

She pointed to a small basin where two more filets soaked in salt water. "I still have those to fry when Annaliese wakes up. Having Hugh and Josephine play with her so long yesterday afternoon must have worn her out. She's sleeping late." She flicked her fingers at him. "But you don't need to wait.

Go ahead and eat while they're hot and fresh."

He sat, bowed his head, then picked up his fork and stabbed into a curled filet. A chunk broke loose and slid through the smear of grease on the plate. He aimed the tines for the chunk, and when he speared it, it crumbled. He set the fork aside and gave her a sheepish grin. "I think these might be a little too . . . done."

Fanny stared at the fish, then at his face. Not a shred of criticism showed in his eyes, which made her feel even worse about ruining the filets. She grabbed the plate, hurried to the open doorway, and tossed the food outside. She turned and found him still sitting at the table with his napkin under his chin. He needed breakfast, but she didn't want to fry those other filets and ruin them, too. What could she fix quickly?

She returned to the dry sink and lifted down the tin box holding the bread loaves she'd baked on Saturday. She consoled herself that at least the bread was palatable, thanks to Josephine's help. She cut three thick slices, smeared them with butter, and stacked them on a fresh plate.

Plate in hand, she faced Walter. "I'm so sorry about the fish."

"No need to be." He took the plate, folded

one of the bread slices, and took a bite. "Have you ever cooked fish over an open fire?"

She hung her head. "I have not."

"It takes time to learn to cook."

Was he thinking of Grete's first attempts at preparing meals for him? If so, she hoped the memories were sweet.

He took another bite. "I haven't thrown anything else you've cooked out the door."

She looked at him. A teasing glint lit his blue eyes. Her heart lifted, and a smile tugged at the corners of her lips. "You didn't throw them out. I did."

"I would have if you hadn't."

Despite her dented pride, Fanny laughed. "Well, the next time we have fish, I'll ask Josephine to help me cook the filets. Then you'll be able to eat them."

He popped the last bit of the first slice of bread into his mouth and picked up another. He gestured to the fireplace with it. "Is the coffee ready?"

"It is." She hooked two cups from the shelf with her fingers, then brought them and the coffeepot to the table. She poured the dark, steaming brew into both cups and sat across from Walter. "Bread and butter isn't much of a breakfast, but you'll have a fine lunch. Josephine told me how to make

345

sure the beans are cooked clear through. I'll put molasses and side meat in the pot with the beans and make cornmeal muffins to go with it."

He paused with the cup of steaming coffee halfway to his mouth. "You are a good-hearted person, Fanny. I feel blessed you've chosen to stay."

All teasing had fled, and his eyes shimmered with appreciation. Heat built in Fanny's cheeks, but she couldn't decide if she was embarrassed or pleased by his words. "I . . . I wasn't sure I should. My being here means you have to sleep in the barn."

He put down the cup and rested his elbows on either side of his plate. "May I ask why you decided to stay?"

She took a sip of the coffee, contemplating her answer. It seemed boastful to repeat what Josephine and Enoch had said about her. But it was their claim she'd been sent by God that brought her to the decision. She said honestly, "I believe God told me I should."

He sat gazing at her while the mantel clock gently ticktocked and a bird chirped a cheerful morning song. Then he took up the last slice of bread, his smile sweet. "We should always do what God says."

She nodded, unable to look away from the tenderness in his expression. He, too, seemed transfixed. They both sat motionless, smiling at each other.

Annaliese let out a waking-up squeak.

Walter lowered his attention to the last piece of bread, and Fanny, with reluctance, left the table and took the two steps needed to reach the cradle.

Annaliese arched her back and scrunched her face, then opened her eyes. She broke into a huge grin and reached for Fanny. "Nee."

Fanny scooped her up and held her close, cheek to sleep-moist cheek, love swelling in her breast. She sang to Annaliese, nuzzling her belly while changing her wet napkin and gown. The little girl now clothed, Fanny carried her to the table and secured her to her chair.

Walter's plate and cup were empty, but he remained at the table.

Fanny picked up the coffeepot. "Would you like more?"

He leaned over and kissed Annaliese's flattened curls. "No, thank you. I've had plenty." He stood. "Thank you for breakfast, Fanny." He smiled down at his daughter, then settled the smile on Fanny. "Thank you for staying." He turned and quickly strode out the door.

Fanny basked in his simple statement — *"Thank you for staying"* — as she cleaned the cabin. Even more than the words, she thought about the tone he used, the shimmer in his eyes as he spoke. Such simple words, yet they communicated so much. Relief. Gratitude, of course. But also surprise. And — unless she misinterpreted — a hint of worry.

At noon, he refused to enter the freshly scrubbed cabin. He'd spent the morning carting back clay from the creek and then mixing a batch of chinking for the highest logs of the barn. Fanny didn't argue with him. His clothes were covered with clay, ash, and mud. She didn't want bits of dried muck falling on the floor she'd just thoroughly swept, even if the floor was only hard-packed earth.

She carried bowls of the well-seasoned beans to the stoop. She and Walter, along with Annaliese, sat in a circle on the warm rock and enjoyed a picnic. While they ate, she repeatedly lifted her face to catch the sun's rays. The bright ball carving its way across a seemingly endless sky, the rolling grassland, the trees tall and majestic, the spattering of wildflowers coming to life in every direction — they called to her. She wanted to drink in the openness and beauty. Eventually she would leave this farm in Indiana for the crowded city. She wanted to carry many images away with her.

Walter scraped the last drips of sauce from his bowl with his spoon, licked the spoon clean, then set the bowl and spoon on the rock. He pushed to his feet and released a sigh, rubbing the taut front of his plaid shirt. "Thank you, Fanny. That was very good."

She cupped her hand above her eyes and smiled up at him. "The molasses made a difference."

He chuckled. "It did." He drew his fingers down his beard. "Are you doing wash this afternoon?"

"I am not." She wiped a bit of juice from Annaliese's chin. The toddler was getting better at using a spoon, but sometimes she still missed her mouth. "Josephine is coming this afternoon. She promised to share some tomato starts for the garden, and she's bringing a length of fabric. We will put the tomato starts in the ground first. Then she's going to cut out pieces for a dress for me."

His brows descended. "Are there not enough dresses in the trunk?"

He'd been more than generous, allowing her to wear Grete's clothes, but she shouldn't treat them as if they were hers. Someday Annaliese would want something of her mother's. Fanny should do her best to preserve those items. "There are, and I thank you for letting me make use of them. But it would be better for me to have a dress of my own to wear."

An odd expression flickered in his eyes, but his brows relaxed. "I hope you and Josephine will enjoy your afternoon. Would you do something for me?"

She nodded.

He gestured to his filthy clothing. "I would like to have a clean shirt and britches to put on before I come in for supper. Would you bring some to the barn today?"

Only a wife should pick out a man's clothing, but what else could she do? "I will. I'll wrap them in some toweling to keep them from getting dusty. Then if you decide to" — should she say it? — "take a wash before you put on clean clothes, you'll have a towel, as well."

He ducked his head and tapped the ground with the toe of his boot. "That is sound thinking, Fanny. Thank you." He took a backward step, his head still low. "If you need me, I plan to work on the barn until sundown."

■ ■ ■ ■

Walter

Walter jogged the distance from the cabin to the barn. The top layer of chinking had grown crusty during his time away at lunch. He should have eaten faster, but it was too pleasant sitting on the slab of sandstone with a gentle breeze stirring his little Annaliese's curls and sunbeams shining like copper on Fanny's hair. He'd chosen to savor the minutes. Now he needed to add water and make the chinking workable again.

He poured a bit from the ready bucket and used his shovel's blade to stir and fold the thick mixture. What a fool he'd been, expecting Fanny to be content in Grete's dresses day after day. Why would she, or anyone else, want to wear the clothes of a dead woman?

Dead. He hated thinking of Grete as dead. At her graveside, Reverend Lee had told those gathered that Grete was more alive — eternally alive — than she'd been on earth. Walter didn't doubt it. The Bible promised that those who claimed Jesus as Lord would be welcomed into heaven when they died, where death never touched them again. If

Indiana in the springtime was pretty, heaven must be more wonderful than a man could imagine. But being alive in heaven still meant dead on earth, and the thought troubled him.

It probably troubled Fanny, too. At least Josephine was fixing it. He scooped chinking into a bucket, stuck a trowel in his trouser pocket, then tromped around to the side of the barn, where he'd left the ladder. Holding the bucket in one hand and the ladder rail with the other, he climbed the rungs, going slow, careful. His leg had stopped bothering him, thanks to time and Fanny's poultices, and he didn't care to fall and hurt himself again.

As he slapped chinking between logs and smoothed it with the back of the trowel, he silently berated himself. He'd told Fanny to get what she needed when she went to the mercantile last Thursday, but he should have outright said to buy dress goods. She'd agreed to stay until his new wife came. He couldn't know when that would be, but as long as Fanny was here, she should have things to call her own.

The rattle of a wagon intruded upon his thoughts. Josephine was coming. Even though he hadn't emptied the bucket, he jammed the trowel into the chinking and came down the ladder. He trotted out and met the wagon.

"Josephine, good afternoon."

She set the brake and smiled down at him. "Good afternoon, Walter. Gonna have that barn done today, you reckon?"

"I hope so." He started to smooth his beard, caught sight of his grubby hand, and thought better of it. "Josephine, may I ask a favor?"

"Why, sure. You can ask me most anything."

She was a good friend. He could trust her with this duty. "Fanny said you were going to help her start a new dress today."

"Yep, I sure am. Have the fabric right here." She patted a thick fold of cloth that rested beside her on the seat. "I was plannin' to make sheets with it, but I got to thinkin' it's too pretty to hide under a quilt. Those flowers dotted all over the green reminds me of a spring meadow. It'll make a real pretty dress for Fanny."

Considering how many times he'd seen Fanny staring across the landscape, she'd like fabric that looked like a spring meadow. "It's kind of you to share with her. She came with so little." He now understood why she hadn't carried anything away with her from the riverboat. "There are things a woman needs. Things she . . . she wouldn't want to tell me. But you know what they are."

"Are you talkin' about personal things?"

Walter gulped and nodded. "Would you get what she needs? Charge it to my account at the mercantile."

Josephine pursed her lips, frowning. "I'll do that for you. But are you really thinkin' she's gonna be here for a long time? Surely you'll get word about your new wife soon, won't you? I'm not sayin' you shouldn't see to Fanny's needs while she's here. Mercy, the girl's been through so much, bein' held against her will an' then almost —"

"What?" Josephine liked to talk, and usually Walter didn't interrupt, even if she'd been talking for a long spell, but he needed to make sense of something. "Held against her will? Who held her against her will?"

She groaned. "I shouldn't have said that. Fanny told it to me in confidence." She leaned forward slightly. "Let's just say the riverboat captain who indentured her wasn't honest an' leave it there, all right?" She sat up again. "As I was sayin', your new wife's bound to get here before long, so are you sure you want to buy Fanny everything a gal needs? When she gets to her folks, they'll take good care of her."

Walter couldn't deny Josephine was right. Fanny's parents would see to her, and his new wife had to be coming soon. It couldn't be too much longer, considering how many months had already passed. Even so, he gave a firm nod. "I am sure. While she's here, even if it isn't for long, she ought to have her own things."

Josephine smiled. "All right, I'll do it for you, then. Hugh told me to go to town tomorrow an' get chicken wire for your new coop, anyway. While I'm there, I'll kill two birds with one stone."

Walter held up his hand. "Chicken wire? I didn't say anything about chicken wire."

She chuckled. "I didn't say you did. But you should have." She braced one fist on her hip and grinned. "You gotta have a fence around the coop, or the new hens an' rooster you're plannin' to bring home won't stay put."

She was right again. He should've thought of it himself. Grete had even pestered him about putting up a fence around the old coop. He blew out a noisy breath. "All right. Chicken wire, too, but put it on my account and not your own." He reached for her. "Let me help you down from there. Fanny's probably inside wondering what we're talking about."

Josephine took hold of his hands and hopped to the ground. She let go of him and swished the dust from her skirt. "Well, I won't go tell her what you said. She's a proud girl. She'd march right out here an' tell you not to do it. An' I think — especially with all she's been through — she deserves some new things."

She slid the fabric from the seat, then hugged it to her chest. Her expression turned thoughtful. "You know somethin', Walter? As much as I've been prayin' for your new wife to get here, it'll be a sad day for me when Fanny leaves for New York." She headed for the cabin.

Walter watched after her, his heart thudding in unanticipated trepidation. He whispered, "For me, too."

27

Sloan took his bag from the porter. "Where might I find a telegraph office?"

"Right over there, mister." The man pointed to a small building up the street from the train station. "They charge ten cents for four lines."

Sloan wasn't concerned about the price. He tipped the man a two-bit piece, then wove between the many people milling on the boardwalk. The Chicago station, his eighth stop in three days, was certainly the busiest he'd encountered since he left Jefferson City. He entered the telegraph office, blinking as his eyes adjusted from the bright afternoon sunshine to the dim interior.

A man sat at a desk on the other side of a tall counter, his back to the door. Sloan dropped his bag on the floor with an intentional thud. The man spun the seat of his wheeled chair around and squinted at Sloan

357

through round glass spectacles. "Afternoon, sir. What can I do for you?"

"I need to send a telegram to Canton, Missouri." The telegrapher there had been given instruction from Burke to send an errand boy for him if a message came in. Burke then sent an immediate response. Sloan had come to appreciate the quick means of communication during his lengthy time away from the *River Peacock.*

The man slid a piece of paper and a pencil stub across the counter to Sloan. "Write it down."

Sloan wrote,

IN CHICAGO STOP STILL SEEKING SINGER STOP HAVE GOOD LEAD STOP

He paused and considered the last sentence. Did he truly have a good lead? Or was he, in essence, chasing after the pot of gold at the base of a rainbow?

"That it?" the man asked.

Sloan shook his head. He crossed out the line about the good lead and then added,

GIVE UPDATE ON REPAIRS STOP WILL WAIT STOP KIRKPATRICK STOP

He slipped a dime from his pocket and

handed it over with the message.

The telegrapher read it back in a droning monotone that would never pass for a singing voice. Then he tapped the paper with his ink-stained fingertip and looked at Sloan. "You gonna wait for a reply?"

Sloan nodded.

He bobbed his head at the door. "There's a bench in the alley between this office and the building next door. I sit out there and take my lunch most days. Go ahead and wait there. I'll let you know when the answer comes."

Sloan thanked him, picked up his bag, and exited. As the telegrapher had indicated, a bench was against the lapped siding of the telegraph office in the deeply shaded alleyway. He put his bag on one end of the bench and sat next to it. Using the bag as an armrest, he leaned his head against the siding and released a sigh. How nice to sit on something that didn't move, even if it was only a plank of wood.

Riding in a passenger railcar wasn't any faster than taking a stagecoach, but its amenities far exceeded stagecoach travel. Granted, the train was louder. Steel wheels on an iron track created a constant, rhythmic *clack-clack*. Brakes squealed so loudly they could pierce a man's eardrums, and the whistle blasting at will startled him every time. But no more being crowded three abreast on a hard seat or being jounced until he felt as if his brain were scrambled. He'd particularly enjoyed his private berth in the Chicago and Mississippi car. The button-tufted velvet seat with at least four inches of padding, as well as a fold-down sleeping berth, offered privacy and comfort. Yes, so much nicer than being on the stagecoach. He would do his utmost to avoid stage-coaches for the duration of his trip. How much longer would it be?

Since Monday morning, when he'd boarded the train in Jefferson City and set off, once again, in pursuit of this elusive unknown woman, he'd frequently pondered his sensibility. But each time he recalled the glowing praise for her ability, he pushed his uncertainty aside. Whoever she was, he had determined he would hire her. His reputa-tion for providing excellent entertainment was at stake. Not that there weren't other means on his boat for passengers to enter-tain themselves. Gambling was a favorite pastime for the men, but the ladies needed something more genteel.

Fanny's hour-long programs of hymns, love songs, and ballads earned accolades from some of the most elite people in the states of Missouri and Illinois. And no man had ever complained about the men-only show featuring quick-paced tunes of a bawdy nature. Sloan chuckled, recalling Fanny's natural blush as she sang about guzzling wine until one's head spun or enticing a man with a pucker of rose-tinted lips. Her innocent appearance combined with the sultry songs were irresistible.

All at once, he cringed. Fanny had rarely uttered a word of complaint or protest, but when he'd given her the stack of sheet music containing lyrics of a suggestive nature, she'd stared at him in horror. Her voice echoed in his memory. *"I can't be singin' such as these. Me da would have a fit. These are dishonorin' to the Lord."*

He had reminded her their agreement dictated compliance to his commands, and she fell silent. But her eyes continued to spark, and her jaw jutted out stubbornly. He'd sent her to her cabin so he wouldn't have to look upon her mute rebellion. Only fourteen years old, but she'd already possessed morals most likely learned as a wee lass at her father's knee. She probably grew up hearing the same lessons about pleasing God that he had. But although he'd discarded it all, choosing a path of pleasing self, she'd clung to it.

361

For as much good as it had done her. If God was real and took care of His children, as his father had preached, then He should have saved Fanny. A deep sigh heaved from his chest. Such a loss. Not only for him, but for her parents, too. He murmured, his heart heavy, "I was robbed of a singer. *They* lost a child."

"Mr. Kirkpatrick?" The telegrapher stood only a few feet away, folded paper in hand. "I got your response."

Sloan scowled and sat upright. How long had the man been there? He mustn't allow himself to get so lost in thought again. Not in a city the size of Chicago. Someone could make off with his bag or wallet. He stood and took the paper. "Thank you." He slid the telegram into his jacket's inside pocket and took hold of his bag. The telegrapher hadn't moved. Probably waiting for a tip. Sloan gritted his teeth and reached for his vest pocket where he always carried a few coins.

"We aren't supposed to pay attention to the messages folks send." The man took off his glasses and scrubbed the lenses against the front of his pin-striped black vest. "But since we have to read them in order to send them, it's hard not to pay attention. You know what I'm meaning?"

Sloan knew, but he had no idea why the man felt the need to explain. "It's fine. If you'll excuse me, I —"

"The thing is" — the fellow went on as if Sloan hadn't uttered a word — "what you wrote about looking for a singer made me remember something. A while back — somewhere close to the first of May, I think — quite a few people at the railroad station were abuzz about some lady who came in on the train. I didn't hear her myself, but they said she sang while another train rolled away, and her voice was so pretty it moved a few ladies to tears."

Tingles attacked Sloan's frame from his scalp to his heels. The story, so similar to what Lorna had shared, had to be about the same woman. "Did anyone say where the woman went from there?"

The man shrugged. "I don't remember. Like I said, it was a while back. Two or three weeks already." Then he brightened. "But my cousin Coy works as a freight mover for the Chicago and Mississippi line. He's at the station every day from eight in the morning 'til six at night. He might've seen her leave. You could ask him."

Excitement urged Sloan forward. "Where will I find him? How will I know him?"

The man hooked the wire temples of his

spectacles over his ears and adjusted the bridge on his nose. "Look for him on the boarding ramps close to the water tanks. You can't miss him because he's near as tall as Abraham Lincoln and just as skinny. Except he has yellow hair and no beard."

"Tall, skinny, yellow hair, clean shaven." Sloan recited the description for himself, but the man beamed as if he'd taught Sloan something spectacular.

"That's exactly right." He moved aside. "Good luck, mister. I hope you find what you're looking for."

As Sloan headed for the station, he slid Burke's response from his pocket and read it.

DRUNKS CAME ON BOARD STOP BEAT UP CRICKET STOP SPILLED PAINT BIG MESS TO CLEAN UP STOP BOATWRIGHT WANTS MORE MONEY STOP NEED YOU HERE STOP

His feet came to a halt, and he stared at the message in disbelief. Everything back at the *River Peacock* had gone well until now. Why, when he could very well be on the cusp of finding his next singer, did this happen?

Pa always preached that everything befalling a person upon whom God looked with favor was either ordained by Him or could be used by Him. Sloan released a growl of frustration. If there was a God in heaven, He did not look upon Sloan Kirkpatrick with favor.

The Kuhn Homestead
Fanny

God had certainly chosen to favor Fanny by letting her path cross Josephine's. Monday, Tuesday, and Wednesday, the dear woman left many of her own chores undone, drove over, and spent several hours each afternoon helping Fanny sew her dress. Her kindness seemed boundless. Fanny couldn't keep from smiling as she, with Annaliese straddling her hip, walked Josephine to her wagon at the end of Wednesday afternoon.

Josephine wrapped Fanny and Annaliese in a hug of farewell. "One more day an' it'll all be done. Just in time to wear to church service. An' after church this Sunday, you an' Walter an' Annaliese" — she grinned and tickled the little girl's tummy — "are eatin' at our place."

Fanny gasped. "But you've already done so much for me. You shouldn't cook for me, too."

Tears winked in Josephine's hazel eyes.

"Fanny, it'll be a treat to have you with us at our place. Time was when us an' the Kuhns swapped back an' forth cookin' on Sundays. Then Grete died." She sniffed. "I've missed havin' the company. So please say you'll come. Walter an' Hugh ought to be done plantin' the acreage at the Sandersons' place by Friday. Old Man Sanderson pays Walter in cash, but he pays Hugh with half a hog."

A funny picture formed in Fanny's mind, and a grin twitched her cheeks. "The snout half or the tail?"

Josephine threw back her head and laughed. "It gets sliced end to end 'stead of round the middle, so lots of good eatin'." She hiked her skirts high and climbed up on the wagon seat. "Hugh's especially fond of pork chops. I'll be fryin' up a batch. I'm fixin' fried taters an' mustard greens to go with 'em, an' I aim to bake an apple pie."

Fanny's mouth watered. "If you're sure it won't be too much trouble, I'll ask Walter if we may accept your invitation."

Josephine winked. "If it'll make you feel better to ask, go right ahead, but in these parts, since we women are the cooks, we generally make the decisions about who sits at the table."

Fanny lifted her chin. "Then I accept."

Josephine laughed again. She unwound the reins from the brake handle and unlatched the brake. "I'll see you tomorrow, Fanny. Bye-bye, Annaliese."

Annaliese waved her pudgy hand, grinning her dimpled smile. "Buh-buh."

Fanny waited until the wagon rolled from the yard, then put Annaliese down and took her hand. As they walked slowly toward the cabin, Fanny marveled at the turn her life had taken. She had a friend. A true friend.

When she was still at home, because they lived outside the village, her only friends were Flossie and Moira. Well, mostly Flossie, because Moira was only a toddler, barely older than little Annaliese was now, when Fanny went away. For her first three years on the *River Peacock,* she'd spent hours each day with her tutor. Miss Halstead wasn't unfriendly, but she was so much older than Fanny. More like an aunt than a true friend. But in the weeks away from the boat, Fanny had been blessed by Pazzy, Itiah, Kircie, Dathan, and Enoch befriending her, if only for a short time. And now she had Josephine.

And Walter.

Her steps faltered, the thought taking her by surprise. Or was it a surprise? Walter had become her friend. A trusted friend. And maybe even —

She scooped Annaliese up and sped up her pace. She shouldn't allow herself to go in that direction. Not even in her thoughts.

They reached the cabin, and Fanny put the baby in her chair, used a towel to secure her, then gave her some crackers, talking as she did so. "Now that the fabric is put away in the trunk and we needn't worry about getting crumbs on my lovely new dress, you may have your snack, Annaliese. Three crackers and some milk." She poured a bit of milk into a tin cup from the pitcher on the dry sink and set it in front of Annaliese. "Your papa will be home soon and hungry for his supper. What do you think we should have?"

Annaliese gnawed a cracker, her big blue eyes pinned on Fanny's face. The baby wasn't old enough for conversation, but Fanny talked to her anyway. How else would she learn speech? Besides, it pleased her to have someone to talk to after so many lonely years. She chuckled to herself. She'd thought Josephine had lots of stored-up words to say. Perhaps *she* did, too.

She perused the bins, crocks, and tins on the shelf. "Hmm, I could make a pot of rice. There's a bit of ham left from breakfast. I could chop it up and make ham gravy to pour over the rice." She glanced over her shoulder and discovered Annaliese still watching her. "Or would you rather have fried side meat, beans, and the last of the lamb's quarter?"

The little girl banged her hand on the table and loudly jabbered something non-sensical.

"Oh!" Fanny feigned surprise. "You don't want fried side meat, beans, and lamb's quarter? Then rice and gravy it is."

Humming, she gathered what she needed from the shelf, then reached for the water bucket. She released a huff. "Nearly empty. Annaliese, you stay right there, and I'll go fill it at the well. I'll be back before you finish your crackers."

She darted outside and rounded the corner of the cabin, swinging the bucket. The breeze kissed her face and swept a loose strand of hair across her cheek. She anchored it behind her ear and, even though she'd promised to hurry, her pace slowed. As had become her habit, she scanned the area from horizon to horizon and gloried in all she saw, smelled, and heard.

She reached the well, and even the squeak of rope as she turned the handle that brought up the bucket from the bottom became music when combined with a bird's trill, a squirrel's chatter, and the sweet whisper of wind through the trees. She couldn't stay silent, and she began to sing as she sloshed water from the well's bucket into the one she used in the house. " 'We'll find the place which God for us prepared.' "

She tossed the bucket back into the well, smiled at the soft splash when it hit the water, then picked up the kitchen bucket by its rope handle and turned for the cabin, still singing. As she did, she caught sight of a movement in the east. Walter was coming, with his hat pushed back on his head, a hoe bobbing on his shoulder, his strides long and sure. Her song faded, and a warbling melody reached her ears.

He was whistling.

Something fluttered in her chest. A familiar flutter, one she'd experienced at moments when something rare and beautiful — such as a butterfly unfurling its wings, or a falling star streaking against the night sky, or a tiny green toad peeping from a scattering of dried leaves — captured her attention. She was familiar with the flutter, but never before had the sight of a man, dusty from work, created it.

"I guess when he lost Grete, he lost his whistler, too." Josephine's statement echoed in Fanny's memory. He'd apparently found

his whistler again. Her palm lifted as if on its own accord and pressed against her bodice directly over her heart. Its steady thrum kept beat with his lively tune. She'd found a purpose in caring for Annaliese. She'd found a friend, too, in Josephine. The flutter returned. Though she'd told herself she mustn't let her thoughts run unchecked, she couldn't help wondering if she was also here for something more.

28

CHICAGO, ILLINOIS
SLOAN

"There's five lines runnin' in an' out of Chicago, mister. How'm I s'posed to know for sure which way she went?" Already frustrated by Burke's telegram, Sloan had little patience for this man's less-than-satisfactory answers to his questions about the singer. "Then who might be able to direct me? It is imperative I find this woman." And quickly.

Before coming to the station, he'd sent a second message to Burke, instructing him to promise the shipwright whatever was necessary to keep him working until Sloan could return to Missouri. He also told him to hire the stablehand named Rock, who'd rowed the little boat for him when he searched for Fanny's body, as a watchman. The man's intimidating size should prevent another invasion on his riverboat. Burke was dependable, but he wasn't the captain. Sloan was needed there.

The tall-as-Lincoln man with straight blond hair poking out from beneath his cap scratched his jaw. "Well, I reckon you could ask the ticket-booth clerk. It's been a while since that gal came through here, but ol' Rufus has an eye for a pretty girl." The man leaned in and winked. "He's had three reprimands for holdin' up the line to flirt." He straightened and shrugged. "I don't know what else to tell you, 'cept to say she sure could sing."

Irritation and impatience creating a maelstrom in his gut, Sloan strode off without a thank-you for the information. A line of no less than two dozen people already waited in front of the ticket window. Grumbling to himself, he marched to the rear of the line and took his position. A stout wind peppered him with dust and grit. The combination of people's chatter, train wheels squealing, luggage thudding onto wooden carts, and sporadic whistling blasts created such a cacophony, Sloan only wanted to escape. Should he give up this search? The *River Peacock* was his sanctuary, his peaceful place. It seemed he'd been away from it forever.

As the line slowly moved forward, bringing him closer to the ticket counter, he debated with himself. Continue searching for the singer with a voice like a nightingale, or settle for one of those he'd auditioned and return to the *River Peacock*? He was leaning heavily toward buying a ticket for Jefferson City when he reached the window.

The man on the other side of the counter didn't even look up. "Destination, please."

"I'm not sure." Sloan surprised himself with his response. The pull of this mysterious singer was stronger than he'd realized.

The man lifted his head and fixed Sloan with a frown. "Well, unless you know, mister, there's not much I can do for you."

"There's plenty you can do." Sloan dropped his bag, slipped a coin from his vest pocket, and rested both elbows on the counter. He held the gold half eagle between his fingers and tapped it on the counter. "Two or three weeks ago, a woman came through this depot. A woman with a beautiful singing voice. Do you remember her?"

The clerk ogled the coin. "Hard to forget someone like that."

Hope ignited in Sloan's chest. "Tell me what you remember."

"You mean besides her having a voice that held folks up just to listen to her sing?" The man pinched his chin and rolled his gaze upward. "She was pretty. No, she was beautiful. Had a profile that belonged on an ivory cameo. Full rosy lips, and brown eyes all flecked with gold. I reckon if her hair'd been clean, it would've had strands of reddish-gold in the brown. Yes, sir. A real beauty."

A picture formed in Sloan's mind. A familiar one. His frame went hot.

The ticket agent's smirking gaze landed on Sloan. "If she hadn't looked an' smelled like she'd been living in a barn, I would've been sorely tempted to —"

Sloan didn't need to hear the man's intentions. "To where did she purchase a ticket?"

The man propped one arm on the counter, shaking his head. "Now, that was a strange thing. She asked for a whole passel of tickets for Milwaukee, Wisconsin" —

Milwaukee? Multiple tickets?

— "and one for New York City."

The suspicion that had been budding in the back of Sloan's mind now exploded into a full bloom. The tickets to Wisconsin puzzled him, but the other made perfect sense. He abruptly straightened. "She bought a ticket and left for New York City?"

"No, no." The man waved his hand. "She was out of money, I guess, after buying all the tickets to Wisconsin. She bought a ticket for Baileytown, Indiana."

Sloan slapped the coin into the clerk's

palm. "One ticket to Baileytown. And keep the change." He drummed his fingers on the edge of the counter while waiting for the agent to stamp his ticket. No wonder people said the singer's voice was so extraordinary. He didn't know how she'd survived the fall from the boat. He didn't know how she'd made it clear to Indiana. He didn't know why she'd passed herself off as a married woman or bought "a passel" of tickets for Milwaukee. But he'd put the *River Peacock* up for sale if the person he'd been chasing wasn't Fanny Beck herself.

The Kuhn Homestead
Walter

Before coming in for supper, Walter dipped water from the rain barrel into a small basin and carried it to the barn. He kept the last bar of Grete's homemade lye soap in there for his Saturday-night allover bath. He made good use of it, soaping his face and neck and his arms clear up to his elbows. The strong smell erased the odor of sweat clinging to him.

When Grete was alive, she set a basin and soap out on the stoop for his use. After she died, he put the basin in the barn and set aside the habit. He was too tired, maybe even too heart-sore, to care if he smelled good or not, was dirty or not. And his Liébling didn't care. But now, with Fanny there, no matter how tired he was, he washed up. He did it for the same reason he'd done it when Grete was alive — out of respect for the one who kept things tidy.

Whistling a tune he made up himself, he emptied the pan of dirty water behind the barn. As he went to return it to its spot on the worktable, he glanced in the chickens' pans. A smile tugged at his lips, making the tune go flat. A few dried corn kernels remained in one, and the other held water that looked fresh. They'd been cared for. No matter what other chores kept her busy, Fanny never neglected those clucking birds. She'd even named them — Hildy and Tildy. He hoped no fox or possum stole away with either of the chickens. Fanny would be heartbroken.

The roll of wire fencing Josephine brought from the Feed and Seed in Gideon lay against the barn's foundation near the coop, waiting to be put up. He paused, stilling his whistle, and stared at the roll. He'd need at least six fence posts, sturdy ties to fasten the wire to the posts, and some sort of gate so Fanny could go in and out — a full day's work, for sure. It'd be a while before he could set aside a day to commit to it. But it would keep.

He entered the barn and clanked the basin on the worktable, then set off for the cabin. The front door stood open, and surprisingly good smells escaped, inviting him in. He stepped inside, then paused. The sight of Annaliese in her chair, cheerfully chewing on a spoon, and Fanny leaning over a pot at the fireplace, combined with the rich, savory aroma filling the small space, made something warm and pleasant well in his chest. He stayed just inside the threshold and pondered the feeling. He couldn't attach a word to it, but it was good. It felt right.

Annaliese broke into a huge grin and banged the spoon on the table. "Fa, Fa, Fa."

Fanny rose and turned around, surprise on her heat-flushed face. "There you are." She pushed a few damp squiggles of hair away from her forehead with her wrist. "I thought maybe you got lost between the field and the cabin. I saw you coming quite a while ago."

He laughed softly and crossed to Annaliese. He played with the little curl above her ear. "I was looking at the chicken wire and planning what I need to put up the fence."

She nodded and bent toward the fire again. "And did you complete your plan?"

The question was so wifely that a knot filled Walter's throat. "Yes. I think I did. But it will have to wait some. I'm going to work at Sanderson's again tomorrow and Friday. Hugh and I got his crop in for him, but there is some damage to the roof of his springhouse. Instead of only fixing it, he wants a new roof put on. I said I would do it for him." Sanderson promised to pay him three dollars. Added to the two he had in his pocket, he was building a nice amount in his can out in the barn.

Annaliese stirred the air with the spoon, chanting, "Fa, Fa."

Fanny smiled over her shoulder. "That is her name for you. I've never heard a wee one call her father 'Fa.' It's clever of her."

Pride swelled in Walter's chest. He perched on the stool next to Annaliese's chair and rubbed her back while she played with the spoon. "She's trying to say 'Vater,' I think, but it's too much for her yet. Just as Fanny is too much, so she calls you 'Nee.' "

Fanny carried a pot from the fireplace to the dry sink. "She knows what the words mean, though, even if she can't say them." She settled an affectionate smile on the baby. "She's a very smart, bonny hen."

Walter raised his eyebrows. "Hen?"

Fanny's laughter spilled. She spooned

sticky rice onto plates. "Not one with pinfeathers and a beak. In Scotland, 'hen' is a girl. I said she's a smart, pretty girl."

"Ah." Walter nodded. "In my native language, we would say, *intelligentes, hübsches Mädchen.*"

Fanny paused and shot him a puzzled look. "If German is your native language, when did you learn to speak English?"

"In school." He toyed with the curl above Annaliese's ear. "My parents insisted I learn it. English is the language of America, and we are now Americans."

Fanny returned to the fire and picked up a skillet. She dipped gravy from the skillet and poured it over the rice. "Josephine told me you are a learned man. That you attended school through your twelfth year."

He stood and plucked silverware from the crock on the corner of the dry sink. "My parents wanted me to have a good education, something I wouldn't have had in Germany." He laid the silverware on the table, glancing at her between placing the forks and spoons. "Where did you go to school?"

An odd look flitted across her face. She lowered her head and brought the filled plates to the table. "I didn't go to school. I learned from a tutor."

The answer surprised him. Her speech and intelligence indicated a sound education. But Josephine had said Fanny had been held against her will. He'd envisioned her trapped in a dungeon of sorts. A tutor didn't fit with his imagining. "In Scotland?"

"On the *River Peacock*." She sat on her stool, a nervous smile trembling on her lips. "The food will grow cold if we don't eat. And our bonny Annaliese is hungry, so will you pray, please?"

Walter sat and bowed his head. He stammered through his prayer of gratitude for the food, though. Her choice of words — *"our bonny Annaliese"* — rang in his head, the possessive *our* reverberating like the tolling of a church bell. Fanny had paired herself with Annaliese with the statement. But with a common three-letter pronoun, she'd also paired herself with him.

Fanny

She'd heard Walter pray many times since her arrival at his cabin. She'd never before heard him stumble over words. She knew the reason. *Our,* she'd said. Not *your* bonny Annaliese, but *our* bonny Annaliese. And Annaliese, no matter how much Fanny had grown to love the little girl, was not hers to claim. She'd made him uncomfortable, but he was too kind to say so. It didn't matter. His stutter said it all.

As she ate, she silently chastised herself. His relaxed demeanor as he'd walked toward the homestead, their easy conversation as she prepared dinner, and their shared affection for the curly-haired, blue-eyed baby now making a mess of her rice and gravy had lowered her guard. Of course, she'd already been lowering her guard all week, spending so much time with Josephine.

She jerked her head up. "Oh!"

Walter jolted, and a few grains of rice fell from his spoon onto the table. He pinched them up and put them on his plate, then looked at her. "What is it?"

No condemnation, only curiosity, lit his stunning blue eyes. She swallowed. "Josephine invited me — you — *us* — to eat with them after church this coming Sunday." Now *she* was stuttering. She drew a breath to steady her nerves. "She said she would cook some of the pork chops Mr. Sanderson gave to Hugh in exchange for his work."

Walter gazed at her, unmoving, for several seconds. Then he nodded and spooned another bite. "I am not surprised she made the invitation. Especially after they ate here last week. They and we . . ."

Although the sentence trailed off, Fanny finished it in her head. She might as well divulge what Josephine had told her. "She said you and Grete had meals at their home many Sundays."

He peeked at her, his head low. "Ja, we did."

Fanny gathered her courage. "But if you would rather take Annaliese and go . . . without me, I'll understand. If getting together with the Moores was something special between them and you and Grete, I don't want to intrude upon it."

He sat up and fully faced her. "You are not an intrusion, Fanny. You are doing me a favor by staying. By loving Annaliese. By taking care of the household duties and the chickens and the milk and" — he shrugged — "everything else. Of course you should go. Josephine invited you. It wouldn't be kind to stay away. Unless . . ." He tilted his head slightly, his brows descending. "Unless you want to stay away. To have time for yourself."

She blurted the first thing that popped into her head. "I have had time to myself to last the remainder of my days. I don't want to stay here all alone."

The curiosity she'd witnessed earlier in his expression returned, and she braced herself for the questions that were sure to come. But to her surprise, he smiled and nodded.

"Then we'll all go on Sunday. And I hope you will wear your new dress."

29

MISHAWAKA, INDIANA
SLOAN

The echoing *bong-bong-bong* of a steeple bell awakened Sloan from a restless sleep. He rolled over, groaning. Last night he'd been thankful that if he had to be stuck overnight in a town — why couldn't the trains run on Sunday, too? — at least this one had a tavern. He'd never been one to indulge in alcohol. Alcohol rendered men insensible, and Sloan always wanted to be in control of his senses. But for the first time in his forty-four years of life, he'd gotten himself rip-roarin' drunk.

For a few hours, he'd forgotten the damage to his riverboat, forgotten how he'd been hoodwinked by Fanny, forgotten every frustration from the past five weeks. It had been marvelous. But now morning sunlight streamed past the lace curtain on the hotel window and attacked his eyeballs, restoring his memory and raising a fierce, pulsing throb in the top of his skull. He slid his feet to the floor and clumsily sat up. His head felt as if it weighed fifty pounds. He would never have downed those pints of malt liquor were it not for the anger seeping through every pore of his body. She'd duped him.

All these weeks, snippets from the letters her sister had written had tormented him with guilt and sorrow. He'd felt sorry about the years she'd spent away from family, without friends to call her own. Felt sorry for never considering she had needs beyond the bounds of the *River Peacock.* He'd felt guilty that her life ended before she had the chance to experience the joy of courtship, of motherhood, of reuniting with her parents.

Those emotions mocked him now. But he'd get the upper hand again. He was on her trail. At each of the seven stops since he'd left Chicago, someone had shared a variation of the story he'd heard from Lorna about a beautiful but disheveled young woman who sang with a distinct and pure voice. The newest stories added a detail that helped explain how she was making her way across the country toward New York. Fanny was begging, enticing people to drop coins into a tin cup by singing to them.

He growled under his breath and pushed

to his feet. He wobbled a bit, gained his balance, and crossed to the water pitcher and bowl on the mirrored stand beside the door. He splashed tepid water on his face, then lifted his head. Bracing his palms on the edge of the stand, he stared at his image in the round mirror. Despite the pounding pain in his temples, he smiled at his reflection.

Fanny, the careless little songbird, was throwing out a trail of bread crumbs for him to follow. He would follow until he found her. And when he found her, he would bring her back to the *River Peacock* with him. No more feeling guilty. She would serve every day of the thirty-five years to which her father had unwittingly agreed. No one bested Sloan Kirkpatrick. Not without paying dearly.

His smile turned into a grimace of pain. Oh, his head. Such an incredible ache. It couldn't hurt more if someone had plunged an ax into his scalp. He staggered back to the bed, flopped across it, and let sleep bring temporary escape.

The Moore Homestead
Fanny

Fanny couldn't recall the last time she had so reveled in a day. Every little bit of it —

from Walter complimenting her spring-flowered new dress, to their peaceful walk to the chapel under a cloud-dotted sky of purest blue, to being asked to sing "Sweet Hour of Prayer" after Reverend Lee's sermon about the importance of talking often to one's Maker, to laughter and conversation around the Moores' table — held moments to seal away in her memory and cherish. Even now, performing the tedious task of washing the dishes, pots, and pans was pleasant because she chatted with Josephine while they worked. Her heart held so much joy she thought it would surely burst.

The men had wandered out to the barn when the women began cleaning up, and they'd taken Annaliese with them. Hugh wanted Walter to see the new calf born only yesterday, and Walter wanted Annaliese to see it. According to Josephine, there was a litter of kittens somewhere in the barn, too.

"Our ol' calico kitty, Patches, has 'em hid out there. Her tummy's not round an' tight anymore," she'd said with a little sigh. As soon as they put the clean dishes away, Josephine promised to take Fanny to the barn and locate the litter. "Wouldn't Annaliese like to have a little kitty at your place?"

Fanny's heart thrummed at Josephine's choice of words even though she knew

Walter's cabin wasn't her place. That thought briefly cast a pall over the otherwise bright day, but she refused to dwell on it. Her time in Indiana might be temporary, but Walter's cabin seemed more of a home to her than her room on the *River Peacock* had ever been. She should savor being part of the community of Gideon and, no matter how unconventional her standing, being part of Walter's family.

Josephine slid the last green-speckled plate onto the shelf and turned to Fanny with a big smile. "An' that's that. Work's done. Now we can play." She hung the damp towels and dishrag on nails pounded into the log wall, then looped arms with Fanny. "After we've found the kittens, I'd like to take a walk through the meadow northeast of our place. Wildflowers are bloomin' all over out there. I've spotted touch-me-nots, lady's slippers, snow trillium, Dutchman's-breeches, Royal Catchfly, Indian pipe, jack-in-the-pulpit, rattlesnake master, bloodroot, an' shooting star. Oh, the colors of 'em all together makes me think of what heaven's gonna look like. I want a bouquet to put on the table. Flowers liven up a room, don't you think?"

"I do." Fanny wasn't familiar with the flower names, but Josephine's enthusiasm was contagious. She wanted a bouquet to take home and put in the middle of the table. Or maybe on the fireplace mantel. Or even on the little table beside the bed. She tamped down her desire. "I should ask Walter if it's all right for me to go. Annaliese will need a nap, and he might want to leave when he knows we've finished washing the dishes."

"*Pffft.*" Josephine flicked her hand as if shooing flies. "Walter can put Annaliese down in our bed, an' him an' Hugh can sit on the porch an' jaw while they whittle. Or Hugh might wheedle him into playin' the new board game he got. I don't like it much. It's supposed to be about life, but there's squares your game piece lands on that say you've gone to ruin by gamblin' or you've been disgraced or even sent to prison." She made a sour face and shook her head. "What's the fun in that? I told Hugh I wasn't gonna play it, but Walter might since him an' Hugh played dominoes last week. It'll keep 'em busy for a long time. Long enough for us to mosey through the meadow an' pick flowers."

They entered the barn, which matched Walter's in size but boasted six stalls instead of only two. Its windows — one centered on the back and two on each side — made it much brighter inside. Had there been windows in the barn that burned down? Did Walter intend to put windows in his new barn? With the walls chinked all the way to the top, the place was as dark as a tomb inside. She hoped he'd chop out some openings for windows.

Hugh and Walter were in the far corner of the barn. Annaliese sat on the top rail of a stall wall, with Walter's arm wrapped around her middle. She chortled and waved her hands up and down at something inside the stall.

When Fanny stepped close and looked into the partitioned area, she couldn't resist a little gasp of delight. "Oh, what a darling baby."

The mama cow munched from a box at the wall side of the stall, and the calf lay on a carpet of clean hay, its feet tucked under its chest. The calf, with its big brown eyes in a tan-and-white face, peered up at Annaliese as if studying her.

Fanny curled her hands over the top rail and went up on tiptoe to better see the new arrival. "Is it a girl or a boy?"

"A bull." Hugh bounced his palm on the rail, disappointment pursing his face. "I've always planned to build a small dairy herd. Bulls don't give milk, so he ain't gonna be much help." Then he shrugged and brightened. "But I reckon I can sell him an' buy a little heifer or maybe trade with someone who wants a cow to butcher."

Fanny couldn't imagine butchering something so precious, and she started to say so.

Josephine touched her arm. "You gonna ask Walter about us goin' to the meadow?"

Walter lifted Annaliese from the rail and held her on his hip. She rested her head on his shoulder and tucked two fingers in her mouth. He swayed side to side and sent Fanny a curious look. "What's this about the meadow?"

"Josephine wants to pick wildflowers for a bouquet. I'd like to go with her. But I won't if you're ready to go back to the cabin."

Hugh stepped around Walter, grinning. "He's not leavin' yet. After he skunked me last week at dominoes, I aim to stomp him good at The Checkered Game of Life."

Josephine nudged Fanny and snickered. Fanny hid a smile.

Walter smirked at his friend, then turned to Fanny. "I guess you and Josephine are going to the meadow."

She held her arms to Annaliese. "Do you want me to take her?"

He shook his head. "No sense in dragging her out there when she's ready for a nap.

I'll put her down somewhere."

"On our bed," Josephine said.

Walter smiled at her. "Thank you." He turned to Fanny again. "She'll be fine."

"By the way," Hugh said, "I found where Patches hid her babies this time. They're in the loft. Remember the crate where I store the old blankets an' such I use for the animals when it gets so cold? The crazy cat made a nest of some sort behind it on a wadded-up burlap sack."

Josephine's face lit. "How many?"

"Five. One looks just like her, and then there's a couple all-white ones an' a pair of brown tabbies." He glanced upward. "They're safe for now, but they're gonna need to come down from there. They get big enough to wander, they could fall over the edge. That'll be another week or so, I speculate. I'll keep checkin', an' when I'm worried, I'll move her nest."

Fanny's heart warmed toward the tall, broad-shouldered man. Compared to Walter's slighter frame and shorter stature, Hugh appeared big and tough. But underneath he had a gentle heart. She'd seen it in how he related to Annaliese and now in his concern for a batch of barn kittens. Impulsively she reached out and touched the cuff of his Sunday shirt. "Thank you for caring about the kittens. You'll be a good da some-day."

He ducked his head, but not before she saw moisture glimmer in his eyes. He scuffed his toe against the barn floor, stirring hay. "Thanks, Fanny. I hope to be."

Josephine turned toward the wide-open doorway. "Let me grab the egg basket. It should hold enough flowers for two bouquets. Then we'll go." Her voice lacked its former eagerness, raising concern in the back of Fanny's mind.

Fanny walked alongside Josephine. They followed a path of flattened grass leading behind the barn, past the corral, and beyond the Moores' cornfield. Josephine swung the basket, a seemingly carefree action, but her lips stayed in a firm line. Her cheerful chatter of earlier was stilled.

What had trampled Josephine's enthusiasm about scouring the meadow for a bouquet? Fanny stayed quiet for as long as she could, but the silence reminded her too much of the years she'd spent with no voice but her own for company. She came to a stop and caught hold of Josephine's elbow.

Josephine stopped, too, and turned a mild frown on Fanny. "What?"

"Why are you being so quiet?" Fanny released a nervous laugh. "Josephine, you're never quiet."

Josephine turned her face away, giving Fanny a view of her profile. Her chin quivered. "I'm not bein' quiet inside my head. I'm hollerin' an' fussin' an' askin' all kinds of questions." She looked at Fanny, and tears swam in her hazel eyes. "I'm spittin' mad. What you said in the barn about Hugh bein' a good — What did you call it?"

"Da," Fanny said.

"Yes. Da. You're right. He'd be a good da. I'd be a good ma." The tears spilled. "We both want a family so bad, but all the prayin' we've done don't seem to go anywhere. Reverend Lee talked about prayer in his sermon today, an' even the song you sang said how God bears our petitions an' blesses the soul of the one who calls out to Him. Well, I've been callin' an' callin'. Where's my blessing? Why are my arms still empty? Why ain't Hugh a papa yet? It ain't fair, Fanny."

Fanny lunged forward and captured Josephine in a hug. Josephine dropped the basket and clung to Fanny, her shoulders shaking with the force of her sobs. Fanny patted her back and inwardly begged God to comfort her hurting friend. She longed for words of wisdom that would bring hope and comfort, but she had none to offer. So she held tight and prayed until Josephine's sobs came to a shuddering stop.

Josephine pulled loose and used her apron skirt to clean her face. "I'm sorry. I shouldn't have put all that on you. While I was cryin', I remembered you've had hard times, too. Harder'n mine, I reckon, bein' locked away from your family for so long. I don't know how you keep smilin' when inside you've gotta be achin' to see your folks an' your sisters."

The ache was always there. "I am." A realization dawned in her mind, and she grabbed Josephine's hands. "Josephine, remember when you told me I'm" — she glanced aside, shyness striking — "Walter's godsend?"

Josephine nodded.

Fanny looked into Josephine's eyes. "You're *mine.* You've helped me so much. You didn't have to teach me to bake bread or give me the fabric to sew a dress, but you did. And in so doing, you became the answer to a prayer I've had for years — to have a friend."

Josephine's lips turned down in a sympathetic pucker. "There wasn't anybody on the riverboat who was your friend?"

"No one." Fanny blinked hard and fast, holding tears at bay. She didn't want to go back to the *River Peacock* in her memory, but she couldn't tell Josephine how much her friendship meant without doing so. She took a deep breath. "The loneliness . . ." Her breath whooshed out. "Sometimes I thought I would shrivel and die from it. I begged God to help me escape it — both the boat and the horrible burden of loneliness. He answered. Not right away. He waited until the time was just right."

Awe bloomed anew as she considered being swept to the riverbank where Dathan and Kircie would find her. If He'd answered sooner, she wouldn't have met Enoch's family. She would be forever grateful for the time she'd spent with them.

More amazing happenings, proof of God's fingers guiding her, found their way from her heart to her lips. "If not for God's timing, I wouldn't have come upon Walter's cabin at the exact hour when little Annaliese was crying. I wouldn't have met you." She took Josephine's hands. "I've had so many blessings. God answered my prayers for escape and for friendship, and He answered them exactly the way they should be. Exactly when it was right." Fanny squeezed her friend's hands. "That's why I know He'll answer your prayers, too. I don't know when, I don't know how, but I know He will answer the cry of your heart."

Words from the morning's hymn she'd sung rang through her heart, and she sang, " 'With such I hasten to the place where God my Savior shows His face, and gladly take my station there and wait for Thee, sweet hour of prayer!' "

A smile quavered on Josephine's lips. "I don't know how you can't be mad at God after you were left holed up all alone for so long."

Another revelation whispered through Fanny's heart. "Maybe all those years by myself with only God to talk to let me understand better than most that He is with us."

Josephine tugged Fanny's hands. "Would you pray with me now, Fanny?"

"I will."

Together they knelt and spent sweet time in prayer.

30

THE KUHN HOMESTEAD
FANNY

Monday, as Fanny gave the cabin a thorough cleaning, her mind continually wandered. When they'd left the Moores' cabin yesterday evening, Josephine reminded her to make her shopping list because she'd pick up Fanny on Thursday morning after breakfast for a visit to Gideon's mercantile. Although Josephine didn't say so, Fanny knew that a visit to the mercantile meant they would also go by the post office.

As she scrubbed smoke residue from the fireplace mantel, a question she didn't want answered plagued her. Would a letter from Walter's parents, with word about his new wife, be waiting? She should hope so. More than hoping, she should pray so. Walter had waited long enough. The new wife's arrival would free Fanny from her commitment and let her go on to New York. She hadn't been in Walter's employ long enough to earn the full train fare, but God had brought her this far. She trusted He would take her the remainder of the way. But did she want to go?

She dipped the cloth in the bucket of warm, sudsy water sitting on the table, wrung it out with a vicious twist intended to squeeze the unsettling question from her mind, then returned to the mantel. Of course she wanted to see her parents and sisters. Hadn't she spent the last seven years pining for their presence? Why *wouldn't* she want to continue her journey to them?

From the corner where Annaliese played with her beloved rag doll, a stream of happy babbles flowed. A smile tugged on Fanny's lips, and she paused to observe the little girl. Sunlight spilling through the window turned Annaliese's blond curls into a halo of white. She sat in the spot where Fanny had first seen her, but the barrier was gone, giving her the freedom to get up and move wherever she pleased in the cabin. She seemed content, though, on the little patch of sunlit, rock-hard earth with her blocks, her doll, and a plate and spoon Fanny had given her to pretend to feed her dolly. Annaliese used the latter two as a drum and mallet instead, but Fanny didn't mind. Nothing the little girl did bothered Fanny because she loved Annaliese so much.

A lump filled her throat. She dropped the cloth on the mantel and crossed to the baby. She crouched and ran her fingers through the silky yellow curls, smiled in response to Annaliese's precious crinkled-nose grin, and whispered, "Oh, my bonny hen, how will I find the courage to leave you behind?"

She rose and crossed to the open doorway, then stepped out onto the rock slab and gazed across the rolling landscape. Images of the scene outside her family's little cottage near Inverness bounced in her memory, so similar to the view she now relished. The explosion of colors — verdant grass dotted with pink, yellow, and lavender wildflowers spread beneath a robin's-egg-blue sky — sang to her heart. After experiencing the joy of this vast expanse, how would she contentedly live in a cramped apartment in a crowded city? She hadn't yet seen it with her own eyes, but the descriptions Flossie had given in her letters painted a picture in Fanny's mind.

A shiver rattled her frame, and she hugged herself. Would the home waiting in New York City remind her of her dark, confined room on the *River Peacock*? She gave herself a mental shake. It wouldn't be like the *River Peacock* because she wouldn't be alone. Her family would be with her. And even if the apartment was small and crowded, she would live free, no longer under Sloan's control. She would be fine in New York. She shouldn't think otherwise. Yet even as she returned to her chores, humming as she worked, she couldn't erase the disquieting sense of apprehension lurking in her heart.

Walter peeked in the door at noon with a sheepish grin. "My boots and pant legs are muddy. Last night's rain turned the field into a mess."

Fanny jolted, her pulse skipping a beat. "It rained last night?"

Walter nodded, wariness in his blue eyes. "Ja. A very gentle rain. A peaceful rain."

A peaceful rain. Like the rains that had moistened Ma's garden and coaxed wildflowers to open their buds. A good kind of rain. His gaze was locked on her, as if waiting for a frightened outburst. But none rose. She sent up a silent thank-you to God for a peaceful night and for this peace-filled day. "I must have slept through it."

A smile lifted the corners of his mustache. "You must have. That's good."

Indeed, it was.

He lifted one foot, and Fanny's mouth fell open at the thick coating of drying muck hiding his boot from view. He set his foot down again, losing a few small chunks of dried mud, and shrugged. "I suspect you don't want me in the house since you've been cleaning."

"You suspect correctly." She put her hands on her hips and tsk-tsked. "I suppose we're forced to have another picnic on the stoop."

His shoulders jerked back, and his expression changed to boyish eagerness.

She tilted her head, daring to tease, "Does that suit you, Mr. Kuhn?"

"It does. I'll go wash up at the well." He held up his hands and gave them a rueful grimace. "I might be a while."

She couldn't hold back a chortle. "Take as much time as you need. I was so busy cleaning I lost track of time. I'll make some sandwiches, and Annaliese and I will join you on the stoop when they're done."

"Thank you, Fanny." He trudged out of sight.

Fanny hurriedly sliced one of the loaves of bread she'd baked on Saturday. The loaves weren't nearly as pretty as the ones from the dough Josephine kneaded, but they were edible and Josephine assured her she'd get better with practice. She spread creamy butter churned only that morning onto each slice, then cut thick slices from the remaining wedge of the ring of cheese. She should put cheese on Thursday's shopping list.

After layering cheese between the slices of buttered bread, she stacked the sandwiches on a plate and turned a smile on Annaliese. "Come, my wee bairn. Let's go have lunch with your fa."

Annaliese pushed her palms on the ground, poked her bottom into the air, and rose. She toddled to Fanny, one hand reaching.

"My hands are full, Annaliese." Fanny bobbed the plate. "See?"

Annaliese squawked and flapped her hand at Fanny. For someone with few words, she communicated very well.

Fanny swallowed an amused chuckle. "I know you like holding my hand. I like holding your hand, too. But you'll have to follow me. Come along now. You can sit in my lap while we eat."

Annaliese jerked her hand down, then plopped onto her bottom and began to cry.

Walter appeared in the doorway. "What's wrong?"

Fanny shrugged. "She wanted to hold my hand, but . . ." She glanced at her full hands.

"Let me take that for you." He reached over the threshold and took hold of the plate.

"Thank you." Fanny turned to Annaliese.

"All right, bonny hen. I'll hold your hand now."

Annaliese kicked her heels against the floor and continued to wail.

Fanny recalled Ma handling wee Moira's tantrums. She stepped past the squalling child and poured milk into cups from the pitcher, talking as she did so. "Oh, such a nice day for a picnic. The cheese sandwiches will taste so good with this milk. My, won't Fa and Nee have a pleasant time eating together under the sunshine on this pretty day?"

Hooking the cups' handles with her fingers, she glanced at Annaliese. The little girl blinked up at Fanny, her lower lip quivering and plump tears wobbling on her thick lashes. Fanny headed to the door as if Annaliese wasn't sitting in the way. Fanny moved out onto the stoop, where Walter sat with his feet in the grass and the plate of sandwiches beside his knee.

"Are you ready for our picnic, Walter?"

He peeked through the doorway at his pouting daughter, then stroked his scrubbed-clean fingers through his beard, his eyes twinkling. "I am."

Fanny handed him the cups of milk and then sat, bending her legs to the side. "Would you like to say grace?"

He bowed his head.

Before closing her eyes, Fanny sneaked a glance at Annaliese and caught the little girl pushing to her feet.

Walter finished with a rumbling "Amen," and Fanny opened her eyes. Annaliese stood beside her, her big blue eyes fixed on Fanny's face.

Fanny smiled. "Oh, good. Annaliese has chosen to join our picnic." She lifted the child into her lap and kissed her tousled curls, then looked up and found Walter gazing at her with something unreadable yet captivating and shining in his beautiful eyes. She found herself caught by his expression, as if he'd bewitched her. Awareness climbed her spine like a spider scurrying up its rope of silk, and she quickly turned her attention to the plate of sandwiches.

"Walter, help yourself. When we've finished the sandwiches, we can have the pieces of apple pie Josephine sent with me last night."

Her casual words seemed to break whatever spell had woven itself around them. He lowered his gaze to the sandwiches, took one, and carried it to his mouth. "Save the pie for supper." He spoke around the bite of sandwich. "I want to get back to the field as quickly as possible."

He'd told her at breakfast that he planned to weed the cornfield. She remembered Ma diligently hacking away every weed from their garden lest they choke out the vegetable plants. She broke off a small piece of sandwich and gave it to Annaliese. "Are there lots of weeds?"

"Not an overabundance. And the ground is soft from last night's rain. The softened ground makes it easy to chop the weeds out, but its sloppiness is slowing me down." He took a bite, followed by a regret-laden sigh. "I'd hoped to have the whole acreage weeded in one day, but I think I'll need tomorrow, too."

Fanny smiled, hoping to encourage him. "Do what you can. There's no rule that says you must weed an entire cornfield in one day."

He chuckled, giving her spirits a lift. "You are right about there not being a written rule. But when there's a fence to be built for the new chickens that are coming on Friday, it's best to get it done as quickly as possible."

She released a little cry of delight.

He grinned. "Did I forget to tell you the new chickens are coming on Friday?"

She laughed. "You know very well you didn't mention it." She bounced Annaliese and tipped her head to peer into the little girl's face. "Did you hear your fa, Annaliese? He says more chickens are coming soon. Won't we have fun taking care of them and gathering their eggs?"

Like a storm cloud rolling in, sorrow descended. How many days would she be there to see to these new chickens? Thursday's mail might bring word of Walter's new wife, and if the woman was on her way, she would take care of the flock with little Annaliese's help, not Fanny. The joy of the picnic shattered.

Walter

Walter waited several seconds, but Fanny didn't look up. Where had her cheerful countenance gone? He'd been enjoying their conversation, had deliberately dropped the surprise about the chickens in order to please her, and he'd seen happiness ignite the golden flecks in her brown eyes. But as quickly as it rose, it departed. Was the scent of the rain-dampened ground taking her back to a place of terror again? Maybe she should go inside the cabin.

He tapped her knee. "Is something wrong?"

"Not a thing." She spoke quickly. Too quickly. She meticulously broke off bits of

408

bread and cheese for Annaliese, who sat contentedly in her lap.

"Are you sure?" Women could be moody. He'd learned this while growing up with his sisters and then living with Grete. "If I said something to —"

"You said nothing for which to apologize." Her face lifted, and a weak smile curved her lips. The smile did not reach her eyes. "We both have much work left to do. Maybe we should finish eating and return to our chores."

She was hiding something. He wanted to know what, but he tamped down questioning her further. She might tell him something he didn't want to hear. He nodded. "You are right."

They finished eating in silence. Walter drained his cup of milk, swiped his mouth with the back of his hand, and stood. He usually gave Annaliese a farewell hug or kiss, but with her nestled in Fanny's lap, he would have to lean improperly close to Fanny. He remained upright. "Have a good afternoon, Fanny."

She glanced up. "You, too, Walter."

So formal. He took one step in the direction of the field.

"Oh, Walter?"

He turned back, hopefulness fluttering in

his chest. "Yes?"

"Josephine is taking me to town on Thursday."

He nodded, puzzled by her flat tone.

"I'll make a list of things we need for the kitchen. If there are things you need, would you please write them down for me so I can be sure to . . ."

He waited, but she didn't complete her sentence. He couldn't think of anything right then. He cleared his throat. "Yes, I will do that."

She set Annaliese on the stoop and stood. "Thank you."

"You're welcome."

She stacked the cups on the empty plate, picked it up, and entered the cabin. Annaliese followed her. He remained in place for a few seconds, frowning after them, then headed for the field. What had created her strange shift from delighted to dismal? What had they been talking about when her mood changed? Ah, yes, the new chickens. He had no doubt she'd name each one and spoil them with leftovers from their table and gentle strokes on their backs, the way she did with Hildy and Tildy.

Such a tender soul. His heart swelled as he recalled her means of dealing with Annaliese's little fit of temper. Some might yank a child to her feet and demand she behave, or even deliver a smack on her behind. But Fanny chose a patient response. A soft chuckle left his throat. She was a good mother.

He halted so quickly his soles slid on the rain-dampened grass. He spun around and gawked at the cabin where, right now, Fanny was probably rocking his Liébling to sleep for her afternoon nap. Despondence bore down on him the same way he'd witnessed it descend on Fanny.

He wanted her to stay. He wanted her to stay for Annaliese, but even more, he wanted her to stay for him. His pulse throbbed with the realization that somehow, in a very short period of time, Fanny had worked her way into the center of his heart. An ache settled there, squeezing as if a giant fist had taken hold. His entire frame strained toward the cabin, the desire to take her in his arms and tell her how he felt tingling within him from head to toe.

But he shouldn't tell her. She wanted to go to her family. He'd already pledged himself to an unknown woman from New York.

He let his head drop back, and he closed his eyes and groaned. For months, he, Hugh, and Josephine had been praying for

411

Walter's new wife to come. They'd prayed for his and the new wife's hearts to mesh, as God intended for a man and wife. Why, then, had God allowed his heart to open to a woman who would eventually leave? It must be punishment for his cowardice in not running into the barn to rescue Grete. And his cowardice would hold back the words he longed to say to Fanny.

31

ELKHART, INDIANA
SLOAN

This made no sense. Only he and one other passenger had gotten off at the Elkhart depot, and two more had gotten on before the train chugged its way out of the station. The lack of activity gave Sloan the freedom to pace back and forth in front of the tiny brick depot without interruption of his thoughts. She had to have come this way. It was the route a traveler would take to get to New York. The map on the wall, as well as the stationmaster's confirmation, proved it. A person who left Mishawaka would arrive in Elkhart, just as he'd done. Yet no one — not any of the few station workers, nor any of the townsfolk he'd queried — remembered seeing a disheveled young woman with a beautiful face and memorable singing voice.

He inwardly cursed himself for losing a full day of searching. His splitting headache had kept him in bed all day Sunday. The sickness had convinced him he was not and would never be a drinking man. His lips twisted with self-derision. His father would be pleased with Sloan's discovery.

Unwilling to put his fouled clothes in his bag with clean ones, he'd sought a laundry on Monday morning, then spent most of the day waiting for the laundress to return the items to him. The delay, of course, caused him to miss the outgoing train for Elkhart. So here he was, midday on Tuesday, clearheaded but empty handed.

He crossed to the bench where he'd placed his travel bag upon disembarking from the Michigan Southern Railroad passenger car and eased onto the wooden seat. He squinted against the afternoon sun. He wasn't a stupid man. If he weren't so tired — and angry — he would have no trouble conjuring possible reasons for Fanny not to have stopped and sung at this station. He forced himself to set aside the fiery irritation burning in his chest and think.

With a grunt of aggravation, he slapped his thigh. Of course! How could such a simple answer elude him? She hadn't stopped. If she'd received enough money at the previous station to continue on, there'd have been no need for her to sing at this station.

Leaving his bag beneath the bench, he stomped to the ticket window. "I need to send a message to" — he consulted the map on the wall — "Goshen. Where might I find a telegrapher?"

The elderly clerk shrugged his skinny shoulders. "Right here in the depot, mister." He produced a piece of paper from a drawer under the counter and slid a pencil from behind his ear. He handed both items over. "Write it down, an' I'll send it for you."

Sloan scrawled,

HAS WOMAN PASSENGER SUNG FOR DONATIONS AT YOUR STATION STOP ADVISE IMMEDIATELY STOP

He shoved the paper and pencil at the man. "I'll wait over there for a response."

He tromped back to the bench and sat. Clamping his hands over his knees, he stared across the railroad tracks at a row of small square houses. One, painted white with green trim, resembled his boyhood home in Concord, Massachusetts. The smells from skillets or pots drifting on the breeze took him back to the dinner table in that house. His folks never had much money. Father's preaching barely drew a wage. Yet somehow Mother always managed to put a meal on the table. And Father always offered a prayer of gratitude for it. His father's solemn voice echoed in Sloan's memory. *"For these gifts of Thy bounty and in gratitude for the hands which prepared it, we thank Thee, our Lord and Master."*

His heart twisted in his chest. How he'd hated that prayer. Not the part acknowledging Mother's hands. She'd been a hard worker, always busy and serving. She deserved recognition. But bounty? Yes, the food had tasted good, and his stomach was always filled, but how could Father call their staples of beans, rice, mutton, and corn bread a bounty? Sloan had vowed when he left home he would never put another gristly chunk of mutton in his mouth. And he hadn't. Yet here he sat, breathing in the scent of food from a stranger's cookstove or fireplace, wondering if his folks were right now at their table, eating beans, mutton, and corn bread.

He rubbed his forehead with his thumb and forefinger. He must be tired if he was letting himself drift back to the house in Concord and its scarred, rickety table with its paltry offering. He launched himself from the bench and paced again, seeking an escape from his wandering thoughts. But they dogged him, as relentless as his pursuit

416

of Fanny.

Other words — these from one of Flossie's most recent letters — rose in his memory.

I cannot wait to lay sight on you, my dear sister. Such a reunion we will have when you are free again.

Sloan's feet stopped as if they had a mind of their own. *Free again . . . free again . . . free again . . .*

He stormed to the building and slammed his palm against the wood siding, stilling the echo in his mind. A growl built in his throat, and he let it emerge low and menacing. Fanny didn't deserve freedom after making him feel like a ninny. After bringing him to a place where he was taken to his parents' table in his recollections. Impatience built within him to find her, return to the *River Peacock,* and restore the life he'd known for the past decade. The best decade of his life.

The best decade? Was it really? The question drew him up short for a few seconds, and then he gave a fierce shake of his head. Of course it was. Wealth, popularity, prestige, and power were his, thanks to the success of his entertainment riverboat. He'd dreamed of such success when he was a boy forced to sit on a hard bench Sunday after Sunday and listen to his father preach from the pulpit about the riches of God's grace.

Sloan understood riches. His grandfather and grandmother Kirkpatrick's wealth was great. The summer weeks spent with them from the time he was six until he turned sixteen showed him the delights money could buy. He'd never comprehend why Father had abandoned monetary wealth to store up treasures in heaven. Sloan had experienced poverty and wealth, and he much preferred wealth. And he'd have it again, as soon as he laid his hands on Fanny.

"Mister?" The station agent poked his head from the window. "I got a response here."

Sloan hurried to the window, snatched the telegram from the man's hand, and read it. It only took a moment.

NO.

That's all it said. *No.* Had she made enough to go beyond this station to the next?

He crumpled the paper into a wad and glowered at the agent. "Send the same query to the next three stations along the line."

The agent shrugged. "Sure thing, mister."

Sloan returned to the bench and sank heavily onto the seat. She had to have gone this way. The only question was, how far had she made it? Worry mingled with fury created a foul taste in his mouth. She'd better not be too far ahead for him to catch up.

The Kuhn Homestead
Fanny

Tuesday. Washday. A day of scrubbing away the dust and sweat and stains of the former week. If only Fanny could scrub away the stain of guilt weighing upon her, heavier than the basket of wet bedding she carried across the grass to the row of bushes at the edge of Walter's property.

She walked at a snail's pace, mindful of Annaliese plodding along behind her. The little girl's short legs required twice as many steps as Fanny's to cover the same distance. The slower pace suited Fanny. She hadn't slept well last night. And she was ashamed of herself for it.

Hadn't she been praying for Walter's new wife to come? Hadn't she been praying that the woman would love little Annaliese as if the baby were her own? Hadn't she told Josephine that God answered prayers in the

419

best way, at the best time? So why was she worrying that word of Walter's new wife would be in his mail slot in Gideon? She might as well tell God He didn't know what He was doing. How disappointed Da and Ma would be with her for doubting God.

They reached the row of thick, leafy bushes. Fanny trudged all the way to the end of the row, past Annaliese's little frocks, napkins, and gowns and her own few clothing items spread out and catching the sunshine. She pulled a bedsheet from the basket, gave it several brisk snaps to release it from its tangled wad, and draped it over the green leaves.

When Walter offered to release her from their agreement, she'd known she was supposed to stay. The peace she experienced at the decision could have come only from the One who knew better than she what she should do. Was the absence of peace now plaguing her meant to propel her on to New York?

She wrestled a second sheet from the basket and shook it. The wind caught it, making it billow like a sail, and then it settled neatly across the bushes. Much the way she had settled into a routine in Walter's cabin.

She picked up the basket, carried it several

feet, and set it in the grass again. The quilt from her bed — from Walter's bed, she reminded herself — was next. She laid it out, admiring the patches of varying colors. Such a pretty quilt, bearing the colors of the grass, sky, sun, and clouds. The patches of greens, blues, yellows, and whites appeared so much brighter under the early-afternoon sunshine than they seemed in the cabin. Her gaze drifted back to the patches again and again as she continued placing damp items, one by one, over the thick clusters of leaves.

A fleeting thought trickled through her mind. Perhaps God brought her to Gideon for a time of enjoying the open expanse of nature. Being here had helped her soul heal from her lengthy time sealed away from the beautiful sights of His creation. She'd discovered the joy of friendship, relived some of her fondest childhood memories, and received the blessing of bestowing affection on a little someone who loved her in return.

A smile, a genuine one, pulled at the corners of her lips. She turned, gladness rising and washing away her doldrums. "Ah, my Annaliese, you —" She stilled, her smile fading. Where was Annaliese? Her heart fired into her throat. With her pulse galloping as if she'd just finished a footrace, she turned in a slow circle, her gaze searching every direction.

"Annaliese? Annaliese!" Hysteria built in her chest. She trotted up and down the line of bushes, peeking beneath the foliage as she went. No sign of a little blond head, a flowered dress, or tiny button-up shoes.

Continuing to call for the child, Fanny scanned the area. She forced herself to meticulously examine every square inch. Annaliese's little legs couldn't have carried her far. She had to be close by. Fanny tried to comfort herself, but the attempt proved useless. Her heart pounded so hard her entire frame trembled.

She pressed her fist to her mouth and held back a moan of despair. How could she have allowed the little girl to wander off? Why hadn't she paid better attention? How negligent she'd been, so caught up in fretting she'd forgotten to keep an eye on her precious little charge. It was full daylight, a time when animals were less likely to prowl, but even so, Annaliese was so small. So helpless. And she was lost on the prairie.

"Dear Lord in heaven, what have I done?" The prayer groaned from the depth of Fanny's soul. She didn't want to leave the area. What if Annaliese returned and couldn't find her Nee? But a greater fear — that she wouldn't be able to find the little girl on her own — set her feet into motion. She raced across the ground toward the cornfield, screeching Walter's name at the top of her lungs.

The rising slope of land that hid the plowed patch of ground from sight waited just ahead. Although her chest ached and her throat was raw, she forced herself onward, forced herself to call. "Walter! Walter! Walter!"

She started up the rise, hooked the toe of her shoe in her hem, and fell flat. She tried to stand, but she'd torn the hem, and her foot was caught. Grunting in panic and frustration, she kicked the fabric loose and tried again. Her quivering muscles refused to cooperate. She sobbed out, "Walter!"

Hands curled around her upper arms and pulled her to her feet. Walter held on to her, his brows low, confusion glimmering in his eyes. "Fanny, what is it?"

She grabbed fistfuls of his shirtfront. "Annaliese. I . . . I . . ."

His face above his beard paled. His fingers bit into her arms. "What? What about her?"

She swallowed a sob and willed her tight throat to speak. "I can't find her. I was laying out the wash and . . . and . . . I turned, and she was gone."

"How long ago?"

Fanny shook her head, her muddled brain refusing to process. "I don't know. I don't know!"

He caught her hand and took off at a run. She grabbed her skirts with her free hand and held them out of the way. How could she continue running when she felt as if her lungs would burst? Surely God was giving her the strength, although she couldn't imagine why He would help her, considering how badly she'd failed Annaliese.

They reached the bushes and separated, each calling Annaliese's name again and again. Fanny stumbled across the ground between the bushes and the cabin, crying, praying, hoping she'd come upon the little girl hunkered low, examining a flower or bug in the grass.

Walter bounded across the prairie to her, his expression grim. "I didn't find her, or any sign of her. Not so much as impressions of her feet in the grass. Have you searched in the barn or around the cabin?"

Fanny shook her head. Tears poured in warm rivulets down her cheeks. "I . . . I did not. I went after you."

He turned her toward the cabin. "She might have gone to her cradle. You look there. I'll check the barn. She loves to play in the hay." He took off at a trot.

The muscles in Fanny's legs burned as hot as the sun scorching through her bonnet, but she made them carry her to the cabin. She burst inside, a prayer thundering within her that she'd find the little girl curled in her cradle. She dashed to the cradle and looked inside. Empty, save for the battered rag doll. Her hope fizzled and died. She dropped to her knees and snatched out the little doll. Rocking, she held it to her heart, the way she longed to hold Annaliese.

"Fanny! Fanny!"

Walter's shout jolted Fanny to her feet. Every muscle in her body screamed in agony, but she raced out of the cabin and around the corner. Walter stood next to the barn. He waved to her. "Come quick!"

She suddenly realized he was smiling. A sob filled her throat and escaped on a note of hope. She reached him, and her legs seemed to lose their ability to stand. She fell against his chest. His arms encircled her, and she curled her hands over his shoulders, searching his face. "Y-you found her?"

A laugh, one filled with joy and relief, spilled from him. "I did. You always call her your bonny hen. She must have taken the name to heart." He shifted her gently in the direction of the newly built coop and bobbed his chin at the little door for the chickens. "Look inside."

Still holding his shoulders for support, Fanny dipped her knees slightly and peered through the opening. Another sob broke loose. There lay her bonny hen, curled in a ball on the hay inside the coop. Such relief flooded her that her quaking legs could no longer hold her upright. And her emotions couldn't be quelled. She wrapped her arms around Walter's neck, pressed her face to his chest, and burst into tears.

32

THE KUHN HOMESTEAD
WALTER

Too stunned to do anything else, Walter slipped his arms around Fanny and held her. He rested his bearded chin against her temple while his heart thrummed in double beats. When he'd prayed last night for God to mend whatever rift had suddenly grown between them, he hadn't imagined Him using fear as an impetus. He had imagined, however, what it would be like to hold Fanny. But he'd never believed it would actually happen.

"Shh, shh," he murmured against her cheek, rubbing her shuddering back. "Annaliese is fine. You are fine. There's no need to cry."

"Th-there is." Her voice was muffled, but he made out the fractured words. "I didn't lose her now, but I w-will soon. And my . . . my heart . . . I can't bear it."

Very gently, he took hold of her arms and drew them from his neck. He set her away from him but kept a gentle grip just above her elbows. "What do you mean?"

Her tearstained face lifted to him. "I l-love her, Walter." Her chin quivered, and fresh tears welled in her red-rimmed eyes. "I think I have since the moment I found her crying in that" — a short laugh escaped on a sob — "despicable pen." She sniffled and rubbed her nose with the skirt of one of Grete's aprons. "But I'll have to tell her goodbye when . . . when . . ."

Understanding bloomed. He nodded. "When my new wife comes?" She didn't answer, but the misery in her eyes spoke louder than words would. He sighed and chafed her arms with his palms. "I could never have asked for a better person to love my sweet Annaliese. I . . ." He gulped, desire to share his deepest feelings warring with fear of rejection.

She'd cried in his arms, but she needed comforting. He was the only one there to offer it. Just because she loved his daughter didn't mean she loved him. He'd known from the day he asked Fanny to stay that she would eventually go to New York. He'd already lost one woman he loved. Telling Fanny he loved her, then watching her leave, would open him to the pain of loss again.

He let go of her and took a sideways step,

putting several inches of space between them. "I owe you more than I can repay." He pulled in a deep breath, held it for several seconds, and then let it slowly ease from his lungs. "Since Annaliese is found and all is well, I need to . . ." He gestured in the direction of the field.

She stared into his face, uncertainty pinching her brow, as if waiting for him to say something else. Then she gave a brusque nod. "I have wash to finish. Th-thank you for not being angry with me."

He smiled, his lips trembling. He ran his fingers through his beard. Her brown eyes beseeched him, but he didn't know what else to say. "I'll see you at suppertime." He turned on his heel and hurried off.

Elkhart, Indiana
Sloan

With every negative response from train stations as far as sixty miles beyond Elkhart, Sloan's anger with Fanny grew. She couldn't have simply disappeared, but that was how it seemed. He instructed the station agent to send the message farther on.

The man made a sour face. "Mister, you're using up quite a lot of my time. Isn't there some other way to find the person you're looking for?"

Sloan slammed two Liberty dollars onto the counter. "Just do as I asked. I'll be back in the morning for any other replies." He grabbed up his bag and headed for the center of town. He hadn't intended to spend the night here, but what other choice did he have? Until he knew which direction Fanny had gone, he was stuck.

He stopped. Unless he traveled all the way to New York. He had her family's address. How fortuitous that he'd taken the letters from Fanny's room. Father would say God was looking out for him. Sloan could go to their apartment building, knock on their door, and — He shook his head, grunting in annoyance. What a ludicrous thought. As if God would aid this wandering sheep. As if her father would willingly hand her over. Again.

He stepped up on the boardwalk fronting the row of businesses on the south side of the street and read each name printed on the plate-glass windows. He located a café and entered.

A few people were seated at tables or in booths, and the aromas in the room promised a decent meal. He moved to the counter and picked up the little brass bell sitting on a corner. Even before the clanging ring stopped reverberating, a slight middle-aged woman emerged from a doorway near the back of the dining room and crossed to the desk.

"Welcome, sir. Are you wanting a meal or a room?"

He hadn't realized he could rent a room. How convenient. "Both, if possible."

She beamed. "It's possible." She moved behind the counter and opened a large leather-bound book. On the wall behind her, six hooks with numbers painted above them were screwed into the plaster. Keys dangled from the hooks marked one, three, five, and six. She turned the book toward him and dipped a pen in an inkwell. "Sign here, and I'll get you a key."

Sloan put down his bag and signed his name. As he placed the pen in the book's gutter, the woman freed the key beneath the number one and held it toward him. He didn't take it. He'd signed, but he could still scratch through it. "How much?"

"Fifty cents. And that includes tomorrow's breakfast." She swung the key on its string. "My rooms are neat as a pin, and I don't allow any drinking or carousing, so you'll get a good night's rest."

No drinking or carousing won him over. Sloan took the key. He dug out two twenty-five-cent pieces and plinked them onto the counter. He half turned, surveying the empty tables. It was past seven, and he hadn't eaten since morning. He'd pay another four bits for a decent meal if he had to. "Is it too late for supper?"

"I serve until eight. I have roasted chicken, potatoes boiled in their skins, and breaded tomatoes for tonight's menu."

He'd never cared for breaded tomatoes. Who wanted to eat something so soggy? But the rest sounded good. "I'll take a plate, please."

The woman cocked her head. "Half or quarter?"

Sloan frowned. "Excuse me?"

She laughed. "Chicken. Do you want half a chicken, or a quarter?"

His stomach rumbled.

She laughed again, the sound so merry Sloan almost smiled. "Let's say a half." She eased from behind the counter. "Take a seat wherever you like. I'll be right back with your food — and a cup of coffee?"

Sloan slid his bag onto the bench in a booth, then sat across from it. "No coffee. Tea if you have it. If not, water's fine."

"Tea it is." She hurried off.

Sloan rested his head against the high back of the booth and considered what he was doing. Burke needed him at his boat.

He'd spent more time and money than he wanted to admit chasing after a new singer. If he was honest with himself, a couple of the women who'd auditioned were talented enough to perform on the *River Peacock.* As good as Fanny? No, not anywhere near Fanny's vocal quality. But if people were eating — and drinking — they might not be disappointed.

But he did not want to concede defeat. More than that, he wanted revenge. After everything he'd done for her, how dare she let him think all this time she was dead and lying at the bottom of the Mississippi River? His anger surged again. He wouldn't give up. Not yet.

A different woman, this one much younger than the other but equally friendly, approached his booth and set a platter of food and a cup of tea in front of him. "We ran out of biscuits an hour or so ago, so Ma had me slice some day-old bread for you. I hope that's all right."

Sloan scanned the contents on the platter, and his mouth watered. Even the mound of tomatoey mush looked appealing. "It's fine. Thank you."

"You're welcome." She turned toward the kitchen.

Sloan put up his hand. "Wait a moment,

please. Do you live in Elkhart?"

She grinned. "I was born and raised here. I'll probably live here until they put me in the ground in the cemetery behind the Presbyterian church."

For reasons he couldn't explain, his body gave an involuntary shudder. "Then let me ask you a question." He'd had time to think while he sat at the station waiting for replies from different telegraphers, and something had occurred to him. "Have any newcomers moved in recently? Maybe a young woman, early twenties, brown hair and eyes, pretty, who came in looking for a job?"

The woman tapped her chin, her face puckering. "None that I can think of. Did you lose somebody?"

Sloan huffed a laugh. "You could say so. She was in Mishawaka, but I asked about her at the Elkhart railroad depot. None of the workers there recalled seeing her. But I thought, maybe . . ." His food was growing cold. He could ask more questions in the morning. He picked up his fork. "Never mind. Thank you."

"You're welcome, sir." She started off again, then hurried back. "You know something? There's other ways to travel besides the train. Maybe the woman you're looking for found a different way to get from place to place."

Sloan held his fork without stabbing it into the food, his mind whirling with the possibilities the woman's comment had inspired.

"Ease up on those reins, Mr. Kirkpatrick."

The stable owner's sharp tone set Sloan's teeth on edge. Sloan gave commands — he didn't receive them. But he did as the man said, although begrudgingly. If he wanted to rent this rig, he shouldn't aggravate the horse and buggy's owner. The horse, its coat a brown as rich as Fanny's hair, relaxed its head and snorted softly, as if offering appreciation.

Sloan had never driven a rig, although he had ridden horseback at Grandfather's estate when he was a boy. Maybe he should rent a horse and saddle rather than a horse and buggy. But if he located Fanny, he needed a way to transport her. There was plenty of room for two on the leather seat of this canopied buggy. And there was a sturdy metal frame around the seat to which he could tie her if need be.

He frowned down at the man. "Do you have a length of rope?"

"There's two or three coils in my barn."

Sloan shouldn't need more than six or

seven feet of rope, but he'd take a full coil. "How much to borrow one?"

The fellow scratched his gray-whiskered chin. "Rope? I've never been asked to rent out some rope." He shrugged. "I guess if you're paying for the full rig, I can throw in a coil of rope for the price."

That suited Sloan fine. He drummed his fingers in impatience while the fellow sauntered into the barn and sauntered out again, a coil of twisted hemp hanging from his shoulder. He tossed the rope on top of Sloan's case in the small storage boot behind the seat, then squinted up at Sloan.

"Have 'er back by suppertime or I'll have to charge you extra."

Sloan didn't care what it cost. And he didn't intend to be back by suppertime unless by some stroke of luck, fate, or goodwill he found Fanny in the first community he searched. He refused to hope for such a providential turn of events, though. He gave a brusque nod, flicked the reins, and said, "Hyah," as the stable owner had instructed.

The horse trotted forward, and Sloan guided the beast out of town.

A beautiful morning dawned around him, but he kept his gaze on the horse's glossy rump. He'd lain awake for hours last night, mulling over the café worker's comment about other means of travel. This morning's report from the station agent that no depot masters beyond Mishawaka as far as Lake Erie in Ohio had seen Fanny confirmed something for him. She'd gotten as far as Mishawaka on the train, but after that, she'd traveled some other way.

In his pocket, he carried a map, drawn by the café owner, of all the small towns and stage stops within twenty miles of the train tracks between Mishawaka and the Ohio border. He was starting with the town of Osceola, even though it took him west, because it was the closest community east of Mishawaka. If she wasn't there, he'd work his way east again. First on the south side of the tracks and then, if necessary, the north.

If memory served him correctly, from Osceola he'd travel to Gideon. A snicker built in his throat and escaped. Gideon. Such a name for a town. Father had preached about an Old Testament man named Gideon, calling him the greatest judge of Israel. As Sloan recalled, the so-called great judge was also a big sissy who hid from his enemies on a threshing floor. Wasn't he also the one who tested God by laying out a fleece? Yes. Not only once, but twice.

God tested Gideon, too, forcing him to

enter a battle with only a few hundred men. Hardly an army at all. Supposedly, through this experience, Gideon learned to fully depend on God instead of self.

Countless times, he'd heard Father say, "Whatever you need, Sloan, God'll see to it. All you have to do is ask the Master of your life to provide." He curled his lips in disdain. Father might believe all those Bible stories, but Sloan knew on whom he could depend — no one but himself.

Fanny was here somewhere. She had to be. He would find her by his own ingenuity and prove to himself that he, and he alone, was the master of his life.

33

THE KUHN HOMESTEAD
WALTER

Walter pounded the post into the ground, the vibration of each blow from his hammer sending a shock through his arm. He paused and wiped sweat from his forehead. Only an hour or so past breakfast and already the day was hot and humid. Summer was rapidly approaching. Was his new wife also coming soon?

He smacked the hammer one more time, sending the idle thought away, then hopped off the crate he'd used to make himself tall enough to get a good swing on his hammer. He surveyed what he'd accomplished so far. Two more posts to go, and then he would be able to string the chicken wire. He turned and reached for one of the stripped saplings lying in the grass. Tiny fingers gripped his pant leg and tugged.

He shifted his focus and smiled down at Annaliese. "What do you have now?" She'd brought him several treasures already, and he'd acknowledged each with due attention.

She opened her grubby hand. Three empty snail shells rested in her palm.

He crouched and touched them by turn. "Oh, you found some shells. Can you say 'shells,' Annaliese?"

She lifted the shells higher, grunting.

He chuckled. "Snails lived inside of these, but they must have crawled out." Actually, the chickens probably had something to do with the shells being empty, but he shouldn't say such a thing to his little Liébling. "The shells are pretty, yes? Pretty?"

"Pih-ee," she said.

"Yes. Pretty." He stroked her sweat-damp curls. "Annaliese is pretty, too. Nee's bonny hen. *Mein hübsches Mädchen.*" His heart swelled.

She poked the shells with her fingertip, babbling. Then abruptly she dropped them, brushed her hands together, and headed to another spot. She crouched, her bottom hovering an inch or two above the grass, and picked at some seed heads.

Walter watched her for a few moments, smiling with contentment. When he'd seen Fanny heating irons over the fire at breakfast that morning, he'd volunteered to watch Annaliese. The hot irons were dangerous. Besides, the scare they'd received yesterday when his little girl had disappeared re-inforced how precious she was to him. He couldn't always take her with him. Some of his chores were too dangerous, and others took him too far from the house. But he vowed to keep her with him when he could.

He picked up a post and the crate, took two long strides, and set the crate down. He climbed up, positioned the post, and started driving it into the ground. Between blows, he glanced at his daughter. She'd shifted to her hands and knees, her face nearly touching the tips of the grass blades, examining something. A beetle? A pebble? Another snail shell, or maybe a chicken feather? Or maybe she was seeking a tiny elf. How many hours had he spent searching when he was very young, hoping to discover one of the mythical beings? When had he last had such a fanciful thought? Not since before Grete died, for sure.

His heart caught, his hand stilling mid-swing. The childhood memory and the lightness in his chest were proof of changes happening inside him. He knew what had brought them — prayer. Hugh, Josephine, and Reverend Lee had often told him they were asking God to heal his great sorrow. Vater and Mutter surely were, too. He had to give credit to their prayers, and to God

441

for choosing to touch him with His hand of mercy and healing. But he also credited Fanny. Her presence, mostly cheerful despite the pain she'd suffered before coming here, inspired him to look beyond his sad past to a hopeful future.

A lump formed in his throat. He gave the post several more whacks, driving it deep enough to support the fence, then stepped off the crate. He crossed to Annaliese and sat cross-legged in the grass beside her.

She pushed to her feet, aimed her little behind at him, and settled in his lap. While she toyed with the tips of grass blades, he wrapped one of her golden curls around his finger and divulged the truths she wouldn't be able to repeat.

"I could not imagine loving someone besides your mama. Even when I agreed to send for a new wife, even though Hugh and Josephine promised to pray for my heart to open to loving someone else, I didn't think I would be able to grow to love another. Now I know my heart is able to love again. Because I love your Nee."

"Nee," she repeated, tilting her face and giving him a crinkling smile.

He kissed her forehead. "Yes, Nee. You love her, too, don't you?"

Annaliese babbled her baby talk, rolled

from his lap, and stood. She played with his beard, chattering her nonsense words, occasionally inserting the clearly recognizable "Nee."

Walter cupped his hand around her pudgy waist and sighed. "Yes, you and I both love her. This should encourage me. It tells me I'll be able to grow to love the wife your *Großmutter und Großvater* are sending. But . . ." He looked toward the cabin, envisioning Fanny at the ironing board, no doubt humming as she pressed the wrinkles from his shirts and trousers. "To tell you the truth, Liébling, I'd rather keep loving Fanny. But it's too late." Would word finally be in his mail slot tomorrow? Even if it wasn't, it didn't matter. He'd asked for a new wife. Eventually Vater and Mutter would send one.

He sighed and gathered his little girl in his arms. He whispered against her hair, "It's too late."

Fanny

As she'd done two weeks ago for the trip to Gideon, Fanny readied a basket. But this time, in addition to fresh napkins and a shopping list, she put the balls of butter she'd saved. The butter had stayed cool in the cellar. Now, protected by a towel soaked in cold well water, the nicely molded balls would travel to Gideon and be traded for dress goods at the mercantile.

Fanny didn't need another dress. She had the blue-checked one from the kind woman who'd given Ransom, Enoch's family, and her shelter, plus the one Josephine had helped her stitch. But little Annaliese was outgrowing her frocks. Walter had suggested cutting up one of Grete's dresses, but Fanny couldn't bring herself to do it. Trading for fabric seemed a good alternative.

Josephine arrived shortly after seven thirty, and Fanny was ready and waiting with Annaliese already secured to Fanny's front with the length of muslin. Fanny hooked the basket over her arm and trotted out to meet the wagon.

Walter came out of the barn at the same time. Her heart fluttered. He'd probably come to help her into the wagon. Always such a gentleman. My, she would miss him when she left this place.

Her throat went tight. Since he'd held her while she cried on Tuesday, she'd had a hard time meeting his gaze. If she looked at his beard, she remembered how it had tickled her cheek. The sight of his arms inspired a longing to again be sheltered in his embrace. It was safer not to look at him at all, but it was hard. She intended to talk to Josephine about these feelings and ask her help in overcoming them. In the meantime, she needed help climbing aboard.

Walter strode up close, and she swallowed before offering him a shy smile. "I can use a hand to get up onto the seat."

He put the basket in the back, then guided her foot to the little step. Heat filled her face. A glance at him revealed he, too, was blushing. She lifted her gaze to Josephine instead. Walter took hold of Fanny's elbow and gave a boost. She stepped into the box and settled on the seat. She turned to thank him, but he was already striding to the back. To her surprise, he climbed into the bed.

Josephine angled herself in the seat and sent him a puzzled frown. "You're comin', too?"

He sat and leaned against the wagon's high side, crossing his ankles, as casual a pose as a man could give. But his glowing pink cheeks ruined his attempt at nonchalance. "If you don't mind. I used twine to tie the chicken wire to the fence posts, but I need good strong wire if it's to hold. I also need wood planks to build a decent gate, and more chicken wire for a cover over the whole area. It'll prevent hawks and raccoons from getting in. I figure it's easier for me to pick out those things myself than try to explain what I want, so" — he shifted his hat forward, its brim creating a slash of shade across his face — "I'm coming, too."

Josephine looked at Fanny, her expression bland, and then she shrugged. "All right, then. Let's go."

Fanny couldn't talk to Josephine about Walter with him only a few feet behind her. So instead they chatted about their gardens, the sheet music Josephine had seen in the latest issue of *Godey's Lady's Book,* and how much fabric was required to make three Annaliese-sized dresses. As Fanny asked Josephine's advice about fabric, she hoped she would be in Indiana long enough to finish the dresses. She wanted so much to leave something behind for Annaliese.

When they reached Gideon, Walter rose and perched on the edge of the wagon box. Josephine drew the horses to a stop, and Walter hopped over the edge, walked to Josephine's side, and squinted up at her.

"I'll meet you ladies at the mercantile. Don't worry about visiting the post office. I'll . . . go by there. I can get your mail, too, Josephine, if you'd like."

Josephine nodded. "That'd be fine, Walter. We'll see you when you're done." She snapped the reins, and the horse pulled them forward.

Fanny resisted peeking over her shoulder to see if Walter watched them. A sigh found its way from her mouth.

Josephine shot her a sharp look. "Did you an' Walter have some kind of squabble?"

Fanny raised her eyebrows. "A squabble? We haven't squabbled. Why do you ask?"

Josephine shrugged, her gaze forward. "Dunno, exactly. Just seemed like he was awful quiet, even for Walter. An' you seem to be tryin' to act happier'n you really feel."

Josephine had grown to know her pretty well in the past few weeks. Fanny sighed again. "I think we're both wondering what mail might be waiting. And what it will mean for us."

Josephine pulled the reins and called, "Whoa." She set the wagon's brake in the middle of the street and turned sideways on the seat, fully facing Fanny. "If there's a letter from Walter's folks, you know what it means. His wife's on her way. An' you'll be on your way." Her fine dark eyebrows formed a *V*. "Ain't that what you want?"

Tears filled Fanny's eyes. She blinked several times and cleared her vision. She rubbed Annaliese's back, seeking comfort from the gesture. "Of course it is. I . . . I miss Da and Ma and my sisters so much.

But I . . ." She gulped. "Josephine, how can I want to go and want to stay at the same time? I don't understand myself."

Josephine's jaw went slack. She leaned close and stared directly into Fanny's eyes. "Why do you wanna stay? 'Cause of Annaliese, or 'cause of" — she lowered her voice — "Annaliese's papa?"

Fanny's chin quivered. She gritted her teeth and made the tremor stop. "Both."

Understanding bloomed on Josephine's freckled face, followed by sympathy. "Aw, Fanny, if only you'd come sooner. Then there wouldn't be some other wife comin'. Walter . . . he's honorable."

Reverend Lee had said the same thing.

"He won't break an agreement his folks made with a new bride." Josephine shook her head. "But you probably wouldn't have stayed anyway. Not after so many years away from your folks." She took hold of Fanny's hand and squeezed it. "I'm sorry you're feelin' so confused. I know how much this little one has come to mean to you." Her tender smile landed on Annaliese, then lifted to Fanny again. "But you've traveled this far. Do you really not wanna go all the way to New York City an' be with your mama an' papa again?"

Equal portions of longing and regret

twined in Fanny's middle. She didn't know what she wanted. She pointed ahead. "We'd better get out of the street and see to our shopping" — she forced a weak smile — "before my butter melts."

Josephine stared at her for a few silent seconds, her face pinched with uncertainty, and then she nodded. "You're right. We ain't gonna change anything by sittin' here." She whisked a glance at Fanny. "But just as soon as we have a few minutes alone, you an' me are gonna hash out everything you're feelin', all right?"

Making sense of her confusing emotions was exactly what she needed. "All right."

34

The steeple appeared to rise from the ground, like a buoy on the sea. A chill attacked Sloan despite the warm sun on his face. Father's little church had a steeple, one without a bell, the same as this one, and also topped with a cross. He'd never liked looking at that cross. It always seemed to mock him.

But the sight of a church steeple meant he was close to the town. No one in Osceola had seen anyone matching Fanny's description. The manager of the stage stop outside Osceola claimed he hadn't laid sight of her, either. Sloan stayed the night at the stage stop and then left early that morning for the town bearing the name of a biblical judge.

As the horse clip-clopped over the grass, a movement caught Sloan's eye — something flapping. A flag? He raised up as straight as he could for a better look. Ah. Not a flag but a rug. Someone at the church was shaking the dust from a rug.

His pulse skipped. Whoever was at the church would likely be familiar with newcomers in town. Father and Mother had always made it a point to welcome newcomers and invite them to service. He might not need to go into Gideon at all if this person could answer his question about Fanny. He tugged the reins and guided the horse into a gentle turn. The buggy rolled to a stop as a red-haired woman carrying the rug mounted the church's steps.

Sloan called, "You there, madam. Good morning."

The woman turned and looked at him, a curious but not unfriendly frown crinkling her brow. "Good mornin', sir. What can I do for you?"

He pushed his foot against the brake to stabilize the buggy, then leaned forward, resting his elbow on his knee. "I hope you might give me some information. I'm seeking a friend of mine." No sense in giving her name. Apparently she'd previously used a different name. Who knew what she might be calling herself by now. "A young woman with brown hair and eyes and" — he gave his most charming smile — "the voice of an angel. Does that description match anyone

451

you've recently met?"

The woman draped the rug over the porch's railing and came down the steps. "Why, it sure sounds like the woman who's been watchin' over Walter Kuhn's little girl. She stood up an' sang 'Sweet Hour of Prayer' at the close of the sermon last Sunday, an' oh, my" — she fluttered her hand against her bodice — "it surely did seem as if an angel was singin' to us."

Gooseflesh prickled Sloan's arms. He reined in a shout of exultation and forced an interested yet relaxed tone. "I'd sure like to find her." He reached back and patted his bag. "If she's who I'm hunting, I have some letters her sister wrote to her."

A smile broke over the woman's face. "I'd be happy to give 'em to her." She scurried closer and gestured to a pair of fresh wheel tracks on the east side of the small structure. "Her an' another of our church members went by here a bit ago on their way to town. They'll come this way again goin' home. I could flag 'em down an' —"

Eagerness stole Sloan's manners. "I want to give them to her myself. Besides, I need to confirm it's truly her before I hand over the letters." He feigned a worried scowl. "It'd be a real shame if I left the letters for the wrong person."

"Oh, you're right about that, mister." She fanned herself with her apron skirt, sending up puffs of dust. "I should've thought of it myself."

Thank goodness he'd thought of it. "You said she was heading to town? The town of Gideon?" He nearly laughed as he said the name.

She nodded. "Yes, sir. It's a mile an' a half southeast o' here." She smiled up at him. "I reckon her an' Mrs. Moore are shoppin' at the Gideon General Mercantile. But you know, 'stead of goin' on into town, why not wait for 'em here? I'm pret' near done with my tidyin' up, but the door's always left open. You're welcome to come in the chapel an' sit a spell. It's nice an' peaceful inside."

Go inside the chapel? He hadn't entered a place of worship since he'd left home. Nor had he wanted to. So why did this woman's casual invitation tug at him? He squashed the fleeting temptation. But waiting for the wagon to pass this way made good sense. If he seized Fanny from her companion in the middle of town, someone might alert the sheriff. Assuming they had one. Should he take the chance of being arrested for snatching Fanny right off the street?

He offered the woman a smile. "Thank you, but I'll stay in my buggy. However, I would like to wait here for the women to come back from town. May I park on the shady side of the church?"

"That's just fine. Your horse'll likely enjoy gettin' out of the sun." She headed for the chapel stairs, smiling over her shoulder. "If you change your mind about comin' inside —"

"I won't." He tipped his hat and released the brake. As he urged the horse into motion, he chuckled. How perfect. He'd be shielded from sight by Fanny and whoever she was with until they were upon him. He'd find such pleasure in surprising her with his presence. And out here on the open prairie, there'd be no one nearby to rescue her.

Gideon, Indiana
Walter

How long would he stand here holding the letter from New York without opening it? Walter stared at his name written in Mutter's neat handwriting until the letters seemed to swim. How irrational to not open it. He'd been waiting for months for word about his new wife. Now word had come. He should open it.

He turned the envelope over and slid his finger beneath the edge of the glued flap.

Josephine stepped into the building. "Walter?"

Walter shoved the letter into his shirt pocket. "Are you ladies finished shopping?"

She nodded. "What about the mail?"

After discovering the missive in his own box, he'd forgotten to check hers. "I just got here, so I don't know yet."

She hurried to her box and peeked in, then released a little cry of delight. "Two letters!" She pulled them out and hugged them to her chest, beaming at Walter. "I can't wait to get home an' read these with Hugh."

He wished he shared her enthusiasm. He held the door open for her. "Then I guess we better go." He followed Josephine to the mercantile and her waiting wagon.

Fanny stood beside the wagon, holding Annaliese's hand. They looked so natural together. So right. The letter in his shirt pocket seemed to press like a boulder against his chest, making it difficult for him to draw a full breath.

Annaliese giggled and danced in place, reaching her free hand to him. He scooped her up, offering what he hoped was a casual smile, and glanced at the length of cloth draped over Fanny's shoulders like a shawl. "Did your knot come loose?"

Fanny shrugged, the gesture sheepish. "She needed a napkin change, and afterward she resisted being confined again. She'd been tied to me for so long, I thought it best to let her walk free." She winced, then shrugged again. "Maybe she can stay in the back of the wagon with you for the ride h-home, where she can wriggle."

A lump filled Walter's throat. Before he could agree, Josephine's laughter rang out.

Josephine winked. "I declare, Fanny, you'll be glad when she's trained to use the outhouse, won't you?"

The comment was meant to be teasing, but it stabbed Walter. In all likelihood, Fanny wouldn't still be in Gideon when Annaliese was old enough to wear pantalets in place of diapers. He cleared his throat. "Are your purchases in the wagon, or do I need to fetch them?"

Josephine strode to the front of the wagon. "Our stuff's all loaded. We'll stop by the lumber store for yours. Then we can head for home."

Walter swung Annaliese into the wagon's bed, then turned to Fanny. "Let me help you onto the seat."

But she shook her head and pointed to the toes of her shoes poking from beneath her dress hem. "Since I'm not holding

Annaliese, I can see my feet. Go ahead and climb in with your Liébling. I'll be fine." She hurried to the seat and pulled herself aboard.

I'll be fine, she'd said. Walter swallowed, and his hand drifted to his shirt pocket. He hoped he'd be fine, too.

Gideon Bible Chapel
Sloan

Roughly a half hour previously, the cleaning woman had rounded the building and reminded Sloan the church doors were always unlocked, so he was welcome to go in if he changed his mind. He wouldn't, but he thanked her anyway. She departed, taking her cheerful but tuneless hum with her, and Sloan was alone, save for the drowsing horse, on the prairie.

So quiet. As quiet as nighttime on the Mississippi River. Not that either location was silent. The river's flow always provided a gentle bit of sound. On the prairie, wind whistled through the tall grass. Occasionally a bird called to its mate.

Suddenly the horse raised his head and snorted. Sloan sat bolt upright, his senses alert. Moments later he heard the creak and crunch of wagon wheels, accompanied by women's soft chatter. One of those voices held a familiar musicality. Awareness sizzled through his entire frame. Up until that moment, he'd held a tiny element of doubt she'd survived the fall. After all, it would have taken a miracle, and Sloan didn't believe in miracles. But now all doubt fled. Fanny was alive.

Sloan released the brake and curled his hands around the reins, his fingers twitching with eagerness. Part of him wanted to chase the wagon down, to grab her off the seat in the middle of her lighthearted conversation, but they were still close to town. Whoever drove the wagon might be able to make it to Gideon and round up a search party. Men on horseback would certainly overtake this buggy. No, he'd need to be patient, follow well behind the wagon, and not draw attention to himself. Then when the wagon stopped, he'd survey the location and, with a cardplayer's keen strategy, plot his next move.

35

THE KUHN HOMESTEAD
WALTER

While Annaliese slept in his lap, Walter leaned against the crates of purchases and read his letter. Again.

My dear son,
  Your Vater and I are sorry for taking so long to respond to your request for a new wife. Even more people from Germany have come to the city — ach, it grows more crowded by the day — but many have abandoned the old tradition of match-making for their children, saying the young ones should choose mates for themselves in this land of freedom. Thus, we turned to a woman who arranges brides for home-steaders in the west.
  To our disappointment, the girls on her list were English, Irish, or Scottish. Your Vater said no, we must send a German girl to you. One with blue eyes and gold braids. One more like your Grete. So we

have been waiting for the woman to tell us a German girl wanted to move west and marry a farmer. We had nearly given up hope, as you probably had, too. But at last we received word.

She has found a girl from Germany. A girl so German she does not yet even speak the English language. She is young, has the golden hair and blue eyes your Vater wanted, and is willing to work hard. But the matchmaker will not send her on our say-so, even though we paid the fee. She must hear from you that you want this wife. So in this letter, you will find the matchmaker's address. Send her a telegram and confirm your desire for the girl to come. Then we will make arrangements for her transport to Indiana.

There was more, but Walter focused on the part about his new wife. On the German girl his father had insisted must be sent instead of one from England, Ireland, or Scotland. What would Vater and Mutter think if he said he'd already given his heart to a young woman with a Scottish lilt in her voice, gold-flecked eyes of brown, and reddish threads in her brown hair? But he couldn't tell them. Not after they'd paid a fee to secure this wife.

460

The matchmaker in New York City was waiting for his confirmation. He'd need to ride to Elkhart in order to send a telegram. Gideon didn't have a telegrapher. But it wasn't a problem. Hugh and Josephine would lend him their wagon and team. They would even keep Annaliese while he went. He could take Fanny to the railroad station and send his telegram at the same time. The plan formed so effortlessly in his mind. So why did his heart ache so badly?

"Whoa," Josephine's command came, and then the wagon creaked to a stop. The bed continued to rock slightly for a few more seconds and then stilled. Walter stuffed the letter back into his pocket and gently wakened Annaliese.

She sat up and rubbed her eyes, her mouth widening into an adorable yawn. Oh, how precious she was. Would this new wife love her as much as he did? As much as Fanny did?

He pushed to his feet, lifting Annaliese at the same time. Fanny was already on the ground next to the wagon box, her sweet face lifted to him. He swallowed a knot of agony and forced his tight throat to speak. "Would you take Annaliese? Then I will unload our goods."

She nodded, and he placed his daughter

in Fanny's waiting arms. Annaliese chortled and patted Fanny's cheek. Fanny tipped her head and kissed the baby's palm. Such a sweet picture. His heart caught, and he quickly turned away.

Dear Lord, rid my mind of images of my Annaliese with her Nee. Set my mind and heart on the wife I have prayed will come. Give me the strength to keep my word.

Fanny

Fanny nuzzled Annaliese's sweaty neck and inwardly prayed for courage. She'd begun praying for it the moment she peeked into the back of the wagon as they left Gideon and saw Walter reading a letter. It had come and, without doubt, brought word about his new wife. During the last mile of the ride, an idea began rolling in the back of her mind. She didn't know if it held merit, but she wanted to at least discuss it with Josephine.

Josephine remained on the wagon seat, her hand on the brake and her gaze seemingly on Walter, who had begun unloading the wagon. Fanny reached up and tugged her friend's skirt. "Could we talk?"

Josephine shifted her attention to Fanny. "Sure."

Fanny glanced at Walter. "Not here. Somewhere . . . private."

Josephine shrugged. "I suppose so. If Walter doesn't mind."

Walter might want her to put away their purchases right away. She was still employed by him. She should ask his permission to speak with Josephine. She settled Annaliese on her hip and moved to the rear of the wagon. "Walter?"

He shifted his eyes a bit but didn't fully turn his head, balancing a crate against his belly. "Ja?"

How masculine he seemed, with his shirt sleeves stretched taut over his biceps, his stance wide, and a sheen of perspiration on his brow. Must he be so appealing? So tender, strong in faith, and handsome to look upon? She glanced at his pocket, where the folded pages of a letter showed as boldly as a red silk handkerchief against a gentleman's black suit coat. Would his new wife appreciate and admire him as much as Fanny did? Her heart ached, but she forced a casual tone. "May I spend a few minutes alone with Josephine?"

"I suppose you want to tell her a . . . a proper goodbye?"

So he knew she'd seen the letter. She wished he'd look directly at her. But he didn't. She stifled a sigh. "Do you mind if

463

Josephine and I go behind the cabin and talk?"

"Take as much time as you need." He headed for the cabin.

Fanny put Annaliese down and led her by the hand to the front of the wagon. She squinted up at Josephine. "Let's walk out to the well."

Josephine clambered down and linked elbows with Fanny, as she'd done during previous walks. The friendly gesture touched Fanny deeply. She cherished Josephine's kindness.

They went to the garden patch, and Annaliese circled Fanny's legs, jabbering to herself. Fanny drew in a big breath, organizing her thoughts, and then let them spill out with preamble.

"Walter got his letter, which means his new wife is coming. Which means I should be on my way. But I spent nearly seven years on a boat, the majority of those years either in a small dark room or in a windowless performance room, singing before an audience. I was always" — she sucked in a lungful of the fresh air, then let it ease out — "closed in. From the time I awakened on the bank after my plunge into the river, I've been trying to get my fill of the open spaces and beauty of nature. I'm still not full, and . . . and the thought of living in a big city holds no appeal."

Josephine gaped at Fanny. "None? But your family is there."

Fanny caught hold of Josephine's hands. "But what if they aren't happy there? My da was a sheepherder in Scotland. In Flossie's letters, she talked about how discontented he is working in a factory. I know he longs for open spaces as much as I do. Is there land here, near Gideon, where my family could come and live? Where my da could raise sheep or even grow corn and barley? Instead of me going to them, do you think they could come to me?"

Josephine stared at Fanny for several seconds, her lips pressed tight, while Annaliese passed back and forth beneath their joined hands, her childish babble never ceasing. Finally, Josephine released a huff. "I'll talk to Hugh. He'll know if there's an empty house either in town or somewhere close to it." She squeezed Fanny's hand, and a hopeful smile appeared on her face. "I admit, it wouldn't bother me a bit to have you stay around. I've grown pretty fond of you, Fanny Beck."

Fanny grabbed Josephine in a hug, squashing Annaliese between their skirts. Annaliese squawked in protest, and Fanny let go of

Josephine and lifted Annaliese into her arms. She kissed the little girl's temple, then turned a sad smile on Josephine. "I'm fond of you, too. I don't want to tell you good-bye."

Josephine rubbed Fanny's upper arm, then shot a look in the direction of the wagon. "Fanny, what you told me in Gideon — how you've got attached to Annaliese an' Walter . . ." Worry tinged her features. "Can you stay here an' be at peace, seein' them take up with his new wife?"

"Fanny?"

Walter's call kept her from having to answer, which was just as well, because she had no answer. She hurried around the cabin. "What do you need?"

"Where do you want this?" He held the paper-wrapped package containing the fabric she'd purchase for Annaliese's new gowns.

She gulped. Would she be here long enough to sew the little frocks? Should she ask Josephine to make the dresses or leave the cloth for Walter's new wife? She couldn't think clearly enough to form a reply.

He took a step toward her. "Fanny?"

She shifted her attention to his dear, kind, beautiful blue eyes. She lingered there, locked in his gaze. Then Annaliese patted

Fanny's cheek and said, "Nee," and Fanny jerked her attention to the toddler. "Please put it on the bed. Thank you."

He nodded and strode to the cabin. Josephine came up behind Fanny, put her arm across Fanny's shoulders, and squeezed. "I'm gonna pray real hard for you to know for sure whether it's a good idea for you to stay in Gideon. Because the sparks I just saw shootin' from your eyes tell me it might be harder to live in the open spaces close to Walter than in a crowded city far away from him."

Annaliese squirmed, and Fanny set her on the ground again. After taking the little girl's hand, she walked Josephine to her wagon.

Josephine hugged Fanny, then climbed onto the seat and said goodbye with a promise to ask Hugh about available houses or land.

Fanny watched Josephine's wagon roll past the barn and out of sight, then shifted her attention to the open barn doors. Thuds and clunks let her know Walter was working, putting away the things he'd bought in town. Afterward, he would probably take his hoe to the cornfield. He said a man must be diligent to keep weeds from taking over a field. She should put the food stores away.

She held her hand toward Annaliese.

"Come along now, my bonny hen. Let's go inside."

But Annaliese darted around the corner of the cabin, giggling. Fanny followed her.

Annaliese ran to the far side of the garden, whirled, then ran back to Fanny, calling, "Aaaaaa!" as she came. The tune was unmelodious but so cheerful that Fanny couldn't help but smile. Annaliese plowed into Fanny's skirts for a brief hug, then turned and pattered off again. Fanny watched her, chuckling indulgently. She should make the child obey, but after her being strapped to Fanny and then confined in the wagon, it would do her good to run. So Fanny let her run back and forth across the green grass beneath the bright sun.

Annaliese met Fanny's knees for the fourth time, and Fanny captured her in a hug. "One more time, little hen, then —"

"What a pretty little girl you have."

Chills exploded from her scalp all the way to her toes. The voice. Deep. Authoritative. Cocksure. Her pulse sped into double beats, and her knees went weak. She had no need to look. She knew who'd spoken.

Annaliese wriggled to free herself, but Fanny held tight. She grated a stern whisper, "Go to Fa, Annaliese. Go to Fa." She released the child, her heart begging Annaliese to obey. Annaliese slipped one finger in her mouth and headed for the barn door, gazing back at Fanny.

As soon as Annaliese entered the log building, Fanny forced her quivering legs to turn. And she found herself face to face with Sloan Kirkpatrick. Her mouth was so dry it felt as if her tongue was swollen. She couldn't speak.

He pushed back his jacket and slid his hand into his pocket, his weight settled on one hip, the way she'd seen him stand countless times. An arrogantly confident pose. But today the pistol he usually carried in his boot was caught beneath his belt, next to his pocket. She stared at the weapon, fear coiling through her.

If he fired the pistol, it would certainly alert Walter. If Walter came running, Annaliese would come, too. She couldn't risk either of them being hurt.

Sloan's lips formed a smirk and, with his free hand, he tipped his hat. "I can tell from the expression on your lovely face you hadn't anticipated seeing me today."

Or ever again. She licked her dry lips and forced her vocal cords to produce sound. "How did you find me?"

He chuckled, a low rumble more menacing than mirthful. "Perhaps you shouldn't have chosen to sing your way across the country." He angled one brow. "As I always told you, you have a one-of-a-kind gift."

Her gift, bestowed by God and to be used for His glory, had become her undoing. Tears stung, but she blinked them away. She would not give him the satisfaction of making her cry.

He beckoned her with the tweak of one finger. "Come along, Fanny. You've had your holiday. Time to return to the *River Peacock*."

She commanded her trembling limbs to still and lifted her chin. "And never leave it again?"

"Of course you'll leave it." A smirk lifted the corners of his lips. "When your term of service is up. Or you've outgrown your usefulness."

Fanny released a huff. "You're lying, Sloan. You won't honor our agreement."

"On the contrary, Fainche, you are the one dishonoring the agreement your father signed, which promised seven years' service for each person transported to America." He held up his hand, his fingers spread wide. "Five people. You learned arithmetic. How many years is five times seven?"

Her jaw dropped, and she stared at him. He was lying. He had to be lying. Da would

never have agreed to such terms. "You —
Da, he —"

"You doubt me?" He lowered his hand
and took a step toward her, his expression
smug. "The agreement bearing your father's
X is in the safe of my cabin. I'll show you
when we return to the *River Peacock*. You'll
see you are still bound to me."

The sweet spring breeze caught a strand
of Fanny's hair and tossed it across her
cheek. She anchored it behind her ear,
determination filling her. God didn't rescue
her only to let her be trapped in a private
dungeon again for years on end. She
wouldn't accept it. "I am not bound to you,
Sloan. I've been set free."

"No longer bound?" His hand jerked from
his pocket and settled on the butt of his
gun. He slowly advanced until less than
three feet separated them. "No longer
bound?" His voice was controlled, his
expression friendly, but fury glittered in his
clover-green eyes. "Who brought you to
America? Who clothed you, fed you, housed
you, educated you, and elevated you to
celebrity status? All up and down the Mississippi, when people spoke of the best
riverboat singer, they were speaking of you.
I made you the Darling of the *River Peacock*. You will always be bound to me."

Fanny shook her head. "I am not. The only One to whom I am ever bound is my Lord and Savior, Jesus Christ. There can be no one on earth who holds me forever." As she spoke, awareness bloomed with clarity. How could she have thought she'd been a captive? All those long years serving Sloan, she'd had her freedom. Not an earthly freedom, such as she'd enjoyed these weeks after her fall from the boat, but an eternal freedom from sin and condemnation. The abolitionist, Ransom, had mentioned freedom in Christ, as had Enoch, but somehow the concept hadn't truly reached her heart. Until now.

Even if Sloan forced her onto his boat again, even if he held her in that vile room for the rest of her life, she would still be free. She looked directly into his narrowed eyes and quoted, " 'If the Son therefore shall make you free, ye shall be free indeed.' "

Sloan

Sloan had heard the verse from John 8 often enough during his childhood to know to whom she referred. The recognition rattled him to his core. How many times had Father taught from the pulpit about the freedom found in a relationship with Christ?

472

But Sloan had never understood it. How could binding oneself to servanthood bring freedom? And why should he care?

"Enough talk." He grabbed Fanny's arm and yanked her to his side. The length of light-tan fabric draped like a shawl around her shoulders fell to the ground, but there was no need to retrieve it. He'd not allow her to wear such a pitiful wrap on the *River Peacock.* "I left my buggy just over that rise. You will get in without a fuss. If you yell or try to run, someone could get hurt." He patted his gun and found satisfaction when her face paled. "I'm sure you don't want harm to come to that sweet little girl you called your bonny hen. Am I correct?"

Fanny's chin quivered for a moment, then stilled. "You are."

"Good. Let's go."

It had taken Walter longer than expected to organize the materials needed to finish the chicken coop. His daughter was a distraction. But he'd needed a distraction from his troubled thoughts. Now everything was put away and there wasn't anything else to keep him in the barn. He should take Annaliese to the cabin to Fanny, and spend the remaining sunlit hours in his field.

Walter swished his palms, then turned to Annaliese. "I'm all finished. Let's go find Nee."

Annaliese scampered to him and took his hand. They left the murky barn and stepped into the bright sunshine. Walter's eyes watered, and he blinked several times to clear his vision. When he could focus, his gaze landed on a length of crumpled cloth lying on the ground between the well and the house. It took a moment for him to recognize the length of muslin Fanny used to carry Annaliese. Why had she left it out in the yard? It seemed a careless thing to do. He would take it in to her.

"Wait for me here, Annaliese." He let go of his daughter's small hand and crossed to the cloth. As he bent down to pick it up, a movement in the distance caught his eye. He straightened and stared across the landscape. A man and woman were heading for the rise to the west of the cabin. He recognized Fanny by her blue-checked dress, but where was she going? And who was with her? The man wasn't from Gideon. His fine suit marked him as someone from high society. Not even Reverend Lee, who'd come to Gideon from a city in Massachusetts, wore such nice clothes.

Walter took a step in the direction the two were traveling, cupped his hands around his mouth, and yelled, "Fanny!"

She stumbled to a stop, but the man yanked her arm and jerked her into motion again. She shot a quick, pleading look over her shoulder. He'd seen the expression before — on Grete's face the night of the fire. She'd dashed away from him that night, never to return. And now it seemed he'd lose Fanny, too. But to whom?

Like a lightning bolt striking, a comment Josephine made zinged through Walter's

mind — *"The riverboat captain who inden-*
tured her wasn't honest."

Josephine also mentioned Fanny had been
locked away against her will. Walter's breath
caught in his lungs, and he stared at the
man, who was now nearly dragging Fanny
up the rise. She was going with him, but
not by choice. Without another thought, he
broke into a run. Fear thundered through
his veins and grew with every pounding step
against the ground, making him go cold,
then hot, then cold again. The man taking
Fanny was tall and broad shouldered —
much like the bullies who'd tormented the
poor German boy every day at school. He'd
never been able to stand against those bullies. Did he intend to fight this man? He
didn't know. He only knew he had to get to
her.

The pair reached the top of the rise, and
the man paused and looked backward. His
gaze met Walter's, and derision curled his
lips. Still holding Fanny's arm, he turned
and remained in place, his mocking smile
locked on Walter.

Walter bolted up beside the man, grabbed
his wrist, and jerked his hand away from
Fanny. "Let go of her."

The man brushed the backs of his fingers
over the spot Walter had touched. "I'll thank

you to keep your grubby paws from my suit." He caught hold of Fanny's elbow again and looked Walter up and down. "Who are you?"

"Walter Kuhn. I own this land. Who are you?"

The fellow raised his chin and pushed his jacket aside with his free hand, giving Walter a glimpse of the ivory-embellished butt of a pistol. "I am Sloan Kirkpatrick, captain of the *River Peacock,* and I am here to recover my riverboat singer. Now, scat. I don't have time for the likes of you."

If this was the man who'd indentured Fanny and cruelly locked her away from the sun and flowers for so many years, he deserved to be pounded into the dust. Walter's hands formed fists. His muscles quivered. His chest heaved like a bellows, but he didn't move or speak.

The man released a soft, derisive snort. "You've made a wise choice." He gave Fanny a little push toward a buggy parked at the bottom of the rise.

With a growl, Walter dove into the man's pathway. "Leave her be!" The cold fury in the riverboat captain's eyes gave Walter another chill. Temptation to back away tugged hard. But he stood firm, his eyes locked on the captain's stony glare. "She is

going home to her da and ma." The right-
ness of Walter's stance emboldened him
beyond anything he'd known before. Courage filled him from the soles of his feet to
the top of his head. This riverboat captain
might beat him to a pulp, but he wouldn't
run from the fight. Fanny was worth defend-
ing.

"Well, well, well." A wry laugh blasted
from the man. "It seems my Fainche has
found a champion. But how brave will he
be" — he pulled the pistol from his belt in
a smooth motion — "in the face of death?"
He aimed the barrel at Walter's middle and
cocked the hammer. He angled his head,
his eyes glimmering. "Now will you step
aside?"

Fanny leaped to Walter's side and grabbed
his arm. "Please go to Annaliese. I'll be all
right."

Walter's heart thudded with such force he
marveled it remained in his chest. He
shifted, positioning himself between Fanny
and the captain and held his arms wide, a
gesture meant to shield Fanny. "No, sir, I
will not step aside. I promised to send
Fanny to her family. I might not be much
in your eyes, only a simple farmer, but I
will do what is necessary to keep my promise."

The captain eased forward until the tip of the pistol's barrel touched a button on Walter's shirt. "Even if it costs you your life?"

Sloan

Such a stubborn fool. This bearded man with a colorless face and trembling limbs would soon scuttle out of the way. No man, no matter how harebrained, would willingly take a bullet for someone else.

"Well?" Sloan barked the query. "What's your decision, *simple farmer*? Will you live or die?"

Kuhn held his arms-flung-open pose. He maintained a steady gaze, as well. But he swallowed, an audible gulp that told Sloan how much fear flowed through him. Then his head lifted a fraction of an inch, and he pulled in a breath that straightened his shoulders. "If I have to, I'll die. But I will not step aside, because I am a man of my word."

"A man of my word." The statement struck Sloan like a fist, sending him backward a step. Moments from the day he raged at his father's inability to provide one small want — a new suit for Sloan to wear to his graduation ceremony — clicked in the back of his mind like a series of daguerreotypes. His

father had sat silent and unflinching while Sloan belittled his family's simple lifestyle, kicked at their hand-me-over furnishings, and gestured to his patched, donated clothing.

When he'd finally run out of disparaging words, Father had pushed wearily from his chair, crossed the bare wood floor, and placed his broad warm hand on Sloan's shoulder. Father had said, "Son, when I was the age you are now, I made a vow to serve the Lord with my whole heart, no matter what it cost me. After all, He loves me enough to give up His life for me. How could I do any less than offer my full self to Him? It pains me now to think I could lose my beloved son, but I'm a man of my word. At the end of my life, I might not have much in material things to leave behind, but I pray I'll be remembered as a man of integrity. Because when it comes right down to it, the only things we hold our whole life long, the only things we really have to call our own, are our principles. If we falter on those, we lose ourselves."

During these weeks of searching, how many times had Father come to mind? How many times had something in Flossie's letters to Fanny pricked his conscience? And now this farmer with his arms spread wide brought to mind another Man, one who sacrificed His life for, as Father said, the sins of mankind. Was God, the God his father so faithfully served, trying to get hold of Sloan's heart? Sloan had set off on this journey to locate a singer for his riverboat. But had he been sent to find something more important?

Suddenly Fanny slipped beneath Kuhn's outstretched arm and stood half in front of the farmer, only inches from the tip of the pistol barrel. "Please don't hurt him, Sloan. He's a widower with a little girl. Please don't make her an orphan."

"Fanny!" Kuhn growled under his breath and executed a dance-like move that brought him in front again but with his back to Sloan. Encircling Fanny with his arms, he looked over his shoulder at Sloan. "If you want her, you'll have to kill me first."

A week ago, maybe even a day ago, Sloan would have pulled the trigger. But he couldn't do it. Not today. He uncocked the gun and stepped backward, lowering his arm to his side. "All right, Mr. Kuhn. If keeping your promise means that much to you, I'll let her go."

The man scowled at Sloan and remained in his protective pose.

Sloan ignored him and turned his attention on Fanny. "I had your belongings sent to your parents. I'm sure the box has arrived by now, so it will be waiting for you when you reach New York City."

Fanny gasped and wriggled free of Kuhn's hold. "They must think I'm dead."

Sloan snorted, but the sound lacked real disdain. "Then your arrival on their doorstep will be a welcome surprise." Would his arrival on his parents' doorstep be a welcome or unwelcome surprise? An unexpected one, for sure. He slipped the pistol into his boot and moved to the rear of the buggy. "I have your sister's letters with me. I presume you'd like to have them?"

She lifted the hem of her skirt and hurried to him, her brown eyes alight. Kuhn came with her, his distrustful glare fixed on Sloan. Sloan reached to place the packet into Fanny's hands, but Kuhn grabbed them first and gave them to Fanny. Gritting his teeth, Sloan buckled his bag and turned to Kuhn again. "Where's the closest telegrapher?"

Kuhn's gaze still didn't waver. "Elkhart. About six miles nor—"

"I know where it is." When he returned the horse and buggy, he would make use of the telegraph office in Elkhart and contact Burke. And maybe send word to his parents.

They would likely appreciate knowing their son had thought of them.

Sloan moved to the buggy seat and climbed in. He placed his foot against the brake and picked up the reins. Then he angled his head and met Fanny's gaze. "Enjoy your freedom, Fainche." He'd intended to insert sarcasm into his tone, but an unexpected note of longing ruined the effect.

She hugged the tied bundle of letters to her breast. Sunlight brought out the burnished red-gold highlights in her hair and brightened the gold flecks in her eyes. Her beauty had always been captivating, but the serenity in her expression as she smiled up at him added a new element to her physical attractiveness. "I will. Thank you for reminding me where it's always been found."

Fanny

The moment Sloan's buggy rolled away, Fanny's knees buckled. She sank down on the grass, dropped Flossie's letters into her lap, and gazed at Walter in astonishment. "He left. He really left. He let me go."

Walter seemed to chase the buggy with his frown, as if daring it to turn around and come back. Not until it crossed the next rise did he crouch next to her. He locked

483

his worried gaze on her face. "Are you all right? Did he hurt you?"

"He scared me, but he didn't hurt me." She closed her eyes for a moment, memorizing the wonder of this moment. She was forever free of Sloan's control. But if things had gone differently and he'd taken her back to the *River Peacock,* at least she would go with a full understanding of where freedom resided. No matter where she lived from then on, she would always remember she was truly free.

"Nee. Fa. Nee."

At Annaliese's strident cry, Fanny shifted on her bottom. Annaliese trudged toward her and Walter, dragging the length of muslin. Fanny set the stack of letters aside and held her arms wide. Annaliese ran the last few yards and fell against Fanny.

Fanny kissed Annaliese's sweat-damp curls, grateful not only for the opportunity to lavish affection on her bonny hen but for the distraction the child provided. She felt suddenly shy in Walter's presence. His defense, even willing to take a bullet if necessary to keep Sloan from carrying her away, humbled and astounded her. She already loved him, but his selfless act increased her admiration. No one, besides Jesus, had been willing to die for her. Why

484

had he done it?

He stood and picked up the packet of letters. He gruffly cleared his throat and held the packet to her. "You'll be happy to have these again."

She stared for several seconds at his broad work-roughened hand and the rumpled satin ribbon drifting over his knuckles. A smile tugged at her lips. The ribbon matched the pale blue of the Indiana sky as dusk approached. "I am. Just as you are" — she swallowed a knot of mingled hope and heartache — "happy to have received a letter today."

She hugged Annaliese, pressing her face against the child's curls. God's timing in sending Walter's new wife was perfect. If Sloan had taken her away, little Annaliese would be cared for anyway. She should be grateful. Joyful, even. But a fierce ache filled her heart.

Annaliese wriggled and reached for her fa. Fanny relieved Walter of her letters, and he perched Annaliese on his arm. Then he offered Fanny his hand. "I guess now . . . we go home."

Fanny placed her hand in his and allowed him to help her to her feet. Her limbs still trembled, but she released his hand and

485

forced a smile she didn't feel. "I guess . . . we do."

They walked to the cabin side by side, Walter carrying Annaliese, and Fanny cradling her letters against her breast.

At the little stoop, he turned to Fanny. She found herself trapped by his steady gaze. Why had he risked his life for her? She wanted to ask, but his unsmiling countenance, the agony and remorse and hopefulness glittering in his blue eyes, silenced her.

"Are" — he cleared his throat — "you ready?"

Ready for what? To go to New York? To say goodbye to him, Annaliese, and the Moores? To bid farewell to this glorious countryside exploding with the marvelous colors and scents of spring? She wanted to say, "I am not," but the words wouldn't form.

"It's all right if you're not."

Hope ignited in her chest.

"If you haven't recovered from your scare and aren't yet ready to see to Annaliese, I can take her with me to the Moores. It's only a two-mile walk to their cabin. Or, if you're afraid of being alone, you can walk with us to the Moores. I know Josephine would welcome your company."

His comments, kindly stated yet so different from what she'd hoped to hear, left her reeling. And oddly weary. She sat on the edge of the stoop. "Why are you going to the Moores?"

He glanced aside, then met her gaze. "That man — the riverboat captain — came onto my property, accosted you, and threatened me with a gun. He can't be allowed to do such things. I want to borrow one of the Moores' horses, ride into Elkhart, and tell the sheriff what happened here." He paused, shifting his attention to somewhere beyond her. "I also need to send a telegram."

"Oh . . ." Fanny placed her letters in her lap. The return address, written in pencil, stared up at her from the top envelope.

Michael and Johanna Beck
1 Essex St. Unit 3B
Manhattan Borough
New York City

Such a specific address. Such an unfamiliar address. Her parents' names pulled at her heart, but nothing about the place raised feelings of yearning. She blinked up at Walter, at Annaliese's little fingers twisting the whiskers that nearly touched his chest. Longing swept through her, almost dizzying in its intensity. But it was misplaced. Word of his new wife had come. And Josephine was right. Fanny couldn't live here and watch another woman take her place. She should make ready to leave his cabin.

She pulled the top envelope from the stack, then stood and held the missive out to Walter. "When you go to Elkhart, would you send a telegram to my parents? Let them know I'm alive and . . . and . . ." Her heart twisted in her chest. "I will write to them soon."

He took the letter, his brows low. "I will see to it, Fanny."

She turned away and scanned the landscape, memorizing the rolling hills thickly carpeted with grass and dotted with wildflowers, the sky forming a canopy over them, and the wispy clouds that mimicked ribbons floating on a breeze. Such a beautiful picture. One she would pull from her mind's eye and examine when the crowded streets of the big city pressed in on her.

She dared another peek. At the father and daughter. A smile formed without effort. She would remember, too, the darling little yellow-haired girl and the dark-haired man with their matching vivid blue eyes. Then she thought of Josephine. Affection rose and filled her. She would also remember this friend, and the ones who'd been her companions over the hundreds of miles between Missouri and Illinois. So many memories to cherish.

Fanny sighed and lifted her face to catch the warm sunshine. She closed her eyes. If she had to leave, she would do so with gratitude in her heart for all God had given her. But, oh, how she would miss them.

Fanny chose to keep Annaliese while Walter made his trek to Elkhart. She didn't want to sacrifice a single minute of time with her wee bonny hen. While Annaliese played with her toys, Fanny put all the purchased goods in their proper places, then prepared a pot of beans with chunks of pork and a full cup of molasses. She sang the song she'd learned from Pazzy over and over. Each time she reached the words "All is well," she sang them at the top of her voice, willing them to be true.

Walter returned an hour past their usual suppertime and entered the cabin with a timidity that took Fanny back to their first days of acquaintanceship. He sat at the table next to Annaliese, as he always did. The girl patted his arm and babbled, frequently interjecting "Fa" in the midst of her chatter, but he sat silently, not tweaking the baby's curls or tickling her belly or otherwise acknowledging her. He kept his head angled toward the open doorway as if something outside held his attention.

Fanny scooped beans into bowls, balanced a slice of buttered bread on the edge of each, then carried them to the table. As she set down his bowl with a firm clunk, he abruptly met her gaze.

She slowly sank onto her stool. She'd intended to stay silent until he chose to speak, but a question wrenched itself from the center of her soul. "Why did you put yourself between Sloan and me?"

He stroked his fingers through his beard, confusion marring his forehead. "Why should I have not?"

"Because he's" — she sought an appropriate description. The man wasn't evil. His letting her go proved it. But neither was he a saint — "unaccustomed to not getting his own way. He might have shot you, Walter." Her voice quavered, ugly images plaguing her mind. "What would Annaliese have done if he'd shot you?"

Tenderness crept across his features. He looked at his little daughter and smoothed his hand over her hair. "She would have been cared for."

Fanny swallowed a knot of sorrow. "Because your new wife is coming, and she would see to her." She spoke what she was certain he'd meant to say.

He turned a mild frown on her. "No."

Annaliese grunted and pointed to the piece of bread on her bowl. He gave it to her, then slid his hands across the table and took hold of Fanny's. The bowls of beans in the way forced them to set their elbows wide and lean toward each other. "Fanny, all my life I've been a coward. When I was in school, I ran from bullies. Here in Indiana, when my barn caught fire, I ran from it to save myself. Even the letter I sent to my parents, asking them to find a wife for me, was cowardly. Because courtship is frightening, not knowing whether the woman will find you pleasing or not. I could avoid rejection if they did the choosing."

She considered what he'd said, her heart swelling with compassion, but she didn't know what to say in response. She gave his hands a gentle squeeze she hoped would communicate understanding.

He shifted his hands, linking his fingers with hers. His callused thumbs rubbed gently back and forth, back and forth, as rhythmic as the little wooden mantel clock's soft ticktock. "For years and years, I've prayed for God to make me a brave man. A man He could be proud to call His own,

492

like David in the Bible — a man after God's heart. If I could be brave, then I could be proud to be me."

Fanny shook her head in amazement. "Walter, you should be proud to be you. You're a gentle man but a strong man. You're a man who keeps his word. You —"

"No!" He hung his head, his face twisting into a grimace of despair. His thumbs stilled, and his fingers tightened on hers. "A man who keeps his word would have prevented the woman he'd promised to cherish and protect from running into a burning barn to rescue a horse." His face lifted, and the shame and anguish reflected from his eyes pierced Fanny like a knife. "She'd be alive today if I'd been braver. Stronger." His hands went limp, and he bowed his head.

Fanny sat with her fingers laced with his, her heart aching for him. And for her. If she would leave his cabin and never live here again, she would leave something of value behind. She whispered, "David."

Walter raised his head and sent her a puzzled frown. "What?"

A smile formed as words from the Psalms, penned by King David, crept through her memory. They'd been spoken over her grandmother's grave when she was a young child, and she'd never forgotten them. "You said David was a man after God's heart. In Psalm 139, David wrote, speaking of God, 'In thy book all my members were written, which in continuance were fashioned, when as yet there was none of them.' Me da told me God knows the length of a person's life. He knows the first day and the last day, and for those who love God and serve His Son, the last day only means stepping into a life more glorious than we can know on this earth. Did Grete know God? Did she serve His Son?"

Walter's blue eyes brightened with unshed tears. "Yes. Her faith was strong."

"If she trusted Him, then you need to trust His wisdom in taking her home to Him. There was nothing you could have done that would change the number of the days of her life." Fanny formed a careful question. "You didn't send her into the barn, did you?"

He shook his head hard. "No. No, I tried to stop her."

"Then you honored your pledge to protect her. What she did, she did on her own." She squeezed his hands. "It isn't your fault, Walter, that she's gone. You must stop blaming yourself or . . . or branding yourself a coward. The man I saw today, standing up to a bully who held a loaded pistol in his hand, is a brave man. An honorable man. A man I am proud to . . . to . . ." She gulped. Could she say it? She'd promised God she wouldn't tell any more falsehoods if He got her to a place of safety. She spoke truth straight from her heart. "To love."

Walter

Walter stared at her, at her beautiful face shining with love. Love for *him*. He knew she loved Annaliese. The knowledge had helped give him the courage to confront the riverboat captain. If Walter had died, Kirkpatrick would have gone to prison, and Fanny would have taken Annaliese and raised her as her own. He'd held no worries about his precious Liébling because of his surety that Fanny loved her. But to know she loved him sent a shaft of pure joy through him.

"Walter?" Fanny's quiet voice intruded upon his jubilant reckoning. "You didn't fully answer my question. Why did you risk your life for me today?"

He'd done it because the fear of losing her was greater than the fear of that taller, stronger, sneering man with a pistol. He'd done it because he loved her. Only a coward would hold back the truth of how he felt about her. He didn't want to feel cowardly.

He didn't want to *be* cowardly. But neither did he want her to misunderstand why he would tell her he loved her now.

Annaliese finished the bread. The beans had sat long enough they wouldn't burn her mouth. He slipped his hands free of Fanny's light grip and slid the bowl and spoon in front of his daughter. She held the spoon in her left hand and scooped up beans with the right, cheerfully smearing them over her face as she fed herself.

Convinced Annaliese was fine, he sent up a silent prayer for God to help him find the right words. "Fanny, I want to tell you about the letter from my parents. You should know what it says."

Her expression reflected uncertainty, but she offered a small nod. "All right."

He moved his stool next to hers. She gripped her hands in her lap and set her gaze on his face, her lips pressed tight and her eyes seeming to beg. He offered an assuring smile, patted her clenched hands, and cleared his throat. He shared his parents' failed efforts to locate a wife on their own and told her the arrangement they'd made with a matchmaker.

"The matchmaker said she wouldn't send someone only because my parents requested it. I, as the husband, had to be the one to

496

say I wanted a wife. That was the other reason I wanted to go to Elkhart. So I could send a telegram to New York to the matchmaker my parents found."

She sat staring at him in silence. Did she not understand?

He squeezed her hands. "Fanny, I sent the telegram. To the matchmaker."

She swallowed. "You told her you wanted the wife to come."

She didn't understand. He shook his head. "I told her I did *not* want the wife to come. It wouldn't be fair for her to come here when I have fallen in love with someone else."

She jolted, and her fine brows lifted. "S-someone else?" A little cry left her lips. She sat straight up, her eyes searching his face. "Do you love me, Walter?"

Ah, she finally understood. "Ja, I do." He raised his hands to her face and cupped her cheeks. "I think I already knew, but when I realized Sloan was going to take you away from Annaliese and me, I had no doubt. I couldn't let you go. Not with him."

The pale lamplight brought out the little flecks of gold in her brown eyes. He would be content to spend time every evening for the rest of his life admiring those dots of gold. But for now there was more he needed to say.

A tear rolled down her cheek. He caught it with his thumb, then gathered his courage and did what Sloan had refused to do when she lived on his boat — set her free. "But I made an agreement with you. I have enough money to pay for a ticket to New York. I'll take you to the train station in Elkhart tomorrow if —"

"I do not want to go!"

The exclamation startled him so much he nearly lost his seat.

She grabbed his elbows and held tight. "I love me da and ma. But I can't live in a big city. Not after living in such a lovely, wide-open place. And not so far away from you and my bonny hen. I —" Her voice broke on a sob. She shifted her gaze toward Annaliese, and musical laughter spilled. She pulled loose and pointed.

Walter looked, and he couldn't hold back a hoot of laughter. A bowl sat upside down on Annaliese's head like a hat. Drying sauce formed paths from her head down her face, and beans dotted her shoulders and the front of her dress. He'd never seen such a mess. He rose, chuckling. "Liébling, Liébling, what did you do?"

Fanny hurried to the washstand and

dipped a rag.

He took the bowl from his daughter's head and, frequently chortling or exchanging amused smiles, together they stripped her clothes and mopped away as much goo as possible. The entire time, Annaliese grinned up at them, clearly pleased with herself.

When they'd finished, Fanny turned toward the bureau where Annaliese's clothes were stored. "I'll fetch a fresh gown and —"

"The gown can wait." Walter caught her hand and drew her back. "Please finish what you were saying. You no longer want to go to New York?" Hope beat in his chest like the moth now struggling to reach the flame on the other side of the lamp's glass globe.

She shook her head slowly, smiling up at him. "Not to live. I told Josephine I'm going to write to my family and ask them to come to Indiana. To the rolling plains that take me to Scotland in my mind. I pray they'll come, but if they don't, this is my home now. God brought me here to this beautiful place. To love Annaliese." She moved closer and placed both palms against his chest. "And to fall in love with you. This is where I'm meant to be."

She lifted her head, closed her eyes, and began to sing, " 'We'll find the place which

God for us prepared.' "

Walter loved her voice, loved to hear her sing, but right now he wanted something else. He slipped his arms around her waist, tilted his face to hers, and silenced her tune with a kiss. After a moment's pause, she went up on tiptoe and eased her arms around his neck. The kiss lingered, and he tasted salt. From her tears or his? He couldn't be sure, but it didn't matter. They were happy tears. He'd found love again and, in so doing, discovered the man he'd always prayed to be.

Fanny lowered her heels to the floor and leaned back a bit. With a sweet smile gracing her face, she sang, " 'All is well! All is well!' "

EPILOGUE

ELKHART, INDIANA
FANNY

A train's whistle drifted across the plain and stirred excitement in Fanny's breast. She crouched next to Annaliese and pointed to the lines of silver track entering the town from the east. "Watch, now." Fanny's warm breath formed little puffs in the frosty air. "The train is coming."

Annaliese put her finger in her mouth and danced in place, her bright-eyed gaze bouncing from Walter to Fanny to the snow-lined tracks. Finally they were coming, and just in time for Christmas.

Fanny still marveled at how neatly things had fallen into place. By the time she received the letter from her parents expressing their desire to leave New York, Hugh and Josephine had already made several inquiries. To Walter and Fanny's surprise, Old Man Sanderson made a visit to their cabin and confessed his arthritis was getting the best of him — "My oldest girl's been pesterin' me to move to Augusta, where she can keep an eye on me. Only thing keepin' me here's been my hogs. But if your folks, Mrs. Kuhn, would see to my critters an' house, I reckon I could rent the place to 'em."

So instead of herding sheep, Da would care for pigs, and he couldn't wait to leave the factory behind.

Fanny couldn't wait until she lived mere miles from her family. She'd be able to visit them often, thanks to the wonderful wedding gift she'd received from Walter. She loved the russet gelding — she'd named him Rupert — and the little buggy that could be fitted with sleigh runners when the snow was deep. Like it was today.

Snow and her family together for Christmas. Walter's Vater and Mutter planned to visit in the spring and meet their new daughter-in-law. Things couldn't be more perfect.

Beneath their feet, a vibration signified an approaching locomotive, and then a shrill blast pierced the air. Annaliese raised both hands to Walter and cried, "Fa!"

He scooped her up as Fanny rose and moved to the edge of the wood-planked platform. She leaned forward, head craned, mittened hands clasped at her throat, heart pounding in eager anticipation. Another shrill blast sounded right before the shiny black engine rounded the bend. Fanny tossed a smile over her shoulder at Walter and Annaliese, then watched the train pull into the station.

She scanned the frost-edged windows of the passenger cars as they slowly eased by on shrieking wheels, seeking the first glimpse of her parents and sisters since she was barely out of girlhood. Would she recognize them? Would they recognize her? The locomotive squealed to a stop with a burst of hissing steam that created a cloud of fog.

"Fanny! Fanny!"

The cry came from her right. She spun toward the sound, and Ma emerged from the wispy curtain of white. A cry of joy left Fanny's throat, and she raced across the crunchy snow, arms outstretched.

Ma captured her in a hug, and then another pair of arms wrapped around them both — Da, his mustached face bearing a smile as big as the canopy of sky. Fanny laughed and cried and alternately pressed her face into their necks and pulled back to reacquaint herself with their precious faces.

Then she tugged loose and sent a searching look back and forth. "But where are

Flossie and Moira? Didn't they come, too?"

Da barked his laugh and held his gloved hand toward a pair of young ladies with matching brown eyes and red-brown hair. "Did y' lose yer sight, lass? They're standin' right beside y'."

Fanny gaped at her sisters. In her mind, they'd remained little girls. But now Moira resembled Flossie when Fanny had seen her last, and Flossie — Fanny gulped and took a hesitant step toward the sister she'd witnessed grow up through letters. She touched Flossie's glossy upswept hair, then her rosy cheek.

"Oh, my goodness, Flossie. You . . . you're so beautiful."

A shy smile lit Flossie's eyes. "Only because I look like you." And she lunged at Fanny. They hugged, rocking to and fro and laughing into each other's ears.

A hand tapped Fanny's shoulder. She released Flossie and turned toward her littlest sister. Moira angled her chin, put her hands on her hips, and gave a dimpled grin. "And what of me? Am I beautiful, too?"

Fanny laughed and lifted Moira off her feet with a hug. "You're enchanting." Moira giggled, and Fanny set her back on the snowy ground. She kept her arm around Moira's shoulders, though, and gestured to

Walter to join them. "Ma, Da, Flossie, and Moira, I want you to meet my husband, Walter Kuhn, and my wee bonny hen, Annaliese."

Fanny's cheeks ached from smiling as she watched Walter and Da exchange a solemn handshake that turned into a bear hug. Ma hugged Walter, too, then cooed over Annaliese. Flossie and Moira crowded close, reaching to stroke Annaliese's rabbit-fur bonnet or hold her mittened hand. The poor little girl whimpered, stared at the strangers, and clung to her fa's neck.

Walter apologized, but neither Ma nor Da was offended.

Ma patted Annaliese's back and said, "There'll be lots o' time for gettin' acquainted now that we're here." She aimed a watery-eyed smile at Fanny. "All of us together ag'in."

Joy exploded in Fanny's chest. They'd been apart for seven long years — years of growth and change and challenges and tears. For a moment, sadness tried to take hold for the time they would never recapture, but then lines from Pazzy's freedom song whispered to her heart — " *'Why should we mourn or think our lot is hard? 'Tis not so; all is right!'* "

There, under a clear winter sky, with

crystals of snow beneath Fanny's feet and the ones she loved gathered near, she set aside sadness and focused on her blessings. God was good, and all was well.

She slipped her hand through Walter's elbow, briefly pressed her cheek to his shoulder, then smiled and said, "Come. Let's go home."

READERS GUIDE

1. Fanny's plunge from the riverboat into the Mississippi River sent her on a journey she never could have imagined. Has an unexpected, unpleasant experience ever sent you in a different direction? Could you see God's hand in the experience?

2. Sloan tricked Fanny's father into signing a thirty-five-year commitment of service. Because Sloan duped the family, was Fanny obligated to fulfill the agreement? Why or why not?

3. Fanny unwittingly became caught up in an Underground Railroad operation. She didn't have to stay with Enoch and his family. Why do you think she chose to do so?

4. Walter branded himself a coward because he had run in fear from the bullies who'd

tormented him during his childhood. Was this a fair designation? Why or why not? Have you ever placed a certain "brand" on yourself? How can we keep from defining ourselves negatively and instead view ourselves through God's eyes?

5. Sloan grew up in a home with few material possessions but a great deal of love. Why do you think he was dissatisfied with his life? How did scriptures and spoken words from his past affect him as he sought a new singer? Have you ever been influenced by remembered words from the Bible or a loved one? In what way?

6. When Fanny heard a young child crying, why did she decide to investigate? If you heard a child in distress, how would you respond?

7. After deciding to let Fanny go, Sloan considered contacting his parents. Do you think he followed through with it? What kind of reception do you think he received?

8. Freedom is a theme throughout the story — Fanny's freedom from Sloan, Enoch and his family's freedom from bondage, and Walter's freedom from a cloak of fear.

Ransom told Fanny, "I'm free because Jesus forgave my sins." Later, Fanny realized she would still be free even if held captive again by Sloan. What is the difference between physical freedom and spiritual freedom? Have you found freedom in Christ? How has it affected you?

ACKNOWLEDGMENTS

I always thank family first, so thank you, *Mom and Daddy*. Mom, we've been apart for almost three years now. I miss you as much today as the day you graduated to heaven, but you always reside in the center of my heart. Daddy, the faith you and Mom demonstrated bolsters and guides me. I am so grateful you're mine.

Don, Kristian, Kaitlyn, Kamryn, and my precious granddarlings, you are the joys of my life. I love you muchly!

Candace and Kevin, thank you for letting me borrow your sweet baby girl's name for this story. Although your Annalise Hope is in heaven, her influence on earth continues.

Speaking of names in the story . . . thank you, *Hugh and Patti Jo Moore,* for lending yours. They fit the friendly, helpful couple next door so well.

Jalana, if you hadn't wanted to visit the steamboat museum during our one-on-one posse retreat in 2017, this story's seed might never have been planted. So thank you! As for the rest of the posse . . . let's get together soon!

To *Becky, Abby, Leslie, and the entire team at WaterBrook,* thank you for all you do to bring these stories to life and put them in readers' hands. I appreciate you very much.

And, *Tamela,* this is book number fifty-seven. Were it not for your efforts, there might not be more than one. Thank you for believing in me and being my champion. God bless you!

Finally, and most importantly, thank You, my *Father God.* You freed me from sin's chains and gave me new eternal life in Christ. My freedom song will always be "my hope is built on nothing less than Jesus' blood and righteousness." I love You, Lord. May any praise or glory be reflected directly to You.

ABOUT THE AUTHOR

In 1966, **Kim Vogel Sawyer** told her kindergarten teacher that someday people would check out her book in libraries. That little-girl dream came true in 2006 with the release of *Waiting for Summer's Return.* Since then, Kim has watched God expand her dream beyond her childhood imaginings. With more than fifty titles on library shelves and more than 1.5 million copies of her books in print worldwide, she enjoys a full-time writing and speaking ministry. Empty nesters, Kim and her retired military husband, Don, live in small-town Kansas, the setting for many of her novels. When she isn't writing, Kim stays active serving in her church's women's and music ministries, crafting quilts, petting cats, and spoiling her quiverful of granddarlings. You can learn more about Kim's writing at www.Kim VogelSawyer.com.

The employees of Thorndike Press hope you have enjoyed this Large Print book. All our Thorndike, Wheeler, and Kennebec Large Print titles are designed for easy reading, and all our books are made to last. Other Thorndike Press Large Print books are available at your library, through selected bookstores, or directly from us.

For information about titles, please call:
  (800) 223-1244

or visit our website at:
  gale.com/thorndike

To share your comments, please write:
  Publisher
  Thorndike Press
  10 Water St., Suite 310
  Waterville, ME 04901

3468